GLORIOUS PRAISE FOR ANGELA BENSON AND *THE AMEN SISTERS*

"Courageous! . . . The next level of Christian fiction . . . If you're looking for a juicy novel, this definitely fits the bill."
—*Bahiyah Magazine*

"5 Stars! An excellent story of failure, judgment, redemption, and release from shame."
—FaithfulReader.com

"Benson is a talented writer."
—*Black Issues Book Review*

"A remarkable novel . . . Benson masterfully tackles an often taboo subject . . . an enaging, powerful Christian novel that will leave you saying amen."
—Urban-Reviews.com

"A powerful and compelling novel."
—ArmchairInterviews.com

"A rich, multifaceted work of Christian fiction that is both timely and realistic. Highlights God's power to transform lives and the importance of forgiveness."
—RawSistaz.com

more . . .

"Benson aptly captures both the passion and pain that folks bottle up in their lives, and the importance of dealing with situations as they arise. Kudos to Ms. Benson for dealing with one of the last remaining taboo topics in today's church in such a straightforward and compassionate manner."

—FallenAngelReviews.com

"A talented author . . . Benson is a leading author of . . . Christian fiction, and her insight into God's impact on our lives makes her work a requirement for growing collections."

—*Library Journal*

"She is just as compelling a writer in Christian romance as she is in contemporary."

—*Affaire de Coeur*

"Angela Benson is a good storyteller . . . She has not created plaster saints but real men and women who grapple with real-life issues."

—TheRomanceReader.com

The Amen Sisters

Angela Benson

Walk Worthy Press

West Bloomfield, Michigan

GC

GRAND CENTRAL
PUBLISHING

NEW YORK   BOSTON

Copyright © 2005 by Angela Denise Benson
Reading Group Guide Copyright © 2007 by Hachette Book Group USA.
All rights reserved. Except as permitted under the U.S. Copyright Act of 1976, no part of this publication may be reproduced, distributed, or transmitted in any form or by any means, or stored in a database or retrieval system, without the prior written permission of the publisher.

Grand Central Publishing
Hachette Book Group USA
237 Park Avenue
New York, NY 10017

Walk Worthy Press
33290 West Fourteen Mile Road, #482, West Bloomfield, MI 48322

Visit our Web sites at www.HachetteBookGroupUSA.com and www.walkworthypress.net.

Printed in the United States of America

Originally published in hardcover by Hachette Book Group USA.

First Trade Edition: November 2007
10 9 8 7 6 5 4 3 2 1

The Library of Congress has cataloged the hardcover edition as follows:

Benson, Angela.
    The Amen sisters / Angela Benson.—1st ed.
        p. cm.
    ISBN 0-446-53153-7
    1. Women clergy—Fiction. 2. Church members—Fiction. 3. Suicide victims—Fiction.
  4. Witnesses—Fiction. I. Title.
    PS3552.E5476585A83 2005
    813'.54—dc22
                                                            2005009378

ISBN 978-0-446-69947-1 (pbk.)

The book is dedicated to women everywhere who have felt betrayed by people they loved and trusted. I pray that *The Amen Sisters* gives you a chance to name your betrayal and give it to God. There is no hurt that He can't heal, no pain that He can't ease. He gives the strength to fight, the strength to forgive, and the strength to go on. My prayer is that you may find hope and help in Him.

ACKNOWLEDGMENTS

The Amen Sisters marks my first venture with the Walk Worthy Press/Warner team and I'm pleased to report that it was a delight.

Denise Stinson, Walk Worthy Press publisher, you were right about many things, including the title. Thanks for all your support. Our first time out was a good one, and I look forward to the next one. We make a good team.

Frances Jalet-Miller, editor, thanks so much for the care that you took with my story. I trust you completely. Your wisdom and insight are appreciated and I'm blessed to have found you. I'll be very disappointed if we don't work together on my next book.

Deb Dwyer, copy editor, thanks for your kind words and good eye. You found inconsistencies in my manuscript that I surely would have missed, and my story is better because of you.

I offer a special thanks to the other members of the Walk Worthy Press/Warner team who worked to get *The Amen Sisters* into print and into bookstores. I don't know you all by name, but I want you to know that I appreciate your efforts.

The
Amen
Sisters

PROLOGUE

Y ou're a liar, Toni," Francine Amen said, forcing a calmness she didn't feel to project in her voice. She pressed her palms down on the counter that separated the kitchen from the dining room in the two-bedroom apartment that she shared with her childhood friend Toni Roberts. "I don't believe you."

Toni, standing on the dining room side of the counter, took a step closer to her roommate. "Why would I lie to you, Francie? Tell me that."

The plea in her friend's soft brown eyes was almost more than Francine could bear. "I know you, remember? You and me go way back. It wouldn't be the first time you've lied about something like this." Francine didn't turn away from the stricken look on her friend's face. She knew her words needed to be spoken. "Well, if we're talking about truth here, we should talk about truth."

Toni wrapped her arms around her midsection and said, "You may not believe me, Francie, but I *am* pregnant and Bishop Payne *is* the father. We've been having an affair for months."

Francine laughed a dry laugh. "An affair? Come off it, Toni.

Bishop told us all how you've been coming on to him. And you know what? He didn't condemn you for it. He asked us to pray for you. And what do you do to him in return? You come up with these lies. I pray to God you haven't told anyone else this pack of garbage. That man has a wife and kids, and all of them have done nothing but love you. You have to know the damage these lies of yours will do to them."

"I'm not lying, Francie," Toni said, her eyes clouding with tears. "You know me," she pleaded. "You have to believe me. I knew nobody else would believe me. I've known for weeks now, and I've wanted to tell you so badly, but I just couldn't. I know what people say about me around here. I've overheard them saying I'm not a real Christian, that I don't have the fire. I heard it from them, but I never thought I'd hear it from you. You're the one who shared the gospel with me. You're the one who told me that life in Christ could be different. You know I've changed."

Francine's heart ached for her friend, but she couldn't let emotions deter her. Toni had to suffer the consequences of her actions. Tough love was exactly that—tough. "If you've been having an affair with Bishop like you say you have, then you haven't changed that much after all, have you?"

Toni turned away, seeming to deflate right before Francine's eyes. "You know how he is, Francie. He can be so charming. I loved him as the man of God he seemed to be, and then I simply loved him. It was like I couldn't help myself."

"I don't believe you and neither will anyone else. I don't know what you think you're going to get out of this."

Toni turned back to her. "I need a friend, Francie. I need someone to hear me out, be on my side. He wants me to have an abortion. He said he'll deny anything ever happened between us."

"I can't help you, Toni. I won't be a party to whatever game it is you're playing."

"But you're all I have," Toni pleaded. "I can't go back home now. This would kill George and Momma. I have nowhere else to turn."

Francine inhaled deeply. "Not this time, Toni. Not this time. I've stood by you through a lot of your drama, most of it of your own making, but not this time. This time you're on your own."

Toni opened her mouth as if to defend herself, but then she shook her head. "What does it matter?" she said, the defeat in her voice wrenching Francine's heart.

As Francine watched, Toni turned her petite frame away and headed off, shoulders slumped, toward her bedroom. Francine closed her eyes and issued a brief prayer on Toni's behalf. She didn't know what had gotten into Toni, but she prayed her friend would soon see the error of her ways and repent. Francine loved her, but she couldn't support her. Not this time. She and Toni had grown up together, been friends for as long as Francine could remember, but Francine had to face facts. Toni wasn't ready to give her life to the Lord, and Francine couldn't be held back because of it. She heaved a deep sigh, knowing that even though it hurt, she had done the right thing. She could have ignored Toni's actions, but that would not have been love. She knew from Psalms that the harsh truth from a friend was better than sweet words from an enemy.

As she reached for the phone to call Cassandra, her friend and prayer partner, to tell her about the conversation with Toni, Francine heard what sounded like the backfire of a car, followed by a loud thump, both coming from the direction of Toni's room. Wondering what Toni was doing to make such noise, Francine forgot the phone and headed for her friend's room. When she got no answer to her knock, she turned the doorknob. She screamed as she realized the sound she'd heard hadn't been the backfire of a car at all.

CHAPTER 1

Three months later

Francine Amen straightened her shoulders and exhaled a deep breath as she walked from her room on the patient wing of the Southwest Ohio Mental Health Clinic, through the patient activity ward, on her way to her morning appointment with Dr. Jennings, her therapist of record for the last eighty-five days. As she made her way across the breezeway, she gave slight nods of greeting to the patients and nurses much too familiar to her.

The stale odor of despair mingled with the fresh, but antiseptic, smell of Lysol that characterized the patient area contrasted greatly with the cinnamon aroma that greeted her when she passed through the glass double doors that served as the boundary between the mentally unwell and those who treated them. Sometimes the casual elegance of the lobby outside the staff offices—potted plants, rich artwork on the walls, deep-cushioned chairs and settees in bright multicolored patterns—was almost enough to make her forget where she was and why she was there. Almost but not quite. Straightening her back even more, Francine strode toward the sign-in desk with one thought on her mind: In three days she would leave this place that had become an unlikely home and refuge for her.

"Morning, Francine," the duty nurse, Margaret, a grandmotherly woman of about sixty, said to her. "Dr. Jennings hasn't gotten here yet, but we're expecting her any minute now. You can go on into her office."

"Thanks, Margaret. How are you this morning?"

"Busy, but good. I hear you're leaving us on Sunday. You know, I'm happy to see you go, but we sure are gonna miss you around here."

Francine smiled. "Believe it or not, I'm going to miss you too, but that doesn't mean I want to stay any longer."

The older woman chuckled. "I know what you mean. Now, you go on into the doctor's office. I have to run some papers over to the patient wing. Dr. Jennings will probably beat me back here."

Francine followed the older woman's directive and went into the doctor's office to wait. As she took her seat on the couch, she remembered her first visit to this office. Then she'd wondered if she was supposed to stretch out on the couch. She smiled at her ignorance. Before her stay here, her knowledge of therapists had been limited to what she knew from prime-time television. Fortunately for her, Dr. Jennings was neither Frasier Crane nor Bob Hartley.

Francine looked toward the door as it opened and the bubbly Dr. Jennings stormed in. "Sorry I'm late," the five-foot redheaded dynamo said. Then, without preamble, she took a seat in the chair across from Francine and said, "So, you're going home Sunday."

Home, Francine thought, back to Georgia. A place she hadn't visited in the last five years. This hospital was more familiar to her than home was. "That's what they tell me."

"So how do you feel about it?" Dr. Jennings glanced down at the yellow legal pad that seemed to always be on her lap, a habit Francine found unnerving. It was as if the woman couldn't remember Francine's issues and had to check the pad to remind herself.

How do I feel about it? Francine thought to herself. She was ready to leave, but ready to leave wasn't a feeling. She'd been in therapy long enough to understand the difference between feelings and thoughts. "I'm a bit anxious," she said, glancing down at her recently manicured hands, courtesy of the hospital services staff, "but I guess that's to be expected."

"Why anxious?"

Francine shrugged her shoulders and glanced out the plate glass windows overlooking the recently mowed north lawn of the institution. "Why shouldn't I be anxious? I'm a thirty-three-year-old woman running home to her sister after being let loose from the funny farm. I think that's enough to be anxious about."

When the doctor didn't respond, Francine turned to her. "What? No more questions?"

Dr. Jennings looked down at her pad again. "This is your time, Francine. If you want to spend it making sarcastic remarks, go right ahead."

Francine turned the corners of her lips down and sank back into the couch. She rubbed her hands down her jean-clad thighs. "Okay, you're right. Sorry."

"Don't be sorry," Dr. Jennings said. "Recognize what you're doing."

Francine knew Dr. Jennings was referring to the way she used sarcasm to handle emotions and situations that made her uneasy. "I'm anxious about going back home. I don't look forward to living with my sister. I don't look forward to seeing the people that I was so ugly to before I left. I dread seeing Toni's family."

Dr. Jennings leaned forward, in full empathy mode. "I know that'll be hard for you, seeing Toni's family again."

Hard was a mild word to describe what Francine felt about seeing Toni's mother and brother again. The last time she'd seen them was when they'd come to Dayton to get Toni's body. They'd come to her wanting answers about what led their daughter and sister to suicide. By then, Francine had learned that Toni had indeed been pregnant, and the reaction of her friend Cassandra to the news had pretty much convinced her that Toni hadn't been lying about Bishop Payne being the father. Toni's family had been devastated after they'd dragged those gory details out of Francine. Out of their devastation had come their accusations. Francine, who had already tried and convicted herself, accepted their condemnation without a word of self-defense. The last thing she remembered from that day was George, Toni's brother, calling her a murderer. Her next memory was waking up in this hospital, her arms restrained, her sister asleep in the chair next to her bed.

"Hey," Dr. Jennings said, interrupting her thoughts. "You've come a long way in your therapy, Francine. The biggest step in that journey for you was accepting that Toni's suicide wasn't your fault. That's ground you cannot afford to lose."

Francine met the doctor's gaze. "I know I didn't cause Toni's death, but knowing that only makes my guilt bearable. The fact remains, if it were not for me, Toni would still be alive. That's something I'll always have to live with."

"Thinking like that isn't good for you, Francine," the doctor warned. "You have to know that."

Francine let the familiar words settle in her spirit. "You tell me it's not my fault, but all I hear is that it's not *all* my fault. Toni was in Dayton because I dragged her here. She was in that church because I encouraged her to be there. She trusted Bishop Payne because I trusted him. And when she needed a friend, I wasn't there for her."

"But you didn't put the gun to her head."

"I know that," Francine said. "Toni did that all by herself, but she did it because I didn't believe her, because I refused to believe her. I was the only person she had, and I wasn't there for her."

"So you're going to beat yourself up about that for the rest of your life?"

Francine shook her head. She knew she had to try to be like Paul and forget the sins of the past and move forward. "No, I won't do that, but I will take responsibility for what I did. That's why going home is going to be so difficult. I have to make amends for the hurt I caused, to Toni's family, yes, but to the others as well. That's the only way I'll be able to live with myself. Unfortunately, I have no idea how they're going to respond to my overtures."

"You're not responsible for how they respond," Dr. Jennings said. "You're only responsible for your own actions. You have to remember that."

Francine signaled compliance with a downward tilt of her head.

"So have you decided where you're going to start?"

Francine squeezed her eyes shut. Then she quickly opened them. "Cassandra."

"Are you sure you want to tackle her first?"

Francine tipped her chin up. Cassandra had been her closest friend at Temple Church. In fact, Cassandra's testimony about how she'd come to be a member of Temple Church and her devotion to God had been a major factor in Francine's decision to join the group. Francine had looked up to the woman as a mentor in Christ and cherished her friendship. Therefore, her betrayal had hurt the most. "I have to do it. I have to confront her. I have to hear the truth from her."

"What are you going to say to her?"

"I'm going to ask her if she knew."

"Do you think she did?"

Francine's heart ached at the answer to that question. "I know she did. She had to have known. I can still remember the look on her face when I told her what Toni had told me. She knew. I could tell by the look on her face that she knew, and I have a feeling she wasn't the only one who knew."

"So why ask her if you already know the answer?"

"Because I have to hear the words from her and I have to know why. I loved them all. They were my family. I walked away from my biological family so I could be a part of their church family. I have to understand how they could do what they did, how they could sit by and let Bishop Payne do the damage he did when they knew what was going on. I have to know. I need to make some sense out of it in order to get on with my life."

Dr. Jennings looked down at her pad again. "You know, Francine, there's a real possibility you won't be able to make sense of it. At least, not in the way you want. What if you don't get the answers you need?"

"I don't know," she said. "I guess I'll have to deal with it, but I have to try. I can't walk away without trying."

The doctor flipped the top sheet of her pad over. "Have you lined up a therapist at home the way I suggested?"

Francine looked down at her folded hands. "My sister did the legwork. She's very worried about her crazy sister."

The doctor lifted a brow.

"Okay, maybe Dawn doesn't think I'm crazy, but she is worried about me."

"It's natural. She loves you."

"I know she does."

"And?"

Francine looked up and met the doctor's eyes. "It makes me feel guilty. I hadn't spoken to her in five years, but when I needed her she was right there. Cassandra did one thing right when she called Dawn. I'm not sure what I would have done without my sister's support. She's been a good sister to me, even though I haven't been a good sister to her."

"From what I've seen of your sister, I don't think she's keeping score. She only wants you to get better."

"It certainly looks that way," Francine said. She and Dawn had always had a complicated relationship. Though they were fraternal twins, Francine the older by a couple of minutes, they had never really shared the symbiotic closeness that many twins experienced. Mostly, they'd been competitive. The differences in their appearances only added to the competition. Tall and sleek, Dawn had a polished, sophisticated look with stark features, while the petite Francine was muted in comparison. "She's my sister and she loves me, but you never know with Dawn. She always seems to be working some angle." Francine lifted her shoulders in a light shrug. "Maybe she's working through some residual guilt from marrying my fiancé."

"I thought *you* ended that relationship."

"I did, but she didn't waste much time stepping in, now did she?"

Dr. Jennings jotted something on her yellow pad. "I thought you and Dawn had talked this through. Your living with them is going to be difficult enough without these feelings lurking beneath the surface."

"Whoopee, what fun that's going to be!"

Dr. Jennings arched a brow.

"Okay, I'll stop with the sarcasm. I don't look forward to moving in with them. I hate the fact that I'm flat broke. I hate even more the reason I'm flat broke. When I left town with Bishop Payne and the others, I was so sure I was doing the right thing. I knew I was right and I didn't lose any time telling everybody else how wrong they were. Lord forgive me, I was so self-righteous. I can hardly believe I said some of the things I did. And now I have to go back and face all my mistakes. It's a bit daunting."

Dr. Jennings studied her quietly. "You know, Francine, this

anxiety is not a bad thing. You do have some challenges ahead of you, and recognizing them will only make you better equipped to meet them. Now, back to the therapist. Did you find one with a Christian orientation?"

"Dawn had a couple on her list, but I didn't pick one of them."

Dr. Jennings leaned forward. "Why not? Your faith has been a large part of your life for all of your life, Francine. It's reasonable that what's happened has caused you to reevaluate a lot of what you believe, but if you're going to be whole again, you're going to have to work through the faith issues in a rational way."

"You may be right," Francine said, "but I'm not ready for anyone to explain what the Bible means to me, or to interpret what God is saying. I did that with Bishop Payne and look where it got me. Thank God, I know now that's something I have to do on my own."

"Not all religious people are like Bishop Payne or the others at Temple Church."

"I know that in my head," Francine said, "but my heart is another matter. I have to do this my way."

"All right," the doctor said. "I'm not going to push." She glanced at her pad again. "I guess that ends our session for today. We'll meet again before your Sunday discharge."

As Sylvester Ray entered his home Friday evening, he rubbed his hand across the back of his neck, trying to wipe away the stress of the day. As manager of Amen-Ray Funeral Home, the family business he co-owned with his wife and sister-in-law, he had a lot on his shoulders. Though the business had recovered the ground it lost during the fallout of Francine leaving town, things were not going as well as he knew they needed to go in order for the funeral home to thrive. A quick solution would be to sell out to Easy Rest, the public company that had taken over a large number of smaller funeral homes in the Southeast, but he wanted that to be the answer of last resort. He knew that a move like that at this point in time would more likely than not lead to the end of his marriage of four years. He had no doubt that his wife, Dawn Amen-Ray, would consider such a decision the last straw. So Sylvester was left to find another solution if he wanted to keep his wife. And he did want to keep her. Doing so just seemed to get more difficult every day.

On his way through the kitchen, he opened the refrigerator and pulled out a bottle of mineral water. He drank it as he walked past the closed door of the upstairs bedroom that was now his wife's and on to the master bedroom that was now his alone. His eyes widened in surprise and welcome when he saw Dawn standing in the doorway of the closet they had once shared, their bed littered with her clothes. His heart quickened at the sight of her in a pair of denim cutoffs too short and too worn for her to wear anywhere but in the house. The sight of her and her long, sleek, cinnamon-toasted legs made him yearn for the times when things had been good between them. Then he would have pulled her into his arms and they would have spent the rest of the evening making very good use of their king-sized bed. But things weren't good between them and he had as much a chance of getting her into that teak bed as he did of finding a million dollars under one of the pillows.

"What are you doing?" he asked.

She turned to him, her bright brown eyes full of the accusation they usually held for him these days. "What does it look like I'm doing?"

He sighed as he walked fully into the room. He drank the last of his water and then tossed the bottle into the teak wastebasket in the corner of the room. How many times would he have to ask for forgiveness? Would she ever forgive him? Did it even matter? "It looks like you're putting your clothes in that closet, but I'm sure that's not the case since you no longer consider this room yours."

She turned away from him and continued with her clothes. "You know Francine is coming home."

He dropped down on the edge of the bed. "So that's what this is about? You're going to put on a happy face for Francine. You don't want her to know we're not sleeping together."

She turned a glare on him. "Do you?"

"Why should I care what Francine thinks about our marriage? I care what we think about it. I care what you think about it."

She turned away again. "There was a time when you cared a lot about what Francine thought."

Yes, he'd been devastated when Francine had deserted him, but out of that devastation had come his relationship with Dawn. "That was a long time ago, Dawn. We're married. I love you."

"So you say."

He got up, went to her, and turned her to face him. "I do love you. What do I have to do to make you believe me?" He read her answer in her eyes and dropped his hands away from her. "I can't undo it, Dawn. I made a mistake. Can't you forgive me?"

"It's so easy for you to say. *Forgive me, Dawn. I love you, Dawn,*" she mimicked. "But you know what? It's not easy for me to believe you're sincere. You were telling me you loved me for months, and loving me physically, while you were having an affair right under my nose, with somebody I knew. How can I believe anything you say? Would you believe me if the tables were turned?"

Sylvester felt the resentment rise up in his throat. Dawn often taunted him with the idea of her and another man. "I would want to. I would want to believe that we could get back what we'd lost. I'd want to believe that."

"But could you? Would you really want me if you knew I'd

been with someone else for months, that I'd been with you *and* somebody else for months?"

Sylvester turned away from her. The idea of her with another man turned his insides. He didn't even like to think about it. His repulsion at the idea of her being with another man was the only thing that kept him holding on to a marriage that seemed, at times, unsalvageable. He could imagine the hurt, betrayal, and yes, anger, he'd feel if she'd done what he did, so he was willing to give her time to forgive him. He just didn't know how long he could hold on without some sign of encouragement from her.

"I didn't think so." Dawn stomped into the closet. "Men! I can't believe you. You go out and do what you do, not expecting to get caught, and when you do, you expect to be forgiven. You tell me I'm being cruel, but I know for a fact that I'm treating you a million times better than you'd be treating me if I'd had an affair."

"You don't know how I'd react."

Dawn propped her hands on her hips and stared him down. "Puh-leez, Sylvester. I remember how you reacted when Francine left town with that traveling minister. She was out of your system so fast it made my head spin. I still wonder if you didn't go after me to get back at her."

She'd questioned his motives when he'd first begun to pursue her. He'd convinced her then that what he felt for her had nothing to do with the feelings he'd had for her sister. Now all of her insecurities were coming back, and it was his fault. He still didn't know why he'd done it. Why had he put his marriage in jeopardy for a few hours of sexual release with a woman he didn't even really care about?

Dawn tapped one slender foot against the plush carpet. "Tell me, Sylvester, do you still have feelings for Francine? Am I going to come home one day and find you and her—"

"Don't say it, Dawn. She's your sister, for goodness' sake. If you don't have any faith in me, at least have some in her. Besides, if you're so worried, why're you inviting her to stay with us?"

"You know why. It's her home and she has nowhere else to go. You know she has no money and no job. She gave all her money to that church and she lost her job a long time ago because she was too busy ministering to go to work." She dropped her hands to her sides. "And I was supposed to be the irresponsible sister. Who would have ever thought it would turn out to be Francine?"

"Not me, that's for sure. Francine was as predictable as Wednesday night Bible study."

"Until our grandparents died."

Sylvester felt the grief his wife still carried for the grandparents who'd reared her and Francine. Both women had taken the deaths hard. Dawn had settled down and tried to become the granddaughter they'd always wanted her to be, while Francine had broken out of the mold they had for her and had begun to spread her wings. Though Francine's actions had been more self-destructive in the end, Sylvester knew Dawn had her own set of demons. He knew she had many misgivings about her relationship with the older couple, many wrongs she wished she'd righted before they died, but she hadn't had the chance and that haunted her. He saw it in her eyes now, the regret, making him want to pull her into his arms and tell her that it would be all right. But he didn't have the right. She'd push him away as she'd done many times before. He stripped off his slacks in preparation for bed. "Are you sleeping in here tonight?" he asked as he passed her on the way to the bathroom, though he knew the answer.

"I'll sleep across the hall until Francine gets here."

"Surprise, surprise."

Ignoring his comment, she said, "I'm going to leave to pick her up straight from the Leadership Team meeting tomorrow morning, so we'll have to go in separate cars."

He turned back to her. "Are you sure you don't want me to go with you? I can still get away."

She shook her head. "I can handle it on my own."

Sylvester grunted his assent as he closed the bathroom door. Though he loved his wife and knew he had to pay for his mistakes, he didn't know how long he could continue to live in a loveless marriage.

CHAPTER 2

Sylvester sat forward in intense concentration. He hadn't been too enthusiastic when he'd heard a representative from BCN, Black Christian Network, a newly founded cable television station, would be speaking at the Leadership Team meeting this morning, but now that the guy was talking, Sylvester was more than interested. Not because of what the rep said about BCN, but because of the idea that the guy had given him for Amen-Ray Funeral Home. The speaker, whom Sly had nicknamed Mr. Slick partly because he wore his graying hair slicked back like Al Sharpton and partly because of the used-car-salesman cadence to his voice, overwhelmed the quaint and homey environs of the banquet room of Rob's Country Buffet with his grandiose multimedia presentation. But Sly had to hand it to the man, he definitely had his ducks all in a row.

"So that's our proposal for BCN," Mr. Slick said, wrapping up his presentation. "Are there any questions?"

Sylvester had a few, but since none of them related directly to BCN, he kept his mouth shut. Rev. Thomas, the dapper sixty-year-old pastor at Faith Central, spoke up first. He flipped through the fancy package of color slides Mr. Slick had given them. "So you'd fund this station through individual donations, selling programming time to churches and other black Christian groups, and advertisements?"

"That's right," Mr. Slick said. "That's three sources of revenue. Our projection has most of our initial funding coming from individual donations and selling programming time but then by year three moving to a situation where most, if not all, of our funding is from advertisements. As that percentage grows, we'll decrease the amount we charge churches and other groups for programming."

Rev. Thomas nodded. "I'm a bit concerned about these individual donations. What do people get in return for donating?"

"The blessing of giving."

Rev. Thomas laughed. "That's a good one, but if Faith Central is going to even consider being involved in this, we'd have to see the donors getting more in return. We've seen too many ministries built on the backs of working Christians that have, in the end, only served to line the pockets of those in charge. We can't be a part of anything that would abuse people that way."

"We don't look at it as abuse," Mr. Slick said. "It's an opportunity for people to help in spreading the gospel. That'll be their reward."

"What will be your reward?" Rev. Thomas asked, leaning back in his chair, his fingers steepled across the bridge of his nose.

"Of course, I'd be on the payroll and collect a salary based on the role I play in building the business."

"I'd like to see the donors reap a similar benefit," Rev. Thomas said, looking around the circle of now-bare banquet tables at the deacons, trustees, and ministry and lay leaders constituting the Leadership Team at Faith Central. "If their donations are going to serve to get the business built, those donors should reap financial benefits once the station becomes profitable. It's only fair. Are you open to discussing these types of benefits?"

Mr. Slick didn't look as though he wanted to open a discussion on the issue, but he was smart enough to know that such an answer would effectively end all possibility of Faith Central participating in the venture. From the way Mr. Slick had described it, the station would live or die based on the support of small- to medium-sized congregations like Faith Central. The larger churches with the larger budgets could afford existing broadcast outlets, so they really had no incentive to participate in something like BCN. Smaller congregations like Faith Central could benefit from a collective of many churches participating in such a venture.

It was the idea of the collective that intrigued Sylvester. He saw direct application of that concept to the funeral home. Small family-owned funeral homes like theirs were struggling today, due in large part to market pressures being exerted on them by the larger corporate funeral homes seeking to take over the business. If the smaller funeral homes could bind together, maybe they could form a collective that could better battle the corporate guys than they could as individual funeral homes. It was definitely an idea worth pursuing.

"Does anyone else have any questions or comments?" Rev. Thomas was asking the group. Sylvester didn't have to look around the room to know there would be no more questions. As usual, Rev. Thomas had quickly cut to the heart of the matter. If his pastor had one pet peeve, taking money from church folks was it. Sylvester knew then and there that Faith Central would not be a part of BCN, not the way it was currently organized.

Rev. Thomas looked back at Mr. Slick. "I think we understand your plan, Rev. Campbell. Unfortunately, in its present form, it doesn't look like a match for where we see ourselves going at Faith Central."

"Don't you see that this station could broaden your ministry?"

Mr. Slick asked, spreading open the jacket of what Sly guessed was a two-thousand-dollar suit and slipping his hands into the pockets of his slacks. The challenge in his stance matched the challenge in his voice. "Just imagine how many new souls you could serve. One day BCN will be as big and as effective as CBN."

"It could," Rev. Thomas agreed, "and I pray it does, but other things could happen as well. I've seen Christian nonprofit start-ups turn into major profit-making entities."

Mr. Slick's jaw twitched. "Do you have something against solid business decisions, Rev. Thomas?"

"Not at all, but if anyone is going to profit from this venture at any point in the future, there have to be provisions in place for the donors to reap their fair share. Without such a provision, you're building a business on the backs—and pocketbooks—of working Christian men and women, many who would give beyond their means. Despite the benefits that might accrue to us by our involvement with BCN, Faith Central can't be a party to taking the money of poor people and giving them nothing in return."

"You'd pass on this opportunity because of that?" Mr. Slick asked, looking around the room as if waiting for someone to say no. All he got was nodding heads.

As if sensing sure defeat, Mr. Slick dropped his hands to his sides. "We came to Faith Central because you're the type of progressive, forward-looking church we want involved with BCN. I'll take this issue under consideration with my team and get back to you."

Rev. Thomas accepted the compromise with a nod of his head. "We'll be happy to listen to the options that you come up with. In fact, we have some folks here today who can help you work through those issues if you're looking for some input. Stuart Rogers"—he inclined his head to the left, toward the bespectacled young deacon seated two tables away from him—"has done a lot of legal work with nonprofits, looking at exactly this point. I'm sure he'd be willing to share his experiences with you."

Sylvester slid his gaze to Stuart, his close friend and prayer partner, who was already nodding his assent. Now Mr. Slick's feet would be held to the fire. Between Pastor and Stuart, the guy would show his true colors. If his interest was ministry, then that would be quickly seen and Faith Central and BCN might be on the verge of a long and spiritually profitable association. Likewise, if his interest was strictly money, then that would be seen even more quickly and all discussions would end.

Rev. Thomas dismissed the meeting shortly thereafter with a group prayer. Dawn brushed against Sylvester as she stood and took her place in the prayer circle next to him. She put her hand on his forearm to steady herself and flashed him a loving smile. All a show, he knew, so none of their friends would know of the problem in their home. As Rev. Thomas prayed for the work of Faith Central, Sylvester prayed for his marriage. Afterwards he and Dawn followed the crowd out. As he walked Dawn to her car, he saw Stuart corner Mr. Slick and had to grin.

"What are you grinning about?" Dawn asked.

"Stuart just cornered that BCN guy."

She gave him a smile and leaned up to press a wifely kiss on his cheek. Weary of the playacting, Sylvester pulled her into his arms and kissed her as he'd wanted to kiss for the last month. This time she didn't pull away. Though he knew the only reason she didn't was that others were watching, he didn't care. If this was his only chance to touch her, he'd take what he could get.

"Hey, you two," Rev. Thomas called. "You're worse than the newlyweds. This is a parking lot. Haven't you heard of Christian decorum?" he teased.

Sylvester reluctantly lifted his head and looked into his wife's eyes, not hiding the love he felt for her. Her own eyes were clouded, but he was hopeful because he had felt a bit of a response from her. Not a lot, but enough to give him hope that one day she'd be his again.

"You'd think the woman was leaving you for a year instead of a couple of days," Pastor said, clapping him on the back. "Why don't you go with her?"

Sylvester smiled, his eyes still locked with Dawn's. "Maybe I ought to."

Pastor stepped in front of him and gave Dawn a hug. "You get going so you can hurry and get back. We'll take good care of your man here."

Mother Harris, the eighty-year-old woman who had served as Faith Central's First Lady for her late husband's thirty-five-year tenure as pastor, joined them. Rev. Thomas gave the older woman a kiss on the cheek and then moved on to chat with another parishioner. "Dawn, you make sure Francie knows we love her," Mother Harris said. "And you tell her she'd better not be long in coming to see me either."

"Yes, ma'am," Dawn said to the older woman. "I'll give her your message."

"And you, young man," she said to Sylvester. "You keep kissing your wife like that. Marriage is hard work, so you'd better have some fun at it when you can."

Sylvester grinned as the older woman walked off in the direction of Stuart and Mr. Slick.

"I guess I'd better get on the road," Dawn said.

Still smiling, Sylvester opened the door of the white Cadillac she'd chosen from among the funeral home's fleet, then closed it after she was inside. "You have your cell phone?" he asked. She held the phone up so he could see it. "Good. Call me if you need me and be sure to call me when you get there." Without agreeing, she gave him a brief smile, put the car in gear, and pulled out of the restaurant's parking lot.

Sylvester stood looking in the direction of the car long after it was out of sight. When he looked around, he saw that only Stuart Rogers was still present.

"Some kiss," Stuart said with a lifted brow. "Does this mean all is well in Amen-Ray land?"

Sly turned to his friend. "I wish. But not yet."

"Didn't look that way to me."

"Looks can be deceiving, Stuart, you should know that. My wife's a good actress. She doesn't want anyone to know we're having problems, so she puts on a good front. Believe me, that kiss never would have happened if we had been alone."

"Didn't look like acting to me."

"That's because you're an optimist and you love both of us."

Stuart clapped him on the back. "That could be part of it. Let's go get our coffee. I have another meeting later this morning."

Sylvester followed his friend back into the restaurant, where they took a booth in the back. Though Dawn had warned him not to tell anyone of their differences, Sly had shared the gory details with Stuart because he'd had to tell someone. So Stuart knew about the affair and he knew about the resulting trouble Sly had in his marriage, but Dawn didn't know that Stuart knew.

"You seem to be hanging in there," Stuart said once they were seated.

"It's not like I have a lot of options."

"You always have options," Stuart said. He'd said those words when Sly had told him about the affair and how he'd found himself in a situation that was too strong for him.

"So you keep telling me."

"Are you ready for Francine's arrival?"

Sly had told Stuart all about his past with Francine and the troubles that were bringing her back home. Stuart hadn't met her though, since he'd joined Faith Central shortly after Francine had left town. "About as ready as I can be. Her staying with us has an unexpected upside."

"What's that?"

"Dawn's moved back into our bedroom. For purely practical reasons, mind you. She doesn't want her sister to know we're having problems." He ran his fingers around the rim of his coffee cup. "But she'll know soon enough. We can't spend all our time hidden in our separate corners of the bed." He rubbed his hands across his bald head and down his face. "Why did I do it, man? Why did I risk everything the way I did?"

Stuart stirred his coffee. "That's a question only you can answer, Sly. You probably already know the answer."

Sly shook his head. "It just happened. One minute I was a happily married man and the next minute I was an adulterer, lying to my wife on a daily basis."

"Sorry, but I don't believe it. It doesn't happen that way. First comes the desire, then the action, then the devastating results. And that's from the Book of James, not the Book of Stuart."

"Did it ever happen to you?" Sly asked the question he'd wanted to ask since he'd first told Stuart about his sin. He'd been reluctant to ask it, because he didn't like to bring up Marie, Stuart's wife, who had died about two years ago.

Stuart shook his head. "Not that I didn't have the opportunity. Women are always available and many of them don't seem to mind the wedding ring. Some of them even seem to prefer relationships with married men."

"Tell me about it," Sly said.

"I never cheated on Marie and I was never really tempted, but I admit some of the female attention was flattering. It made me feel good to know that other women found me attractive."

"You didn't let it go further than that, and I did."

"Hey, I feel you. I'm a man and I understand physical attraction. I also know that just because the attraction is there, you don't have to act on it. For some reason, you did, and you have to figure out why you did or you may just do it again."

"Never. I know now that I have too much to lose."

"You had to know it then too, Sly, but for some reason, it didn't matter. At least, not at that moment."

Those words were harsh to Sly's ears but he knew there was some truth in them. He hadn't been able to think about Dawn when he was with Fredericka. They never spoke her name when they were together. It was as if he had two lives, one with his wife and one with his woman, and he wanted to keep them both, had actually tried to keep them both. But he'd learned his lesson. He would never again jeopardize what he had with Dawn. "All I need is for her to trust me again. If she does, she'll never regret it."

"You have to give her a reason to trust you again. She trusted you before and look what she got. How does she know you won't cheat on her again given the right circumstances?"

"Because I won't let it happen. She has to trust that I won't."

Stuart shook her head. "No, she doesn't. You have to show her that she can trust you again."

"I've tried everything," he said. "I don't know what else to do."

Stuart pushed his coffee cup away. "That's probably a good place to be. If you're like me, it's only after you've done everything that you can think to do, that it occurs to you that maybe you need some help. Want to pray?"

Sly's eyes skittered around the restaurant. Stuart always wanted to pray in public and it always made Sly self-conscious. It was one thing for a group of men to pray together, holding hands in a circle, but it was quite another for two men to hold hands and pray in the back booth of a restaurant. They compromised by putting a hand on each other's shoulder instead of holding hands.

"Father, thank you for this time with my brother this morning," Stuart prayed. "We come asking you for a breakthrough in Sly and Dawn's relationship. You know both their hearts, Lord. You know the problem, you know the cause, and you know the solution. Please open Sly and Dawn's hearts and minds so that they can see that solution and walk in it. Make them a stronger team because of what they're going through. In Jesus's name. Amen."

Sly studied his friend, taking in the wedding ring he still wore. He realized that recently most of their prayer time had been spent on his issues, with very little time given to the things that concerned Stuart. He vowed to begin rectifying that imbalance today. He valued the brotherhood that he shared with Stuart, and he wanted their relationship to remain steady. "It's been more than two years since Marie died, Stuart. Have you thought about getting married again?"

"I've thought about it, sure, but I'm not ready yet." He idly twisted the platinum wedding band on his finger. "I still love my wife."

"You'll always love her, but that doesn't mean you can't be happy with someone else."

"Maybe."

"No maybe about it. My marriage is in awful shape right now, so I'm the worst person in the world to give advice, but you need to give it a try. You can't withdraw from life. I hate that you resigned from the youth ministry team. You didn't have to do that."

"Yeah, I did," Stuart said with certainty. "That job is better handled by a couple. Marie and I were a team in that ministry. I couldn't continue in it without her. I didn't have everything those kids needed within me. They need that male-female perspective. CeCe and Nate are doing a great job with them. "

"Still, you didn't have to take yourself out. I don't think God required that of you."

"It was best, Sly. One door closes, another opens. I believe that. The Lord will show me what to do next. Besides, I haven't deserted the kids. I'm there for them if they need me. They know that. I haven't given up the teen fathers' group either."

"Thank God for that."

"I do thank Him. Daily. The kids fill up a lot of my time, not to mention my heart. I'm a little worried about Monika though. She's being really clingy with me these days. I've tried to get her to confide in CeCe, but she still looks to me."

Sly knew about the teenager who'd started coming to Faith Central a few years ago. She attended Faith Central but her mother didn't. "What's up with her?"

"Teenage angst, as best I can see it. She and her mother are having a rough time. Monika wants to know who her father is and her mother won't tell her. It's causing the girl a lot of pain."

"How old is she?"

"Fifteen," Stuart said. "The age when girls crave attention from men. I pray she doesn't start looking for love in all the wrong places."

Sly knew exactly what Stuart meant and his heart went out to the girl. "How about we spend some time praying for her?"

Stuart nodded and again, with hands to shoulders, the two men prayed.

Sitting in the parking lot in front of the Southwest Ohio Mental Health Clinic on Sunday morning, Dawn Amen-Ray finally gave in to the urge she'd fought throughout the nine-hour drive from Georgia to Ohio and through the sleepless night she'd spent in a nearby hotel. She pressed her fingertips against her lips, closed her eyes, and relived the kiss she and Sylvester had shared. She still loved him, still wanted him. Even though he had cheated on her for months, she still loved him. She wondered when she'd turned into such a wimp of a woman. What kind of woman continues to live with a man who cheated on her? A woman who loves the Lord and who believes marriage vows are a covenant between a man, a woman, and God? She certainly hoped so, because that's the woman she wanted to be.

She sighed deeply. If she couldn't be honest with herself, who could she be honest with? What kind of woman continues to live with a man who cheated on her? A woman who still loves her husband. She'd loved Sylvester for as long as she could remember, but for most of that time Sylvester had loved Francine. Dawn had done all sorts of outrageous things to get his attention, but he'd never been interested. Though Francine was an attractive woman, Dawn had known that it wasn't Francine's looks that had captured Sylvester. No, Sly had chosen Francine because he'd seen that even though Dawn had the better packaging, Francine was the better person. Dawn looked good; Francine *was* good. That had been the case for as long as she could remember. Her grandparents had often told her that she was "just like her mother" and she'd instinctively known that wasn't a good thing. From the pictures they had, Dawn knew she looked more like her mother than Francine did, and apparently her personality reminded her grandparents of the wild daughter they'd never been able to control, the daughter who'd died of a drug overdose, leaving them to rear two baby girls in their old age.

As she'd grown older, she'd gotten tired of the comparisons that both labeled her "just like her mother" and challenged her to "be more like your sister," and she became the wild child that everybody seemed to expect her to be. She smiled as she remembered her grandmother's often uttered lament "If I weren't already gray-headed, chile, you'd make me gray." Her grandparents had been good to her, despite her rebelliousness. She wished she'd had the opportunity to show them that she'd learned what they wanted her to learn. She'd finally grown up and seen the wisdom of taking the path of the virtuous woman talked about in Proverbs 31. Unfortunately, it had taken their deaths to force her to do so.

After their deaths, she quickly grew tired of playing the role of hellion. She realized she wanted what most women wanted:

a home, a family, someone to love her, children. She'd even come to accept Sylvester's engagement to Francine. She loved her sister, despite the petty jealousy she oftentimes felt toward her, and she loved Sylvester. She'd convinced herself to be happy for them, though she did wonder what married life would be like for them. Frankly, she thought they'd bore each other to death within a year, but it wasn't her place to say so, especially since she couldn't trust her own motives.

Then heaven had opened and smiled down on her. Francine had left town with the traveling evangelist, an act that had almost devastated both Dawn and Sylvester, but the storm cloud had had a mocha-chocolate lining. She and Sly had found comfort in each other. Friendship had blossomed between them and that friendship had grown into something deeper. At first, she'd been afraid that Sylvester was transferring his feelings for Francine to her, but he'd proven to her over time that he was in love with her, so when he'd asked her to marry him, she'd gladly accepted. She'd contacted Francine with the news, but she'd never heard anything back from her sister. Without her sister to share her wedding day, she and Sylvester decided on an intimate ceremony with his family and the closest members of their church family. It had been the happiest day of her life.

She and Sly had been on their way to having the life she'd imagined for them. They were in love, they shared a deep and abiding love for Jesus, and they worked side by side in the family business. Dawn had followed in her grandmother's footsteps and taken on the responsibility for interacting with the grieving families, which she considered the "heart" of the funeral business. Sylvester continued in his manager role as the "brain" of the business. Before Francine left, Francine and Sly had shared the manager function, with Francine managing one of their two locations and Sly managing the other. After she left, Sly had taken on both jobs before deciding to consolidate the management function at one location for efficiency. Dawn was proud of the job he was doing. Or she had been. Everything had been wonderful until she'd found out about the affair. Then her world had fallen off its axis. Everything she'd taken comfort in was gone—poof! She still loved Sylvester, there was no doubt of that, but she now wondered if he'd ever loved her. Had their entire life together been a façade? She'd asked herself and God that question many times, but no satisfactory answer had settled in her spirit.

Dawn sighed. It was too much to think about right now. She needed to focus on Francine. How odd that Francine would need to come home at the moment Dawn's marriage was weakest. Francine had told her that she had no feelings for Sylvester, but Dawn wasn't sure. The two of them had been a couple forever. She wasn't sure it was possible for feelings that deep, held for that length of time, to be easily forgotten. Perhaps they only lay dormant until stirred up by some outside force.

"Stop it," Dawn said aloud to herself. "They'll be locking you up if you keep thinking this way."

Shoving away the negative thoughts, Dawn took a deep breath and got out of the car. Though this facility was one of the better ones—its price tag confirmed that point—she still found it depressing. She'd spent a week here when Francine had first been admitted, with once-a-week visits thereafter, so the place held a familiarity for her.

"Morning, Mrs. Amen-Ray," the duty nurse, Margaret, said to her. "I bet you're here to take your sister home."

Dawn bit back a sharp retort. Margaret was only doing her job, though her perpetual exuberance grated on Dawn like tart lemons on an empty stomach. "I certainly am," she said. "Is she ready?"

Margaret pressed the button that opened the second set of glass doors. "She's in her room waiting for you. If you'll leave your keys with me, I'll have one of the men load her bags. They're all ready."

After handing Margaret the keys to the Cadillac, Dawn stared at the double doors, almost afraid to walk through, a feeling that assaulted her every time she came here. As she made her way into the inner sanctuary of the asylum, the antiseptic smell burned her nostrils, making her want to hold her nose. When she reached her sister's private room, she stood outside the closed oak door and forced a smile on her face. Being strong for her sister and putting on the face of optimism was a role that had been thrust upon her, but one she believed she played with Oscar-worthy skill. She couldn't let Francine know that sometimes all she wanted to do was curl up in the bed bedside her and let somebody take care of her too.

Confident her smile was in place, she pushed open the door. "So, are you ready to blow this pop stand?" she asked, fighting to keep her smile in place as she met her sister's eyes. The doctors said Francine was ready to go home, to face everyday living again, but Dawn didn't like the dimness in her eyes. Would it ever go away?

Francine slid from the side of the bed where she sat, hands folded across her denim-clad thighs in a manner best described as prim. The low-maintenance French braid that had become her trademark hairstyle only added to the conservative look. "I've been ready," she said.

Dawn's anxiety lessened at her sister's eagerness and the flicker of light that flashed in her eyes. "Your carriage awaits," she said with a mock bow.

Francine lifted a small green duffel bag that Dawn knew held Francine's Bible and personal journal, and her brown leather purse, the few belongings representing the sparseness of life she'd experienced during the ninety days she'd been a guest at this mental health hotel. "Let's go."

Dawn took the duffel from her sister's hand and held the door open for her. As she followed Francine past the nurses, the other patients, and their murmured well wishes, hope began to build in her chest. As she passed Margaret for the last time and wished her the last "Have a good day," she knew that this part of their life was over. When the sisters walked through the set of glass double doors that separated the mentally ill from the mentally well, Dawn turned to Francine and took one of her hands in hers. "Are you ready to go home, sis?"

Francine looked up at the sky and inhaled a deep breath, reminding Dawn of a criminal recently released from prison. "More than ready," Francine said, "but I need to make one stop first."

CHAPTER 3

Dawn pulled the Cadillac to a stop in front of the rambling two-story Tudor on Marshall Street that had been like a second home to Francine. She'd lived here, loved here, and grown here in ways she hadn't imagined were possible. When she looked at the place with its peeling paint, full gutters, and sagging shutters, she still felt the excitement she'd often felt when she attended one of the frequent Bible study classes held here. How the Word of God had come alive for her in this place! And not just in words, but in deeds.

Although only eight members of the Temple congregation officially lived in the four-bedroom home, the place was always brimming with the activity of many more. On any given day, they'd have ten to fifteen people staying over. Sometimes more. Bishop Payne was there a lot too, since the house also served as a meeting place for the church on many occasions, but he lived with his family in a separate house a few miles away.

Living together the way they did was a challenge, but Francine was up to it because she considered herself to be living the life Luke described in the second chapter of Acts, where the saints met together in houses and shared everything they had. There had been times when she felt she was living the life the early Christians had lived. Oh, how good those times had been!

She'd been reluctant to move out of the house to an apartment with Toni, but Bishop Payne had encouraged the move. At the time, she'd thought it was because Toni wasn't thriving in the house; Toni didn't cope well with crowded conditions. Now she wondered if his motive had been more personal and more sinister. Had he encouraged the move so he'd have better access to Toni, knowing that Francine would still spend the bulk of her time at the Marshall Street house? All the evidence indicated he had.

"I'm going in with you," Dawn said, moving to open her door.

Francine shook her head, both to clear her thoughts and in response to Dawn's statement. "No, this is something I have to do on my own."

"But—"

"No buts." She pressed her palm across her sister's forearm. "I love you for wanting to be with me, but I need to do this alone. It should only take a few minutes."

Dawn squeezed Francine's fingers. "How many is a few? I need to know when to come looking for you."

Francine smiled. "If I'm not out in half an hour, call in the National Guard."

Dawn snorted. "I'm not waiting that long. If you're not back here in fifteen minutes, I'm coming in after you. I don't trust these people and you shouldn't either."

"Okay," Francine said. "Give me fifteen minutes and then you can come in."

After Dawn nodded agreement, Francine opened her door and headed for the house. The yard was unkempt as usual, with weeds overtaking grass and hedges nearly hiding the windows, but there were no people around, which was odd. She guessed it was a good thing that the group—she refused to use the term *ministry*—no longer held its draw.

She walked up the four oak steps and across the wooden porch to ring the bell, not sure who would answer or what their reaction to her would be. None of them had come to visit her in the hospital, and she could think of only two reasons why they hadn't. First, everything Toni had said was true and everybody but Francine knew it. Second, she had been discredited among the congregation, and the people whom she had once considered her family now shunned her. She suspected both reasons were true.

After peeking through the sidelights, Cassandra opened the door. "Francine," she said. Just that one word, with no emotion at all.

"Yes, it's me." Francine stepped across the threshold and into the house without waiting for an invitation. "Long time no see, Cassandra. How's it going?"

Cassandra stepped back. "You shouldn't be here, Francine."

"Why not?" said Francine. "Unless my memory's failing me, it took my name on a mortgage to get this place out of foreclosure a few years back. By the way, I suggest you find somewhere else to live, or get somebody else to sign on the dotted line of another mortgage, because they'll be foreclosing on this property again any day now." Cassandra's eyes widened. "You didn't really expect me to continue paying the mortgage, did you?" Francine continued. "Where would I get the money, Cassandra? We were behind even before I went into the hospital. You knew that, since you were one of the four people who committed to splitting the payment with me, and I can't even remember the last time you contributed."

"I thought things would work themselves out."

Francine gave a dry laugh. "Guess you didn't pray hard enough."

Cassandra straightened her spine. "Okay, Francine, say what

you came to say and leave. Some of the saints are coming by later and you shouldn't be here when they get here."

"Are you talking about my brothers and sisters, my family?" Francine took a deep breath. The snide remarks were getting her nowhere. "I only have one question, Cassandra. Did you know about Bishop and Toni? Did you know he was sleeping with her?"

"It wasn't like that," Cassandra began. "Toni was lying. She seduced him. He confessed everything to all of us and we've forgiven him."

Francine wasn't buying that nonsense. "That's not what I asked you, Cassandra. You can save the party line for somebody who is as stupid as I used to be. I want to know if you knew he was sleeping with Toni." When Cassandra didn't say anything, Francine added, "It's just you and me. You can tell me the truth. I'm sure my name has been dragged through the mud so much in my absence that nobody here would believe me if I told them what you said anyway. Besides, I just got out of the crazy house. Nobody anywhere would believe me. So be honest with me. You owe me that much."

Cassandra took a deep breath. "You don't understand," she said. "Bishop has a lot on him. His needs are greater than other men's needs. He thought Toni understood."

Even though Francine had known the answer to her question before she'd asked it, Cassandra's rationalization made her throat ache with unspeakable anger. "Why didn't you tell me, Cassandra? Didn't you think I deserved to know?"

Cassandra looked away. "At first, I thought you knew. Then when I realized you didn't, I didn't see any reason to tell you. Everybody knew, Francine. The only reason you didn't know was because you didn't want to know."

"That's not true," Francine said. "I didn't know. I didn't have a clue."

"Only because you closed your eyes to them," Cassandra accused. "Your head was stuck in the Bible so much that you never looked up to see what was going on around you. Everybody knew about Toni and Bishop, and everybody knew she was taking it too seriously. Everybody knew but you."

"Was Toni the only one?"

Cassandra shook her head.

"How many?"

"Does it matter?"

"How many?"

"I didn't keep count."

"You?"

"That's none of your business."

That response gave Francine her answer. "I pity you, Cassandra. I pity you for the way you're letting Bishop use you, and for the way you're enabling and allowing him to use others. I know God's watching and all of you are going to get yours. There's no way you're going to get away with what you're doing."

Cassandra laughed, a demonic sound that Francine had not heard before. Tight tension lines pulled Cassandra's beautiful smooth skin into a ghoulish frown. "You don't know what you're talking about. You don't know what plans Bishop has. Do you think something like this hasn't happened before?" She laughed again. "You really are stupid. We'll lay low for a while, give Bishop time to repent fully since you people really like a good repentance scene, but we'll be back in business in no time."

"Is that what this is about to you, Cassandra? Money?"

Cassandra bared her teeth in a sneer. "It's easy for you to look down on me. You had a good job before you met us. You had money. When Bishop found me, I was living on the street doing what I had to do to survive. The life I have with him is much better than the life I had on the street."

Francine's anger began to dissipate as she listened to Cassandra. "What kind of life is it, Cassandra? Don't you feel any guilt for what happened to Toni?"

Cassandra tossed her mane of jet black hair over her shoulder. "Why should I feel sorry for somebody as stupid as Toni?"

Francine knew trying to get Cassandra to accept any responsibility for Toni's death was hopeless. "Good-bye, Cassandra," she said. "Thanks for calling my sister and telling her I was in the hospital." Then she turned and walked out of the house. She didn't look back, not even when Dawn pulled the car away from the curb. This was her past and she was leaving it behind. For good.

The sisters made the normally nine-hour drive back to Georgia in eight hours. Dawn had started to question Francine about what had happened in the house, but the one-word answers clearly told her that her sister didn't want to talk. By mutual agreement, they made the trip to Atlanta in relative silence. Other than a couple of bathroom and sandwich breaks, they drove straight through. Dawn had called Sylvester from the road, so she wasn't surprised to find the house well lit when she pulled into the drive.

Sylvester met them as they entered the house. As if it were an everyday thing, he pressed a soft kiss on Dawn's lips and then one on Francine's cheek. With one arm draped around Dawn's shoulders, he gave Francine a welcoming smile. "I'm glad you're here," he said. "You're looking good."

Francine brushed back the strands that had escaped from her French braid as she smiled back at him. "Thanks, Sylvester, but I'm sure I look a wreck. It's been a long drive."

He dropped his arms from Dawn's shoulders. "Why don't you two go sit down and relax while I get your things out of the car? There are some appetizers on the counter in the kitchen along with a pitcher of iced tea."

"I can help you—" Francine began.

"And insult my masculinity?" Sylvester teased. "I don't think so."

"Come on, sis," Dawn said, pulling her through the kitchen. "Let Mr. Macho be macho. I could do with putting my feet up and sipping on a cold glass of iced tea."

Francine rubbed her hand on the back of her neck. "That does sound nice. I'm more tired than I thought."

Dawn looked back at her. "Do you want to go to bed?"

"Not right now. I need to relax and rest up first."

"I know the feeling," Dawn said, kicking off her shoes and leaving them in front of the kitchen's center island. She went to the counter, filled a salad plate with celery sticks, cheese, and some dip, and handed it to Francine. "Here. You can start with this." She pointed toward the den. "Take a load off. I'll bring in the iced tea."

Dawn watched her sister with a heavy heart, thinking of everything she'd been through recently. She so wanted Francine to have some peace in her life. As she looked at her sister now, she realized how much she'd missed her and how glad she was to have her back home. The noise of Sylvester entering the house got her attention. She turned to him. "Thanks, Sly," she said.

He inclined his head toward the family room. "How is she, really?"

"Better, but a little battered. She wanted to stop by her old church meeting place before we left."

"Why would she want to do that?"

Dawn shrugged. "That's what I asked her, but she said she had to do it."

Sly studied her beautiful face. Even after a day's drive her makeup was still perfect and not a strand of her shoulder-length auburn curls was out of place. But the tiredness was there in the eyes. "How about you? How are you doing?"

Dawn straightened, fighting the part of herself that wanted to curl into his chest and have him hold her. "I'm fine. Just a little tired. We're going to sit and drink some tea. You're welcome to join us."

"Let me take these bags up to her room and I'll be back down."

"Okay."

He touched her cheek with his palm. "It's going to work out, Dawn." He dropped his hand, picked up the bags, and headed up the back stairs.

Dawn looked after him, hoping that he was right. Shaking her head to clear her thoughts, she poured two glasses of iced tea, grabbed herself a salad plate of veggies and dip, and went to join Francine in the family room.

"Here you go," she said, handing Francine a glass. She sat down in the easy chair opposite where her sister sat in the matching recliner and propped her feet up on the ottoman. "Now, this is exactly what the doctor ordered."

"Thanks for coming to get me, Dawn," Francine said, her eyes soaking up the changes in the room. Dawn had swapped the mint green drapes for deep rose ones that better matched the paisley upholstery on the sofa and chairs. "Thanks for everything. You've really been there for me and I appreciate it."

"I'm your sister, Francine, you don't have to thank me."

"Yes, I do. I haven't been much of a sister to you the past few years, and you would have been well within your rights to ignore my call for help, but you didn't. I thank you for that, because I didn't have anyone else to turn to."

Dawn got up and walked over to her sister, squatting down beside her chair. "No matter what happens, we're family. I haven't always been the best sister myself, so I figure we're even."

Francine leaned over and hugged her sister. "Thanks."

"No problem," Dawn said, standing up. She went back to her chair and dropped down into it just as Sylvester joined them.

"I put your bags in your old room, Fancy," he said, sitting down on the ottoman in front of Dawn. His use of the nickname he'd used for Francine when they were dating pierced Dawn's heart.

"Thanks, Sly," she said. "I was telling Dawn how much I appreciate what she's done for me. I should have included you as well."

"No problem," he said. "We're family."

"So I've been told," Francine said, fighting a yawn that seemed to come up out of nowhere. "I guess I'd better get to bed. I want to get an early start tomorrow."

"Why get up early?" Dawn asked. "Sleep in. I plan to."

"I need a job," Francine said, "and the quicker I find one, the better."

Sylvester sent Dawn a quick glance before asking, "What's this about a job? We assumed you'd be working in the funeral home. We've already put you on the payroll. All you have to do is let us know when you want to start and what you want to do. In fact, I had a business idea that I wanted to discuss with you."

Francine shook her head. "Thank you, Sly, but I can't work in the funeral home."

"Of course you can," Dawn said, hiding her surprise at Sly's mention of a business idea he wanted to discuss with Francine. "We've worked there off and on all of our lives. Big Daddy trained you to run the business."

Francine shook her head again. "I know, but I can't do it now. Not after Toni. I saw her lying there. No, I can't do it. Not now. Maybe one day, but not now."

Dawn exchanged another look with Sly. "You don't have to, but you really don't have to start looking for a job now either. Why not take some time to settle in?"

"I had enough empty time when I was in the hospital. I need to be productive again, the sooner the better. You know what the Bible says, you don't work, you don't eat. Besides, my creditors are going to be tracking me down about that house in Dayton and I'm going to need some money to pay them."

Dawn was about to object, but Sylvester took her hand and squeezed it, effectively cutting her off. "We understand, Fancy. Let us know if we can help."

Francine yawned again. "I guess I'd better head for bed." She picked up her empty glass and saucer and stood. "I'll see you two in the morning."

"Night, Francie," Dawn said. "Welcome home."

Dawn snatched her hand out of Sylvester's as soon as her sister left the room. He turned to her. "What?" he asked.

"Fancy?" she practically sneered, unable to stop herself. "You're flirting with her right under my nose."

"You've got to be kidding me."

"Admit it, Sylvester," Dawn said. "I was always your second choice, maybe even your third choice. If Francine hadn't left town, we never would have gotten together."

"All that means is that I would have married the wrong sister. It's you I love, Dawn, and I don't know how I can tell you that and make you believe it, but it's true."

Dawn studied Sly in silence as she waited for her emotions to settle down. "I'm tired and sleepy. I think it's time I go to bed."

"I'll go up with you."

She turned back to him. "Look, Sylvester, I'm sleeping in our room, but all I'm doing is sleeping. I don't want you to get any ideas about what to expect."

Sylvester sighed deeply, rubbing his hand down his face. "No, Dawn, you've been perfectly clear about what you want from me and what you don't. I don't think my expectations could get any lower. Go on up to bed. I'll clean up down here and come up later."

Fighting the urge to smooth the worry lines from his forehead, she muttered a "Thanks, Sly," walked around him, and raced up the stairs to their room.

CHAPTER 4

Francine lay in her old bed staring at the ceiling. Her room was just as she'd left it, almost as if it had sat waiting for her return for five years. Same burgundy draperies, same dark oak sleigh bed, same Varnette P. Honeywood prints. All symbols of the stability and certainty that had been hallmarks of her life. Yes, the room was the same, but she wasn't. This room belonged to the pre-Temple Francine, a woman who no longer existed. Today's Francine, post-Temple Francine, was a brand new person. Today was literally the first day of the rest of her life. And how was she going to start the day? She rolled onto her side and reached over to the nightstand for the small, blue, spiral-bound notebook that served as her personal journal. The journal that held the list of amends she needed to make. She frowned as she looked at the daunting list of people she had wronged. Like a 12-stepper, her recovery required that she go to each one personally and make amends. She opened the drawer of the nightstand, found a pencil, and drew a line through Cassandra's name. She'd thanked her for calling Dawn and that's all she owed her. Though her questioning hadn't led to a satisfactory end, she had gotten all her answers confirmed. That done, she placed the journal back in the nightstand and pulled out her Bible so she could begin her morning devotions.

She glanced at the clock after she finished her devotions and saw that it was five-thirty, much too early to get started, but she really didn't see herself going back to sleep. She got up, pulled on her favorite navy terry cover-up, and made the trek downstairs. She found Sylvester seated at her grandparents' old oak dinette table sipping on a cup of coffee. Dawn was nowhere in sight. Checking to make sure she was fully covered, she joined her brother-in-law. "Morning, Sly," she said.

He flashed her a smile. "Good morning to you. Sleep well?"

"Very well. It must have been sleeping in a room without bars on the windows that did the trick." She laughed at her own joke, but the sound was hollow to her ears.

Sly reached for her hand. "I'm sorry you had to go through so much, Fancy," he said. "I never wanted to hurt you."

She looked down at their joined hands, remembering the life they had shared together as well as the one they had planned to share. "I never wanted to hurt you either. I'm sorry I left the way I did, Sylvester. You deserved better."

He dropped her hand. "You're right. I did, but things have a way of working themselves out."

"I'm glad you and Dawn found each other."

"So am I," he said, a winsome smile on his face. "You know, before you left I never thought of Dawn as anything other than your bratty twin sister."

She quirked a brow.

"Okay, maybe I thought she was a pain in the butt."

Francine laughed. "Now you're being honest."

"She's nothing like you," he continued. "Maybe that's what attracted me at first." He lifted his eyes to hers, allowing her to see his pain. "You hurt me, Fancy, really badly. I won't lie to you.

I expected to spend the rest of my life with you, have children with you. And you walked away as though I meant nothing to you. Recovery was a long time coming."

A cup of coffee in hand, Francine sat down next to him. "I loved you, Sly, but I guess I didn't love you enough. After my grandparents died, I couldn't think right. I felt trapped, like my life was slipping away. What I saw before me, even being your wife, didn't seem to be enough. I needed purpose."

"That church gave you purpose?"

She scooped two teaspoons of sugar into her coffee and stirred. "For a while. For a long while, in fact. I know you're not going to understand this, because it's hard for me to understand, but I had some really good times there."

His nose crinkled above a frown. "You're right. I don't understand, but I want to."

Francine studied him closely. Dr. Jennings was the only person to whom she had described the details of the goings-on at Temple. She wondered if Sly could handle hearing about some of what she'd experienced. Something in her spirit told her that he could. "I don't know where to start," she said.

"Try the beginning. What made you go with them?"

She closed her eyes briefly and then opened them. "It was a lot of things, but mostly it was the way all the young people handled the Bible. I'm talking people our age and younger. These weren't people at the end of their lives, deciding it was now time to follow God, but people at their prime. Take Cassandra for instance. She was beautiful, smart, she had everything going on for her, but she chose to be with God and the people of God." She gave a self-deriding laugh. "Now I know I was only seeing what I wanted to see."

Sly tipped her chin up. "Don't do that. You aren't the first one to be fooled. The Bible talks about people like those coming along to deceive God's people."

"Yeah, I know it does," she said, thinking of the passage in

Mark. "I just never thought I would be one of the ones deceived. When I first met them, the people from Temple Church, I remember thinking that they must really love God if they knew the Bible the way they did. It seemed reasonable that they knew it so well because they read it so often." She glanced at Sly. "I guess that was pretty stupid," she said. "The Bible says clearly it's not knowing the Bible that makes a difference, but living it. Demons know the Scripture but that doesn't make them lovers of God."

"You've got that right," Sly said. "But there are a lot of people in a lot of churches who talk the Bible but don't live it."

"You know, that's what I think got me. I thought Temple was different. I guess I thought it was the *real* thing, a church where everybody had a heart to follow God. You know I loved Faith Central and Pastor Thomas, but some of the folks up in there were 'bout as crazy as the day is long. I thought it was different at Temple."

"But it wasn't."

She nodded. "Actually, it was different. It was worse because the intentions of the leaders and many of the followers at Temple were evil. Bishop Payne knew the Scriptures and pretended to love God, but deep in his heart, he only loved himself. When I think of the way he preyed on Toni and the other women, it makes me ill. But he preyed on many others as well. He was an equal opportunity predator. Some people were used for sex, like Toni, while others were used for money, like me. And I've got the stack of overdue credit card bills to prove it. But we were all used for Bishop Payne's pleasure, not God's. Bishop Payne presented an imitation of life in Christ, and I bought it, hook, line, and sinker. I still can't get my mind around how I allowed it to happen. I'm not sure I ever will."

"You're too hard on yourself. Just be glad that you got out when you did."

She sobered. "But look at the cost—Toni's life. That cost is too high."

They sat silent for a few minutes. Then, observing Francine over the rim of his cup, Sly said, "You've changed."

"I hope that's a good thing."

"It is. I was worried about you even before you left. You weren't yourself and I kept wondering where my Fancy was. I wanted her back."

"Do you see her now?" Francine asked, not sure what she wanted the answer to be.

He shook his head. "No," he said sadly. "My Fancy is gone, forever, I think. The Francine in front of me now is somebody new."

"Look what a few months in a mental institution will get you."

"Don't joke about it."

"I have to. Otherwise, I'll go crazy. Literally. No pun intended."

"Was it awful?"

She rocked her coffee cup from side to side. "Not really. The surroundings were the last thing on my mind when I got there. In fact, nothing was on my mind. I wanted to disappear."

"Suicide?"

She shook her head. "After seeing Toni—I don't think so. I just wanted life to end. I wanted to fade away, or hide away. That image of Toni—I don't know if I'll ever get it out of my mind. You know, living around a funeral home all my life, I'm used to dead people. But Toni, the blood. I don't think I've ever been that close to death before. The bodies I'd seen had all been long dead. Toni was fresh." The pity in his eyes made her stop talking. "I'm sorry," she said. "I know you don't want to hear this."

"It's all right. Death is our business, or part of it. If we can't talk about it, who can?"

"I don't know if I'll ever be able to look dispassionately at a body again."

Sly pressed a hand to her shoulder. "I understand. You do what you have to do to take care of yourself. That's all Dawn and I want."

She placed her hand on top of his, grateful for his friendship. "Last night you mentioned something about a business idea you wanted to talk over with me. I've got time now, if you do."

"Are you sure? It's funeral home business."

She smiled at the caring that was so much a part of who she knew him to be. She may have changed, but he hadn't. "I think I can talk about the business without too much distress. So what is it?"

He lowered their joined hands to the table. "I have this idea about starting a collective of family-owned funeral homes."

"Why would you want to do that?" she asked as she got up and poured herself another cup of coffee. "We've always been family owned and operated."

"That wouldn't change," Sly explained, "but the funeral business has changed, Fancy. Smaller funeral homes are being bought by these major corporations, left and right. In fact, we've had offers from Easy Rest, the conglomerate that's sweeping through the Southeast."

"You aren't thinking of selling out, are you, Sylvester?"

He smiled. "Now you sound like your sister. It would probably be the smart thing to do. Our finances are not at their best right now."

"When did things get bad?" Francine asked, "Before I left—" She met his gaze. "Is that when the trouble started, when I left?"

"It's not your fault. I was out of it for a while after you first left, and I let some things get by me. Our reputation slipped a little."

Francine sat back in her chair. "My ranting all over town, calling people sinners, didn't help, did it?"

He folded her hand in his. "It's not your fault. That died down."

"You know, Big Daddy always said that in the funeral business, your reputation was money in the bank. What have I done to ours?"

"Nothing that can't be fixed," he assured her. "In fact, things are looking up from that perspective, but the marketplace is changing, and we have to change with it if we're going to thrive and not merely survive. If I had spent the last few years looking to the future, instead of trying to recover from the past, we wouldn't be in this situation, but that's water under the bridge. We have to go on from here."

Francine felt responsible, no matter what Sly said. "How can I help?"

"This collective idea, will you think about it with me? You always could help me think through situations and scenarios. I missed that when you were gone."

Francine laughed at the memory of their work discussions. "Yeah, I remember, all right. Two heads were always better than one when one of them was yours."

Sylvester laughed over the long-standing joke they shared. "So you're smarter than I am. I'm man enough to admit it and not have my ego bruised." He'd always accepted that Francine's mind was much quicker than his. Rather than her intelligence challenging his ego, he'd enjoyed sharing ideas with her and getting her opinion. He had to admit that together they'd done a much better job of running the funeral home than he and Dawn had been able to do. Though, he realized now, he'd never really encouraged Dawn's participation in the decision making. She seemed content to follow his lead, and he was content to let her. In fact, now that he thought about it, the way she trusted him to take care of the business gave him a rush, a sense of importance and strength that fed his ego. Looking at his dark brown hand linked with Francine's lighter one, he wondered at the different roles the sisters had played in his life and the roles he had played in theirs.

"Morning."

Dawn's voice from the doorway surprised both Sylvester and Francine, and they pulled away from each other. The look that passed between Dawn and Sylvester was one that Francine couldn't identify, but the tension that emanated from them was very real. "Morning, Dawn," she said. "I interrupted Sylvester's morning coffee with my sob story and we ended up talking business. I promise not to start each day this way. I'd hate for the two of you to dread seeing me in the mornings."

Dawn came fully into the room. She was dressed in a provocative rose floral pajama outfit. The top had spaghetti straps and clearly showed that she wore no bra, while the short bottoms did little more than cover her rear end. "Don't be silly, Francie," she said.

Francine noticed her sister didn't look at Sly as she poured herself a cup of coffee.

"Do you have plans for the day?" Dawn asked.

"I thought I'd drop by Mother Harris's bookstore," Francine said, giving up on trying to identify the source of tension between Sly and Dawn. "She's still in the same place, isn't she?"

Dawn nodded. "She'll be glad to see you. I told her you were coming home and she made me promise to tell you to come see her. She's always asking about you, Francie. She missed you when you were gone."

Francine felt a pain in her heart. Mother Harris had been like a second grandmother to her, and she'd left town and not even looked back. "She'll be my first stop."

Sly chuckled. "If I know Mother Harris, she might also be your last stop. That woman knows she can talk."

Francine laughed because what Sly said was true. "It'll be a good way to spend the day. I always liked going down to the bookstore, spending the day with her. She'd put me to work and we'd talk about everything under the sun. It'll be fun."

Sly pushed back his chair and rose to his feet. "Speaking of fun, I guess I'd better head to the funeral home." He looked at Dawn. "Are you coming in today?"

She looked at him for the first time since she'd entered the kitchen. "A little later. Is there something you need me to do?"

He shook his head. "I just wondered." He leaned over and pressed a kiss on her forehead. "I'll see you when you get there then." He turned to Francine. "Give my best to Mother Harris. And don't forget to let me know what you think about that idea."

When he was gone, Francine turned to her sister. "I'm glad you two found each other," she said.

Dawn put down her coffee cup. "Are you really?"

Francine was taken aback by the accusation in her sister's question. "Of course I am. Why would you even ask such a thing?"

Dawn shrugged. "He was yours first."

"But he's yours last and that's what matters. I hope you don't think I have any ideas about Sly, because I don't. The best thing about my leaving town is that we didn't get married. I'm not sure I could have made him happy, and I'm not sure he could have made me happy."

Dawn pulled out a chair and sat down across from her sister. "Why do you say that?"

"I don't know exactly. You probably know Sly better than I do, but he's not the easiest man to know. He doesn't share his feelings very well and that used to drive me crazy. You have to remember the fights we had about it. We could talk business until the cows came home, but getting Sly to share his feelings was worse than pulling teeth."

"Yeah, I do remember those arguments now, but you know, I'd forgotten."

"I remember them clearly. He would brood but he wouldn't talk. It irritated me no end." Something in Dawn's eyes made

Francine wonder if Sly was as closemouthed with Dawn as he had been with her. "I hope he doesn't still do that."

"Sometimes. It's a part of who he is, I guess. The stress of the funeral home gets to him sometimes, but he doesn't talk a lot about it." *At least, not to me.* "We've been getting some pressure to sell out to this corporation. Sly thinks it's the best thing for us, but I couldn't bear it, Francie. This funeral home is ours. It would be like selling Big Daddy and Big Momma. I can't do it. What about you? What do you think?"

"I'll go along with whatever you and Sly want. It doesn't seem fair for me to even have a say, since I haven't contributed to the work in such a long time."

"Big Momma and Big Daddy would roll in their graves if we tried to cut you out. It was always their plan that this be ours together."

"Do you think they'd want us to sell?" Francine asked.

"I'm not sure. Sly thinks they'd be more concerned about us being happy. I don't know what to think. I just know that the idea of selling makes me almost physically ill."

"Have you and Sly been arguing about this?"

Dawn met her sister's gaze. "Why do you ask?"

Francine shrugged off her concern, not wanting to make a big deal out of nothing. "I just wondered. Don't mind me. I've made so many mistakes in my own life that I don't want to see other people making them."

"You think arguing with Sly about the funeral home would be a mistake?"

"Maybe not a mistake, but definitely a waste of time and energy. I look back on the last five years of my life and I see a big waste sign—wasted time, wasted money, wasted energy. That's an awful feeling, Dawn. I'd hate for you to look back on this time with Sly with that same feeling." Francine put down her coffee cup and stood. "Hey, you'll have to ignore me. I've been in intensive therapy for the last three months so I'm prone to overanalyzing." She pressed a kiss on her sister's forehead. "I'm going to get dressed. I'll bet Mother Harris still gets to the store early, and I want to surprise her."

"The keys to one of the Cadillacs are on the stand by the door. The number's on the key ring."

"Thanks, Sister."

"Puh-leez. We run a funeral home. The one thing we have plenty of is Cadillacs. Enjoy yourself today."

Laughing, Francine rushed up the stairs, eager to continue the first day of the rest of her life.

Just as Francine expected, Mother Harris was at the bookstore long before the 10 a.m. opening time. Her Lincoln Town Car was a dead giveaway. Francine smiled when she thought about the petite older woman behind the wheel of such a big car. Mother Harris had been a minister's wife for thirty-five years when her husband died. She said they'd driven Town Cars all her married life so she didn't see any reason to stop now. Like clockwork, every three years she traded in her signature burgundy Town Car for a brand new one exactly like it. The older woman's predictability now gave Francine a sense of comfort, while in the past she'd considered it quirky.

As she got out of her car Francine felt a high level of anxiety, wondering how Mother Harris would receive her. When she thought of the cruel things she'd said to the older woman, she had to bite back tears. She knew the door to the store was unlocked, so she didn't bother knocking. The door chimes signaled her entry. Mother Harris peered at her from the counter that was located near the back wall of the store, a position that gave her a clear, wide-angle view of everything that happened in the room.

"Francie?" she called. "Is that you, Francie?"

"It's me, Mother Harris," Francine said, rushing forward.

"Oh, praise the Lord, it *is* you!" Mother Harris opened her arms wide and Francine stepped into them as though she'd never been away. When she felt the smaller woman's arms wrap around her, the dam she hadn't realized she had inside seemed to burst and she began to cry. Not those polite tears that sometimes flowed out of happiness. No, these tears were accompanied by wailing sounds that indicated the depth of Francine's sorrow.

"Now, now, it's gonna be all right," Mother Harris was saying. "You're home now and everything's gonna be all right."

Francine still couldn't stop her tears. "I'm so sorry, Mother Harris," she said between hiccups. "I'm so sorry."

"I know you are, sweetie. I know you are."

"I was afraid you would hate me," she said, when she could complete a sentence. "I know I'd hate me."

Mother Harris stood back and wiped Francine's tears with her weathered hands. "I could never hate you, child. You should've known better than that. Love and hate can't dwell in the same vessel. You know that, don't you?"

"Oh, Mother Harris," Francine said, pulling the older woman close again. "I've missed you so much. How could I ever have left you?"

"Well, children have to spread their wings sometime. You just chose a pretty strange way to spread yours."

Laughing, Francine stepped back. "Nobody but you, Mother Harris. Nobody but you could have me laughing like this when my life is in such a shambles."

"Now, stop saying that, Francie. Your life is not in shambles. The way I see it, your life is standing pretty tall about right now." She cupped Francine's cheeks in her hands. "We're so glad you're back. Whyever did you stay gone so long?" Mother Harris took Francine's hands and guided her to a high-backed oak stool behind the counter. Taking the matching stool next to

Francine's, the older woman said, "Tell me what you've got planned."

"What makes you think I have plans?"

"I know you, Francie. I bet you have a notebook with all your plans written in it. You always were the little organizer. Everything had to be in order for you, everything had to make sense. I hope you've learned that some things don't make sense, no matter how hard you try to make sense of them."

"I think I'm learning the hard way."

Mother Harris laughed. "That's you too. Your grandmother used to have me laughing so hard with stories of you and Dawn that she made my sides hurt. You were her little *logic* bird and Dawn was her little *feeling* bird."

"We drove her crazy, her and Big Daddy."

"They loved every minute of it, and don't you ever think different. You two girls were the lights of their lives. Not that you didn't keep them up many a night praying. I have to say, though, that Dawn kept them on their knees a lot more than you did."

"I wonder what they're thinking of me now. I know I've let them down."

"Don't even think like that," Mother Harris chided. "They're sorry you had to take such a hard road, but they're glad you've come out on the other side and so am I. It's good to have you back home where you belong, Francie. We've missed you, girl, and we need you."

"Need me?"

"Of course we need you. We needed you when you left, but you couldn't see it. Thought you had to be on a traveling ministry team to serve God. I hope you know now that that's not true."

"More than you know, Mother Harris." And with that truth came the bitter knowledge that the last five years didn't have to happen.

"Well, that doesn't matter. What matters now is what you're going to do. So tell me what it is."

Francine took a deep sigh. "I have to get a job and I have to make amends to all the people that I hurt when I left, not necessarily in that order."

Mother Harris beamed. "That's my girl. I knew you'd come out of this still trusting the Lord."

Francine didn't have the heart to tell Mother Harris of the uncertainties she still held. The older woman was so happy; Francine couldn't burst her bubble.

"Now," Mother Harris was saying, "I could use somebody full-time in the store here. You wouldn't be interested in that, would you?"

Francine couldn't believe her luck. Of course, she knew it wasn't luck; it was God. "It'd be perfect, Mother Harris. I love it here, and I love being around you all day."

"That's sweet of you to say, Francie, but if you're going to be here full-time, I probably won't be."

"What'll you be doing?"

"Let's just say I need to do a little wing spreadin' of my own. So when can you start?"

"You're serious?"

"As a heart attack, and at my age a heart attack is pretty serious."

Francine chuckled as a deep sense of well-being settled within her. "Okay, I can start today."

"You're sure you don't want to try to find a job somewhere else? You haven't even asked about the salary or the hours."

"They don't matter. This is where I need to be. You may want to think about it though. No doubt a lot of people that I offended will come through those doors. They may not like that you've hired me. I'd hate for my presence here to affect your business. Maybe we should try my working here on a trial basis?"

Mother Harris waved her hand in dismissal. "Forget a trial basis. You start today and that's final. Anybody doesn't like it, they can take it up with me and God. Between the two of us, we'll set them straight."

Francine leaned over and hugged the older woman.

When Mother Harris pulled away, she said, "Now, enough of this sitting and chitchatting. Let's start to working and chitchatting. We have a lot to do. You'd better lock that front door. We're going to be in the back for a while."

Francine laughed as she slid off her stool. As directed, she went and locked the front door and then she followed Mother Harris back to the storeroom.

CHAPTER 5

Since Francine decided to go job hunting, Dawn changed her mind about sleeping in and instead decided to pamper herself with a visit to her favorite day spa, Kings and Queens, for a facial, manicure, pedicure, and massage. Dolores King, the proprietress, a tall, big-boned woman with perfect mahogany skin, met her at the door. "Morning, Dawn," she said, holding the door open for her. "You're our first customer of the day."

"Morning to you," Dawn said to the woman who'd started Kings and Queens on a shoestring budget about six years ago and grown it into one of the most popular day spas in southwest DeKalb. "Thanks for fitting me in."

Dolores smiled at her. "If we had VIP customers, girl, you'd be one of them. You know we have to make room for you. You are blessed to get Tomika for your massage though, she has a cancellation."

"That is a blessing," Dawn said. "I know how booked up she gets. You have me down for my regular appointment next week, don't you?"

"Yep," Dolores said. She led Dawn to one of the dressing rooms near the back of the salon so she could shed her clothes and slip into one of Kings and Queens's plush white terry-cloth robes. "How'd your trip go?" Dolores asked when Dawn joined her at the first in a line of eight pampering stations, each equipped for facials, manicures, and pedicures.

"It's over," Dawn said as she took a seat in the station's lightly vibrating massage chair. Dolores lifted her feet and placed them in the warm herbal water that would make them baby soft. "That's about the best thing I can say about it."

"Well, at least your sister's home."

"Thank God for that," Dawn said.

Dolores picked up Dawn's right hand and placed it on the tray table in front of her and began removing last week's polish. "You should have brought her with you. I bet she could use some pampering time."

"That's a great idea," Dawn said. "I've had so much on my mind that I didn't even think of it. Can you fit her in with me next week?"

"I'll check," Dolores said. She put Dawn's hands in cool foamy water to soak and then headed for the receptionist's desk to check her schedule.

Dawn heard the door chimes that indicated the arrival of another client. "Hey, Dolores," said a voice Dawn had come to hate. She braced herself to face the woman who had betrayed her. "Girl, do I need a massage this morning!" added the woman.

"Rough weekend?" Dolores asked.

"You said it, girl. This one was a killer. We were in church all weekend. I mean every minute."

"What? Were you having revival?"

"No, girl, the Women's Retreat at Berean Bible," said the woman. "I told you about it, and, girl, you know how those

things go. Get a few of us sisters together and we can talk up a
storm. We gabbed from sunup to sundown. You should've been
there."

The voices grew louder as Dolores led Fredericka Andrews
back to the pampering stations. "Next time you have a retreat,
I'll have to supply you with some spa gift certificates," said Dolores. "It'll be great advertising for me. Now let's get you back
here. Missy'll be out in a minute."

"Great—" Fredericka's voice dropped off when she saw
Dawn. "—idea."

"You two know each other, don't you?" Dolores asked.

Dawn boldly met Freddie's green-eyed gaze. A black woman
with green eyes? Puh-leez, stop with the colored contacts! "Yes,"
she said, fighting to maintain a straight face, "our church choirs
have competed in the city's Battle of the Church Choirs for the
last few years. Freddie's husband, Walter, directs their choir."
She wondered if Fredericka and Sly had been sleeping together
since that first competition. He'd denied the affair had gone on
for that long, but she couldn't be sure. "Walter's choir did a great
job last year, Freddie."

Freddie nodded, taking a seat at the station next to Dawn's.
"Thanks, yours did well too."

"But we didn't make the finals and y'all did. I believe in giving credit where credit is due. Are y'all competing this year?"

"Of course," Freddie said. "Walter and the choir look forward
to it every year. How about y'all?"

"It's the same," Dawn said. "Looking forward to it each year
keeps everybody on their toes." Dawn couldn't believe she was
actually carrying on a conversation with this woman. Though
the affair was an unspoken secret between the two women,
Dawn was pretty sure that Fredericka had no idea how often
she, Dawn, talked to Walter. Dawn ached to gloat to the
green-eyed witch that she knew Walter had moved out and

was staying with one of his buddies. He hadn't filed for a divorce yet, but he was thinking about it. Dawn sympathized with Walter, and she felt Fredericka was getting what she deserved.

Missy joined them then. "Morning, ladies," the twenty-something girl said. "Sorry to keep you waiting, Freddie." She took the stool in front of Fredericka.

"Freddie was telling us about the Women's Retreat at her church," Dolores said.

"I heard," Missy said. "Sounds like it was a lot of fun. Just women?"

Freddie nodded. "Not a man in sight. None were invited."

"Sometimes those women fests are good," Dawn said, unable to resist taking a jab at Fredericka, "but sometimes you need men around to keep it interesting."

Before Freddie could rise to the bait, Dolores inserted, "Well, all I know is that sometimes it's good to get away from the men. They tend to crowd a woman's mind." She cast a wink at Freddie. "But then I'm not married to fine men like the two of you. You two know you got yourselves some good men." She glanced from Dawn to Freddie and back again. "Don't y'all go all humble on me now. You can say it. You know you've got yourselves some good men, don't you?"

If you only knew, Dawn thought. But she met Freddie's eyes and said, "I know it."

"Some women have it too good, Missy," Dolores said. "Handsome, successful husbands. It's enough to make a single woman like me jealous. How about you?"

"Jealous ain't the word," Missy said, her beaded braids jangling as she scrubbed one of Freddie's feet. "I should go straight to the animal shelter to get a date because all I seem to get are dogs."

Dawn chuckled along with the rest of the women. Fly girl Missy's relationships rivaled the best soap operas.

Fredericka added, "Then you should have been at the retreat, girl. We talked that subject inside and out."

"Now I know I shoulda been there," Dolores said. "I thought it might have been a bunch of happily married women like you and Dawn bragging about your husbands. I knew I couldn't deal with that."

Freddie met Dawn's eyes for a brief second, and then turned her attention to Dolores. "It was nothing like that, girl. It was for all women, married and single. The message for single women was about what it means to wait on God."

"Is that all?" Dolores asked. "I already know all about waiting." She huffed. "I could write a book about waiting."

As the Fredericka-witch continued to spout on about what she had learned at the retreat, Dawn tuned her out. *Freddie had some nerve. All up in the salon talking about church, all up in the church talking about God, and sleeping with my husband. If only lightning would strike her dead. But that would be too good for her.* Dawn was glad Freddie's husband had left her. A divorce would serve her right. Dawn cut her eyes at Freddie, wondering for the millionth time what Sly had seen in her. All Dawn saw was a long, thin redbone. She saw nothing in Freddie that came close to giving her competition. Evidently, Sly had seen something.

"Hey, Dawn," Dolores asked, turning Dawn's thoughts back to the conversation. "Does Sylvester have any friends you could introduce me and Missy to? You know what they say about birds of a feather."

"Sorry, but Sly's not doing much flocking this year. He's spending most of his time at home." She eyed Freddie. "With me."

Finished with Dawn's nails, Dolores lifted one of Dawn's feet out of the warm herbal bath and placed it on the footrest. "Don't rub it in. We're already jealous enough. So what else did you talk about at the retreat, Freddie? How do we keep waiting? Sometimes I feel like I've spent my whole life waiting."

"Maybe if I knew the answer to that," the overly dramatic Missy said, "I wouldn't keep making the same mistakes with men." She sighed so hard and long that the other three women laughed again.

"What we talked about this weekend was that waiting means serving God and doing what He wants you to do," Fredericka explained.

"You know," Dolores said, "I've heard that all my adult life, but it doesn't stop me from being lonely. I go to church, I'm involved in the women's group, I feed the hungry on Wednesday nights, but when I go home after a day's work and an evening's service, lonely meets me at the door. You'd think a teenaged daughter would take the edge off the loneliness, but Monika's developing her own life and her own interests and most of them don't include her dear mother."

Dawn found herself drawn into the conversation. She wanted to tell them that marriage was no answer to loneliness. She knew that you could be married and lonely and she knew for a fact that it was a worse lonely than the loneliness she remembered from being single.

"Being married is not a cure for loneliness," Freddie said, surprising Dawn with her honesty. "Married women deal with it too. I haven't figured it all out, but I'm trying to read my Bible and pray when I get lonely. The only way we can know if God will be there for us in those times like He said He would is to give Him a try."

"Well," Dolores said, "you have to let me know how it goes, because I don't see how reading the Bible is going to end the loneliness."

"It's not magic," Freddie agreed, "but I figure that I have to decide whether I want to find a way to deal with the loneliness in God's way, or keep finding ways to deal with the guilt I feel when I deal with it in my way."

"Amen to that," Dolores said. "Sometimes lonely does make you do things you know aren't right."

"I can sure give a second to that one," Missy said.

Freddie glanced at Dawn again, her eyes seeming to want something. "I've been there too," Freddie said. "Lonely can make you do things you never thought you'd do, and you end up hurting yourself and others, even though you didn't mean to. A lot of innocent people get hurt and, no matter how hard you try, what you did is still there and you can't take it back."

"Okay, girl," Dolores said, "you're getting too deep for me." Laughing, she turned to Dawn. "Are you sure Sylvester doesn't have any friends for us?"

Before Dawn could answer, Tomika came out. "I'm ready for you, Dawn," the massage therapist said.

"Saved by the bell," Dolores said. "You'll have to tell us next time."

❧

"Thanks, Mrs. Thompson," Francine said, handing the older woman her receipt and a copy of Michelle Stimpson's *Boaz Brown* for her granddaughter at Howard University. "Have a blessed day."

Mother Harris walked up to Francine as Mrs. Thompson left the store. "I'm so happy to have you here, Francie. I'm so glad you're back."

"I'm glad to be back. If I had known then what I know now, I wouldn't have left in the first place."

"Hey, no looking back today. Remember what Paul said in the Book of Philippians. You've got to look forward. You have your whole life ahead of you and the Lord has a lot in store for you. If you keep looking back, you'll miss it."

The chime on the door signaled the arrival of a new customer. "Sorry I'm late," a girl of about fifteen said. "But I had to stay after school."

Mother Harris narrowed her eyes. "Stay after school?"

The young girl giggled, causing her locks to sway around her face. "I wasn't in trouble. They had a meeting for people who wanted to join the Pep Squad. I didn't know it was going to last so long. I'm sorry."

Mother Harris smiled. "You're not that late, anyway. Come over here," she beckoned. "There's somebody I want you to meet."

"Ms. Francine Amen, meet Monika King. Monika's helping me out this summer. She takes summer school classes in the morning, and then works in the store three to four afternoons a week."

"Hi, Ms. Amen," Monika said. She put her book bag on the counter and extended her hand.

"Hello, Monika," Francine said, taking the younger girl's hand. "Call me Francine or Francie, most people do."

"Francie is going to be working full-time in the store."

Monika turned back to Mother Harris. "Then you won't need me?" she said in a distressed voice.

Mother Harris draped an arm around the girl's shoulders. "I'll always need you, but with both you and Francine at the store, I won't have to be here as much. You know I'm getting old."

The young girl rolled her eyes. "You'll never be old, Mother Harris. You act younger than my momma. Way younger."

Mother Harris laughed. "Don't tell your mother that."

"I'm not crazy," Monika said with a laugh. She picked up her book bag. "So what do you want me to do this afternoon?"

Mother Harris checked her watch. "I'm going to leave the store to you and Francine. Your job is to help Francine close up tonight. This'll be her first time and you know the ropes. How does that sound?"

Francine saw the way the girl's eyes widened with pride that Mother Harris trusted her with such a job. "Great," Monika said. She turned her head toward Francine. "I'll help you."

"Thanks, Monika," Francine said. "It's taking me a while to get the hang of the cash register, so I may need your help with that too."

"No problem," Monika said. "It's a breeze. I'll help you." She turned to Mother Harris. "Who's going to take me home? Do I need to call my momma?"

Mother Harris looked at Francine. "I think Francie'll do it. You're not too much out of her way."

"As long as you can give me directions, you have a ride, Monika," Francine said.

"Great," Monika said. "It's easy to get there." That settled, she turned back to Mother Harris. "What about putting out stock?"

"Francine and I did most of that this morning, but we left a few boxes just for you." Mother Harris tapped her on her nose.

"Yeah, right," the girl said, smiling. "Thanks for thinking of me. I guess I'd better get started."

Francine watched the girl head for the back room. "She's a wonder," she said to Mother Harris. "How long has she been working with you?"

"Just this summer. She and her mother haven't been here that long. I met them after you left town. Monika came to church with some of the kids from the youth ministry a few years back, and she's been coming ever since even though her mother worships somewhere else. She's a really good kid."

"I can see that she is," Francine said. "It's obvious that she loves you. You're more than a boss to her."

"I certainly hope so," Mother Harris said. "Well, I'm going to leave now. Think you'll be okay?"

Francine nodded. "No problem," she said, copying Monika's words. "We won't let you down."

Mother Harris leaned up and kissed her cheek. "I didn't think you would. Don't forget to have fun."

Francine smiled to herself as she thought about Mother Harris and her bookstore for the misplaced. She had no doubt that Mother Harris had embraced her and Monika for similar reasons. The door chime got her attention again. This time the customer was a tall, athletically built man with a mustache and silver wire-rimmed glasses. She guessed he was in his late thirties, early forties. Pretty cute, she thought, taking in the wavy hair.

"Welcome," she called to him with the standard customer greeting. "May I help you?"

He shook his head. "I'll just browse. Are you new here?"

"Just hired today. I guess you're a regular."

"You could say that." He extended his hand. "Stuart Rogers."

Taking his hand, which she noticed bore a wedding ring, she said, "Francine Amen." She'd have to forget about how cute he was.

"Not Dawn's sister?" he said, eyes alert.

Francine wondered what he had heard about her. "Yes, Dawn's sister."

"Well then, I'm especially pleased to meet you. Sly and Dawn are good friends of mine. Small world."

That answered her question. If he was close friends with Dawn and Sly, he had to know her history. That depressed her a bit. "Getting smaller all the time."

"You certainly didn't waste any time finding a job."

Francine laughed. "You know Mother Harris, so you should be able to figure out how that happened."

His laughter told her that he did. "I love that woman," he said.

"Me too."

"Hey, Stuart," Francine heard Monika's voice from behind her.

"Hey yourself," Stuart said, giving the young girl a wide smile.

"I thought it was you," she said, rushing to him and giving him a big hug. Francine watched as he returned her embrace and then pulled away and looked down into Monika's face. "You're pretty happy today," he observed. "What happened? I know you have good news for me."

Monika beamed. Francine could think of no better word for it. "I'm going to be on the Pep Squad," she said. "It's going to be so much fun."

Stuart brushed a hand across the girl's locks. "Good for you. I guess this means you'll have to go to all the games then."

Monika grinned. "It's a tough job, but somebody's got to do it."

Stuart ruffled her locks playfully. "The community thanks you for taking on the tough task."

Monika glanced at Francine. "Did you meet Francine? She started today. Mother Harris left her and me in charge of the store. I have to show Francine how to close up."

Stuart, who had given the young girl his full attention, looked up at Francine for the first time since Monika entered the room. "We've met," he said, giving Francine a smile. He looked back at Monika. "Want to help me find a book?"

The girl nodded. "What you looking for?"

Stuart told Monika what he was looking for and the two of them left to browse the shelves. Francine watched them, wondering at their relationship. Monika certainly held Stuart in high esteem, and he seemed to hold a high level of affection for her. He had to be a relative. When she heard Monika's girlish laughter, she looked over at them and saw Stuart's arm draped around the girl's shoulders. Yes, he had to be a relative.

"Here it is," she heard Monika say.

"Thanks, kiddo," Stuart said.

Francine watched as Monika led him back to the counter. "Do you want me to help you ring this up, Francine?" she asked.

"I think I can handle it," Francine said. "But you're welcome to do it, since you helped him find the book."

Monika shook her head. "That's all right. I still have one more box of books to shelve, so I'd better get back to work." She turned to Stuart. "You're still taking me to lunch tomorrow, right?"

"I wouldn't miss it," he said.

"Good," Monika said, "because I have a lot to talk to you about."

Stuart grinned after her as she headed off to the back.

"Is that all?" Francine asked.

He nodded.

As she rang up his purchase, she asked, "So, are you and Monika related?"

"Depends on how you look at it. I consider her family, but we're not related biologically."

Those words didn't sit too well with Francine. She thought he'd been a bit too familiar with the girl not to be a blood relative. "Oh," she said.

"Oh?"

Francine shrugged as she took his credit card. "You two seem close. I thought you were related." *If you're not, I think you're being a bit too familiar with a teenaged girl.*

"She used to be in my youth group at church."

"Used to be? She's no longer in it?"

He shook his head. "I no longer head the group."

"Well, Monika certainly thinks a lot of you." Francine wondered why Stuart was no longer director of the group, but she didn't ask. He could have been asked to resign. She'd get the details from Mother Harris or Sly and Dawn. Cassandra had accused her of putting her head in the Bible and not seeing what was going on around her. Well, she wouldn't be accused of doing that again. Stuart's relationship with Monika set off all kinds of warning bells in her mind, and she wouldn't rest until she addressed each and every one of them. No one else would be lost on her watch.

"I think a lot of Monika, too," Stuart said. "She's a good kid. You'll see that for yourself as you get to know her."

Francine smiled as she handed him his receipt. "Have a blessed day."

He looked as if he were going to say something, but he took her receipt, nodded, and then turned and left the store.

CHAPTER 6

Stuart's encounter with Francine and Monika weighed heavily on his heart as he sat in his courthouse chambers later that afternoon, after finishing the cases on his docket. He knew Francine's history from Sly, so he had a pretty good idea what she was concerned about, and he wasn't quite sure how to handle it. She actually thought he had inappropriate intentions toward Monika! He would have laughed if it wasn't so serious an allegation, and it had been an allegation even though she hadn't uttered a word of accusation. It was in her eyes and in the words she hadn't spoken.

He was concerned about his relationship with Monika but not because it was inappropriate. No, he was concerned because of the way it looked. He would be more comfortable if Monika reached out to CeCe and Nate, but she wouldn't. She'd grown attached to him and Marie, and he didn't see himself withdrawing from her, not after the way she'd suffered when Marie died. Besides, he had stayed before the Lord long enough to know that he needed to be in Monika's life and that she needed the relationship that he had with her. The kid didn't have a father and she needed to know that a man—a good man, a godly man—cared about her and thought she was valuable. Stuart knew if she didn't get that validation from a good man, a bad one would definitely give her an imitation of it. He wanted much more for Monika than that, and he thanked God her mother did too. In the Psalms, David referred to God as father of the fatherless, and Stuart believed God was using his relationship with Monika to show the teen that she had a father in God.

All that aside, it still felt awkward to know that Francine thought he was a predator. He was going to have to do something to correct her wrong assumption. He'd talk to Sly before he said anything though. He didn't want to do the wrong thing. He closed his eyes. Oh, how he missed Marie. She'd been a part of him. Their lives together had been clear and purposeful. Their shared ministry was more their life than his position on the bench. His role as judge provided him the opportunity to touch lives and gave him a certain standing in the community that opened doors that otherwise would have been closed to him, but it was his life and ministry with Marie and the kids that sustained him. They had always known what their lives together would be, and they'd been living out that life to the fullest when Marie was diagnosed with ovarian cancer. Even then, they hadn't faltered, believing the God they served would heal her. He hadn't. In time, they'd come to accept that as well.

Now that Marie was gone, so was his direction in life. He didn't see himself alone in the ministry they once shared. He didn't fit there anymore and he didn't know where he would fit. He thanked God for his work as jurist because it had kept him sane in the months immediately following Marie's death. He'd found himself assigned to the high-profile case of the outgoing DeKalb County sheriff accused of murdering the incoming sheriff who had defeated him in the most recent election. That case, which had literally been dropped into his lap, had increased his stature considerably in Georgia's political circles. He'd even gotten a letter from the governor commending him on a job well done on a case that could have set Georgia politics back a good twenty years.

Stuart felt good about what he had accomplished, but it still didn't give him the sense of personal fulfillment that the ministry with Marie had. He wasn't sure if anything would ever match it. Stuart knew that Judge Mac's plan to visit him was causing all these thoughts to surface. Though no one in an official capacity had said anything to him, it was rumored that he was on the governor's short list to finish out the remainder of Judge Elway's term on the Georgia Supreme Court, which made him the candidate of choice for the seat in the next election cycle. Judge Mac's impending visit served to confirm the rumors. What other reason would the man have for visiting Stuart? Judge Leander "Mac" Maccalister, now retired, was the head of the Atlanta political machine and everybody knew it. When Stuart's clerk buzzed him that Judge Mac had arrived, he rose to his feet and opened the door for the older man. "Hello, Judge Mac," he said, extending a hand. "I'm honored to have you drop by."

"The honor is all mine, Stuart," Judge Mac said, taking his hand.

Stuart led him into the office, but instead of going back to the chair behind his desk, he chose the more intimate setting of the two burgundy leather chairs facing each other in the front left corner of the room. "Would you like something to drink?" he asked his visitor.

"Nothing for me, but you go ahead."

Stuart shook his head and took a seat facing Judge Mac.

"Today is your day, Stuart," Judge Mac told him bluntly. Sitting across from Stuart in his signature black suit and tie, the older gentleman had a presence that filled Stuart's courthouse office, making it feel much smaller than it actually was. "I see no need to pussyfoot around the issue. You know that Judge Elway is not running for reelection and you also know that, as a courtesy to the governor, he will resign his seat before the end of his term so that the governor can name a replacement. Of course, this is standard policy, as it gives the governor's appointee a slight advantage in the next election, as he'll be the incumbent."

Stuart nodded his understanding of the facts as presented.

"What you don't know is that we've been watching you since you were first appointed to the bench. You've made good decisions from day one and you kept yourself out of any political catfights. Given the district you're in, that took major skill."

"Thank you, Judge."

"No need to thank me. I'm only stating facts. We were impressed with you before you got the sheriff murder case, but you exceeded our expectations with the way you handled that case. It was a political landmine that could have ended your career or boosted you into the stratosphere. I'm here today to show you what the stratosphere looks like."

"I don't know what to say."

"You don't have to say anything yet. Hear me out first. I know you've heard the rumors and I'm here to tell you they're true. The governor has a short list of three men to fill Elway's seat, and your name is at the top of that list. You're the youngest one on it and you're the only African-American."

Stuart's heart raced as he listened to Judge Mac. He understood what Judge Mac was telling him: If he didn't accept the governor's offer, the number of African-Americans on the Georgia Supreme Court would remain at two, but if he took it, it would be the first time three ethnic minorities were on the court.

"Now, the first thing we need to know is whether you're interested. We don't need a commitment yet, but we do need a statement of interest," Judge Mac said. "We'll need a commitment within the next month or so."

Stuart swallowed. How could he not be interested? "Yes, I'm interested."

"Good, good," Judge Mac said. "I was sure you would be. No man in his right mind would turn down an opportunity like the one I'm giving you. You may think you do, but you don't have any idea of the power you'll wield as a Georgia Supreme Court jurist. With power comes privilege and with privilege comes responsibility. You made the short list because we knew you could handle all three. Men fail in the job, or become corrupted by it, when they can't."

"I appreciate your confidence in me, Judge."

"This is merely the first step, Stuart," Judge Mac explained. "We've already started the vetting process and now we'll step that up. If there's any skeleton in your closet, we'll find it, but it'll save us a lot of time if you tell me. Is there anything in your past that might in any way be construed as an embarrassment to the governor or to yourself?"

Stuart shook his head. "Not that I can think of."

"We don't think so either. Our guys are pretty thorough, but we always like to look deeper than our opponents will look, and I'm telling you that they will dig deeply. You can count on it. The days of nonpartisan judicial campaigns are long gone. So you think about my question and if anything, and I do mean anything, comes to mind, you let me know. Now, this is important: You think of anything, no matter how small, you tell me and let me decide if it's worth knowing. In this case, it's truly better to be safe than sorry. Understand?"

"Yes, sir."

"Good, good. I believe that answers all of my questions. Do you have any for me?"

"Is there anything I should be doing?"

Judge Mac shook his head. "Keep doing what you're doing.

Don't change a thing. We're buying the man you are, not making you into the man we want you to be. That's a much harder job, but I've had to do it before and I can do it again if need be. It's just not needed in your case. Judge Elway is not resigning until the end of this year, the beginning of next year, which gives us about six to nine months to prepare. Anything else?"

Stuart shook his head. "Not really."

"Okay, then. I'll get you a schedule for the next six months that lays out our strategy, and I'll be in touch with you pretty regularly to keep you up-to-date on where things stand. The governor won't make a formal announcement until we get closer to Elway's resignation date. Until that time, we want to keep the rumors going but we don't want to confirm any of them. Of course, you can discuss this with the people closest to you. We just don't want you to make any public statements until we're ready to do so. That also gives you some time to make sure this is a step you want to take, because once you do, your life will never be the same."

"That's fine with me," Stuart said.

Judge Mac pushed up on his cane and got out of his chair. "The sky's the limit for you, Stuart," he said, gruffness in his voice. "I don't say this lightly. You've got what it takes to go beyond the Georgia bench, if you want it."

Stuart wasn't sure what to say, so he said nothing.

"You're surprised, aren't you?"

"To put it mildly."

"Well, that's good, too. We don't need career politicians on the bench, and we don't need men with long-standing aspirations for more and more power."

Stuart followed the older man to the door and held it open for him. "I appreciate your confidence in me, Judge Mac. I won't let you down."

Judge Mac turned to him when he reached the door. "Don't

worry about letting me down, Stuart. You were doing what you needed to do before you met me. We need men like you. The problems we face as a society are big and getting bigger every day. It's going to take big men to find reasonable and workable solutions. You're a big man. That's the only reason I'm here."

Stuart closed the door after Judge Mac left, and continued to meditate on his words. Stuart Rogers, a Georgia Supreme Court jurist? Who would have thought it, Marie? He lifted his head and uttered a short prayer for guidance and in thanks.

Anger radiated from Dawn when she walked into the funeral home later that afternoon. Ms. Fredericka had ruined her spa time. The woman had the nerve to try some contrition act on her as if she could make up for sleeping with Sly. Well, Dawn wasn't going for it. You don't ruin somebody's life and then expect her to forgive you. The woman must be stupid or think that Dawn was. Her line obviously hadn't worked on her husband, so why did she think it would work on Dawn?

"Mrs. Tate's here, Ms. Dawn," her assistant said from her office doorway.

Dawn forced a smile for the girl's sake. "Thanks, Tina." As Dawn followed Tina to the outer office, she thought again how right she'd been to hire the teen part-time. She helped out a lot around the office, didn't cost them a lot of money, and gave Amen-Ray an opportunity to support the community by hiring some of its young people. Tina was one of three on their payroll. Two young men did various odd jobs.

"Mrs. Tate," Dawn said, clasping the younger woman's hands in hers. *Lord, give me wisdom.* Still holding one of her hands, she led the woman into her office. Instead of taking her to the chairs at the desk, Dawn led Mrs. Tate to the sitting area she'd recently sectioned off in her office for times like this. She seated Mrs. Tate on the soft leather sofa and sat down next to her.

After she was seated, Mrs. Tate said, "Call me Glenda. I feel like we're friends."

"Okay, Glenda, but you'll have to call me Dawn."

The woman lowered her head and tears built in the back of Dawn's eyes. Her heart ached for this young woman, only married two years when her husband was killed in a tragic car accident.

"I don't mean to bother you," Glenda said, still not looking up. "But I couldn't sit in that house and I didn't have anybody else to talk to." She looked up then with tortured eyes. "I miss him so much. I loved him so much. He was such a good man." Her eyes filled with tears and she began to weep.

Dawn leaned close and pulled the grieving woman into her arms. "It's hard to lose the ones we love. We keep thinking it's a dream. We'll wake up and they'll be back." Dawn knew that was how she herself felt, and her husband was alive and well. It was her dreams that had died.

Glenda peered up at her. "That's why I like to sleep. When I sleep, he's with me. I can pretend he's still with me."

Dawn blinked her eyes a few times to keep her own tears at bay. These days, she knew a lot about pretending. But this wasn't about her. It was about Glenda. Like her grandmother before her, Dawn found this part of her job the most fulfilling, even though it was also the most difficult and most draining part of it. She liked to think the Lord used her to comfort the people who walked through her door. "That's common, Glenda. Though you don't believe it now, there'll come a time when you'll know he's with you and you're wide awake."

Glenda sniffled. "I know Ted's with the Lord, but I want him with me. I don't care that he's in a better place. I want him here. We had such a wonderful life planned." The woman pulled out of Dawn's embrace. "It's not fair. It's really not fair."

"No, it's not fair." Dawn tried, but she couldn't stop her own tears. Her personal losses crowded her mind. Her grandfather taken so suddenly, followed so quickly by her grandmother. And now her marriage seemed to be dying a slow, agonizing death.

Neither woman said anything for a while. A lot of things happened in life that weren't fair, and you had to learn to live through them, Dawn thought.

"I feel so empty," Glenda said. "I can't even feel God. Now when I need to feel Him most, I can't feel Him."

"I know what you mean, Glenda. I've been there." *I am there.* "But you know, He's right here with you nonetheless." Dawn reached behind her, picked up a framed picture of a sunset beach, and handed it to Glenda. "Read this."

She saw Glenda's lips quiver when she realized what it was. "I've seen this before," she said as she read Mary Stevenson's "Footprints in the Sand."

"It's one of my favorites," Dawn said as the woman began to weep again, this time more quietly. "It's the times when we don't feel Him that He's doing our work and His. He'll never leave us alone when we need Him. Like the poem says, when we only see one set of footprints, they're His footprints and He's carrying us. Now's the time to hold to that truth, Glenda. You don't have to feel Him to know He's there, but when you're ready, you'll feel Him, because He's right here." Dawn rested her hand lightly across Glenda's heart. "He promised that He'd never leave us and that He'd not put more on us than we can bear. We have to hold tight to both those promises."

Dawn sat quietly while Glenda dried her tears. "He's here in you too," Glenda said, pointing to Dawn. "You've been such a comfort to me, Dawn. Since the first day I came in here, you've made me feel better, like I could really get through this." She stared at Dawn for a long minute. "I sense you've had your own share of grief. That's why you're so good with others. Your grandparents were wonderful people. I know they'd be proud of you for what you're doing with the funeral home."

Dawn breathed deeply. She didn't want to start boo-hooing. "I still feel their presence. I like working here, knowing they once worked here too. In a way, I feel, all of us feel, that we're carrying on their work in an important way. It helps to keep them close. That doesn't mean I don't miss them. It's just not as piercing as it was at first."

Glenda nodded and the two women sat together in quietness, Dawn enduring her own kind of grief.

A few hours later, Sly walked into Dawn's office and found his wife sitting on the sofa, crying softly. He often found her like this and her tears cut him more deeply than any harsh words she spoke. Tina had told him about Glenda's visit earlier in the day, so a part of him hoped she was the reason for Dawn's tears, but a part of him knew that her tears were because of what he'd done. Praying for strength, he went to her. "What's wrong, baby?" He rubbed his wife's shoulders. "Are you sure this isn't too much for you—dealing with all the families? You don't have to do it by yourself. You don't have to do it at all if it makes you this sad."

Dawn sniffled. "It's not that. The work is rewarding."

Sly sat down next to his wife. He took her hand in his and rubbed.

"What happened to us, Sly? How did we end up like this? Did we start wrong so we had to end wrong?"

Sly held her hand tighter. "You didn't do anything wrong. I did, but it's nothing we can't fix."

"You sound so sure."

Sly pulled her close since she seemed to be in a mood to accept his touch. "I'm sure because I love you."

She looked up at him. "I love you too, Sylvester," she said, reciting the words he'd wondered if he'd ever hear from her lips again. "I love you so much. I always have, but I don't know if it's enough."

"It's enough," he said. "It has to be enough."

She pulled away from him and wiped her eyes. "I saw Fredericka today."

He sat back on the couch, knowing the brief interlude of peace between them was over. "Where?"

"I went to the spa this morning after Francine decided to spend the day with Mother Harris." She sighed. "It still hurts, Sly. It hurts as much as it did when I first found out. Shouldn't I feel the pain less each day? Why does it still hurt so much?"

Each of her words worked its way into Sly's heart, and he felt her pain and his own. "I don't know what to tell you. I don't have any answers. I'm willing to try counseling if you are. Maybe that'll help."

Dawn shook her head. "I can't tell our business to strangers. I can't."

"We have to do something, Dawn. We can't go on like we are forever."

She sighed deeply. "Walter left Freddie."

"I know."

She looked up at him. "How did you know? I thought you hadn't spoken with her."

Now it was his turn to sigh. "I suppose I know from the same source as you. Walter told me. Didn't he tell you?"

She nodded. "I didn't know you had spoken with him."

"Well, he did most of the talking." Actually, what he had done was shout, and Sylvester hadn't even been able to defend himself. "Dawn, I need you to consider the counseling. I don't know what we're going to do if you don't. Every day I feel you pulling farther and farther away from me. I'm afraid you're going to get so far away that we'll never be able to get back together.

It's not what I want to happen, but it's what I fear will happen if we don't fight for what we have, for what we had. You have to decide how much you want this marriage. I know how much I want it."

"That's easy for you to say."

He shook his head. "No, it's not. Every day I have to wake up and look at myself and know that I caused all of our problems. Some days it's hard to even get out of bed, but I do, and I do it because I still have hope for us, hope in us."

She chuckled, a dry chuckle, but a chuckle no less.

"What's funny?"

"I was just thinking that if we go to counseling, both of the Amen sisters will be in therapy. I wonder if that would surprise our grandparents? Probably not, huh? They always said we drove them crazy. I guess we drove ourselves crazy too."

"Don't say that," he commanded. "You're not crazy. I broke our marriage vows. You didn't. If anybody is crazy, it's me. If I could fix all this by myself, I would, but I can't. I need your help. I need you to trust me, or at least, to want to trust me again. Until you get to that point, I don't think there's anywhere else for us to go."

A quiver of what felt like fear flared up in her as she looked up at him. "Are you telling me you're getting tired of waiting?"

He cupped her face in his hands and stared deeply into her eyes. "No, I'm not telling you that. I'm telling you that I'm afraid that you're walking so far away from me that we won't be able to reconnect. That's what I'm saying and that's all I'm saying. I slept in the bed with you last night, Dawn, our bodies less than a foot apart, and I've never felt farther away from you. I know you have to feel the distance."

She felt it all right. "Believe it or not, I don't like it either. I just don't seem to be able to do anything to change it."

"That's why we need counseling."

She looked away and his hands fell from her face. The

thought of listening to Sly talk to another person about his relationship with Freddie was too much for her to bear. "I'll think about it, Sly. That's all I can do at this point."

He pressed a kiss against her forehead. "It's a start, baby. It's a start." *Please, Lord, we desperately need Your help.*

CHAPTER 7

Stuart had a lot on his mind as he left the courthouse: Judge Mac, Francine and Monika, Marie. Too much. He needed to decompress before he went home. He wanted to talk to Sly, but given the problems his friend was having with his wife, Stuart was reluctant to go by their house. He decided to drive by the funeral home. If Sly's car was still there, he'd stop and talk. If it wasn't, he'd wait until tomorrow.

Fortunately, as Stuart slowed down in front of the funeral home, he was able to pick out Sly's Cadillac from all the others present by his vanity plate, RAY ONE. He pulled into the space next to Sly's and made his way into the foyer of the funeral home. He went first to Sly's office, and when he didn't find him there, he went back to the preparation room where the embalming was done. Though Sly had embalmers to do the task, he was a licensed embalmer himself and often took part in the work. That's where Stuart found him. The smell of formaldehyde greeted him at the door, and he wondered again how they kept the smell from permeating the entire funeral home. He knew that was Dawn's doing; the smell of fresh-cut flowers, not formaldehyde, was the aroma that visitors remembered.

Since Sly was observing and not actually carrying out the procedure, Stuart decided it was okay to interrupt. He rapped on the doorframe to get everybody's attention. "May a layperson enter?" he asked when all three of the men present looked up.

"No need," Sly said, glancing over at him. "I was about to leave." He turned to the two men with him. "If I'm not here when you leave, be sure to leave your status report in my box. I appreciate you guys working over like this."

"What brings you by?" Sly asked when he reached Stuart. "It's been a while since you've been here."

Stuart fell into step with Sly and followed him back down the hallway to his office. "I was in the neighborhood," he said.

Sly opened his office door and went straight to the mini-refrigerator that he kept there. He tossed a bottle of mineral water to Stuart and then took out one for himself. Loosening his tie, he dropped down in his chair and propped his feet up on his desk. "Now, what really brings you by?"

Following Sly's lead, Stuart loosened his own tie, sat down in a chair on the opposite side of the desk, and propped his feet up too. "This is the life," he said. "A great way to end the day. All we need is a television and some football."

Sly chuckled. "Or a pool table."

Stuart grunted his agreement. "It's been a tough day."

"Tell me about it," Sly said, taking a swig from his water bottle. "Want to bet on who had the worse day?"

Stuart shook his head. "The way my day's going, I'd lose."

Sly chuckled. "Really, what happened?"

Stuart dropped his feet to the floor and leaned forward. "I was approached today about taking over Judge Elway's seat on the Georgia Supreme Court."

Sly's hand stopped with his bottle of mineral water midway to his mouth. "What?"

"You heard me."

"The Georgia Supreme Court? Are you serious?"

"It looks that way."

Sly dropped his feet to the floor and walked around his desk. "Get out of that chair so I can congratulate you." When Stuart stood, Sly clapped him on the back. "I'm proud of you, man. I know you'll do a great job."

Sly leaned back against his desk as Stuart sat back down. "Nothing's official yet," Stuart said, "so you can't spread the word. I was approached and asked if I was interested."

"You'd better tell me you told them you were."

"I did."

"What else could you say?" Sly said, shaking his head. "You're not crazy. I can't believe it. I'm going to be good friends with a Supreme Court jurist. Does this mean no more parking tickets for me?"

Stuart laughed. "No, but I think it means no more parking tickets for me."

Sly chuckled. "I'll be glad when you get a position where you can help me. It looks like the only thing I'll get out of your new status is bragging rights. My friend, the Supreme Court judge. Hey, we needed you when we had that hanging-chad thing in Florida."

"It's the Georgia Supreme Court, Sly, not the U.S. Supreme Court."

"Oh yeah," Sly said. "I guess that's right. Anyway, who knows, maybe you'll be the next Thurgood Marshall."

"Let's not get carried away."

Sly studied his friend, thinking of the pain he'd suffered over the last few years. If anyone deserved good things, Stuart did. "This news should have made for a good day. If this is the worst thing that happened to you today, I think we should have had that bet. I know I would have won. Are there some downsides to this that I don't see?"

Stuart dropped his head back against his chair. "It's good news, man, but it's so different from how I imagined my life would be. All my plans included me and Marie. Moving up the court system was never really on our timeline."

"It seems God has other plans."

"So it seems."

"You don't sound so sure?"

Stuart sat up and rolled his shoulders forward. "About as sure as I am about anything these days. I'm just going to follow it and see what happens. Either I trust God and the plans He has for me, or I don't, right?"

"Right."

"Then I'll trust God to guide me and try not to get ahead of Him. That's usually where I get in trouble."

Since Sly had taken a similar approach to life himself, he said, "Sounds like a plan to me."

"Hey, I met your sister-in-law today. I dropped by the bookstore earlier. I don't think she likes me."

"Why do you say that?"

Stuart frowned at the memory of the ominous look on Francine's face when she'd rung up his bookstore purchase. "I get the feeling she thinks I have evil intentions toward Monika, who also works at the bookstore. I saw Monika there today too and we were our normal friendly selves. Apparently, a bit too friendly for Francine."

Sly tipped his chin down. "It's what she's been through. A lot of evil stuff went on in that—I hate to even call it a church—in that place, and it has to have colored the way she sees things. I wouldn't take it personally. She'll come to know you and Monika, and she'll understand."

"That's pretty much what I figured. I wanted to say something to her, but I couldn't see myself declaring that I wasn't a pervert."

Sly chuckled. "No, I don't think that would have gone over

well. Just give it time." He cast a sideways glance at Stuart, a thought he hadn't considered before forming in his mind. "She's cute, isn't she?"

"Who?" Stuart asked.

Sly rolled his eyes. "Who do you think?"

"She's pretty cute."

"You'll have to come over to the house for dinner one night. Seeing you in another setting will help to ease her concerns about you."

"Are you matchmaking?"

"Who? Me? Never."

Stuart chuckled. "You'd better not be. Now, what happened to *you* today?"

Sly shrugged off thoughts of Dawn and their relationship; they were not going to be the topic of conversation this evening. "Same old, same old. Let's talk about something else."

Stuart knew Sly was referring to his ongoing problems with Dawn, so he wisely changed the topic. "I'm sitting down next week with the BCN guy, Rev. Campbell."

"Oh, you mean Mr. Slick," Sly said, grinning. "You know, he reminds me of that television evangelist that used to come on when we were kids. I can't remember his name but he used to sell prayer cloths."

Stuart chuckled. "Man, you come up with some crazy stuff. The guy wasn't that bad."

"No, he wasn't," Sly admitted, serious now. "Which church does he pastor? I've forgotten."

"Pilgrim Baptist in southeast Atlanta. He has a nice-sized congregation. I'm surprised Amen-Ray hasn't done any funerals there."

Sly nodded. "We have, but not that recently. I can't believe I forgot the man. What did you think of his idea of a collective of churches coming together to make this network happen?"

"It's a common approach. On the surface, there's nothing wrong with it. It works very well when executed properly."

"I've been thinking about applying that idea to the funeral home."

"Come again?"

Sly went back around the desk and took his seat. "I've told you about the conglomerates that are sucking up family funeral homes all over the Southeast. Well, what if a bunch of small, family funeral homes banded together and operated as a collective?"

Stuart considered the idea. "What exactly would this collective do? Would you still be independents or would you be parts of the collective?"

Sly leaned forward. "Independents, definitely, but we could do collective purchasing and advertising, and maybe some other things. I'm envisioning a logo that we would all use that would identify us as being a part of the same collective. For example, something like 'Amen-Ray Funeral Home, a Good Sense Funeral Home,' where 'Good Sense' is the name of the collective. We'd want a better name than 'Good Sense,' but you get the idea."

"It could work," Stuart said. "Have you talked to any other funeral homes about it?"

Sly shook his head. "I've only mentioned it to Francine. She has a good head for business and I've asked her to help me think the idea through. I'd like you on board as well. Naturally, we'll pay you for your time." He paused. "At your pre–Supreme Court rate, of course."

Stuart chuckled. "Of course. But seriously, you know you don't have to pay. I do this kind of thing all the time. I won't be able to take you far in the process, but I can identify some points you might want to consider early on."

Sly nodded. "I'd like for Francine to be in on the discussion. Do you have some time this week or next to sit down with us?"

"I'll have my clerk check my calendar. If we can't find any time during the day, we can surely find a free evening."

"Thanks, man," Sly said. "This idea could be exactly what we need to take the funeral home to the next level."

Stuart leaned forward. "Is Dawn going to be in on the discussions too?"

Sly shook his head. "I don't want her to worry."

"She's your wife, Sly."

He shook his head again. "Now's not the right time. She's agreed to think about marriage counseling and I don't want to do anything to take her attention from that. I think this would."

"I don't agree with you," Stuart said, "but it's your decision. I'll have my clerk call you tomorrow."

"Great." Sly stood and lifted his arms in a stretch. "Now, on that note, how'd you like to do dinner?"

"I thought you'd be ready to get home."

"Not tonight. Dawn has choir practice and Francine is closing the bookstore for Mother Harris so I'm alone for dinner. You look like a cheap date. How about it?"

Stuart laughed. "With an offer like that, how can I turn you down?"

"Why do we have to do math?" Monika asked Francine. "I mean really. Why do we need it?"

"You tell me," Francine said. "I'm sure you can think of a couple of reasons." She had enjoyed Monika's company this afternoon. After the teenager had finished putting up all the stock, they'd passed the afternoon trading customers and doing homework. When Monika had a customer, Francine checked a homework problem. Francine had volunteered to take all the customers, but Monika had told her that she needed those breaks to keep her mind fresh. Even though Francine hadn't quite believed her, she'd gone along with the plan and they'd had a very pleasant time together.

The chime sounded and Monika quickly closed her math book. "My turn," she said.

Francine looked down at the notes the girl had written on her tablet. Monika might not like math, but she was good at it. She watched Monika welcome the customer, a woman, and direct her to the biblical prophecy section. Judging from their friendly greeting, the two were already acquainted. There was something familiar about the woman that made Francine think she also knew her, but she couldn't recall her name.

The chime sounded again and a second customer entered the store. Francine's eyes widened when she saw that it was George Roberts, Toni's brother. For a brief moment, Francine felt Toni was with her again, in George's eyes, the same soft brown as his sister's. Those eyes had made him a killer with the girls when they were growing up. Not even Francine had been immune to the unique combination of George's eyes, his caressing baritone voice, and his football player's physique. Those traits apparently had the same effect on the voters. A politician since he graduated college, George had never lost an election.

The softness of the brown in his eyes turned to a hot blaze—maybe the softness had been her imagination—as George stalked toward her with an angry glare on his face. "I didn't believe it when they told me," he said, his voice loud enough to attract the attention of Monika and her customer. "How can you even show your face around here after what you've done?"

Francine shook her head in defense of herself, but it was a feeble attempt since part of her believed he was right. She wasn't without responsibility in Toni's death. How could she make this angry man understand that she hadn't known? Should she even try? "This is not the place, George," Francine said, taking in the wary look on Monika's face. She inclined her head toward the back, and Monika took her cue and headed to the back room, leaving the customer standing there watching them.

"That church you took my sister to wasn't the place either, but that didn't stop you, did it?"

"I'm sorry, George," Francine said. The pain in his eyes—yes, she saw it now—was almost identical to the pain she'd seen in Toni's eyes that fateful day in Dayton. More than anything, Francine wanted to ease it, but she knew she couldn't. She settled for "I'm so sorry."

"Well, sorry isn't good enough. It won't bring my sister back. It won't give my mother grandchildren." He spat across the counter. "You are the one who should be dead, not my sister."

"I know—"

"You don't know anything," he yelled. "You don't know anything, you hear me?" He jabbed a finger in her face. "You pimped her to your pastor. How could you do that to her? What did she ever do to you?"

Francine absorbed each of George's accusations as body blows delivered to her midsection. "I'm sorry, George, I didn't know. You have to believe me, I didn't know."

His crazed eyes widened. "What are you—stupid? You should have known! The man was sleeping with half the women in your church, including your own best friend. How could you not know?"

"I trusted him," she said, helpless against the facts he presented. "I trusted him too. I didn't know."

George brushed his hand across his eyes, but not before Francine saw the tears. "You should have known. You were responsible for her. You brought her to that church so that man could abuse her."

"I know," Francine said, and tentatively reached out a hand to comfort him, but he shoved the hand away. "I'm so sorry."

"You're right about that. You *are* sorry. You're a sorry excuse for a friend and a sorry excuse for a sister." George glared at her.

"I pity Dawn because she had to take you in, but you ought to be ashamed of yourself for taking advantage of Mother Harris the way you are. What did you do? Beg her for a job? Give her some sob story and force her to take you in? She'd better watch her back. Being around you can be dangerous to her health."

The customer, a middle-aged woman—Mrs. Reid from the high school, Francine remembered now—joined them at the counter. "You should go, George," she said. "You shouldn't be saying these things here."

He turned to her. "It's the truth. Everything I've said is the truth. She killed my sister."

After casting Francine a quick glance of shocked pity, the woman put her hand on George's forearm. "Come on with me," she said, as if she were speaking to a child.

"She killed my sister," George said, his words wavering. "Toni was such a sweet girl. You remember her, don't you? Toni was so sweet and she killed her."

"It's all right, George," the woman said, leading him to the door. "Yes, Toni was a sweet, sweet girl."

Francine watched the door, her heart breaking for George and his family. Her grief over Toni's death washed over her afresh, just as she knew his had upon learning of her return to town. *Help him, Lord.*

"Francie?"

Monika's weak voice captured her attention. She turned to the younger girl, saw the fright in her eyes. "It's all right," Francine said.

"Mr. Roberts said—"

Francine closed her eyes. She owed Monika an explanation. She didn't want the young girl thinking a murderer would be driving her home, but she had no idea what to tell her. "I knew Mr. Roberts's sister," Francine said, praying for the right words. "She was one of my closest friends and she killed herself a few months ago."

Monika's eyes widened. "Killed herself? Suicide?"

Francine nodded.

"I never knew anyone who committed suicide. Why did Mr. Roberts say you killed her?"

Francine sighed. "He knows that I didn't kill her. He blames me for her death because I was her friend and when she needed help, I wasn't there to help her."

Monika scrunched up her nose as she considered Francine's words. "How did she kill herself?"

"It makes me sad to talk about it, Monika," Francine said, being honest. "It's about closing time. Why don't we close up and you can ask me questions on the drive home."

Monika nodded, and true to her words, she held her questions until she was in the car with Francine. "Why did your friend kill herself?"

Francine wondered how much of the story to tell a fifteen-year-old. "She had a problem that she thought she couldn't solve. She felt very alone and thought no one would help her. She felt so scared and so alone that she killed herself."

"Man," came Monika's dazed reply.

Francine glanced over at her. "Toni was wrong, Monika. Things get bad but they are never that bad."

"Was she pregnant?" Monika asked.

Francine almost veered off the road. "What makes you think that?"

"There was a girl at school who almost died. She was trying to kill her baby."

In high school? "I'm glad she didn't die. There's no problem worth killing yourself over or your unborn baby." When Monika didn't respond, Francine glanced at her and said, "Monika?"

"I heard you."

"What are you thinking about?"

The girl shrugged but didn't say anything. Francine began to pray in earnest. A picture of a laughing Stuart, his arm around

Monika's shoulders, flashed through her mind. "You know that if you have a problem, you have a lot of people you could turn to. You know that, don't you, Monika?"

"I guess," the girl said.

"No, you don't guess, you know. You have Mother Harris, you have me," she said. "You have parents who love you and friends too."

"I don't have parents," the girl said. "I have a mother, but I don't have a father."

Francine calmed down a bit. This she could handle. "I didn't grow up with my father either," Francine said.

"Did he die?" Monika asked.

"I don't know, I never knew who he was. My mother died before I was old enough to ask her, and my grandparents, who raised me and my sister, didn't know who he was."

"My momma says my father died when I was a little girl."

"You sound like you don't believe her."

Monika cut her a wary glance. "She won't tell me his name or anything. I may have grandparents and cousins, but she won't even tell me. I'm not a baby. She can tell me stuff."

Francine knew she was out in deep waters, but she couldn't end the conversation when the girl was opening up to her. "Have you told your mother how much you want to meet your father's side of your family?"

"Lots of times, but she doesn't listen. She never listens to me. I don't think my father is dead. I think she's telling me he is because she doesn't want me to know him."

"Now, why would she do that, Monika?"

"Because maybe I'll want to go live with him and she'll be all alone. I may have brothers and sisters and she's all worried about herself."

Francine's heart turned over at the teenaged angst. She didn't see any assistance she could offer in regard to Monika's mother, so she changed the focus. "Would you like to have brothers and sisters?"

"That'd be neat. Everybody thinks being an only child is so cool, but it's not, not really. I would like a sister *and* a brother." She turned to Francine. "There's this girl at school who has a bunch of sisters and brothers and they all look alike. I'd like to see somebody who looks like me. I don't even look like my momma. I bet I look like my father, but I'll never know because she won't tell me."

Francine began to remember what it was like being Monika's age. Even though she'd loved her grandparents, there had been times when she'd yearned for her own parents. "I used to wonder about my father too," she said. "I wondered what he looked like, if I looked like him. You see, we have pictures of my mother, and my sister looks like her, but I don't. I always thought that I must look like my father."

"But you had your grandparents. I don't even have grandparents. It's me and my momma, all alone."

"Some people don't even have a mother, young lady."

"I know I should be grateful," Monika said, "and I do love my momma, but it's like a part of me is missing. I have to know about my father. It's like a big hole inside me and sometimes it gets so big that I feel I'll get lost in it."

"Have you told your mother all of this?"

She shrugged. "Some of it, but then she starts to look all sad, like she's going to cry, and I give up. She's never going to tell me."

"Don't give up on your mother, Monika. Talking about your father may be hard for her. It may bring up painful memories. She may not know how to tell you. Ask her again and tell her how you feel."

"It won't help."

"You won't know unless you try."

Monika was silent the rest of the trip home. Francine turned onto the girl's street and then followed her directions to her driveway. The lights were on in the two-story colonial, so she assumed Monika's mother was home. "Are you okay?" she asked Monika. "About what happened at the store?"

Monika nodded.

"What about your mother? Are you going to talk to her again?"

"I'll think about it."

"And you'll tell me what happens?"

Monika nodded and reached for the door handle.

Francine reached for hers too.

"I'm not a baby. You don't have to walk me to the door."

Francine was about to respond when the front door of the house opened and a woman about her age, or a little older, came out. When Monika got out of the car, the woman walked forward. Francine got out of the car.

"Francine," the woman said. "I'm Dolores King. Thanks for giving Monika a ride home. Mother Harris called and told me you'd be bringing her home some evenings." Dolores draped an arm around Monika's shoulders and pressed a kiss to the top of her head. "She didn't give you any grief about her math tonight, did she?"

"Momma!"

Francine laughed as Monika rolled her eyes and broke free of her mother's embrace. "See you tomorrow, Francie," she said, heading for the door.

"Teenagers," Dolores said, looking fondly after her daughter. Francine had no doubt the woman dearly loved Monika.

"She's a great kid," Francine said.

Dolores beamed and her resemblance to Monika was so stark that Francine wondered how the teenager could not see it. "Yes, she is."

"We had an incident at the store tonight," Francine said, feeling a bit awkward but knowing Dolores deserved to know so that she could talk to Monika. "George Roberts came by."

"That couldn't have been good."

"So you know about me and his sister?"

Dolores nodded. "I'm so sorry for what happened."

"Thanks, but you should know that George said a lot of things, some of which Monika overheard."

"What did he say?"

She took a deep breath. "The two biggies were when he accused me of killing his sister and pimping her to my pastor."

"He actually said that?"

"Those words exactly. I'm so sorry Monika was anywhere around. I sent her to the storeroom but I'm sure she overheard a lot of what he was saying, since he was yelling most of the time."

"I'll talk to her."

"We talked a little on the ride home about the suicide, and she mentioned some girl from school who had almost died trying to abort her baby."

Dolores sucked in her breath. "So awful. Kids."

Francine debated whether to tell Dolores the other things Monika had said, but she didn't feel she had any choice. Toni's suicide was too fresh on her mind. If she could offer any help to this family, she had to do so. Trying not to betray Monika's confidence, she said, "Monika also talked about her father tonight."

The other woman's face fell.

"I know this is none of my business," Francine rushed on, "but I thought you'd want to know. He's weighing heavily on her heart."

"I'll talk to her."

Francine smiled. "I knew you would."

Dolores backed toward the house. "Thanks for bringing Monika home and thanks for telling me what she said."

"Not a problem at all."

"You'll have to come to my spa, Kings and Queens. Your sister's one of our regular customers. She was in this morning and made an appointment for you to come in with her next time. We give first-time-customer discounts."

"I look forward to it. Talk to you later. And tell Monika good night for me."

CHAPTER 8

Dolores forced herself to go upstairs to her daughter's room. This was a conversation she didn't want to have, she had avoided having, but she'd known that one day she'd have to tell her daughter the truth. Was tonight the night? Monika's door, as usual, was closed when Dolores reached the teen's room. Knocking, she called her daughter's name.

"Come in," Monika said.

Dolores opened the door and found her daughter sitting cross-legged on the bed, reading a book—or pretending to. She looked like an African princess on a punk rock throne. The loud purple and pink that covered her walls set off the hot pink comforter dotted with royal-purple throw pillows. Yet these bright colors clashed mightily with the Afrocentric sisterlocks covering her head, the spattering of African prints on her walls, and the antique figurines scattered across every available surface. How she loved this multifaceted child! Dolores thought as she moved to sit on the bed next to her daughter. She rubbed her hand across the sisterlocks the teen had worn for the last year. "Tough day, huh?"

As was her way more and more often now, Monika shrugged. "Francine told me what Mr. Roberts said. Do you want to talk about it?"

Monika put her book down and gave her a militant stare. "I want to talk about my father, my grandparents. Why won't you tell me?"

Dolores stopped rubbing her daughter's head and gave a heartfelt sigh. "What do you want to know?"

Monika sat up in reaction to her mother's question. Dolores knew it was because mother had surprised daughter for a change. "You're going to tell me? Really?"

"I'm going to try."

Monika looked skeptical. "The truth this time?" she asked.

Dolores nodded. "What do you want to know?"

Monika hugged one of her royal-purple pillows to her chest. "Is he really dead?"

Dolores closed her eyes and breathed out a soft "No."

"I knew it," Monika said, tossing the pillow away. "I knew it. Why did you lie to me, Momma?"

Dolores smiled at her teenager whose voice now sounded as if it belonged to a five-year-old. "I thought it was the right thing to do. A lie was much easier than the truth, so I took the easy way out."

"You're always telling me not to lie, and you lied."

Dolores didn't flinch from her daughter's accusatory tone. "You're right," she agreed. "You shouldn't lie and I shouldn't have lied to you. My only excuse is that I told myself I'd tell you the truth when I thought you were old enough to handle it."

"When would that have been?"

Dolores smiled at the challenge in her daughter's voice. "The time seemed to change every year. This year I decided to tell you when you graduated from college. Probably next year, it would have been when you got married." Monika's lips turned up in an almost smile, and Dolores seized the small encouragement.

"Whatever I did, whatever lies I told, you have to believe that I love you, Monika, and I did it because I thought it was best for both of us."

"Well, it wasn't best for me. I want to know my father. Who is he?"

Dolores latched onto her daughter's hand and held it tightly in her own. "I promise to tell you the truth, Monika, but just because I tell you the truth doesn't mean you're going to get to know your father." Dolores so wanted to say "sperm donor," but she couldn't hurt her daughter that way.

"What do you mean?"

"I mean that life is complicated. You're only fifteen and I worry even now that you're not old enough to handle this."

"I can handle it," Monika said defiantly. "Tell me about him. Who is he?"

"Your father is a man I met when I was a young woman. He was very handsome, but much older than me." She tightened her hold on her daughter's hand. She'd promised the truth and she prayed the truth wouldn't ruin her daughter's opinion of her. "He was married, Monika."

Monika only nodded. "I figured it had to be something like that."

"How did you figure that?"

She lifted her slight shoulders in a shrug. "I'm not a baby, Momma. I know stuff. I knew it had to be something like that. Did he have other children?"

Dolores nodded. "Three sons. They were in middle school when I met him."

"So what happened?"

"Two years after I met him—I was twenty-three—our relationship changed."

"You mean you started having sex with him."

Dolores nodded. "He was my first, and even though I knew it was wrong, I convinced myself that it was right because we loved each other." Only he hadn't loved her, but how did she explain this to the daughter who was the fruit of that relationship?

"Did he?" she asked. "Love you, I mean?"

"He cared about me, I think," Dolores added, "but no, he didn't love me." She hoped this one little lie wouldn't come back to haunt her, but how could she explain to her daughter that he hadn't cared for her at all?

"What about me?" she asked.

Dolores debated another lie. "I told him, but we decided it was best if nobody else found out. So I never told anyone but him that he was your father."

"Not even your foster parents?"

Dolores nodded. "Not even them. By that time, I was living on my own and we didn't really keep in touch."

"But you never told anyone who he was?"

Dolores shook her head. "He had a wife and children. I couldn't hurt them that way. I knew he was married, Monika. I was hurt, but I knew he was married."

"He wasn't a very good guy, was he?"

Dolores hated the pain in her daughter's voice. "He was young then, Monika, even though he was much older than I was. I like to think that he's grown into a better man. We both know that God can change a person's heart; I can only pray that He's changed your father's."

"Did he see me when I was a baby?"

Dolores nodded. "He took care of us when I was pregnant and for a while after you were born. He loved holding you." Another lie, but for the right reason.

"So what happened to him?"

"He was married, Monika, and I couldn't continue to live that way and neither could he. He had big plans for his life and you and I didn't fit in with them, so we ended the relationship."

"Just like that?"

Dolores shook her head. "No, it was much harder than it looked. He got a better job and he and his family moved away."

"Did you keep up with him over the years?"

"Not really." Another lie.

"Do you know where he is now?"

Dolores nodded.

"You haven't told me his name. What's his name?"

"Edward."

"Edward what?"

"Does it matter?"

"Yes, it matters. He's my father. He's alive and I want to meet him."

Dolores shook her head. "He's married, Monika. He has a family. You can't go meet him."

"Why not? He wasn't thinking about his family when he was having sex with you. Why should he be worried about them now? I want to meet him, Momma. I need to see him. Please."

The anguish in Monika's voice tore at Dolores's heart. She hadn't known how much this meant to her daughter, or more truthfully, she hadn't wanted to know how much it meant. She pulled her daughter close to her and said the words she hadn't wanted to ever utter, "He may not want to meet you, Monika. He has a family, position in the community. He's not going to want that upset."

Monika pulled back. "How do you know? Like you said, God could have changed his heart. He may want to see me. I bet he's thought about me over the years. I'm his only daughter. He didn't have another daughter, did he?"

"No, he didn't. Just the three sons."

"I have to meet him, Momma. Just one time."

Dolores pulled her daughter into her arms again. "I'll see what I can do, Monika, but I can't make any promises." She kissed her daughter on her head. "I love you, Moni. I love you so much. I don't want you to ever forget it."

Dolores felt her daughter's arms tighten around her, and took comfort in the girl's neediness. "I love you too, Momma."

Francine was near tears when she walked into the living room of the Amen-Ray home later that night. She'd only been home one day and already her past had come back to slap her in the face. She'd known she'd have to face Toni's family, known it would be difficult, known they were still hurting. She'd even thought she was prepared for it, but she wasn't. She wasn't prepared for the crushing brutality of George's words, or the pained look on Monika's face, or the aching concern on Dolores's when she learned what her daughter had overheard. The past had reached out and dirtied somebody else's life, a child's, and it wasn't fair. All that, after the day had gotten off to such a good start. Mother Harris. The job. Monika. All in all a great day, and then the past had ruined it. It wasn't fair!

"What's not fair?"

Francine looked up at the sound of Sly's voice, surprised to learn she'd spoken her thoughts aloud. "It's nothing," she said, rushing to the stairs, hoping she could get to her room without more questions. She couldn't handle them tonight. Tonight she wanted to give in to the despair she felt. She wanted to cry tears of self-pity. What she didn't want was to burden Sly or Dawn.

Sly's arm caught hers as her foot hit the bottom step. "Hey," he said, turning her around. "What's the matter?"

She shook her head. "Let it be, Sly, it's nothing. I want to go to bed."

He looked at her more closely and she lowered her eyes. "You've been crying," he said.

She tried to give him a smile. "PMS."

He smiled in return, remembering the times in the past when he'd teased her about her moodiness, labeling it PMS. He'd only done so because he knew it teed her off. "Not you," he said. "Tell me what's wrong. You know I'm not going to give up until you do."

Francine breathed deeply. "You have better things to do than listen to my problems. I was serious when I told you and Dawn this morning that I didn't want everything to be about me."

He tipped her chin up and she looked directly into his caring eyes. It was almost her undoing. "We're family, Francie. You need help. We're there for you. Now tell me what's wrong."

"It's—" she began, trying to deny her pain, but then Sly shook his head slowly back and forth, and she collapsed in his arms. His arms tightened around her and she took comfort in the strength of them. "Oh, Sly," she said. "It was awful. Just awful."

Brushing a soothing hand up and down her back, Sly led her to the living room sofa and sat down next to her. He continued to rub his hand across her shoulders. "Tell me," he said.

The entire sordid story tumbled out between her tears. "The worst was that Monika had to hear all of the ugliness George spewed. I know he's hurt and I feel for him, but he didn't have to say those things in front of Monika. She's a child. He should have known better."

"He wasn't thinking, Francie."

"I know, but that doesn't help Monika. I had to tell her about Toni's suicide. Then I had to tell her mother that I told her. Now her mother's going to have to talk to her. Why should a fifteen-year-old have to deal with that filth? Monika and I didn't even get into the 'pimping' comment that George made. I know she's going to ask about it, though. She's a bright girl."

Sylvester continued to rub her shoulders. "She'll ask and you'll tell her in a way that she understands." He tipped her chin up again. "You didn't do anything wrong, Francine. You have to remember that. You didn't do anything wrong."

Francine stared at the brick fireplace that dominated the north wall of the living room, noticing that Dawn had replaced the old silver fireplace screen with a bright gold one. "Maybe I shouldn't even work at the bookstore. I told Mother Harris that something like this might happen, but even I didn't expect it to happen the first day, and I never expected it to be so loud and ugly."

"Like that would matter to Mother Harris. Do you really think she'll want you to quit because of this?"

Francine knew Mother Harris wouldn't want her to quit. That wasn't the older lady's style. She'd want Francine to stay and she'd stand by her, but was it fair to subject Mother Harris, Monika, and the bookstore customers to the hatred directed solely at her? She thought it wasn't.

"If it's taking you this long to answer, you must not know Mother Harris as well as I thought you did."

Francine wiped at her nose with the back of her hand. "I know her, but that doesn't mean she's always right."

Sly arched a brow. "She's right more than most people I know, including you. Look, you had a rough day. Don't try to make any decisions right now. Things will look better in the morning."

"Easy for you to say."

Sylvester dropped his hand from her shoulder and sank back into the plush cushions of the couch. "When did you become so selfish?" he asked.

She turned back to him. "What? I'm not being selfish. I'm trying to think of other people—Mother Harris, Monika."

"Not that. I'm talking about your attitude toward your problems. You seem to think you're the only person with problems, the only person who faces disappointments. Well, I didn't have the best day today myself, but I can't quit my job and hide out in my room because of it. You've got to shape up, Francie. Everybody has problems. Just because yours sent you to the hospital doesn't mean you have the market cornered."

The depth of Sly's words and the length of his discourse took Francine off guard. Sly didn't open up this way. At least, he hadn't with her in the past. He'd kept a tight rein on his emotions, or tried to, even when it had been obvious something was bothering him. As she looked at him now, she did think he looked tired. "I'm sorry, Sly. You're right. I am being selfish. You should have let me go on up to bed and then I wouldn't have burdened you with this."

He sighed. "There you go again. It's not about you going to your room or even about you burdening me. It's about you thinking your problems are somehow more critical than others'. They're problems and they should be acknowledged and dealt with, but problems are a part of everyday life. We face them, we learn what the Lord wants to teach us from them, and we move on."

She didn't say anything for a while. Then she looked back at him. "Want to tell me about your day?"

He shook his head.

"What about what you said about us being family and leaning on each other? Does it apply to everybody but you?"

"It's not that," he said. "I *can't* talk about it."

"Why not?"

"I just can't."

Francine shook her head. "You haven't changed, you know that, Sly? You still keep everything all bottled inside. One day it's going to explode on you."

Sly smirked. "Maybe it already has."

Francine didn't have a response for those ominous words. She sensed that whatever was bothering Sly ran deep. Something told her that it was the funeral home, Dawn, or maybe both. She knew from past experience that trying to pry it out of him was useless, so she tried another tack. "Dawn upstairs?" she asked.

Sly shook his head. "Choir practice."

Francine smiled. "She's still choir director?"

"That'll never change."

Francine took comfort in the certainty of her sister's musical skills. It was good to know that some things stayed the same. She slapped Sly on his knee. "Want to tell me more about this funeral-home-collective idea then? We didn't have much time this morning."

He sat forward, rested his hands on his knees, and looked over at her. "Maybe now's not the time to talk about it. You've had a long day and so have I."

"Humor me," she said. "I'd rather go to bed thinking about the collective than my day."

"You do have a point with that."

"So?" she encouraged.

He sighed. "There's not much to talk about. I met with Stuart Rogers today and he's going to look over the legalities for us so we'll know what to watch out for." He turned to her. "He told me he met you today at the bookstore. What did you think of him?"

Francine realized she'd forgotten about Stuart, but her concern about him returned with Sly's question. "I didn't think much. You know him better than I do. What do *you* think?"

Sly shrugged. "I consider him a friend and brother. I've known him since he starting coming to Faith Central about five years ago, right after you left, in fact. He and his wife and Dawn and I spent a lot of time together. His wife died two years ago."

Francine turned to him, remembering the ring Stuart still wore. She guessed he still missed his wife. That softened her heart toward him. "I'm sorry to hear that."

"It was a rough time for him," Sly said. "But he's getting better every day."

Though Francine was feeling more kindhearted toward Stuart, she wasn't ready yet to dismiss her concerns about him. "He said he used to be the youth leader."

"He resigned after his wife died. He says he thinks the kids need a man and a woman, a husband-and-wife team, and that he couldn't give them what they needed alone, without his wife at his side."

"You believe that?" Francine said, her esteem for Stuart rising.

"I don't agree with his assessment, but I know he's doing what's in his heart. He loved those kids, loves them still, and only wants the best for them. There's no question in my mind about that."

"He's pretty close to Monika," she said—she hoped—casually. She didn't want to levy any accusations at this point.

"He and Marie, that's his wife, were close to her. He couldn't just pull away after his wife died. He knows Monika's needy where men are concerned, and he wants to be there for her. It's nothing more than that."

Though Francine still wasn't sure, she would give Stuart the benefit of the doubt. She'd still watch him though. She had to. "So when's this meeting to talk about the funeral home?"

"Don't know yet. Stuart's clerk's gonna call tomorrow with his calendar."

"His clerk?"

Sly nodded. "Yes, he's a Superior Court judge in DeKalb County."

"Youth leader and judge, what a combination."

Sly eyed her again. "So what did you think of him, seriously?"

"He seemed to be a nice enough guy. I didn't feel the need to arm the security system when he walked into the store."

Sly chuckled. "He'll be relieved to hear that. You know, a lot of women find Stuart attractive. It was pretty funny, but pitiful too, the way they ran after him after Marie died."

"He's not ready for a relationship—he's still wearing his wedding ring."

Sly elbowed her in the side. "So you noticed?"

Francine bumped his shoulder with her own. "Don't even think about it," she warned.

"Think about what?" he asked innocently.

Francine stood and cast him a wary eye. "I'm going to bed."

"Hey, no need to run off just when the conversation's getting good."

Francine chuckled and then she leaned over and pressed a kiss on his forehead. "Good night, Sly," she said. "Thanks for being a good brother."

CHAPTER 9

One more song, Sister Dawn. Just one."

"No way," Dawn said, lowering the cover on the piano keys. "That'll make it extra song number four. You may not need your sleep, but I need mine, so I'm going home."

Her words were met with good-hearted mutterings from the members of Faith Central's Gospel Chorus. The group had made it to the semifinals of the city choir competition for the last two years, and they were determined to make the finals this year. Therefore, Dawn never had problems getting people to practice; she had problems getting them to go home.

"See you on Sunday," a few of them said as they left the church.

As usual, she was one of the last ones out of the building, along with a couple of choir members who hung around to keep her company while she locked the door and walked to her car. As she crossed the parking lot, she was met by a familiar but unexpected face. "Walter," she said. "What are you doing here?"

"I came to talk to you," he said, nodding a greeting to the others with her.

Dawn turned to her choir members and said, "You all can head on out. I'll be fine."

They murmured good-bye and Dawn was left standing with Fredericka's husband, the man who had given her the news that had changed her life. "What do you want to talk about?" she asked.

He fell into step beside her as she continued to her car. "Can we go somewhere for a cup of coffee?"

She turned to him. "It's late. I have to get home."

"It won't take but a minute. Please."

Dawn looked at this man, saw her pain mirrored in his eyes, and knew she couldn't turn him down. "I'll follow you over to Friendly's."

As Dawn drove to the restaurant, she thought about her own personal D-day, the day the bomb had been dropped on her marriage, her life. Walter had come up to her in much the same way he'd come up to her tonight, but then when he'd asked that she go somewhere with him, she'd turned him down out of hand. She was not in the habit of going for late-night coffee with men other than her husband, even if she did know them, and she wasn't going to start that night. He'd stopped her rejection of his offer with that one fateful question: "Do you know where your husband is?"

Something about the way he'd asked the question told her that she should get in her car and leave. Instead, she'd turned to him and asked her own question, "Why?"

"Because he's with my wife," he'd answered.

"You're lying."

"No," he'd said. "I'm not."

At that moment, Dawn had believed him. She'd gotten in her car and followed him to a Holiday Inn Express not far away. Surprisingly, she'd seen her husband's car parked in the lot. In their separate cars, she and Walter had watched and waited. They hadn't had to wait for long. A hotel room door opened and Freddie and Sly walked out. Sly walked Freddie to her car, pulled her into his arms, and lowered his head to kiss her, but the kiss never happened. Walter had bolted out of his car and slammed his fist into Sly's jaw, sending him sprawling onto the ground in surprise. Dawn hadn't been able to move. She heard the shouting, but couldn't make out the words. Then Walter had pointed toward her car and Sly's head had followed the direction of his hand. Their eyes had met and life as she'd known it had ended.

She shook herself free of the past as she pulled into the restaurant parking lot. Walter waited for her at the door and escorted her inside. They quickly took a seat in the back and ordered coffee. "How are you doing?" she asked.

"I've been better," he said.

Though his words were surely the understatement of the year, Dawn knew exactly what he meant by them. She'd definitely seen better days herself. "So what did you want to talk about?"

"Fredericka told me she saw you today."

Dawn nodded. "At the spa. You can imagine my surprise."

"She says she's changed. She wants to get back together."

Dawn didn't believe for a minute that Freddie had changed. "You going to do it?"

He slumped back in his chair, looking older than his thirty-five years. His full cheeks hung down in a sick-puppy-dog style and his brown eyes were faded. "I've loved her all my life," he said, "but I don't know if I can."

"Then don't," she said.

He was quiet for a minute, and then he said, "I see you haven't left your husband."

"There's more than one way to leave."

He grunted. "So you've got him on lockdown."

Dawn refused to go into details about her relationship with Sly. She sipped her coffee.

"You know what I wish?" he asked. Then, without waiting for her answer, he said, "I wish I'd never found out. Isn't that stupid? I should be wishing that it hadn't happened, but what I wish is that I hadn't found out."

Again, Dawn knew exactly what he meant. "Wishing won't make it so."

He met her eyes. "How do you get past it?"

"You're asking the wrong person. I'm doing the best I can, making it through each day."

"She wants me to go to counseling."

"Sly wants me to go too. Maybe they've been talking to each other."

Walter leaned forward. "Do you think so?"

Dawn shook her head. "No way. Sly wouldn't dare."

"How can you be sure?"

Dawn sighed. "Because I believe Sly wants our marriage to work and he knows there'd be no chance of that if he even spoke to Fredericka on the street."

"Sounds like you two are working things out."

She sipped her coffee again. "I wouldn't go that far."

"You know," Walter said, rubbing his hands down the side of his coffee cup, "sometimes all I want is to pay her back. Sometimes I feel that if I slept with somebody else, then I could forgive her for doing what she did."

Similar thoughts had crossed Dawn's mind, but hearing the words come out of Walter's mouth made the notion real. She'd feel better if she could pay Sly back too, or at least she thought she would. "So you're thinking of having an affair?"

He shook his head.

"But you said—"

"Just one time so I could throw it in her face and get it out of my system."

"Think it'll work?"

"Can't hurt any worse than I hurt now."

"That's a point."

He studied his cup of coffee, which he hadn't touched, then he looked up at her. "You interested?"

Dawn met his eyes. "You can't be serious?"

He leaned forward. "You know I am. Don't look so shocked. I know you've thought about getting back at your husband. This would be the perfect opportunity. One night. You and me. We do it, get it out of our systems, go home, and work on our marriages."

Dawn was alarmed and also frightened that she didn't feel outrage at Walter's suggestion. She pushed her coffee cup away. "You're crazy," she said, but she didn't really think he was.

"Think about it," he called after her as she rushed out of the restaurant.

More than an hour after Francine headed off to bed, Sylvester prowled the first floor of his home, anxiously awaiting his wife's return. Only fifteen minutes ago, he'd called one of her choir friends and found out they'd left her standing in the church parking lot talking to Walter Andrews over an hour ago. Sly didn't like the idea of his wife with Fredericka's husband. Their last get-together had ended in disaster, though he really couldn't blame Walter for that. He wished Dawn would hurry and get home. What did Walter want with her? What did she want with him?

Sylvester didn't like the ideas floating around in his head, but he couldn't shake Dawn's taunts about her and another man. But Walter? No way. Not Dawn. Sly didn't really believe she'd do anything so vicious, but he sure wished she would hurry and get home.

He sat down on the couch, propped his feet up on the ottoman that Dawn used instead of a coffee table, and told himself to wait patiently. Easier said than done. He got up and went to the windows, not knowing what he expected to see. As he turned from the window, he heard the garage door go up, and turning back, he saw the headlights of Dawn's car. He rushed through the kitchen to the garage door to meet her.

"You're late," he said when she entered the house. "I was worried."

She peered up at him. "You shouldn't have been. I'm not that late."

Following her up the stairs, he asked, "So how was choir practice?"

"Choir practice was choir practice," she answered, after they'd entered their bedroom and he'd closed the door. "Francie in bed?"

"Yeah, she got in over an hour ago." He decided not to tell Dawn about Francine's day because he didn't want the conversation diverted to Francine and her issues. "She wondered where you were."

Dawn stepped out of her shoes and took them to the closet. "I was at choir practice," she called from the closet.

"So I told her, but you're later than usual." He watched her go into the bathroom, just beyond the closet. "I thought you may have gone out afterwards."

A few minutes passed before Dawn returned to the bedroom, dressed in a pair of her most revealing shorty pajamas, ready for bed. He wondered if she dressed so skimpily just to tease him. He wouldn't put it past her.

"I went for coffee," she said, "but it was no big deal." She sat down on the side of the bed and looked at him, as if daring him to question her further. "You have something to ask me, Sly, ask me. Don't keep beating around the bush."

He turned away from her and started to unbutton his shirt.

He was not going to interrogate her. He wasn't even sure he wanted answers. He couldn't deal with her and another man. He couldn't.

Dawn sighed. "Who'd you call?" she asked.

He turned to her. "What are you talking about?"

"I asked who you called. Evidently you called somebody from the choir and they told you that I left with Walter."

"I called Larry," he said. "You were late and I was worried."

"Worried about what?"

He turned to her. "Something could have happened to you. I'm your husband. Of course I was worried."

She laughed a harsh laugh. "So you were worried about my health? I'm not even believing that, Sly. At least be honest."

"So what were you doing with him all this time?"

She crossed her legs and leaned back on her elbows in what Sly thought was a deliberately provocative pose. "Are you worried, Sly? Worried that maybe I was doing what you were doing?"

"Don't play games with me, Dawn. You begged me to ask the question, so answer it. What were you doing with him all this time?"

She rocked her legs back and forth. "Maybe I'll let you wonder. Does it bother you to think about it, Sly? Me and Walter—"

"Shut up," he said, "just shut up." He stomped out of the bedroom, slamming the door behind him. He stood and stared at the closed door, his breath coming out in stiff puffs. He wanted to shake some sense into her. He really did. He started to open the door, but stopped himself. He wouldn't play games with Dawn. He was tired of paying for what he'd done. If the only peace she could get was from hurting him, then maybe his marriage wasn't worth fighting for. Why should he fight for a woman who only wanted to hurt him? She said she loved him, but if she did, how could she deliberately look for ways to stick the knife in his heart?

Isn't that what you did? a soft, calm voice he knew well asked. No, he told himself. He hadn't thrown his relationship with Fredericka in Dawn's face. Hurting her had been the result of what he'd done, but it hadn't been the purpose. Dawn wanted to hurt him, and she knew exactly how she could do it.

Sylvester walked to the bedroom across the hall, the one that Dawn had occupied until she decided she wanted to put on a front for Francine. Well, the gig was up. He wasn't going to play games with her anymore. He wouldn't pretend to be married to a loving wife so she could save face. He was more interested in saving his marriage. Since he'd been the one to do wrong, he'd allowed Dawn to use her pain as an excuse to walk all over him. Well, that ended today. He couldn't take back what he'd done. He was willing to work to earn her trust, but he wouldn't continue to subject himself to her abuse. He knew then that if Dawn decided to have an affair to get back at him, their marriage was over. Maybe it wasn't fair, given what he'd done, but that was the way it was in his heart.

He took a deep breath and then headed back across the hall to the master bedroom. Dawn was in bed, seemingly unbothered by the harsh words that had passed between them. After giving her no more than a cursory glance, he went straight to the closet. When he came back out with an armload of his clothes, Dawn sat up in the bed and asked, "What are you doing?"

"What does it look like I'm doing?" he said, marching straight to the door. He opened it, and leaving it open, he strode across the hall and deposited his clothes in that closet.

"What do you think you're doing?" she asked again, when he came back to the master bedroom.

"I'm moving across the hall," he said, en route to the bathroom to get his toiletries.

"Why?"

His jaw tightened at that stupid question and he didn't bother to respond. He merely gathered his toothbrush and shaving kit and brought them to the guest room bath. When he turned to go back and get more of his things, he almost bumped into her. She was standing in the guest room with her arms folded across her chest.

"You've made your point, Sly," she said. "Nothing happened between me and Walter and you know it. We went for coffee. That's all."

"Good for you." He stepped around her and headed back to the master bedroom. She followed him and stood quietly while he gathered a few items from each of the dresser drawers. Then she followed him back across the hall.

"Are you trying to embarrass me in front of my sister?" Dawn asked. "I'm sure she's heard all this noise you're making. What do you think she's thinking about us?"

He turned on her. "I don't care what she thinks. I do care, though, that you're more concerned about what Francine thinks than you are about this marriage. Well, I'm tired of it, Dawn. You're going to have to decide. You either forgive me, or it's over. I won't live with these taunts or your attitude. I love you but I won't do it."

She folded her arms again and looked mutinously up at him. "I have to take you sleeping with another woman but you can't take a few harsh words?" she scoffed. "You've got to be kidding."

He refused to let his guilt make him back down. "I'm not kidding. I know I was wrong. I've apologized. I've put up with your foolishness. I've put up with this front that you want others to see, but tonight I'm done."

"What does that mean?" she asked. "This morning you were talking about counseling. Are you now saying you want a divorce?"

He looked down at the woman he loved more than he'd thought possible. "I think I've been pretty clear about what I want. The question is, what do *you* want? To be honest, I don't have a clue. I feel like you're playing with me. This afternoon you're saying you'll think about counseling and tonight you're suggesting that maybe you're sleeping with somebody else. That doesn't work for me, Dawn. I can't stand on the shifting sands of your emotions. I've tried this your way, but now I'm going to do it my way."

"What does that mean?"

"It means that since you don't want to be with me, we won't pretend that we're together."

"You're moving out?"

He wanted to shake her for being so dense. "Would it even matter to you if I did?"

"Of course it would."

"But only because of what Francine and others would think, right? Well, I no longer care what they think and I'm not going to pretend everything is okay with us when it isn't."

"So you decided this all by yourself and I have no say in it?"

"The days of your say have passed. They started fading when you started throwing other men in my face. I'm done with it, Dawn. If you decide you want me, let me know and I'll move back across the hall. If you decide you want somebody else, I'll move out so you can have him. But I'm done with the games." Sylvester could tell by her expression that he had surprised her. Well, she needed to be surprised. "Look," he said, "we're both tired. Why don't you go to your room so that I can go to bed?"

"Are you sure this is the way you want it?"

Sly shook his head. "But it's the way it is." He opened the door so she could leave. Then he slammed it after she walked through.

CHAPTER 10

Francine took a deep breath and said a silent prayer before she entered the kitchen the next morning. In fact, she'd been praying all morning, most of it for Sly and Dawn. She'd hoped against hope that both of them would either be gone before she came down or still in bed. Her prayer wasn't to be answered. Sly sat at the table, absorbed in the morning paper. "Morning," she said, in what she knew was an overly bright voice. "We have to stop meeting like this."

He smiled at her. "Feeling better this morning?"

She nodded. "Thanks for loaning me a shoulder last night. I appreciate it."

"No problem."

After pouring herself a cup of the coffee Sly had brewed, Francine sat down across from him. "You were right, Sly," she said. "I have been selfish. I needed to hear you say that."

He put the paper down. "So you heard us arguing?"

She dropped her eyes and said, "I didn't mean to."

He gave a dry chuckle. "I guess we may have gotten a little loud."

She looked up at him and saw the humor in his voice reflected on his face. "You surprise me, Sly. You think this—whatever is going on with you and Dawn—is funny?"

Sly shook his head and his eyes grew dark. "No, I don't think it's funny, but sometimes you have to laugh to keep from crying."

"I knew you were arguing but I couldn't make out the words to know what you were arguing about. I guess that's a good thing, since you two deserve your privacy. Can I help?"

"This is between me and your sister."

"Is it that serious?" she asked.

He met her eyes. "It's serious. Very serious."

"Will you be able to work it out?"

"I don't know."

"What do you mean, you don't know? You do love Dawn, don't you?"

Sly got up and poured himself more coffee. "Of course I love her. I think I love her more today than I did the day I married her."

"So what's the problem?" Francine asked. "Did she kick you out of the bedroom or did you move out?"

"That's not your business," Dawn's voice called from the doorway.

Both Sly and Francine turned to Dawn. "I'm not trying to be nosy, Dawn," Francine said.

Dawn walked fully into the room. "For someone who's not trying, you're certainly doing a good job of it."

"No need to jump down Fancy's throat, Dawn. This is between you and me. You got something to say, then say it to me. Don't take it out on her."

Francine watched her sister's eyes flash at Sly. "My husband, the protector. Spare me." She turned to Francine. "See what you missed out on, Francine? This"—she shot a glance at Sly—"could have been yours."

The venom in Dawn's voice scared Francine. Her sister was more upset than she'd ever seen her. "Whatever your problem—"

"Spare me," she said again. "I don't need your lectures on my marriage. Don't get in the middle of something you don't understand."

"You're going too far, Dawn," Sly warned.

"No, Sly," she said, "I think you're the one who went too far." She turned to Francine. "Maybe we should answer your question, but you'd better be sure you want the answer. Are you sure, Francie?"

Francine didn't know what to say or do. "Maybe you were right, Dawn," she said, standing. "This is really none of my business. I'm sorry for putting my nose in. I was only trying to help."

"We don't need your help, do we, Sly?" Turning to her husband, she added, "Three people are too many in any marriage, wouldn't you agree?"

Sly shot Francine a pleading glance. "Give us a minute, will you?"

Francine quickly took hold of the chance to escape a situation she didn't understand and wasn't sure she wanted to understand. "No problem. I need to get to work." She looked at her sister. "Dawn?"

"Go ahead, Francie," she said. "I promise not to kill him." She looked at Sly. "Today."

"Dawn—" Sly warned.

"I'm joking. Go to work," Dawn said to Francine. "Have a good day."

Dawn watched her sister as she left the room. Then she turned to Sly. At the frown on his face, she asked, "What's your problem? You were about to tell her everything before I came in, so why did you get so bent out of shape when I was going to tell her?"

"Maybe I don't like the way you were going to do it."

"Let's see," she said, pressing her index finger against her chin. "How many ways can you tell your sister that your husband stepped out on you and then he moved out of the bedroom because you didn't fall all over yourself accepting his sorry apology?"

His eyes blazed. "That's not the way it was and you know it."

Dawn slapped her palm to her forehead. "Look, I must be having mind trouble. Are you telling me that you didn't sleep with Ms. Fredericka or that you didn't move out of our bedroom? Help me, because I really want to get this right."

Sly pushed back his chair and stalked to her. "You're pushing, Dawn, and you're pushing hard. Don't be surprised when I push back." Without giving her a chance to respond, he left the kitchen.

Dawn dropped down into the seat that had been Francine's and rested her face on her folded hands. Why was she being so evil to him? When she'd heard Francine's question, something inside her had snapped. She didn't want her sister to know that Sly had gone to another woman, didn't want Francine to know that she, Dawn, hadn't been able to satisfy him at home. She didn't want to see the look of pity on her sister's face when she got that piece of information. She didn't want to see it on anyone's face, which was why she was determined to keep all this sordid business between her and Sly.

She still loved him and she wanted to believe his apology, but she couldn't trust herself to do so. What if he really didn't love her? What if he'd married her on the rebound and never loved her? What if he'd cheated on her before? What if he cheated on her again?

She bet he wouldn't have cheated on Francine. They'd been together for years, and during that time, Sly had never had eyes for anybody but Francine. One thing Dawn had never doubted was Sly's love for Francine. No, it was only his love for her that she doubted. Though she wanted another answer, some miraculous sign from God, she couldn't get around this one fact: If Sly had loved her the way she loved him, he never would have cheated on her.

Sly slammed the door to his office at the funeral home after he walked inside later that morning. To say he was in a bad mood was an understatement. How dare she? he thought to himself. How dare she? Dawn was pushing and she was pushing hard. He was beginning to wonder if she really wanted to push him out of her life. Maybe she wanted their marriage over but didn't have the heart or the guts to say so. Or maybe she was so concerned about public opinion that her pride wouldn't allow her to admit to a failed marriage. Whatever it was, he knew he wouldn't be able to put up with it for much longer. He faced enough stress in the world outside—he knew he didn't need stress at home. Neither did he want a divorce. He loved his wife.

Sly rubbed his hand down the back of his neck. What was he going to do? Well, he couldn't come up with a solution now because he had a meeting—another meeting—with the execs from Easy Rest. The people couldn't take no for an answer. The knock on his door told him they had arrived. He took a deep breath to clear his head and then he opened the door. "Good morning, gentlemen," he said to the two men who had visited him on two other occasions.

"Mr. Ray," one said. "Thanks for agreeing to meet with us again."

Sly led them to chairs in front of his desk and then he went around the desk and sat in the burgundy leather chair that had been his grandfather's, studying the two men sitting across from him. They'd come in from Boston in their fifteen-hundred-dollar suits, thinking to impress the local yokels. "If you want to keep spending your money on trips to our fair city, Mr. Thompson, I can't help but be hospitable to you once you get here."

Thompson chuckled. "Well, I think you'll find this trip of great interest." He glanced at his partner and then he turned his attention back to Sly. "We went back and looked at the numbers again and were able to come up with a better deal— the best deal you'll ever see from us. The final deal you'll see from us."

The hair on Sly's neck stood up at the threat. He was definitely not having a good day. Two threats in one day and it wasn't yet noon. He watched as Thompson wrote a figure on a slip of paper and slid it across the desk to him. He didn't pick it up, but met Thompson's gaze and said, "I must not have made myself clear the last time you were here, Mr. Thompson." He slid the slip of paper back over to the man. "We're not interested."

Keeping his eyes on Sylvester, Thompson smiled a knowing smile. "Humor me. Take a look anyway." He slid the slip of paper back to Sylvester.

Sylvester bridged his hands over his nose and stared at the slip of paper. He knew he shouldn't look at it. His decision was already made. Looking at that piece of paper would do one of two things: make him angry at what he considered another lowball offer or make him regret having to pass on an offer too good to refuse. The latter he really didn't expect. He glanced up at Thompson. "I don't need to look at it," he said. "What part of 'we're not interested' don't you understand?"

Thompson glanced at his partner, who said, "We're trying to operate in good faith with you, Mr. Ray. We're willing to negotiate. Be reasonable. You're a small family-owned business. We know the past few years haven't been the best for you. We even acknowledge that you're doing pretty well despite the recent rockiness. Right now. But how do you think to survive in the changing climate of the mortuary business? The independent, family-owned funeral home will soon be a thing of the past."

Sly thought about his grandfather, who'd taught him everything he knew about the funeral business, and about Dawn, who considered the business a member of the family. Then he leaned forward in his chair and rested his folded arms on the desk. "I understand the mortuary climate, Mr. Thompson, and I think we're positioned not only to survive, but also to thrive."

Thompson sat back in his chair, smugness swallowing his face. "While I admire your optimism and confidence, Mr. Ray, it takes more than optimism and confidence to be successful. Your family has been in this business long enough to know that. From what I've heard about your grandfather and his partner, Mr. Amen, I'm sure they would have recognized our offer as a good one."

Sylvester stood, signaling an end to the meeting. He could listen to these suits talk about his business, but he couldn't listen to them tell him about his family. He extended his hand. "Thank you, gentlemen, for stopping by, but I have a business to run."

Having no other option, Thompson shook his hand. "You're making a mistake, Mr. Ray." He glanced at the paper on the desk. "That's a one-time offer. You don't take it today and it's gone."

"I guess that's a chance I'll have to take." Sly stayed behind the big desk that probably had endured many such skirmishes, while his visitors made their way out of his office and out of the funeral home. He sat in his chair and watched from the window as they climbed into their rented sedan. He sincerely hoped he had done the right thing by rejecting their offer. He swiveled in his chair and stared at the slip of paper they'd left behind. Though he knew he should throw it in the trash without looking at it, he picked it up and opened it. As he balled it up and tossed it in the trash, he wished he hadn't opened it. He picked up the phone and called Stuart's clerk. He wanted a meeting about the funeral-home-collective idea as soon as he could get it.

Dawn watched from the windows as the two visitors drove away from the funeral home. She knew they were from Easy Rest but she hadn't known they were meeting with her husband. Why hadn't Sly told her? She sat down at her desk. Probably for the same reason he'd decided to discuss his business idea, whatever it was, with Francine instead of with her. It had been their pattern throughout their marriage—Sly took care of the business and she handled the families. So why did his excluding her bother her now? She'd thought the task distribution was working, that their lives were working, but she'd been wrong. Maybe she'd also been wrong to allow this split in duties. She pushed away from her desk with the intent of rectifying her error.

Since Sly's office door was open, Dawn had the opportunity to observe him unnoticed. His chair was turned so that his profile was to her, his fingers steepled across his nose, a frown on his face. Despite all the indicators of deep concentration that marred his features, she found his mocha skin, bald head, and brown-black eyes as appealing as she always had. She tapped on the door and he looked toward her with a start.

His frown grew more pronounced. "Don't start with me, Dawn."

Her heart ached a bit at his reaction, though it was no less than she deserved. "I was out of line earlier," she admitted.

His eyes narrowed and she knew he didn't trust her words.

"I can admit when I'm wrong," she said when he didn't speak.

"What's up with you, Dawn? These mood shifts of yours are

THE AMEN SISTERS 131

beginning to scare me. Last night you're threatening to sleep with another man. This morning you're angry because you think I'm about to tell your sister our problems, and then you immediately turn around and threaten to tell her yourself. I don't get you."

She walked fully into the room. "Well, I don't get myself a lot these days. I'm doing the best I can, Sly."

He smirked. "What do you want?"

She sat down in the chair in front of his desk, remembering the times in the past when he'd asked that question in a teasing voice with a twinkle in his eyes and love on his mind. She shook off those thoughts. Those days were gone. "I saw the Easy Rest guys leaving. I didn't know you were meeting with them. What did they want?"

"What do you think they wanted? They want what they always want."

"I thought you'd told them we weren't interested in selling. You haven't changed your mind, have you?"

He swiveled his chair so that he faced her. "You're the only person in this room whose mind seems to change with every blowing wind. We agreed that we weren't going to sell and I haven't changed my mind. If I had, I wouldn't do anything behind your back. I'd tell you."

"Thanks for that, Sly."

He leaned forward. "I know how much this funeral home means to you, Dawn. It means a lot to me too. Your grandfather and mine and our grandmothers put their lives into this place. I don't want to lose it any more than you do. Maybe there was a time when I thought we should at least entertain Easy Rest's offers, but we talked about it and you were right. This place is our heritage. We have to hold on to it."

"You still feel that way?"

"Why are you asking me this now? I've told you I haven't changed my mind."

"I'm asking because I want to know. You don't tell me things about the business."

"You've never been interested before."

"Well, I'm interested now."

He studied her. "Why is that?"

"Because I don't want to be the kind of wife who knows nothing about her financial situation."

"Those sound like words from a lawyer, a divorce lawyer. Have you spoken with a divorce lawyer, Dawn?"

She sat back in her chair, shocked at the way his mind had turned. "No."

He studied her, saying nothing.

"You don't believe me?"

"Why should I?" he asked. "Maybe you're ready to get out of this marriage. Maybe you're so interested in the financial side of the business because you want to make sure you get your fair share in the divorce settlement. You think I'd try to cheat you, Dawn? Do you really think I'd stoop so low as to try to cheat you out of what our families built together?"

"No, I don't think that," she said. "I don't know where you're getting these crazy ideas. I haven't spoken to a divorce lawyer and I'm not in here looking for hidden assets."

She could tell he wasn't sure if he should believe her, and that broke her heart. They were far apart now and she knew she had contributed to that distance. "Then why all the questions?" he asked.

"Because," she said, "I'm your wife and your business partner. Why should parts of the business be off limits to me?"

"It's not off limits, Dawn," he said. "You've been content in the past to leave the business end to me. What's changed? Do you think my cheating spread to the funeral home?"

Dawn felt those words as a slap to her face. "I can't believe you brought that up! I can't believe you even fixed your mouth to say those words to me."

He smirked. "Doesn't feel good, does it? Well, think how I feel every time you throw the words back at me."

She took a deep breath and gave her emotions time to settle. "Look, we're getting off track. I came in here to find out what the Easy Rest people wanted and to tell you that I want to be more involved in the business end of things."

"And I asked you why."

"Because it's my business too. I have as much invested here as you and Francine do. I don't see why I should be shut out."

He gave a slick smile. "So that's what this is all about. You want in because I asked Francine to work on a business idea with me." He shook his head sadly. "What are we doing, Dawn, when you don't even trust me around your sister? What does that say about where we are, where our marriage is?"

"It's not about you and Francine."

He lifted a brow.

"It's not *all* about you and Francine. It's about me. I want to be more involved, Sly. Why are you giving me so much grief about it? Are you hiding something from me?"

He shook his head, but not quick enough for her to believe him.

"I won't be shut out," she said, standing.

"I hear you."

"So you'll include me?"

He nodded.

"Thanks," she said. "That's all I wanted. I'll let you get back to work."

"Dawn," Sly called to her.

She turned back to him.

"Instead of being jealous of your sister, you need to talk to her. George Roberts got in her face at the bookstore last night. It really upset her."

Dawn remembered the harsh words she'd spoken to Francine this morning and winced. "I didn't know."

"Now you do."

Dawn nodded. "I'll talk to her. Thanks for telling me."

"No problem."

She turned away from him, intending to leave. Then she turned back. "Sly?"

He looked up.

"I really am sorry about this morning."

He nodded.

Knowing that was all she was going to get, she turned and left the office.

CHAPTER 11

I'm sorry that had to happen, Francine," Mother Harris said, pulling her into a hug. She leaned back and looked into Francine's eyes, squeezing her hand. "You're going to have to be strong, young lady. George is hurting. He's a good man, but he's allowed the hurt to harden his heart. What you have to do is pray that the Lord will soften it again. Can you do that?"

Francine nodded. Mother Harris's reaction to her run-in with George had been no less than Francine expected. She hadn't told the older woman about Dawn and Sly's troubles, but she knew she'd get around to telling her eventually. She figured one set of problems was more than enough to put on the shoulders of her dear friend, even though those shoulders were among the strongest Francine had ever encountered. "What about Monika? She had to listen to all of that and she has enough going on in her life as it is."

"Don't you worry about Monika. The Lord's got her back. You be the friend to her that I know you can be, the friend she needs."

Francine wasn't so sure she could be that friend, but having failed at friendship before, she certainly wanted to give it a try. "I'll do my best."

"Not good enough. You've got to trust the Lord and let Him do His best. Proverbs tells us to trust in the Lord and not lean to our own understanding. Now, that doesn't mean that you can't use the mind that God gave you. It just means that you have to make sure that what you conclude lines up with what the Bible tells us before you do anything." She patted Francine's cheeks. "Now put a smile on that face and get to work." She glanced at her watch. "I've got to go. The bus for the convention leaves the church at four and I still have to finish packing. Will you be okay until Monika gets in? She should be here after lunch, around one or so. Sister Elaine'll be helping out the rest of the week."

"I'll be fine," she said. *As long as George doesn't show up again today.*

"I knew you would be," Mother Harris said. She reached under the counter for her purse. "You know, I love this store but I also love having some time to do other things. Thanks for helping me out."

Francine was amazed at how Mother Harris looked at things. "You're the one who's helping me. I needed this job and I needed to be around you and Monika."

"Don't we serve a good God?" Mother Harris said. "He's met all of our needs with your coming here. Now, that's what I call smart."

Francine didn't have a response and thankfully Mother Harris didn't require one. "I'll see you at church when I get back on Sunday, won't I?" the older woman asked. "It'll be good to have you back at Faith Central. We've missed you there."

"*You've* missed me," Francine said. "I don't know about everybody else."

"Now don't you go worrying again. Trust the Lord, child. It'll be all right."

Francine frowned. "I still remember how I stood up during the Sunday morning testimony service and told everybody they were going to hell if they didn't repent."

"So?" Mother Harris said. "It's true. If they don't repent, they will go to hell."

Francine pushed at the strands that had come out of her French braid. "You know what I mean. It's the way I said it. I was accusing everybody—Pastor, you, everybody. I thought I had uncovered some secret of the gospel that everybody else had missed." She closed her eyes. "I still can't believe I was so stupid, so gullible."

Mother Harris squeezed her hand. "Well, you were."

Francine narrowed her eyes at Mother Harris, surprised at her words.

"Well, you were," the older woman repeated. "Remember, the truth will set you free. Now you have to take the real truth, the truth you know in your heart, and use that to make things right."

"How am I supposed to do that?"

"You fix it the same way you broke it. When you thought you were right, you stood up and told everybody, shouted it to the world. Well, now that you've found out you were wrong, you can do the same thing."

"What does that mean? Do you want me to stand up in front of the church and tell everybody I was wrong?"

Mother Harris smiled. "It's not what I want that matters." She patted Francine's cheeks again. "Now I've got to go. You'll take Monika home tonight, won't you?"

"Sure," Francine said.

"Good. Now I really have to go."

Francine shook her head as she watched Mother Harris leave

the store. Only Mother Harris would issue such a challenge and leave. Smart woman, that one. She knew Francine would spend the day thinking about her words.

The rest of the morning passed relatively quickly for Francine. Being the only one in the store kept her pretty busy, and by twelve-thirty she was looking for Monika. Her stomach told her it was time to eat. She'd have the teen drop by the sandwich store and pick up lunch for them. The chime sounded and Francine looked up, hoping that it was Monika. It wasn't.

"Hey, girl," came the voice of one of her old friends, LaDonna Moss. "I heard you had the easiest job in town."

Francine braced herself, unsure what else LaDonna had to say. She and George had been dating forever. "Hi, LaDonna," she said. "It's good to see you."

"Is it?" LaDonna asked.

Oh, no, Francine thought, not again. Her first thought was that she was glad Monika wasn't there. "Look," Francine said, "if you're here to tell me about myself, you're too late. George beat you to it."

"I know," LaDonna said. "I'm sorry about that."

Francine raised a brow.

"I am," LaDonna said. "George and I are supposed to be getting married in September. That's only three months away and, I have to tell you, Francie, things are not looking good for us."

Francine dropped down on her stool. "I'm so sorry, LaDonna."

"It's not your fault, girl," LaDonna said. "Unlike George, I don't blame you." She gave Francine a wry smile. "I don't blame you *now*. Though for a minute there, I used your face as the target on my dartboard. Thank God, everything I learned in all those psych classes paid off. For a while there, I had to counsel myself."

"I'm sorry, LaDonna," Francine said again, even though she knew the words weren't enough. "It's all my fault."

"Now, don't go feeling all sorry for yourself. I might have to come down hard on you for that. I never could stand self-pity in a person."

Francine chuckled. "It's nice to see you haven't changed."

LaDonna came around the counter and sat on the stool next to Francine. "Why should I?" she asked. "I've got it going on."

Francine laughed. "It's good to see you, LaDonna."

"Didn't look that way when I walked in the door."

"I was worried about your reaction. We didn't part on the best of terms."

"Please, girl. I didn't pay you or that trash you were talkin' any attention. If I listened to everything everybody told me, I'd be stone crazy."

"You're serious?"

"As serious as my Gucci pumps and the Ph.D. in psychology that I have hanging in my office," she said. "Besides, life's too short. My only regret is that I haven't been able to help George. Since Toni's death, he's living in his head, not talking to anybody about what he's feeling. I've suggested counseling but he says he's an action man. Did you know he tried to bring criminal charges against Bishop Payne and that church?"

Francine shook her head. "I had no idea."

LaDonna's lips turned down in a frown. "Probably because nothing came of it. They hadn't broken any laws, so there were no charges to file. Believe me, George used every political connection he's cultivated in his four terms in the Georgia House of Representatives. If there had been any case to build, he would have found it. The best he could do was put the IRS on notice, so at least they'll have those guys breathing down their necks."

"I wish he had found something," Francine said. "What about civil court?"

She shook her head. "No standing. Toni may have had a case but George didn't. He also thought about filing a formal complaint with a national church association, but he couldn't do that because as an independent church Temple didn't belong to any national association."

Francine felt George's frustration. She too wished there were some way to make them all pay. "I feel so sorry for him," she said. "He and Toni were so close, even during those teenaged years when brothers and sisters often drift apart. I can remember him fixing our broken dolls for us when we were in elementary school. I can remember him bristling up at some guy who'd come on to Toni when we were in high school. It hurts to think that I was the cause of the biggest rift between them. First, I got her to leave home and come along with me, Bishop Payne, and the others." She looked away. "Then I didn't stand with her when she needed a friend. I should have been there for her and I wasn't."

"You know," LaDonna said, "you sound the way I think George feels."

"How is that?"

"Guilty. He was always there for his little sister, prided himself on taking care of her. Though I doubt he'll ever admit it, I know he blames himself for not being there for her with this Temple thing. Since he wasn't there to protect her in life, he's become obsessed with avenging her death. He has to make someone pay, Francine."

"I know the feeling," Francine murmured.

"Love is hard, isn't it?" LaDonna said. "All the good things in life seem to be, don't they?"

Francine guessed LaDonna was talking about herself. "How are you holding up?"

"You know me," LaDonna said. "I'm like the tree planted by the rivers of water in Psalms 1. Girl, I'm here for the long haul."

"I heard that," Francine said. "Hey, I want to thank you for pulling together that list of psychologists for Dawn to give to me."

"No problem," she said. "It was pretty easy to do. Have you talked to anybody?"

"Not yet." Francine shrugged her shoulders. "I'm not sure I will. I've been talking to Mother Harris a lot and it's helping."

"I can't argue with that. Mother Harris is a wise woman, wise in the ways of the Lord. Sometimes all you need is a safe place to talk and be heard. When you don't have that, or when you have it and don't use it, like George, you run into problems. That's when counseling can help."

Francine agreed with LaDonna. Maybe she wouldn't have ended up in the hospital if she'd had that safe place. Maybe Toni wouldn't have ended up dead if she'd had a safe place for herself.

LaDonna looked down at the two-carat diamond that George had placed on her finger. Then she looked back up at Francine. "Francine, I've got to ask you something," she said. "I know I have no right, but I love George so I have to ask."

Francine held her breath. "What?"

"George's mother has decided that she can't attend Faith Central if you're going to start coming back there."

Francine fisted her hand to her mouth to fight back a cry. "Oh no," she murmured. "What have I done?"

LaDonna reached over for Francine's hand. "I know it's not right," LaDonna said, "but that's the way it is. She says it would be too hard for her to see you, be around you."

"So she's leaving Faith Central? The Robertses have been members of the church for as long as I can remember."

LaDonna sucked in a deep breath. "I know, and so have I, but if Mrs. Roberts leaves, I don't think George will be too far behind. I'll have to go with him, Francie, and Faith Central is my family church too. I don't want to go. I want to get married there, but now I don't know if that can even happen."

Francine looked away, thinking about the awful impact of her decision to leave town five years ago with Bishop Payne and his team of traveling evangelists. She'd deserted Sly without a word, breaking his heart and leaving him in the lurch in the managing of the funeral home. She'd abandoned her sister when she was still grieving over the deaths of their grandparents. With her words of hell and damnation, she'd swiped at the hearts of all the people who loved her. The final blow had been Toni. She'd led her like a dumb lamb to the slaughter, and knowing that she had been just as dumb didn't ease the guilt she knew she would always carry. Now her sister's marriage was crumbling and she wondered if she played a role in that too. Had Dawn spent too much time in the hospital with her and away from Sly? Had the problems with the funeral home, problems she'd caused, put too much of a strain on the marriage? Now Mrs. Roberts, George, and LaDonna were leaving Faith Central. Added to all of that, Monika's fresh pain at hearing George's condemning words. Would the impact of her foolishness have an end? She met LaDonna's gaze and said, "You haven't asked your question."

LaDonna said gently, "I know it's not fair, Francine, but I have to ask. Do you have to stay here? Wouldn't you be more comfortable somewhere else where people don't know what happened, where you don't have to face so many memories?"

Francine didn't know why the request surprised her, she should have expected it. "This is my home, LaDonna," she said. "I didn't have, still don't have, anywhere else to go. Believe me, I didn't want to come back here."

"I have some money saved," LaDonna offered. "I can help you to get settled somewhere else."

"But my family—"

"What about Toni's family?" LaDonna challenged. "Their lives have been ripped apart, Francine. You don't know the half of it and some of it I can't even share with you. But I can tell you this: George is almost a walking zombie. He's been using his work to dull his pain, but that's not good and it's not helping. Mrs. Roberts is not much better." She sighed. "George isn't a cruel man, Francine, you know that. He's one of the kindest, sweetest men I know, but this thing is changing him. I don't think your being around is going to help him or his mother."

"I don't know what to say," Francine told LaDonna.

"Just think about it," she said. "You're not a cruel person either, Francine. I know you'll do the right thing." LaDonna stood up. "I'd better get out of here. I have to meet a client at one-thirty."

Before Francine could respond, the door chimed, causing her and LaDonna to look in that direction. Monika rushed through the door, tears streaming down her face, and ran to the back room. Francine called after her, but the girl didn't answer. When she was about to follow the teen, Stuart rushed in the store after Monika. "Where is she?" he asked.

Francine's heart began to beat fast. Had he harmed her? She turned to LaDonna. "I'm sorry, but I'm going to have to see to her."

"No problem," LaDonna said. "Anything I can do?"

Francine quickly balanced protecting Monika's privacy with the possible assistance that LaDonna could offer. "Why don't you man the counter for me," she said. "If I need you, I'll call." Then she rushed to the back room.

"Leave me alone," Monika was saying to Stuart, who was trying to pull her into his arms.

"She said to leave her alone," Francine demanded. "So leave her alone."

Stuart turned wide eyes to Francine and she wasn't sure if they were full of guilt or pain. Not having the time to figure it out, she rushed to Monika. "Did he hurt you?" she whispered. "You can tell me if he did."

The girl kept crying.

"I didn't hurt her," Stuart said. "It's not what you're thinking."

She cut him a hard glance. "How do you know what I'm thinking?"

"Stop!" Monika yelled. "Just stop it!"

Stuart pushed past Francine. "Monika, talk to me," he said. "Tell me what's wrong."

The girl turned in his arms. "He doesn't want to meet me. My father doesn't want to meet me. He hates me."

Francine met Stuart's eyes over Monika's head as the teen buried her face in his chest and cried. She wanted to cry herself. Instead, she walked over and patted Monika's back.

"He doesn't hate you," Stuart said. "Nobody could hate you."

Monika pulled back. "Then why won't Momma let me meet him? Why won't he talk to me?"

"I don't know, Monika," Stuart said. "Have you asked your mother?"

"She won't tell me the truth. She lies, makes excuses. I don't believe anything she says. He hates me. I know it. That's why she won't let me meet him. He doesn't want to meet me."

Francine met Stuart's eyes and she knew from the look in them that he was as much at a loss as she was. *Call Dolores,* he mouthed. Francine nodded and went out front to do as he asked. She gave LaDonna a brief overview of what was going on and then called Dolores. When she hung up, she said, "I think Monika's going to be all right. Thanks for staying. I know you have an appointment."

LaDonna slid off the stool. "If you're sure—"

"I'm sure," she said. "Go on. You need to take care of your business."

After LaDonna gathered her purse, Francine led her to the door. "You'll think about my offer, won't you?" LaDonna asked when they reached the door.

Francine nodded, but her mind was on Monika. After

LaDonna left, she flipped over the Away sign on the door, giving herself an hour. When she returned to the back room, Stuart was still holding Monika, but the teen had quieted. "She tired herself out," he said.

"There's a cot," Francine said. "She can rest until her mother gets here."

With Stuart's help, Francine opened the cot and then he laid the teen on it. "She's out, isn't she?" he asked, looking down at the youngster fondly. "She's had a rough few weeks."

"You really do care about her, don't you?"

Stuart met her eyes. "Yes," he said simply.

"I was wrong about you. I'm sorry."

He shook his head. "Don't be sorry. You care about her too, and you were acting out of what you feel for her. Sometimes it's better to be overly cautious."

"I'm still sorry that I jumped to the wrong conclusion."

Monika stirred, and they both looked down at her.

"Let's go out front so she can rest," Stuart whispered. "We'll be able to hear her if she needs us."

Francine nodded, following him out to the front of the store.

"You can open up again," he said. "I'll stay with you until Dolores arrives."

Francine glanced at the door. "Let's wait until Dolores gets here before we do that."

"Okay," he said. "Mind if I sit?"

She shook her head. "Not at all."

"It's a mess, isn't it?" he asked.

Francine nodded. "I'm afraid something she heard last night may have triggered it." She told him about George's visit.

"You can't blame yourself," he said. "Besides, I don't think that was it. This thing has been bothering Monika for a while now. I didn't realize how much. So many kids are raised in single-parent homes these days that I forget that it's not easy for all of them."

"She wants family, more family than she has."

Stuart squeezed his eyes shut and then quickly opened them. "Her mother is a good woman. This is going to break her heart."

"I met her last night," Francine said. "Do you know Monika's father?"

Stuart shook his head. "Not a clue."

"Why wouldn't he want to know her? I can't imagine anybody being that selfish, especially when her need is so great."

"Let's not jump to conclusions. Monika can be overly dramatic at times, so let's wait to see what Dolores says."

"Good idea," Francine said. "I guess I've gotten pretty good at jumping to conclusions."

"What you're good at is taking the blame for everything. Why do you do that?"

She was about to give him an answer when he stood. "There's Dolores," he said.

Francine rushed to the door to let her in.

"Where is she?" Dolores cried. She had left the spa so quickly that she still wore the white Kings and Queens smock that she usually donned when working. "Where's my baby?"

"Calm down, Dolores," Francine said, wrapping her arms around the woman. "She's fine. She's resting in the back."

"What happened?"

"It's about her father," Francine said. "She thinks he hates her."

Dolores moaned. "Where did she get that? I didn't tell her that. I told her I'd talk to him. I haven't even talked to him yet."

Francine met Stuart's eyes again. He'd been right.

"Well," Dolores said. "Let me go talk to her. Thank you both so much. She thinks a lot of both of you."

"We love her too, Dolores."

Dolores nodded, but her attention was already on her daughter and she moved in that direction.

Stuart looked at Francine. "They'll be all right."

"I hope so," she said.

Without asking, Stuart took her hand in his and began to pray. "Father, show your strength to Dolores and Monika. Build bridges between them so they can hold on to each other during this trying time. Show them the love that is all around them. Show Monika that she has all the family she needs in you and your people. Help us to be that family. In Jesus's name. Amen."

When Francine looked up at him, he grinned. "Thanks," he said. "I needed that prayer right now."

"I think I did too," she said, still holding his hand, "though I hadn't known that I did." There was something solid, safe in Stuart's touch. Even more, there was something solid and sincere about the prayer he'd prayed. Just a few simple words but she felt they'd reached the throne of God.

Dolores and Monika came out of the back room, daughter wrapped in mother's arms. "I know she was supposed to work today," Dolores said, "but I think I'd better take her home."

Francine dropped Stuart's hand, reluctant to sever the three-way connection with God. "Of course you should." She looked at Monika. "Feeling better?"

The girl burrowed closer to her mother, but she nodded.

Dolores glanced from Stuart to Francine. "Thanks again. I appreciate both of you being there for her."

Francine watched them as they left, still feeling the power of the prayer she'd shared with Stuart. Mother and daughter would be all right. She was sure of it. It might get rough for a while, but they'd be okay.

"Are you going to be all right here by yourself?" Stuart asked her.

Seeing Stuart with new eyes, she nodded. "I'll be fine."

"I could stay and help you."

She lifted a brow.

"Mother Harris has drafted me into service on a couple of occasions, though I think I'd be better with the customers, leaving the cash register to you."

She shook her head. "Thanks for the offer, but I'll be okay."

"You're sure?"

"I'm positive." When he turned to leave, she said, "I'm really sorry, Stuart, for the things I thought. You deserved better."

His smile told her he didn't hold it against her. "And I'm sure I'll get it. Let's just say you owe me one and leave it at that. Deal?"

She smiled back. "Deal."

CHAPTER 12

E. Theodore "Ted" Campbell checked his watch again. His three o'clock appointment with Judge Stuart Rogers was quickly turning into a four o'clock. According to his clerk, Judge Rogers was in a motion hearing that had gone on much longer than expected. Ted knew he could leave and reschedule the meeting, but he wanted to get Faith Central on board with BCN as quickly as possible. One thing he'd learned since he'd undertaken this venture was that reputable churches attracted reputable churches. The first question pastors typically asked was, "Who's already on board?" Faith Central's Rev. Thomas had been the exception. Ted hadn't even expected the question about individual donors. Nobody else had raised it.

Now that he thought about it, Ted realized that he should have been prepared for the unusual with Thomas. The man had a reputation that was second to none. Though his church had only about three thousand members, making it small compared to the mega-churches in the Atlanta area like New Birth with more than twenty thousand members, he wielded a lot of influence with the other pastors in the city as well as with the community in general. It was important to get Thomas on board. The venture needed the credibility and stature he would bring.

Ted sighed, remembering the days when he could have used his own credibility and stature to anchor the deal. But those days were gone. He was no longer the pastor of one of those mega-churches. His reputation, tarnished by what he considered "a powerful man's weakness for beautiful women," was not enough. Though he had embarked on a trek to rehabilitate his name, he wasn't there yet. BCN would put him back there though. If he made a go of the station, he could build his church from the television audience. In five years, his church, The House of Hope—he'd already come up with a name for it—would be bigger than The Potter's House. Compared to him, T. D. Jakes would be a small-time pastor. Ted could see it now. Like Job, he'd have everything he'd lost and more. In order to have it, he needed BCN to succeed, and for it to succeed, he needed Rev. Thomas and Faith Central on board. That meant he needed Judge Rogers, and so he continued to wait.

He wished Nona had come with him. They would have been more effective as a team. Christian leaders liked to see a husband and wife working side by side, sharing a ministry. Nona knew this, but she refused to cooperate. Ted knew her unwillingness was because she wasn't yet ready to put her trust in him again. The past still hung between them. Though he understood his weakness and didn't come down too hard on himself, Nona wasn't as understanding. Throughout the Bible there was case after case of the man of God being led away by the temptation of a beautiful woman. David, a man after God's own heart, had suffered from the same failing. At least, Ted thought, he hadn't tried to kill anyone's husband. Too bad he couldn't get Nona to see that.

He knew Nona would get over her sulks though, because she

enjoyed being First Lady of a mega-church as much as if not more than he enjoyed being pastor of one. His three sons and his mother were another story. The four of them had led the call for him to step down from his last church and had almost caused Nona to leave him. There wasn't much he could say about his mother, but those boys had been out of line. What call did they have to judge him when they hadn't even experienced much of life yet?

"Rev. Campbell."

Ted looked over at the clerk's desk.

"Judge Rogers can see you now," the young man said. "You can go on in."

Rev. Campbell picked up his portfolio from the seat next to him and headed for the office. Judge Rogers met him at the door with an outstretched hand.

"Sorry I kept you waiting," the judge said, leading Ted into the office. "My last session went much longer than I had anticipated. Unfortunately, that happens a lot." After seating Ted at a chair in front of the desk, Stuart moved to his chair behind it. "I'm glad you waited."

"Not a problem," Ted said. "I'm a busy man myself, so I know how the days can get away from you."

"I bet you're a busy man. Being a pastor is a full-time job, and then you have BCN on top of it. That's a lot for one man."

Ted wondered if Stuart was challenging him, but chose to respond as if he weren't. "My congregation is small," he explained, "and we have a good support team. I also have an Advisory Board with me on BCN, so I'm not alone. Most importantly, I have a strong First Lady standing with me. None of this would be doable without her."

Stuart nodded, and Ted felt the mention of Nona had won him a point, just as he'd hoped it would. "So have you thought about Rev. Thomas's concerns?" Stuart asked.

Ted opened his portfolio and pulled out a sheet with the new numbers. He handed it to Stuart. "I've done more than think about them. The Advisory Board reviewed Rev. Thomas's concerns, found them valid, and made the changes you see there."

Ted watched as Stuart studied the sheet of paper. Though Ted hadn't wanted to commit to giving shares of the network to the donors, he hadn't felt he had much of a choice. Giving up 20 percent of something was better than having 100 percent of nothing. He wasn't a fool.

"The numbers look pretty generous," Stuart said. "So twenty percent of the shares of the network would be held in reserve for the individual donors?"

Ted nodded.

Stuart put down the paper. "I worked on a project—Genesis House—you may have heard of it."

Ted nodded again, wondering where Stuart was going with his line of inquiry. Everybody in the Atlanta area had heard of Genesis House, the nonprofit Christian community service organization run by Nate Richardson and his wife, CeCe.

"I worked with them on a similar deal for donors, except in that case we had a couple of additional provisions," Stuart continued. "First, as long as Genesis House is a nonprofit according to federal regulations, then the donors' share is nonredeemable, but if it goes public, the donor share is redeemable on demand. Second, instead of giving the donors a flat percentage the way you've laid out here, we made their share proportional to their contribution to the operating budget."

Ted and his group had considered that last option, but quickly discarded it. If things didn't go exactly as he'd planned, individual donations could easily end up 50 percent or more of the budget. Instead of responding to Stuart's idea, he decided to wait for the man's question. It wasn't long in coming.

"Have you considered such a split for BCN?"

Ted surreptitiously squeezed his upper thigh with his hand to stop the involuntary shaking of his leg that usually occurred when he was annoyed. "No," Ted said. "That one didn't come up."

Stuart handed him back his sheet of numbers. "Maybe you should think about it."

Ted took the sheet. He should not have met with Rogers in his chambers. The location definitely gave the advantage to the judge. "Are you saying this is a deal breaker?"

Stuart shook his head. "Not at all. What I'm saying is, fair is fair. People should get out based on what they put in. Can you think of anything fairer?"

Ted squeezed his leg tighter, wishing it were Stuart's neck. "You have a point," Ted said, trying to come up with a way around the request. "We'll work on the language."

Stuart opened his desk drawer and pulled out a sheet of his own. "Here's the contract clause I drew up for Genesis House, with a few modifications to make it specific to BCN. It spells out the terms pretty clearly and takes care of all the legalese I'm sure your lawyers will want to see. You're more than welcome to use it. Show it to your lawyers. I'm sure they'll tell you that everything is in order."

Ted took the sheet. "I'll do that," he said, barely glancing at the sheet before tucking it in his portfolio.

Stuart smiled. "I'm glad. Is there anything else we needed to talk about?"

Ted shook his head. "I'll have my attorneys look this over and we'll get back to you."

Stuart stood and extended his hand. "Good, good," he said. "I look forward to talking with you. You have an innovative idea here that could go a long way toward building the kingdom of God. I'd love to see it be a success, but as you know, it'll only be as sound as its foundation. We all want to be a part of something that has a strong foundation, right?"

Ted stood and took Stuart's hand. "You're right about that,

Judge Rogers. We'll look this over and get back to you soon. We want Faith Central on board."

Stuart escorted him to the door. "I'll look to hear from you," he said. "Have a great day."

As Stuart walked back to his desk chair, he wondered about Ted Campbell. It had been obvious the man didn't like his request for yet more changes, but he had gone along with it, or pretended to. He'd wait until he saw the next set of revisions before he made his final judgment of Campbell. He'd give the man the benefit of the doubt until he proved himself otherwise.

Campbell and BCN moved to the back of his mind when he reached his desk and all his thoughts turned to Monika. He picked up his desk phone and dialed Dolores's number. She answered on the first ring. She must have been sitting right next to the phone.

"Hi, Dolores," he said. "It's Stuart Rogers."

"Oh, hi, Stuart," she said. He heard the tiredness in her voice. "I just hung up from talking to Francine."

"Sorry to bother you, but I wanted to check on Monika. How is she?"

"Oh, Stuart, like I told Francine, I just don't know. She's so emotional."

"Well, she's a teenager."

Dolores gave a dry laugh. "Tell me something I don't know. I know it's hard being her age, but she's been such a good kid. This is so new for her and for me."

"What are you doing about her father? You know that's what's on her mind."

"I know," Dolores said.

"If there is anything I can do—"

"No," Dolores said. "This job is mine and mine alone. I knew this day was coming. I just kept fooling myself that I could put it off longer. I guess I was wrong."

"You're not alone, Dolores," Stuart said. "If you need some help—"

"I appreciate it, Stuart, but I have to do this myself. Besides you've done enough. I appreciate what you and Marie were to Monika, what you still are to her. I admit that I was a little jealous of how quickly she grew attached to you two, but I got over it when I saw how much good it did her."

"I know you love Monika, Dolores."

"Sometimes so much it hurts. All I ever wanted was to be a good mother to her. I don't think I've done a very good job. My past is coming back to haunt me."

"The past can't hurt an honest heart before the Lord," Stuart said. "Remember Romans 8 and 1, where it says, 'There is now no condemnation to them which are in Christ Jesus, who walk not after the flesh, but after the Spirit.'"

"I'll try," Dolores said. "I think I hear Monika. Do you want to talk to her?"

"Just tell her I called. I'll talk to her tomorrow."

"Okay, if you're sure."

"I'm sure," he said. "I'll let you go."

"Thanks, Stuart," Dolores said, and hung up.

Stuart prayed silently for Dolores and Monika as he hung up the phone. He wanted them both to feel the Lord's presence with them as well as the love from the people that God had placed around them. He added a special prayer for Francine and the role she was beginning to play in the young girl's life.

Francine was helping a customer when Dawn walked into the bookstore that evening. She looked up at Dawn and gave her a questioning smile. Dawn returned it with an open and apologetic one. She browsed the fiction section while she waited for Francine, though she didn't read much fiction, preferring autobiographies. She'd recently finished Shirley Ceasar's story and was now working on CeCe Winans. She admired both women.

"Hey, sis," Francine said, coming up behind her.

Dawn turned. "Hey yourself. How's it going?"

Francine picked up a nonfiction title that had somehow made its way to the fiction shelves. "We've had a busy day but things are settling down now. What brings you by?"

Dawn rested her hand on her sister's arm. "I'm sorry about this morning, Francine. I wanted to apologize. The argument was between me and Sly. I shouldn't have taken it out on you."

"Don't worry about it," Francine said. "Is there anything I can do? About you and Sly, I mean?"

Dawn shook her head. "Not really. The problem is between us and we should keep it that way."

"Are you sure?" Francine asked. "Sometimes it's good to talk things through with someone not directly involved."

"I appreciate your offer, Francie. I really do, but this three-way relationship with me, you, and Sly is complicated enough as it is."

"Would it help if I moved out? You and Sly deserve some privacy to work out your problems."

Dawn shook her head. "No way should you move out. It's your home too. We both want you there. We just don't want you in the middle." She squeezed her sister's arm. "Even though I act like a crazy woman sometimes, I do love you, Francie. I hope you know that."

Francine placed a hand on top of her sister's. "Of course I do, and I love you too. That's the only reason I'm asking questions."

"I know, but can we agree to keep this door closed between us? At least for now?"

Francine nodded. "But know that if you ever change your mind—"

"I know, I know." She pulled her sister into a brief embrace. "Now how about some dinner? Isn't it nearing closing time?"

Francine looked at her watch. "It certainly is, but you don't have to take me to dinner. Do you want to—?"

"No, I don't want to spend the evening with Sly. You promised to stay out of it, Francie. That means all the way out."

"Okay, okay," Francine said. "I'm out of it. Since you're so determined, why don't you help me close up so we can get out of here quicker?"

Dawn grinned as she pulled a book off the shelf. "I could take a seat on that stool over there and read while you close up."

Francine laughed. She took the book from her sister's hand and placed it back on the shelf. "You could, but you won't. You take the vacuum cleaner and I'll handle the rest. Deal?"

"Deal," she said. "Point me to the instrument of torture."

Francine laughed. "It won't be that bad."

The two of them quickly set the bookstore to rights and headed out for dinner. They decided on the Chinese restaurant a couple of doors down so they wouldn't have to drive.

"This is the best offer I've had all day," Francine said after they were seated in the restaurant. "I didn't get much of a lunch."

"That busy?"

Francine told Dawn a little about the incident with Monika.

"I hate that for Dolores and the girl, but I'm glad Stuart was there with you. What do you think of him?"

Francine peered up at her sister. "Not you too?" she said.

"What?" Dawn asked.

"The other night I got the impression Sly was thinking about playing matchmaker. Now you're sounding like you are."

Dawn smiled. "Maybe it's your own thoughts. I only asked what you thought of the man."

Francine wasn't sure her sister's intentions were as innocent as she claimed. "He seems like a good guy. He really cares about Monika and she needs his friendship a lot right now."

The waiter came to the table and took their orders, leaving

crispy fried noodles, hot mustard, and sweet and sour sauce on the table. Dawn dipped a noodle in the sweet and sour sauce. "Sly told me what happened with George last night. I'm sorry."

"Don't be," Francine said. "I should have expected it. And that's not all. LaDonna came to see me today."

"Oh no, what did she have to say? I like LaDonna, but she thinks George walks on water, and nobody does that. She goes a bit overboard if you ask me."

"She says that Mrs. Roberts will stop going to Faith Central because I'm back. She doesn't want to run into me."

Dawn's heart went out to her sister. "She'll come around, Francie. It'll take some time."

Francine shook her head. "I want to believe that, Dawn," she said, "but I can't." She went on to share with her sister more of what LaDonna had said to her.

"LaDonna has some nerve! You don't have to go anywhere. You're not leaving. This is your home and Faith Central is your family church as much as it's hers. If a person can't come home to heal, where is she supposed to go? And LaDonna calls herself a Christian. Puh-leez! Home girl needs to check herself."

Francine took comfort in her sister's outrage on her behalf. "They're probably not the only ones who want me gone. I wouldn't be surprised if some others had a few words for me that they want to get off their chest."

"Yeah, well, you don't have to sit back and take it."

"Yes, I do." At her sister's wide eyes, she explained, "It's no more than I deserve, Dawn. You have to remember the way I was up in people's faces before I left. What goes around comes around. I'm just reaping what I sowed."

"Puh-leez," Dawn said again.

"I'm serious." Francine tossed a couple of the crispy noodles in her mouth. "I was talking to Mother Harris about it earlier today, before I talked to LaDonna. She said something that got me thinking."

"What?"

"She said I should fix things the same way I broke them."

"What does that mean?"

"I think it means that I need to make some kind of statement of apology at church on Sunday."

Dawn sat back in her seat. "You really want to do that?"

"Not really, but I did stand up and confront everybody when I left. Maybe they deserve as bold an apology as the condemnation I heaped on them. Maybe it'll make a difference to George and his family."

"And maybe it won't." Dawn sipped her tea. "Why bring all that attention on yourself? But it's your call. You're a stronger woman than I am."

Francine chuckled. "I don't think I could fade into the background even if I tried. George and LaDonna have made that very clear. I left in a thundercloud of emotion, and people are going to notice my return. No, I think Mother Harris is right. I need to take responsibility for what I did."

"So you're going to stand up in church and apologize?"

"I've been thinking about it, but what LaDonna said has me wondering if I should just leave it alone. Maybe it would be best for everybody if I did leave town. What if my trying to make things right is only making them more wrong?"

Dawn reached across the table and grabbed hold of her sister's hand. "Listen to me," she said, "you're not going anywhere. If you feel you need to speak to the church, then you speak to the church, but you're not going anywhere. You hear me, Francie?"

Francine nodded to appease her sister, but her mind was far from made up when it came to whether she should leave town. "I hear you."

Dawn leaned back in her chair. "Good. Now, what are you going to do about church on Sunday?"

"I don't know," Francine said. "Maybe I should talk to Pastor first. I haven't seen him or Sister Thomas yet. I'd like to talk to them privately before making any statement in the church."

Dawn nodded. "We can go over there after dinner."

Francine knew her sister was pushing her to take action for fear that she'd let LaDonna's words influence her. "It'll be too late."

Dawn shrugged. "They're night people. They'll be up. Besides, if you're going to make your public apology on Sunday, tonight will be the best time to talk to Pastor. It's the only night he doesn't have Bible Study or scheduled counseling sessions."

"You're right," Francine said, "but you don't have to go with me."

"I know I don't have to," Dawn said. "I want to. The Amen sisters are a team. Don't you forget that."

Francine smiled at her sister. "Thanks. We'll go over after dinner."

CHAPTER 13

After an exhausting day at work, Sly needed some physical exertion and he thought a game of pickup basketball would do the job. Knowing he could usually find a late afternoon game at the Genesis House Community Center, he left the funeral home headed in that direction. Stuart was pulling out of the community center parking lot when Sly drove up.

He stopped and rolled down his window as Stuart did the same. "Man, I wanted to shoot some hoops this afternoon."

"Rough day?"

Sly nodded. "You up for a few more baskets?"

Stuart shook his head. "I wish I could oblige you, man, but those guys about wore me out. After a hot shower I may be able to tackle a game or two of pool, if you're interested, but that's all I can offer."

"I'll take you up on it. You got any home-cooked meals in the fridge?"

"Afraid not, my friend." His empty refrigerator was a reminder of the fact that the single women at church were no longer preparing meals for him—a fact that Sly knew well.

"I thought so," Sly said. "Why don't you head home and shower? I'll be there with dinner in about forty-five minutes."

"Sounds like a plan," Stuart said. "Since the guys kicked my behind at basketball, I'll have to whip yours in pool as a way of reclaiming my manhood."

"Keep dreamin', Rogers."

Sly rolled up his window on Stuart's laughter. Two hours later, a little food, a few games of pool—even though he was losing—and the companionship of a good friend had eased the cares of the day from Sly's shoulders. He watched Stuart sink another easy pocket. Either Stuart was playing better than he ever played or Sly was losing his touch.

After sinking the last ball, Stuart lifted his arms in victory. "I'm good, man," he told Sly. "So good, I'm going to have to look for higher-quality competition. You're Little League compared to me."

"Don't get carried away," Sly said, placing both cues in the rack. "Everybody has a lucky day sometime. Today is yours."

Stuart blew on the knuckles of his right hand and then rubbed them against his chest. "Not luck, my man," he said. "Skill—S-K-I-L-L."

Sly reached into the mini-refrigerator that Stuart kept in his rec room and pulled out two cans of cold soda. He tossed one to Stuart and said, "That ought to keep you quiet for a minute or two."

Stuart popped the tab and took a big gulp. "So what's on your mind? It definitely wasn't this game of pool."

Sly popped the tab on his soda. "Admitting it was my lack of concentration and not your superior skill that led to you winning?"

Stuart perched on the corner of the pool table. "No way. Just trying to give a brother an excuse. So what's up?"

Sly was reluctant to talk about his day. A night away from his troubles was what he needed. "Can't a brother come by and shoot some pool without there being something up?"

Stuart clapped him on the shoulder. "Good try, but the answer to that one is no. You'd be at home with your lovely wife instead of here with me if all was well. I know you enjoy my company, but you don't enjoy it that much."

Sly focused on his soda. "I think she's talked to a divorce lawyer."

Those words wiped the smile off Stuart's face. "You're joking, right?"

Sly shook his head. "I wish."

"Wait a minute. Tell me what happened."

Sly started from the beginning and told Stuart the story.

"I think she's right," Stuart said. "You overreacted. Her interest in the business doesn't mean she's seen an attorney."

Sly snorted. "No, it means she's afraid I'm going to seduce her sister. Man, I can't win! All I'm trying to do is take care of business at the funeral home without having her worry, and she thinks I'm trying to seduce her sister."

"Maybe that's not what she thinks. Maybe she simply wants to share that part of your life."

Sly wished Stuart was right because it would be a sign of hope for his marriage, but he couldn't be sure. Not with Dawn. "Why now, though, when things are so bad with us?"

"Only Dawn knows that." Stuart dropped down on the couch. "Why is her interest such a problem for you, Sly? She wants to be involved. Why don't you let her?"

"Because the business of running the funeral home is my turf. I'm supposed to take care of it. She's supposed to trust me to take care of it."

"Says who?" Stuart challenged. "You make this sound like some type of rule. Was it part of your wedding vows that you'd take care of the business?"

"No, but it was understood. Her job was to take care of the families and mine was to take care of the financials. I haven't done anything to make her not trust me in this area."

"So we're back to trust again."

Sly nodded. "She doesn't trust me with her sister, she doesn't trust me with the business. Where do we start to rebuild, Stuart?"

"Maybe it's the funeral home. You two need a place where you can work together toward a common goal, learn to rely on each other again. Maybe working on this collective project with Dawn is the perfect vehicle. It'll give you something to focus on other than your relationship."

Sly considered his friend's words. "I hadn't thought about it that way. Maybe I did overreact."

"Maybe."

Sly grinned at his friend. "No need to rub it in." He put his hand on the back of his neck. "These days I don't seem to be able to think straight about much of anything. I know part of it is just the frustration I feel because Dawn and I aren't sleeping together. I miss my wife, man."

"You're singing to the choir, brother," Stuart said. "I know about sexual frustration. For a long while time Marie was sick, we couldn't be intimate and it almost killed me. I literally thought I was going to die. But it wasn't just about sexual release. I needed to be close to her, to show her how much I loved her, desired her. But that avenue was cut off for us. It was more than difficult."

"Tell me about it. That's my life now. How did you get through it?"

Stuart smiled a satisfied smile that told Sly his memory was sweet. "I have to give God all the credit. He enhanced every other intimacy we could share. Other things began to have greater intensity. The warmth of her breath against my neck when she slept with her head on my shoulder. The shared tears of joy because we'd found each other and the profound shared sadness that our forever was not going to be as long as we wanted. It was enough."

"But is it still? I mean, man, it's been two years."

Stuart twisted the wedding ring on his finger. "Of course I think about intimacy. I'm a man and those desires are coming back with strength, but God is good and I'm handling it. My life is full. Like the single person Paul talks about in First Corinthians 7, my mind and heart can focus on God and the people and activities He has placed in my life. Right now, it's enough. When it's not, I'll know that too."

"I guess I'm just not as strong as you."

Stuart punched him in the shoulder. "Our situations are different. You have a wife."

"A wife who doesn't want to sleep with me."

"Yet. But she wants to work with you and that's a start. Love her through that. Allow the Lord to turn that work into intimacy. Give it to Him."

Sly downed the rest of his soda. "I hear you, man. I hear you. So when do you think you'll be able to meet with me, Francine, *and* Dawn to get started on the collective project?"

"Didn't my clerk call you? Late Monday afternoon works for me."

"He may have left a message, but I was busy all afternoon. I'll check with Dawn and Francine, and leave a confirmation message with your clerk. I'm sure Monday'll be fine though. I'll nail down a time with the women."

"I'm in Room 17," Dolores said into the receiver, and then she hung up the phone. She closed her eyes and wondered that she was again in this no-name hotel in the boondocks on the outskirts of Atlanta. All because of some man. Shaking her head, she opened her eyes. No, this time wasn't because of a man. Her love for her daughter had brought her back here today, and that love would give her the courage to do what she knew had to be done.

She'd decided to contact Edward Theodore Campbell, Teddy to her, after Monika had fallen asleep. She'd taken a chance and called his cell phone, something she'd never done from her home when they were seeing each other. He'd told her to always call from a public phone so that her number wouldn't show up on his cell phone bill. Tonight she hadn't had a choice. Her daughter's well-being was at stake and Monika was well worth any risk Dolores might be taking. Besides, the truth was going to come out anyway. She'd resigned herself to that eventuality. Now she had to get Teddy to do the same. She'd been surprised when he'd answered and readily agreed to meet her at their old trysting place. After making a quick phone call to Tomika, asking her to stay with Monika for a couple of hours, Dolores had headed out to meet him.

At the soft rap on the door, she rushed to it and pulled it open. Teddy smiled at her, the same smile that had captured her heart over fifteen years ago. He was a handsome devil, she had to give him that, with a body that she knew he spent hours in the gym to maintain. Despite her best intentions, her heart flipped over in her chest and her fingers itched to weave a path through his meticulously groomed hair. "Thanks for coming," she said as he quickly entered the room, closing the door behind him.

"You call, I come," he said with a smile. He reached out to touch her cheek. "I didn't think I'd hear from you again. I'm glad I did."

She stepped back away from his touch. "I didn't call for that."

He stuffed his hands into his pockets. "Then why did you call?"

She looked into his eyes. "It's about Monika."

His smiled faded as he sat down on the queen-sized bed covered with a faded brown floral comforter. "What about her?"

"She's asking questions about her father again."

"I thought you told her that her father was dead."

Dolores twisted her hands together. "I did, but she didn't believe me. I had to tell her the truth."

He raised wide eyes to her. "What exactly did you tell her?"

"I told her that her father wasn't dead. I told her that we were in love but that he was married and had another family."

"What else?"

She exhaled a deep sigh. "I didn't tell your full name, if that's what you're asking."

He visibly relaxed and sat back on the bed. "Good. You should have stuck with your original story."

She stared at him, wondering how she could have ever imagined herself in love with this selfish man. "She's at the age where she wants to know about her father and his family. She feels that she's missing out on part of who she is. I'm worried about her, Teddy."

"She'll be all right," he said. "A lot of kids grow up all right without a father. I did. You did."

"But look at us, Teddy. Look at us. I had a long-term affair with a married man, a minister no less, and bore his illegitimate child. You're a serial adulterer. How can you say Monika'll be all right and use us as examples?"

"Because we're survivors. Look at you, you have your own successful business, and I'm a respected member of the community. We made something of ourselves."

"Who are you kidding, Teddy?" she asked. "I was only able to start my business because of the guilt money you gave me. And you're only respected in the community because nobody knows the real you. If people knew the real you, the real me, what kind of respect do you think we'd get?"

He sighed. "That's what I'm trying to tell you. You can't tell Monika about me. We have too much at stake. My reputation can't take another hit. Not when I'm so close to having everything I want."

Dolores shook her head. "She's hurting so much, Teddy. Can't you think about her instead of yourself for once?"

He got up from the bed and walked to her. "I am thinking about Monika. What's she going to think when she finds out I'm a minister, when she finds out I have other children? How's that going to make her feel?"

"She knows about your other children. I already told her. Do you know what she asked me? She asked if she were your only girl." Dolores felt tears well up behind her eyes. "She thinks you'll want to know her because she's your only daughter. I've never asked you for anything, Teddy, in all the years that we've known each other. I never asked you to leave your wife. I never threatened to tell, but I'm asking you today. No, I'm begging you today. We have to tell her. She needs to meet you, get to know you."

Ted was steadily shaking his head. "You can't tell her about me."

Dolores straightened her shoulders. "You can't stop me," she said, defying him for the first time since she'd known him. "Our daughter is more important to me than your reputation or mine, and she ought to be more important to you."

"She's important to me. You're important to me. Haven't I been there for you when you needed me? You said yourself that it was my money that got your spa started. I've done my part, Dee. Now you have to do yours."

Dolores shook her head. "You haven't seen how she is, Teddy. She's not going to get past this."

He took hold of both her shoulders. "She will. You have to be strong and not give in to her."

She looked up at him. "I'm not strong, Teddy. If I were, Monika wouldn't be here and we wouldn't have this problem." She stepped away from him. "I'm going to tell her."

He studied her for a long moment, and then he said, "I'll deny it."

His words sent Dolores stumbling back to the only chair in the room. She collapsed into it, feeling as if she'd been punched in the stomach.

"I don't want it to come to that," he said calmly, "but you have to know that I can't give up my life because of some period of teenaged rebellion that Monika is going through."

Dolores couldn't speak. What could she say? Who was this man standing before her? She'd known he wouldn't want to step forward, but a part of her felt that when pushed to the wall, he'd do the right thing. Again, she'd been wrong. "You're serious?" she asked. "You'd deny that Monika is your daughter?"

He nodded.

"A paternity test would prove that you're lying."

He shook his head. "I'm not worried. I know you, Dee. You love your daughter and you won't subject her to the humiliation."

Your daughter, not our daughter. "You'd be humiliated too."

"You're right. I'd be humiliated if I had to take a paternity test, but that's just the beginning. I'd also lose everything I'm working toward. For me, it's a no-win situation. I lose if I voluntarily tell her, because someone is bound to find out. On the other hand, I lose if I'm forced to take a paternity test, because that too will be found out. But it doesn't have to be that way, Dee. Stick to your story and both Monika and I win. When I'm back on top again, I'll make sure that you get what's coming to you. I've never been stingy with you, have I?"

Was he so blind to everybody's needs but his own that he really couldn't see that Monika needed more than his money? Instead of answering his question, she asked, "You don't feel anything for Monika, do you, Teddy?"

He lifted his shoulders in a careless shrug. "I don't really know her."

Dolores looked down at her hands. "I guess you don't." She wanted to cry, but she refused to let him see her tears.

"Look," he said. "It's late. If you don't have anything else to talk about, I have to get back home. Nona's gonna throw a fit as it is."

"There's nothing else," she said.

He reached over and touched her shoulder. "It'll be all right, Dee, you'll see."

Dolores couldn't make her lips acknowledge the meaningless words. She didn't respond and she didn't look up at him. Soon his hand dropped from her shoulder. She heard him walk toward the door. He opened it and then he said, "I'm sorry, Dee."

She looked up at him then, the fire in her eyes meeting the weakness in his. "You're right," she said. "You are sorry."

With a frown on his face, the only man she'd ever loved shook his head and pulled the door closed behind him. Dolores sat staring at the door as tears rolled down her cheeks. What had she done to her daughter and how would she ever be able to fix it?

CHAPTER 14

Francine awakened early on Sunday morning, much too early to get up. She lay in bed, her eyes wide open, and the gratefulness she felt in her heart surprised and warmed her. "Lord," she said aloud, "it's been a while since I've talked to you this way, felt your presence, and you know what, I've missed it. I didn't realize how much I'd missed it until Stuart held my hand on Tuesday and prayed. At that moment, I felt closer to you than I've felt since Toni died." Her eyes grew full and her throat clogged up with tears. "I thought you had forgotten about me, Lord. For the last few months, I've been holding on to what I knew to be true about you, but not really feeling you. I thought you were so upset with me that you didn't want to hear from me anymore. When I saw Toni laying there in all that blood, I prayed so hard for her to be all right, but she wasn't. And I felt like you no longer heard my prayers. At that moment, I felt more lost than I've ever felt in my life. It was awful to feel separated from you. Thank you for letting me feel your closeness again. I need you so much.

"There is so much going on here, Lord, so many problems

and I feel like I'm the cause of so many of them. Dawn and Sly are having trouble and I can't help but feel I'm a part of their problems. Please be with them, Father, and help them to work through their problems. I know my leaving hurt them both and I thank you for bringing them together to comfort and love each other. Show me what I can do to help them. Then there's Toni's family. Lord, my heart does ache for them. I pray, Lord, that you would heal their hurt, even though I don't know how you can.

"Lord, my heart aches for Dolores and Monika and the situation they find themselves in. Please work it out for them, Lord. Like Stuart prayed, help us to be the family Monika needs and let her feel the Father love that comes from you that surpasses what she's missing from her biological father.

"Finally, Father, I thank you for the people you've placed in my life to love and guide me. Mother Harris—I can't even express how good she's been for me. Stuart too, even though he doesn't know it. And Dawn and Sly. I've tried to let them know how much I appreciate their love and support. My life is good, Father, and I'm not sure I realized how good until now. Thank you so much for loving me and sticking by me. Give me strength as I speak to the congregation this morning. Help me to be an encouragement to them as you've been an encouragement to me. I pray all this in Jesus's name, Amen."

Francine closed her eyes and began to hum "I love you, I love you, I love you, Lord, today, because you care for me—" Still humming, she turned, opened the drawer of the nightstand, and pulled out her Bible, journal, and a pen. She opened the journal and turned to her amends list and marked through the names of LaDonna, Mother Harris, Sly, and Dawn. Her pen hovered above the names of George and Mrs. Roberts and she wondered if she'd ever be able to mark through their names. After closing her journal and putting it back in the drawer, she opened her Bible and began to read.

Down the hall, Dawn was also awake. Her thoughts centered on Francine and what she planned to do this morning. Dawn admired Francine's courage in admitting her mistakes to the entire congregation the way she planned to do. She knew she couldn't do such a thing. She didn't even have the courage to tell people about the problems between her and Sly. What people thought of her mattered too much, she was sad to say. But Francine didn't really care what people thought. She knew she had to make amends and was willing to do whatever it took. If her sister was going to display that much courage, Dawn planned to give her all of her support. It was the least she could do.

She pushed back the covers on the bed, slipped out, and padded across the hall to Sly's room. She hesitated for a moment and then she lifted her hand and knocked softly. "Sly," she whispered.

"It's not locked, Dawn," he responded.

She took a deep breath and opened the door. Sly sat up in bed, his chest bare, the rest of his body covered with the damask comforter. "I didn't wake you, did I?"

Sly raised a brow. "What do you think?"

Why was he being so difficult? "Well, I wanted to ask if you were going to church this morning."

"Does it matter?"

She nodded.

"Yeah, I'm going."

She bit down on her lower lip. "I know you said that you were going to stop pretending that all is well with us, but I wondered if you'd mind sitting with me and Francine this morning. She's planning to make an apology to the church during the testimony service, and she needs our support because I'm not sure what the response is going to be." She told him about LaDonna's visit.

"LaDonna needs to get a grip on herself. Who does she think she is?"

"My thoughts exactly," Dawn said. "Anyway, I've called Mother Harris and she's going to sit with us in a show of support. Francine doesn't know it yet, but Mother Harris is also going to throw a picnic in her honor, after the service. I know you have a funeral this afternoon, but I'd appreciate it if you'd sit with us at church and drop by the picnic for a little bit. I know Francine would appreciate your support."

"She doesn't have to do this today, does she? She just got out of the hospital. Shouldn't she give herself more time?"

Dawn shook her head. "My sister is a lot stronger than I thought. She wants to do this, Sly. We even went over to Pastor's house Tuesday night and she talked to him about it. He thinks it's the right thing to do."

Sly nodded. "I didn't know you had talked to Pastor."

"You must have gotten in really late on Tuesday night." She knew exactly what time he'd gotten in, but she wouldn't tell him that she'd deliberately stayed awake until he'd returned.

"I spent the evening playing pool with Stuart."

She'd wondered. God help her, she had. "Thanks for telling me."

"I wish you didn't worry so much."

"So do I."

His lips curved up in a sad smile. "We're meeting with Stuart tomorrow afternoon to discuss the business idea that I was talking to Francine about. I'd like you to participate."

She smiled. "Thanks, Sly. I want to participate."

"It's only fair. As you so aptly put it, it's your business too. Now we need to confirm Francine's schedule. Will you do that and then call Stuart's clerk and confirm the time? I really want us to get started with this."

"Is there something you're not telling me, Sly? Is the funeral home in trouble?"

He patted the bed next to him, and without hesitation, she came and sat next to him. "The funeral home is not in trouble, but we need to make some changes and not be content with the way things are. Easy Rest is right about one thing: The small, family-owned funeral home is fading away and being replaced by big corporations. If we want to keep our business, we're going to have to grow and change."

"So what's your idea for growth and change?"

"We'll talk it through tomorrow, but in general the idea is to start a funeral home collective."

"A collective?"

He nodded. "I got the idea from that guy who came and talked to us about BCN. The gist of it is that we start a funeral home collective in much the same way that BCN is starting a church collective."

Dawn smiled. "That's pretty intriguing."

"I'm glad you think so. We have a lot to think about and we're going to need all of our heads to accomplish it."

"Even mine?"

His lips turning in a dour line, Sly said, "Even yours."

She laughed. "You don't have to sound so excited about it, Sly. I promise not to bankrupt us."

He laughed with her. "It's not that. It's just that this way of working together will be different for us."

"But it could be good for us." Dawn eased off the bed, though she was feeling very comfortable where she was. "I'd better get back to my room and start getting ready. I'd like to fix a nice breakfast to start the day."

"You're a good sister, Dawn."

"I try." She felt awkward with his praise. "So you're going to sit with us at church?"

"I'll stick like glue," he said. "That I can promise. I'll have to leave after the service for the funeral, but I'll get back to the picnic as soon as I can."

Dawn left the room without responding, but her heart smiled.

As she sat in a padded pew in the middle section of sanctuary at Faith Central, Francine felt surrounded by love. Dawn and Sly sat on either side of her. Sly held one hand and Dawn's hand covered the other. Mother Harris, Stuart, Dolores, and Monika sat behind them. Mother Harris, Dawn, and Sly knew her plans for the morning, but Francine wasn't sure if Stuart, Dolores, and Monika did. Her fellow parishioners had greeted her warmly for the most part, though she did feel the coldness emanating from a few. From George, she'd gotten the expected hostility. LaDonna, by his side, had given her a weak smile. She hadn't seen Mrs. Roberts.

She turned her attention to Sister Mabeline, the church secretary, famous for her big hats. Today's looked like a fruit bowl. After announcing the upcoming activities for the week, she took a moment to welcome the visitors. Instead of following with the standard offering and sharing time, Rev. Thomas took to the pulpit. "Morning, church," he called to them. He must have found the answering "Morning, church" weak, because he offered his greeting again. "That's more like it," he said when he received a more enthusiastic response. "I was wondering if y'all had gone to sleep already. Most of you at least wait until I start preaching to fall asleep."

The church broke up with laughter at the comment. A lot of things might happen at Faith Central, Francine knew, but falling asleep during service was not one of them. Rev. Thomas was a commanding and charismatic speaker. People did not fall asleep on him. He was like E.F. Hutton: When he spoke, people listened.

"We're going to change the program a bit this morning, church," Rev. Thomas said. "I hope y'all will be able to deal with that. I know some of you like everything done decently and in order."

Again, the church laughed.

"I'd better be clear here," Rev. Thomas explained. "We're going to go on decently and in order, we're just not going to follow the standard program. Can I get an 'Amen' somewhere?"

A chorus of Amen's came from the congregation.

"The Holy Ghost's in charge this morning, the way He is every morning. This morning, the Holy Ghost has a special treat for you. I know it's going to be a special treat for you because it was a special treat for me when He let me in on it. This morning we're going to see and hear the gospel in action, and we're going to have an opportunity to act on what we know to be true about God and true about ourselves as children of God. For those of you who don't know it yet, Sister Francine Amen is back among us today. She's been gone for five years, if you can believe that, and, I'll tell you the truth, Faith Central has missed her."

"Amen," Mother Harris said from behind Francine.

Dawn's hand tightened on Francine's arm and she smiled up at her sister. Francine felt her throat clog with emotion. She had expected time on the program; she hadn't expected such an outpouring of welcome-back love.

"I know some of y'all remember some rocky times before Francine left," Rev. Thomas continued. "But I'm here to tell you this morning that the Lord can make the rocky smooth and He's done that with Sister Francine. Why don't you come on down here, Sister Francine?"

Dawn squeezed Francine's hand again and whispered, "I love you, sis, and I'm proud of what you're about to do."

Francine accepted her sister's encouragement with a smile. Then she stood and made her way down the center aisle. The walk to the front of the church seemed much longer than it was. Rev. Thomas, his royal-purple pastoral robe flowing behind him, came down from the pulpit to meet her in front of the altar. He hugged her. Then he stepped back and turned her to face the congregation, handing her his microphone. When she turned, microphone in hand, she saw that Mother Harris and Stuart had followed her down front. They were now seated in the front row. She eagerly took the courage and support they offered. She needed it, because George, LaDonna, and four of the people sitting in the pew with them got up from their seats and left the sanctuary.

Francine took a deep breath, and then she said, "I don't know where to begin."

"Let the Lord lead," a supportive voice she couldn't recognize called from the back of the church.

She chuckled. "I guess that's as good a place as any." She glanced at Rev. Thomas. "Thank you for everything. You've been a real pastor to me. I'm sorry I had to experience a fake one to appreciate how good you really are." She turned back to the congregation. "When I talked to Pastor about having a chance to speak to you this morning, I thought what I had to do was apologize to you for the hurtful and judgmental things I said before I left. For those of you who don't remember, or who weren't here then, five years ago I walked away from the church that had been my home for all of my life to follow an evangelist who'd come to town claiming revival. While revival is good—"

"Amen, sister," echoed across the sanctuary.

"While revival is good, the message of this group was not the message of the gospel as we know it. According to this group, they were the only ones saved. Their goal was to convert everybody in the churches to the *real* Christianity. Unfortunately, I was suckered in by their half-truths, and suckered in really well. So well, in fact, that I began to preach their message to many of you. I even stood right here and told you all that what you had in Jesus wasn't real." A chill rolled over her shoulders at the memory. "It's still difficult for me to believe that I could be so far gone. But I was. Anyway, when I talked to Pastor, I thought what I needed to do was apologize to everybody for the things I'd said and the harm I'd caused. But this morning when I was reading my Bible, I realized that I needed to do something else. I needed to do more than apologize, I needed to follow the instructions of First John and confess my sins and ask you to pray for me."

A chorus of Amens answered her.

"I say sins because they are many, but this morning I want to focus on two. First, I need to confess the lack of faith that allowed me to be deceived by people who were not of God. I have no excuse other than I took my eyes off the Lord and put them on man. I admit that it was a trying time for me. My grandparents had recently died and I was trying to understand why the Lord would take them both so close to each other. My guard was down and the enemy was able to plant seeds of doubt which men who were not of God were able to exploit. Second, I need to confess the pride that caused me to stand before you and proclaim your damnation. Even if what the false teachers said had been true, I was not delivering the message from a position of love but from a position of superiority. That's pride, a sin, and I have to confess it."

"Preach it, sister," somebody shouted.

"Amen, girl," others chimed in.

"I stand before you now both humbled and exalted, humbled to know how important it is to walk with Jesus on a minute-by-minute basis and exalted to know that as long as we want to walk with Him, He'll walk with us. I'm humbled by His love and exalted by it at the same time. We serve a good God."

"Tell it, sister," a voice chanted.

"Amen, somebody," another said.

"The Lord has taught me something very important out of all of this, and this is where the apology comes in. I see so clearly that we are truly the body of Christ. I look around the sanctuary right now and I can see in some of your faces how the decisions I made five years ago affected you then, and still affect you today. A life has been lost, relationships have been strained, some seemingly beyond repair. Hearts have been saddened in some cases, broken in others. All because of a decision I made. So what I learned is that I am not alone. As long as I claim to be a Christian, my decisions affect you, my brothers and sisters. I ask your forgiveness for those decisions and their effects and I ask you to pray that the Lord will show me how to make amends. Thank you for giving me this time."

She turned to give Pastor Thomas back the microphone so she could go back to her seat, but he put his arm around her shoulder and pulled her close to him. "What we have seen here this morning, church, is the body of Christ in action. Sister Francine has preached the morning's message in her words. She's come before you and confessed her sins and asked you to pray for her. Well, I'm going to go one better than that, the Holy Ghost wants to go one better than that."

With his arm still around Francine's shoulders, he moved to the center aisle. "Sister Francine is not the only one here this morning who needs to confess. Some of you need to join her. Most of you need to join her. You've been holding stuff in too long. You've been dealing with things privately because your pride hasn't wanted others to know of your struggle. Well, this morning, church, the Lord is saying that pride is a sin that you've added to the sin you're trying to keep hidden, and He's saying that the Christian life is not lived that way."

He dropped his arms from Francine's shoulders. "I want my ministerial staff to come down now." When Francine would have moved back to her seat, he stopped her. "You stay where you are." He turned back to the congregation. "Some of your hearts were touched as Sister Francine spoke, and you know who I'm talking about. Some of you didn't want to hear what Sister Francine said, so the Lord had me say it again so you'd be without excuse. You too know who I'm talking about. Well, right now, we're going to have prayer time at Faith Central. If the Lord has been speaking to you this morning about unconfessed sin and pride, then you need to make your way down to the altar so you can join us in prayer. Come on down here right now."

People began moving out of their seats and making it to the altar. "God is good," Rev. Thomas said. "Maybe you haven't followed false teachers the way Sister Francine did. Maybe your sin is much simpler. Maybe it's the ungodly attitude you show to others. Maybe it's unforgiveness you're holding in your heart. Maybe it's the way you're treating your spouse. Whatever it is, you know and the Lord knows. We're going to deal with it this morning so we can put it away. Shame is a hold that sin uses on you. As long as you're ashamed of the sin, it has a hold on you. When you can name it, and walk away from it, you're walking in the power of God. That's what the Lord wants from His people. Sin and shame have no place in the life of a man or woman of God."

Dawn followed Sylvester down the aisle to the altar. Maintaining their positions of support, they each stood next to Francine. Mother Harris stood in front of her and Stuart behind her. Dawn wrapped an arm around her sister's waist and hugged her. "I'm so proud of you," she whispered.

Rev. Thomas moved back to the pulpit. He looked across the congregation, across the faces crowded at the altar. "There's still room at the altar," he said. "Today is not the day to be shy. As you make your public confession this morning, the Lord will release you from the guilt and the shame."

Dolores, still in her seat next to Monika, wanted to go down, but she didn't want to draw attention to herself. What would Monika think? She wanted her daughter's respect; she didn't want her thinking her mother had some secret sin. But Dolores felt in her heart that Pastor was talking to her. She carried a lot of guilt and shame for her relationship with Teddy, guilt and shame compounded by his refusal to acknowledge his daughter. She squeezed her daughter's hand. When Monika looked up at her, she said, "I love you, Moni."

Monika saw the tears in her mother's eyes and her heart responded to them. She hated for her mother to be sad and it hurt to think that she was responsible. She knew her mother was worried about her and she knew that was why she had come to Faith Central this morning instead of the church she regularly attended, Grace Cathedral. Despite the anger that Monika felt toward her mother because she wouldn't tell her about her father, she didn't like to see her cry. "I love you too, Momma," she said.

"One last call for the altar," Rev. Thomas said. "Today is your day. I know some of you are wondering what people will think your sin is. Well, if you're thinking that, then you should be down at the altar because guilt and shame have you bound. The very sin that has you bound is keeping you from your release. You can do it. Get to your feet and come on down. That's good," he said as others made their way to the altar. "There's room. You can still come.

"You know, we serve a good God and this morning He wants to release you and bless you with freedom. There are still some of you who need to make a public confession but you haven't come to the altar. The Lord is so good that He's going to meet you where you are. I want all of the rest of you to stand to your feet at your seat. You're not publicly acknowledging sin, unless you need to, so you don't have to worry about what people are thinking. Just stand to your feet and agree with us in prayer. If you are acknowledging sin, you need to confess it to someone you trust in the Lord before the day is over."

CHAPTER 15

Francine studied her face in Mother Harris's bathroom mirror and blotted her eyes one last time. She'd done what she'd set out to do at the morning service, but her heart ached that George, LaDonna, and their friends hadn't stayed to hear what she had to say. She prayed that one day they'd give her a chance. All that aside, she was grateful for the warm and loving response she'd gotten from many of the members of Faith Central, including the ones attending this surprise picnic that Mother Harris was giving in her honor. "Thank you, Lord," she said, opening the bathroom door.

"You may have fooled them, but you haven't fooled me."

Francine turned at the sound of the angry words. She'd counted her blessings too soon. "Hello, George," she said, a prayer for wisdom going to God at the same time.

"You're not going to get away with what you did to my sister," he said.

"What do you want from me, George?" she asked. "I can't bring Toni back. I can't undo the past. So tell me, what do you want me to do? Just what do you want from me?"

The widening of his brown eyes told her that her question caught him by surprise. "I want you to suffer," he said finally. "I want you to feel as alone as my sister felt. She never should have gone with you. I never should have let her."

George's words made Francine remember what LaDonna had said about his guilt over Toni's death, and she knew her friend had been correct. "It's not your fault, George," she offered.

"Don't try to turn this on me," he said, rebuffing her concern. "I know it's not my fault. It's your fault and you're going to pay. You can take that to the bank."

On those cryptic words, George turned on his heels and exited Mother Harris's home, going away from the party sounds, not toward them. Francine breathed a deep sigh. "Thank you, Lord."

"Hey, Francie," Victor McCoy called to her as she reached the patio door to join the others outside. She'd known Victor since childhood, having grown up with him at Faith Central. He was the perfect antidote to George.

"Hi, Victor," she said. "When did you get here? I didn't see you."

"I just rolled up," he said, leaning in to kiss her cheek. "Can't stay long. Just wanted to drop in and let you know how much I appreciated what you said in church this morning, and to get a bit of Mother Harris's famous fried chicken."

Francine chuckled at the reference to the chicken, finding that much easier to address than his other words. "Her chicken is the best."

Victor rubbed his stomach. "You're preaching to the choir, girlfriend." He took her hand. "Come on and walk out with me. I have to get to work, so I can't stay long."

Francine allowed Victor to lead her outside. He went directly to the table with the meats—chicken, hamburger, hot dogs, sausage, and ribs. He dropped her hand and picked up a paper plate. "I meant what I said. I do appreciate what you said this morning. It gave me a lot to think about, to pray about."

Francine nodded. "I'm glad it was helpful."

"You'd better watch this guy, Francine," a familiar voice said from behind her.

"I can tell by the small amount of dark meat still left here that you've already made your chicken run, Stuart," Victor said, "so you have nothing to say."

Stuart chuckled. "Francine, this guy has a bad reputation for taking all of Mother Harris's fried chicken. Word is he takes enough to hold him over until the next time she cooks it. What do you do, man, freeze it?"

Victor waved Stuart off as he kept loading up his plate. Francine grinned at Stuart and they both watched Victor complete his task and wrap his plate with the foil Mother Harris provided for leftovers. When Victor finished, he looked at Francine. "We'll have to get together," he said. "You're staying at your sister's, right?" When she nodded, he said, "I'll give you a call." He leaned in and bussed her cheek again. "I gotta run now though and you know I gotta see Mother Harris before I do or she'll kill me."

Stuart lifted his arms as Victor turned to walk off. "What? Don't I even get a good-bye?"

Victor smirked. "You start looking like her and we'll talk."

Stuart shook his head, watching Victor walk away. "Now, that's a character."

"Always has been," Francine said. "But he has a good heart."

Stuart looked at her. "He's not the only one."

"What?"

"A good heart. He's not the only one who has one."

Francine met his gaze and saw the truth of his words in his eyes. She didn't know how to respond.

"I've been trying to get to you all afternoon, but you've been pretty much surrounded," Stuart said. "I've felt like I needed to take a number and get in line."

"People are being nice. I sorta feel like the returning prodigal. I guess I am."

"Not a bad feeling, huh?"

"A really good feeling, actually," she said. "I wasn't sure what the response was going to be to my coming back, to what I said in church. The love has been overwhelming."

"We're Christians and that's what we're about."

She cast him a sideways glance. "Not everybody. George and his entourage left."

"Don't let it bother you. That's George's problem, not yours. All you can do is pray for him and be obedient to the Lord yourself."

"Easy for you to say. I bet there are others who feel the same way George does. You weren't around when I left town, so you missed the fond farewell I gave everybody."

He shrugged. "I know the gist of it, but it doesn't really matter what you did five years ago. What matters is where your heart is now, and you let all of us know that pretty clearly this morning. Your heart is with the Lord. What you shared this morning encouraged every one of us, because we've all done things that we wish we hadn't done and many of us still carry the shame of it around with us. You gave us space this morning to confess our faults and get rid of the shame."

"That was the Lord," she said. "Not me."

"But the Lord chose to use you."

Francine's heart quickened at those words and she knew they were true. The Lord had chosen her to say what she said this morning. He'd taken her sin and shame and turned it into something powerful. She now had a much better understanding what Romans 8 and 28 meant when it talked about God working all things together for our good. "He did choose to use me, didn't He?"

"You sound surprised?"

She lifted her shoulders in a slight shrug. "I guess I am. When I left here five years ago full of pride and false teaching, I thought He'd chosen me. But that hadn't been Him. When I came back to town humbled and ashamed, *that* He used. Go figure. Nobody but God works that way."

Stuart grinned. "You got that right."

She looked up at him. "I appreciate what you did for me Tuesday."

"What did I do?"

She explained about the prayer he'd prayed for Monika. "It meant a lot to me. It affirmed for me that God does answer prayer, that He's with us, hears us, loves us. I'm not sure I'd have been able to do what I did this morning without that prayer of yours."

Stuart gave her a slow smile. Taking her hand, he leaned in and bussed her cheek in much the same way Victor had, but it felt different to Francine. So different that she stepped back from him. As if sensing her discomfort, Stuart said, "That's for telling me how the prayer affected you. It's always encouraging to know the Lord uses things He has us do." He pointed to the volleyball net set up across the backyard. "Look at Monika," he said, "you'd think she didn't have a care in the world."

Francine was grateful to turn her attention to the younger girl. "She does look happy," she said. "So does her mother."

"That she does," he said. "Let's go join her."

As Dolores watched her daughter play volleyball, her heart expanded in her chest. This child of her heart meant everything to her. She'd tried to be a good mother, to make up for the circumstances of Monika's birth, but she realized now that was impossible. Her daughter would be hurt and there was no way she could prevent it.

"Hey, Dolores."

Dolores turned to see Stuart and Francine striding toward her. "Hey yourself," she said, forcing into her voice a lightness she didn't feel.

Stuart leaned in and kissed her cheek. "I was glad to see you at service this morning."

She glanced over at Monika. "I thought we needed to be in the same place this morning." Turning back to them, she added, "Maybe we need to go to the same church all the time. It was probably a mistake to let Monika attend Faith Central while I continued at Grace Cathedral."

Stuart glanced at Francine, sending her a silent message to pray. "What's wrong, Dolores?" he asked.

She glanced again at Monika before turning back to them. "Can we go somewhere so we can talk?"

"Sure," Stuart said. "We can go inside."

He took her arm and began to lead her to the house. When she noticed that Francine wasn't following, she turned to her and said, "I'd like you to come too, Francine, if you have the time."

"Sure," Francine said, and fell into step with them.

Apparently very familiar with the older woman's home, Stuart led the two women through the family room and back to Mother Harris's den. He closed the door after the women entered. Dolores sat on the daybed and Francine sat next to her. Stuart was left with the big leather recliner.

Dolores studied her hands, unsure where to start. She took a deep breath. "Now that I've gotten you here, I don't know what to say."

Francine glanced at Stuart and then she placed her hand atop Dolores's. "It's all right. Take your time."

Dolores breathed out a heavy breath. "You had me thinking in church this morning, Francine," Dolores said. "The things you were saying about pride and shame and sin. I was too embarrassed to come to the altar but you were talking about me. All of it was about me."

Francine squeezed Dolores's hand in an offer of comfort as tears spilled down her friend's cheeks.

"It was all about me but I didn't have the courage to go to the altar." She wiped at her tears. "But I did stand at my seat as Pastor asked and I confessed my sin and shame to the Lord." She looked from Francine to Stuart. "Now I want to be obedient to what Pastor said and share it with both of you."

They both nodded, and Dolores was thankful they didn't say anything. She wasn't sure she could go ahead if they did. "You both know that Monika wants to meet her father." When they nodded, she said, "What you don't know is why she hasn't met him to this day." She took another deep breath. Focusing on the picture of Mother Harris with her husband that hung on the wall, Dolores said, "He was married."

After she dropped what she considered to be her bombshell, she cast a quick glance at Stuart and Francine to get their reaction. Instead of seeing the revulsion that she expected, she saw love and concern. She had to bite her lower lip to keep from crying harder. "He was married and he had a family, and I knew all of this, and I slept with him anyway."

Francine squeezed Dolores's hand tighter, but still neither she nor Stuart said anything. "I could say," Dolores explained, "that I loved him, but I know that doesn't make it right. I know now that it was wrong and I knew then that it was wrong. The difference is then I didn't care, and now I do."

"That's the Holy Spirit at work," Stuart said. "When your heart is turned toward God, things that no longer bothered you, sin that no longer bothered you, bothers you a lot."

"I know you're right, Stuart," she said, needing to be honest. "But I wonder if I'd feel this way if I didn't know my daughter's heart was going to be broken because of sin in my life. Talk about the sins of the mothers—"

"Don't say that, Dolores," Francine said. "Don't even think that. God is not vindictive that way. Monika is not paying for your sin."

"Then why does it feel like she is, or she will?"

Stuart got up from his chair and dropped down on his knees in front of Dolores. "God's not vindictive," he said, "but sin can have enormous consequences. It's like Francine said this morning. What she did—her sin—not only impacted her, it impacted all those around her."

"So my sin impacts my daughter?"

Stuart nodded.

"Why?" she asked. "Why does Monika have to suffer for something in which she had no part?"

"That's one question you can ask, Dolores," Stuart said, "but you can also ask how God can use this situation for something good in your life and in Monika's. Think about what He did this morning with Francine. He took something that was ugly in her life and made it an encouragement to those around her, even an encouragement to her."

"But she's my daughter," Dolores cried. "I don't want her to hurt."

"Monika is *God's* daughter too," Francine reminded her. "He loves her as much as you do, if not more."

Dolores sat back on the daybed and allowed the truth of those words to wash over her. This was an angle she had not considered. "She is His daughter, isn't she?"

Stuart and Francine both nodded.

"It doesn't mean that Monika won't be hurt," Stuart said, "but she won't be devastated. God has her back, and her front. He won't leave her alone and He won't put more on her than she can bear. She'll survive and she'll thrive. We have to help her see God in all that's happening. If we're going to do that, we're going to have to see Him in it ourselves."

Dolores took comfort in Stuart's words, knowing he was

right. She knew too that there was more of her story that she needed to tell them. Partial confessions didn't count. "You're right," she said. "I know you're right. I needed to be reminded though."

"We all do at times. That's why we're here for each other. You're not alone in this, Dolores," Stuart said. "I hope you know that."

"I do," she said, "but there's one more thing I need to tell you both about Monika's father. This is going to get bad for her and I don't know what to do. I talked to him yesterday and he doesn't want me to tell her who he is. He says that if I do, he'll deny that he's her father."

Bile rose up in Francine's throat. "How could he be that cruel?"

Dolores shook her head. "That's what I keep asking myself. He says he has too much to lose."

"Too much to lose?" Francine asked. "Is the man crazy? What's more important than his daughter?"

Dolores lifted her eyes to Francine's. "He's not crazy," she said. "He's a minister."

Dawn looked around for her sister, wondering if she was ready to leave. She'd had a great time this afternoon, and she thought the picnic had been a great way to end an almost perfect day for Francine, *almost* because George and his friends had walked out when she'd started to speak. It had been obvious to Dawn and everyone else why they had. She knew their leaving had hurt Francine, and she hoped the picnic was soothing the hurt. Still, she was a bit tired and wanted to go home. She hated to admit it but she missed Sylvester. Though he'd sat with them at church as he'd promised, apparently he hadn't been able to get away from the funeral in time to make the picnic.

"Hey, pretty lady."

Dawn turned to see Walter Andrews standing behind her. "Where did you come from?"

Walter laughed. "You forget that your Mother Harris is my great-aunt Martha. She told us she was having this shindig and invited us over. I came as soon as we got out of service."

Dawn was stuck on the "us" he'd mentioned. She knew it was time to leave now; she wasn't up for another run-in with Ms. Fredericka.

"She's not here," Walter said, as if he'd read her mind. "She went to a funeral."

"Which one?" Dawn asked, and wished she could take back the words.

"That one," Walter said. "I guess I don't have to ask where your husband is. I thought Amen-Ray had the body, but I wasn't sure. I wonder what they're doing."

Dawn refused to be baited. "Your imagination is getting the best of you, Walter. They're at a funeral. What do you think they're doing?"

"Funerals don't last all afternoon," he said. "They could be up to any number of things. I really don't care, but I guess you do."

Dawn fought the uncertainty she felt. No way was anything still going on between Fredericka and Sly. "What do you want, Walter?"

"I told you what I wanted. Have you thought about it?"

"You must be crazy."

"I'm not, and you know it. They found comfort in each other, maybe we can too."

Dawn sent a smirk his way. "I can't believe you're talking to me about this. You just left church and you're talking to me about a one-night stand. What kind of man are you?"

Walter gave her a cruel grin. "I guess I'm like your husband."

Dawn's hand slapped his face before she could stop herself. "Stay away from me," she bit out. Then she pushed past him and rushed toward the house. Mother Harris almost bumped into her as she entered through the patio doors.

"Excuse me, Mother Harris," Dawn said. She attempted to go past the older woman, but Mother Harris held her arm. "Is something wrong?"

Dawn shook her head.

"Dawn—"

"Really, Mother Harris," Dawn said. "It's nothing."

Mother Harris tipped Dawn's chin down. "I know it's not nothing, Dawn," she said. "I'm here for you when you want to talk about it. Anytime."

Dawn nodded and continued through the house and out the front door.

Walter rushed into the house behind her. "What's going on, Walter?" Mother Harris asked.

He kissed her cheek. "Nothing, Auntie."

"Don't lie to me, Walter," she said. "I may be old but I'm not senile. I know something's wrong. You and Freddie haven't been to this house together in I don't know how long. And I saw that slap Dawn gave you. I'll ask you one more time, what's going on?"

"Nothing I can't fix, Auntie. Don't worry."

Mother Harris held him in place with a stare. "I'm not going to worry," she said, "but you can bet I'm going to be praying."

"Well, we all need prayer."

Mother Harris huffed at his offhand comment. "You've changed, Walter, and it's not for the better."

"It's not that bad, Auntie," he said. "I'm going through a rough patch. I'll be okay."

"And Freddie? What about her? Will she be all right?"

Walter straightened his spine. "I can take care of my wife," he said. "You don't have to worry about her."

"I hope so, Walter," she said. "I pray so."

Walter waited a brief moment as he watched his aunt go back

to her guests, but his mind was on Dawn. He rubbed the cheek she'd slapped as he stalked off in the direction she'd gone. He found her standing outside at her car.

"I'm sorry," he said.

"No, you're not."

"I'm sorry if what I said hurt you," he clarified, "but I'm not sorry I said what I did. I'm right and I think you know I'm right."

Dawn paced the length of her parked car, wishing Francine were here so she could get away from Walter. "I don't believe you're saying this to me. Do you really expect me to go to bed with you to get back at my husband? What kind of woman do you think I am?"

Walter grabbed her shoulders and made her look into his eyes. "I think you're a woman who loved her husband and never even dreamed he'd cheat on her. I think you're a woman who's had her world blown to bits by a cheating husband. I think you're a woman who's hurting more than she ever imagined she could and who has no clue how to stop the pain."

Dawn shrugged away from him. "You don't know me, Walter, and you don't know how I feel. You really don't."

"Ah, but I do. I know how you feel because I know how I feel. The love you felt for Sylvester is the love I felt for Freddie. My world has been blown to bits and I hurt more than I ever imagined I could hurt. That's what their affair has done to me. I can only imagine that it's done the same to you. Do you deny it?"

Dawn couldn't deny it. She and Walter did have a shared pain, but a shared pain was no reason for her to hop in the sack with him. She may have been a bit hazy on this point when he'd first mentioned it to her, but now she had clarity. "I'm not going to sleep with you, Walter, so you can get that out of your head."

He touched her cheek. "I think you will," he said. "I can wait until you're ready, Dawn."

She moved away from his touch. "You're an arrogant one, aren't you?"

"Not really. I just know what you're feeling. Like I know that right now you're wondering if Sly and Fredericka are together. You're wondering if they saw each other, if they spoke to each other, what they said. You're wondering if they planned to be there together. You're wondering what it was like for them before and you're wondering what he found in her that he didn't find in you."

Dawn closed her eyes against the truth in Walter's words. He'd captured her thoughts almost exactly.

"I know," he continued, "because I'm wondering the same thing."

CHAPTER 16

Sylvester stood with his hands behind his back and watched the cemetery crew lower the casket into the grave as the mourners made their way to their cars and away from the cemetery. The morning service at Faith Central filled his thoughts, adding to them other thoughts he'd rather not have—thoughts of the affair he'd had with Fredericka. Stuart had asked him how it had happened, how he had allowed it to happen, and Sly had always answered with some form of "It just happened," but as he thought about it now, really thought about it, he understood that it hadn't just happened. Sin never just happened, though it sometimes seemed that way. No, there was always a buildup and now he could clearly see the steps that had led to his downfall.

He'd first met Fredericka at one of the city choir competitions. Dawn already knew her husband, Walter, since she was choir director for Faith Central's gospel choir and he was choir director for his church, Berean Bible. The couple of months leading up to the city competition were always hectic for them, with Dawn spending a great deal of her free time with the

197

choir. Many a night Sly found himself eating dinner alone, and since he didn't enjoy his own cooking, many of those meals were taken in local restaurants. On one such evening, Fredericka had run into him while she too was out and her husband was at choir practice. Instead of eating alone, they'd shared a meal.

They'd commiserated over their busy spouses and made plans to share dinner again. None of this had been done in secret. He'd told Dawn about it and she'd been glad that he and Freddie didn't have to eat alone. Things had changed during that second meal. Fredericka hadn't been the lively woman he'd known her to be. Instead, she'd been distracted, upset. He tried for over an hour to find out what was wrong with her. When he had, he'd almost wished he hadn't. Fredericka had told him about her ailing marriage. Apparently, Walter spent more time at church than he did at home. He wanted children, but Fredericka was concerned that he wasn't there enough for her so how could she expect him to be there for their children? She wanted children, but she didn't want to bring them into a weak marriage. She'd admitted her thoughts of divorce. Sly, who thought she was being overly emotional, had tried to soothe her. She'd seemed to get better with his counsel, and by the end of the evening, she'd had him promising not to tell anybody about her lapse. Not even Dawn. He realized now that Fredericka's request for secrecy should have been his signal.

They'd continued to eat dinner together, off and on. Fredericka often complained about Walter's devotion to the church and lack of devotion to her, and she began to question Sly, asking if he felt the same way with Dawn. He hadn't. Not at first. But Fredericka seemed to plant a seed that grew. Maybe Dawn *was* taking him for granted. Over time, he began to resent the time Dawn spent with the choir, whereas before he'd understood it was just for those couple of months leading up to the competition. Things had come to a head when Fredericka had called him on an evening that Dawn and Walter were rehearsing with their respective choirs. She'd sounded distraught and had begged him to come over before she did something drastic. He'd gone over to comfort her and had ended up betraying his marriage vows on the couch in Freddie's living room. That had been the beginning of the end. After the first time, the second time was easier. Then when the competition was over, they'd started meeting at hotels.

Sly could see the pattern now, how sin had overtaken him. No, it hadn't been a spur-of-the-moment thing. It had been gradual, so gradual that he hadn't seen it coming. Or had he? If the words written in First Peter were true, and Sly knew they were, then the devil walked about as a roaring lion looking to destroy the people of God. If Sly was caught unawares by a roaring lion, it had to mean that his heart had been far from God even before the sexual act with Freddie had occurred. How else could he have missed the attack of a roaring lion?

"Sly."

Sylvester knew who it was before he turned to her. He'd seen her in the church, but he hadn't spoken with her or acknowledged her presence in any way. He knew he never would have approached her the way she was approaching him. A part of him wanted to end the interaction as quickly as possible. He didn't want word to get back to Dawn that he'd spent time talking to her.

"Fredericka."

"So formal," she said, and he felt the pain he saw reflected in her light green eyes.

"That's the way it has to be between us."

"I know," she said. "I know."

"How are you?" he asked.

"You really don't want to know, do you?"

He really didn't, but he couldn't tell her that. "Tell me."

"Not too good."

"I'm sorry," he said. "I heard about you and Walter."

She nodded. "He won't take me back. He says he never will."

"He needs time."

"Is that what Dawn tells you?"

"I can't talk to you about Dawn," he said, not wanting to hurt her, but needing to protect his wife's privacy.

"We used to be able to talk about anything, everything. I miss that. I miss you."

She was right. She had been a friend to him, but that was a road they could never travel again. "You should be having this conversation with Walter."

She looked away. "I know."

The crew was finishing up and Sly knew he couldn't be left alone in this cemetery with Fredericka. He felt her pain but he wasn't the one to ease it. "I'm sorry, Fredericka, for everything. If I could go back and undo it, I would—"

"But you can't," she said with a wry smile. "It really wasn't worth it, was it?"

He shook his head sadly.

"I don't think so either," she said. "So why did it seem like it at the time?"

He shrugged. "I have some ideas on that, but I'm still trying to figure it out myself."

"Well, you let me know when you do."

Sly couldn't commit to that. He could make no promises to her. As if she realized that, she smiled and said, "Be good to yourself, Sly. I hope you and Dawn make it through this."

"You too," he said, wanting to give her more, but having nothing more to give her. When she turned to walk away, he headed toward the crew.

❧

Francine's head throbbed as Dolores related the story of her relationship with her pastor some fifteen years ago, a relationship that she'd resumed when she'd moved to Atlanta some six or seven years ago. The story struck her deeply because of its close resemblance to Toni's story. Only Dolores's story had two major differences. First, unlike Toni, Dolores had chosen to have her baby. Second, Dolores had known she was alone and had not looked to anyone beyond herself for help. Those differences demonstrated that Dolores was a fighter, a survivor. But Francine's mind mostly focused on the key similarities. Both Toni and Dolores had been young women who'd been seduced by pastors they trusted. In both cases, the pastors had gotten off scot-free, while the women had been left to deal with the fallout all alone. That was an injustice Francine didn't think she could bear twice.

"He can't shirk his responsibility like this," Francine declared. "He has to think about Monika."

"That's what I told him," Dolores said, "but he refuses. He's afraid he'll lose his ministry."

Francine wanted to scream her unbelief, but she held herself in check for Dolores's sake. "How can he seriously think he has a ministry that's blessed by God when he refuses to acknowledge his own daughter? Who is he?" she demanded.

Dolores shook her head. "I don't feel right giving you his name."

"Why do you want to protect him?"

"I'm not protecting him," she said. "I'm protecting Monika. If he loses what he has, he's going to take it out on her. I'd rather she never meet him than realize he doesn't care about her."

"But—" Francine began, but Stuart cut her off by putting his hand on her wrist. "It's your decision, Dolores," he said. "But there are biblical ways for us to approach this man—minister— and deal with this. When you're ready, we're ready to deal with him God's way."

"I'll think about it," Dolores said. "Maybe I'll talk to him again. He may change his mind after he has time to think about it."

Francine really didn't think so, and she pitied Dolores if she was hanging her daughter's happiness on a man who hadn't done the right thing in fifteen long years. Stuart's hand holding her wrist made her keep her mouth closed.

Stuart suggested they pray and he led them. Afterwards, the three of them joined the others outside. When Dolores went to see what Monika was up to, Stuart pulled Francine aside. "Are you all right?" he asked.

"No, I'm not all right. I'll never be all right as long as there are people like this guy and Bishop Payne still in pulpits. How can this be, Stuart? How do these men get in pulpits and how do they stay there? I don't get it."

He tossed a leaf into the wind. "Churches, people, are looking for leaders, Francine, and there are many leaders out there who see the church as a good career path. But a pastor is more than a leader, he's a shepherd. The shepherd leads, but he also teaches, comforts, protects. All those things that God does for His children, He expects for His shepherds to carry out with their flock. I think a lot of churches look for good leaders rather than good shepherds. Churches are big business, and people want to make sure business is taken care of."

"So it's the congregation's fault for picking bad preachers?"

Stuart shook his head. "Of course not. Most, if not all, of the blame lies with the leaders themselves. Many of them enter the ministry for the wrong reasons, while others of them are tempted and led astray by the power and position. It happens, more than I want to admit, more than any of us want to admit."

"There ought to be some way of getting those men out, or stopping them from getting in those positions in the first place. We're talking about souls here."

Stuart nodded. "There are ways of getting them out, but that's only after the damage has been done. Truly repentant leaders easily land other congregations, and unfortunately, so do many of the ones who are merely good actors. People in church want to believe that people change, so they're always willing to give a person a second chance."

"So, what's the answer?"

He looked down at her. "What the answer always is: obedience to God. Just as there are men entering the pastorate for the wrong reasons, there are other men who don't enter it when they should. They feel they can reach more people out of the pulpit than in it. These men make the same mistake as the men who think a mega-church means they're doing great work for God. It doesn't. The only great work a man can do for the kingdom is to be obedient to what the Lord has called him to do. If that's pastoring a congregation that never grows above a hundred, so be it. The same if it means pastoring a congregation that's above twenty-five thousand. The same for the guy who thinks he can touch more hearts or make more of a difference as a teacher, or doctor, or lawyer, or judge. The obedience is the measure, not the occupation, not even the results we reap on this earth."

Francine considered Stuart's words. While they sounded good, they really didn't address the issue, not in her mind. "Okay," she said, "I can see that we need to get good people in the pulpit, but how do we get the bad ones out?"

Stuart led her to a picnic table, where he picked up a can of soda on ice after handing one to her. "Easy, we confront the sin in three steps, the way Jesus lays it out in verses 15 through 17 of Matthew, chapter 18."

"Easy to say," Francine muttered.

He tipped his can to his lips. "You're right, but it's only hard because there's a lot of cover-up going on in a lot of these churches with bad preachers. People know, but they don't say anything. Sometimes it's because that 'let he who is without sin cast the first stone' mentality paralyzes them into inaction. Or maybe the 'judge not, lest you be judged' mentality. Or maybe they're like Dolores, and don't want to get caught up in all the fallout. Whatever the reason, the inaction of people who know allows it to go on."

"So what about Dolores? When I tried to press her for the minister's name, you stopped me. How will he ever be confronted if nobody knows his name?"

Stuart gave her a smile that reminded her of an indulgent parent dealing with a precocious child. "Sometimes our timing is not the Lord's. His primary goal is not to *get* that minister. He's concerned about Dolores and Monika and how they come out of this. He's always concerned about souls."

Francine waved her soda can in frustration. "So the pastor gets off scot-free? That's not right. How can that be right?" She was thinking as much about Bishop Payne as she was about Monika's father. Both men still led churches, suffering only minor setbacks, while the women they abused had their lives ruined.

"He won't get off scot-free. None of them do. First Peter 2 and 8 makes it clear that God both delivers the godly out of temptation and reserves the wicked for punishment. The thing is, the Lord may not use us when He exacts his payment. We can be there for Dolores and Monika, loving them with the love of the Lord and encouraging them to trust that love. In time, Dolores will make the right decision and do what the Lord would have her do regarding this man. Besides, he's not going anywhere."

Francine thought about Stuart's words, and though she wanted to exact payment *now,* she knew he was right. "It sounds like you've thought a lot about this," she observed.

"I have. At one time, I thought I was destined for the pulpit."

"I can see that," she said, and she could. Stuart would be one of the good pastors, a true shepherd to his flock. "So what happened to change your path?"

"Life," he said, and she understood he didn't want to talk about it. That made her sad because she thought they were becoming friends. She didn't respond, so they stood together watching the kids run across Mother Harris's backyard. "My vision of my future always included me in the pulpit and my wife, Marie, by my side," Stuart explained a short while later. "That vision died when she died."

"I'm sorry, Stuart," she said. "I shouldn't have asked."

He shook his head. "It's all right. I can talk about her. We had a good life."

"You loved her a lot." She glanced at his ring. "You still wear your wedding ring."

He twisted it on his finger. "I haven't been able to take it off."

"Because you still feel married?"

He tossed his soda can into a garbage pail about five feet away. "I don't think so. I think it represents a part of my life that I'm not yet ready to let go."

Francine thought about the life he'd shared with his wife and compared it to the loves in her life. Sly was the closest she'd come and she knew that hadn't been the same kind of love Stuart felt for Marie. She wondered what that love felt like. She wondered if Dawn and Sly had experienced it, if they still did. "So if you're not going to the pulpit, how do you see your life playing out?"

"The Lord is opening a lot of doors for me now. I lead a teen fathers' group that meets each week and I have a job that gives me a lot of satisfaction. Beyond that, I'm taking it day by day. What about you?"

She drank the last of her soda. "I'm not even taking it day by day yet. I'm still at the moment-by-moment pace. I really don't know. A lot of my life was tied up in Temple Church, and my plans for the future all involved playing some role in that ministry. Now that I'm no longer there, I'm not quite sure what the future holds."

"It sounds like we both need to hold on to the Lord's words to Jeremiah," Stuart said. Then he quoted, "I know the plans I have for you, says the Lord, plans for good and not for evil, plans to give you a hope and a future."

Francine turned to him. "Thanks," she said. "I needed to hear that. I've read it many times, but I needed to hear it. Right now, it feels like the Lord is rejuvenating my spirit by allowing me to make peace with my past so I can walk in the future He has for me, if that makes any sense."

"It makes a lot of sense." He twisted his wedding ring on his finger again. "Maybe I need to make peace with the past myself."

Francine knew he was thinking about his wife. She reached over and touched his hand with hers. "I can't even imagine how it feels to lose someone you love the way you obviously loved your wife, Stuart. Losing my grandparents was worse than anything I'd ever imagined, even though I knew they were going to be with the Lord. Of course it's going to take time for you to see and be excited about a future without her."

Stuart turned his hand over and squeezed hers. "Thanks for saying that."

Sylvester pulled into Mother Harris's driveway about fifteen minutes after Fredericka left him. He had an overwhelming desire to see Dawn, to tell her about seeing Fredericka. Surprise didn't quite capture how he felt when he saw her and Walter engaged in what seemed to be serious conversation in Mother Harris's driveway. Jealousy raged in him like a roaring fire. He could hear Dawn's taunts of another man playing in his mind and he could see how it could happen. It could happen for

Dawn and Walter in much the same way it had happened for him and Fredericka. Walter would plant seeds of doubt and offer a strong shoulder of support. One thing would lead to another and they'd end up horizontal somewhere. With that image in his mind, Sly jerked his car door open and stalked toward the couple.

"I hope I'm not interrupting," he said, though he really hoped he was. He held out his hand. "It's been a while, Walter."

Walter looked down at Sly's hand, but he didn't take it. "Not long enough," Walter said.

"You seem to have a lot to say to my wife," Sly said.

"Not as much as you had to say to mine," Walter countered. "Then again maybe Dawn and I are doing more talking than you and Fredericka did."

Sly took a step toward the man, his hand balled into a fist, itching to wipe that smirk off Walter's face.

"Your husband is a very physical man," Walter said to Dawn. "So physical I can almost understand why he thinks he needs two women."

Sly raised his hand. "You—"

"Stop it, both of you," Dawn yelled. "Sly, stop behaving like a child, and Walter, stop taunting him."

Sylvester dropped his hand and rolled his shoulders to let go of the tension that had bunched there. "Let's make a deal, Walter. You stay away from my wife. I stay away from yours."

Walter smirked. "I don't see how that deal works in my favor, Sly, seeing as you've had my wife and I haven't had yours. Yet."

Sly lifted his hands again and was about to land a blow until Dawn stepped between them. "Leave," she said to Walter. "Now."

Walter looked as if he were going to say something to Sly, but he changed his mind and turned to Dawn. "Think about what I said," he told her. "I'll be in touch."

"Don't bother," Sly called after the weasel. "She's not interested."

Dawn turned on him. "What's your problem, Sly? The man was only talking to me."

"Come off it, Dawn," Sly said. "That guy has more on his mind than talk and you know it. Has he propositioned you yet?"

"I'm not going to answer that," Dawn said, turning away from him and back toward the house.

Sly caught her arm and turned her around. "He has, hasn't he?" When she didn't answer, he dropped her arm. "I knew it. The slimy—"

"Stop with the name-calling, Sly. Walter's harmless."

"Yeah, right."

"He is. He's a bit lost right now. It's something we have in common."

Sly felt her words as a punch in the gut. "You're going to see him again?"

"Maybe. If he needs to talk. I haven't decided."

Sly came so close to her that his nose almost touched hers. "I don't know what game you're playing, Dawn, but you're playing with fire. You may not want to end up in Walter's bed, you may not even have any plans to end up there, but if you keep playing around with him like this, that's exactly where you're going to find yourself."

"Look who's talking," she murmured.

"Because I know what I'm talking about. I didn't set out to sleep with Fredericka. It was the farthest thing from my mind. But it happened, and it happened in small steps that I took without thinking a lot about them."

"I'm not you."

"You're right. You're not me. I didn't have any reason to turn away from you, but you have every reason to turn away from me. You've told me that often enough. Well, whether you want to cheat or not, you're setting yourself up to do it. I can tell you right now though that it's not going to give you what you want. To the contrary, you'll lose more than you'll get. I did. I lost your trust and respect and I lost my own respect and even though I'm working hard to get it all back, I still have no idea if I'll be successful. Believe me, you don't want to put yourself in that position. Take it from somebody who's been there."

CHAPTER 17

Francine was getting out of her car at the funeral home on Monday when Stuart drove up in a sleek red Corvette. She waited for him before going inside for their meeting about the collective. His long legs made confident strides toward her and a smile lit his face. She admitted to herself that she was happy to see him.

He leaned over and kissed her cheek. "I'm glad I'm not late," he said. "I left my office later than I'd planned."

"No, you're right on time," she said, leading him into the funeral home. "Thanks for helping us out. Sly's counting on you."

"No biggie," he said, following her to Sly's office.

She looked back at him as she reached Sly's door. "It's a biggie to us."

Sly stood as they entered his office. "Hey, you two," he said. "Have a seat while I round up Dawn. She's probably in her office."

Francine and Stuart took seats at the round conference table, where each place had been set with a pad, a pen, and a typewritten report.

"This is going to be serious business," Stuart murmured, picking up one of the Amen-Ray engraved pens.

Sly and Dawn were back in the room before Francine could respond. "Hey, sis," Francine said.

"Hey to you, too," Dawn said, taking a seat next to Francine. "Stuart, good to see you."

Sly took a seat between Dawn and Stuart. "Well, I want to thank all three of you for making time to come here today, especially you, Stuart, since I know you have a busy schedule."

"Glad to be able to help," Stuart said.

"I guess we'd better get to it then," Sly said. "I've put together a few notes on the collective idea that I've talked to you all about. You have them in front of you."

Francine looked at the typed sheet atop the yellow pad in front of her.

"Like I told the three of you," Sly said, "I'm looking for ways to expand the funeral home's business and provide some safeguard against corporate funeral homes like Easy Rest. My basic idea, one that I appropriated from a presentation that was made to the Leadership Team at Faith Central, essentially situates Amen-Ray in a collective of funeral homes that work together to leverage their individual resources."

Francine put down the sheet of paper she'd been studying. "I think the idea has some merit, Sly, but can you give us a little bit more on why you think it'll work for Amen-Ray and why Amen-Ray needs it?"

Sly cast a quick glance at Dawn before answering. "Let me answer the second part of your question first. Like I said before, we're getting a lot of pressure from Easy Rest, who wants us to sell out to them. In their deal, they own the funeral home, but we have the option of remaining in management positions, subject to the management in their corporate offices."

"Of course," Francine said.

"Well, all of us here know that once we sell the funeral home,

Easy Rest can do whatever they want. For two years, the name would be 'Amen-Ray, an Easy Rest Funeral Home.' In year three, the name would be simply 'Easy Rest Funeral Home.'"

"What would happen if they bought three funeral homes in the same town?" Dawn asked. "Would they all have the same name?"

"Good question," Sly said, with a smile at his wife. "Their whole point is that there is one Easy Rest. When they purchase funeral homes, they decide whether to keep them open in separate locations or consolidate them into a single location. They make this determination based on a number of factors. If we went with them, we would remain a stand-alone facility for the first two years, but after that, we'd likely consolidate with other Easy Rest funeral homes in the area. It depends on how their numbers shake out."

"So, in effect," Stuart said, "there's only one Easy Rest. Everything operates out of a single corporate headquarters."

"You've got it," Sly said. "Think Wal-Mart for the mortuary business and you've got their concept."

Francine sighed. "I hate to say this, Sly, but it's a pretty good strategy. Why aren't we better off going with them?"

"How can you ask that, Francine?" Dawn asked, before Sly could answer. "Our grandparents built this place and left it for us. We can't sell it to some impersonal corporation. Grandma Willie and Grandpa Grady would roll in their graves."

Francine wasn't so sure, but she held her tongue. She hadn't been involved in the work of the funeral home enough to go against what Dawn and Sly wanted unless she had very strong objections. She didn't. "Just asking," she said to her sister.

"It was a good question," Stuart said, looking at Dawn. "And one all three of you have to answer from both financial and personal perspectives."

"But—" Dawn began.

"I'm not telling you what decision to make," Stuart explained.

"I'm only saying that you have to understand fully the impact of whatever you choose to do. Finances don't have to be the driving issue, and probably shouldn't be, but you should understand the financial ramifications of whatever decision you make."

"He's right, Dawn," Sly said, and Francine heard the compassion in his voice for his wife's feelings. "I've put together a set of numbers based on Easy Rest's last offer. It's in front of you." He waited while they looked at it.

Francine whistled when she read Easy Rest's offer, and she saw Stuart grin at her.

"Yep, that's what we're giving up," Sly said.

"Okay," Dawn said, "it's a lot of money. How do we turn it down in good faith?"

"Well," Sly said, "since I've already turned it down on our behalf, I hope this collective idea gives us the leverage we need. This gets me back to the first part of your question, Francine." He went on to outline for them the benefits of such a collective. "Those are the major benefits as I see them," he concluded. "Stuart's here because he can give us a bigger and probably more accurate picture of the advantages and disadvantages of taking this route." He turned to Stuart.

Stuart opened his portfolio and handed each of them copies of his notes. "What I've given you are some points to consider if you're going to move ahead with this idea. As you'll see, I've listed them in order of importance, as I see them, and from a legal perspective. The first is, you have to decide the boundaries of the collective—its purpose and scope. Second, you have to decide on an organizational structure—equal shares for all or tiers of membership or something in between. Let's tackle the boundaries one first because that'll help us decide on the best organizational structure. For example, will the collective encompass purchasing, marketing, advertising, sales, operations, one of those, some of those, all of those, or something else altogether?"

"I'd thought about it from the purchasing, marketing, advertising, and sales angles," Sly said, "because it's easy to see the economies of scale we can get in those areas."

"Me too," Francine said. "If we could do bulk purchases and joint advertising, marketing, and sales, I'm sure we could get better prices than we get by going alone."

"I agree," Dawn said, "but there's something intriguing about the operations component." She looked at her husband. "What do you think, Sly?"

"It's an angle I hadn't considered, but I can see some possibilities. Tell us your thoughts on it, Stuart."

Stuart sat back in his chair and rested his right foot on his left knee. "This one could be tricky, and probably much more complicated to pull off than the others. It could encompass shared billing and invoicing services, shared embalming services, central and joint training services, that kind of thing."

Sly nodded. "We could even end up with a funeral home consulting service where we consult with funeral homes in trouble or new funeral homes and provide recommendations for changes and improvements."

"I like the concept," Dawn said, "but who would do the work? We're busy enough as it is."

"It might mean staffing adjustments," Stuart said. "But in the long run it could be worth it."

"Can we start at a simpler level and move to the more complex?" Francine asked.

"I'm with Francine on this one," Sly said. "I think the simpler stuff will be an easier sell to other funeral homes because they can see immediate benefit. Once we get some credit for success in those areas, we can begin to think about sharing operations or creating consulting services. We need to start planning for those two now, but I don't think they should be part of our initial rollout. My gut tells me that both of them, consulting and operations-sharing, have so many more particulars that they would seriously delay when we could get started on this."

Dawn looked upon her husband with pride. "I'm with Sly. If we're doing this to fight off the Easy Rests of the world, we need to make a showing fast before too many of our peer funeral homes sell out. It's not clear we have a lot of time."

"Okay," Francine said. "I'm on board with that approach. So what do we do to get started?"

"Not so fast," Stuart said. "We need to decide on an organization structure next. After we do that, we draw up a business plan and then you do a road show."

"A road show?" Dawn asked.

"That's right," Sly said. "We have to sell the idea. Pick a few key funeral homes, ten maybe, that we want to get on board first because we think they'll pull some others. Once we get those on board, we do a full rollout of the collective." He looked at Stuart. "Let's talk organization structure."

The organization structure discussion took much longer than the boundary discussion. After more than two hours of back-and-forth, Sly said, "It seems we have two solid options. One has Amen-Ray as the hub of the collective, and the other creates a separate entity, Everlasting Life, say, as the hub." He turned to Stuart. "From a legal perspective, which option safeguards our interests and assets best?"

"Creating the separate entity is always the cleanest split. I'd go that way."

"But what about the cost?" Dawn asked. "Isn't that option more expensive?"

"Not really," Stuart said. "Remember, each member of the collective will have to pay dues. You'll have to set the dues to cover the operating costs of the hub. Of course, the dues can't be so high that they negate the economies of scale you're going to get by operating as a collective."

216

ANGELA BENSON

"That settles it for me," Sly said. He glanced at Francine and Dawn. "What about you two?"

"Works for me," Francine said. "Dawn?"

"Me too," she said. Then she yawned. "And it's about time too."

Sly checked his watch. "We've been here almost four hours. It's time for a break. Thanks, everybody. We've done some great work. I'll pull together a draft of the business plan over the next week or so and circulate it to you."

Stuart handed him another document. "I happen to have a business plan template for a similar venture that I worked on. You may want to use it as a model. The way I figure it, you have about a couple months of work ahead of you before you're ready to take this show on the road."

Sly took the document. "Thanks, man. We would never have gotten this far without your help."

"Hey, it was fun." Stuart rolled his shoulders. "I could go for a meal. Anybody hungry?"

"I am," Francine said.

"I'm more tired than hungry," Dawn said. "I think I'll head on home."

"Well—" Francine said.

"No," Sly said. "You and Stuart go on out and get something to eat. I'll go home with Dawn. I need to talk to her about something anyway."

The look on Dawn's face said that Sly's need to talk with her was news to her, but she didn't say anything to contradict him. Francine looked at Sly and had the feeling she was being set up. She wondered what Stuart thought but she didn't have the courage to look at him.

"I guess it's me and you," Stuart said, forcing her to meet his gaze. "What do you have a taste for?"

"Something simple," she said. "I eat pretty much anything."

He grinned. "A woman after my own heart."

He turned to Sly and Dawn. "We're going to head out. You two sure you don't want to join us?"

Sly shook his head. "Nah, man." He gave Stuart the soul shake. "Enjoy your dinner and thanks for all your help."

"Yeah, thanks, Stuart," Dawn said, giving him a hug. "We owe you."

"Just a prayer every now and then," he said.

Dawn grinned. "That we can handle."

Stuart turned back to Francine. "Ready?"

She nodded, said good night to Sly and Dawn, and allowed Stuart to lead her out of the funeral home. "I can drive," she said.

He shook his head. "Ride with me. I'll bring you back here and then follow you home."

"That's not necessary—"

Stuart folded his arms across his chest. "Are we going to start our wonderful meal with an argument? If we are, I have to tell you now that I'm going to win. I have substantially more arguing experience. Just ask my colleagues and my opponents."

Francine gave in with a smile. "No arguments," she said. "I'm too tired."

He opened the door of his Corvette and she slid in. "Boys and their toys," she muttered.

"What was that you said?" Stuart asked when he slid into the driver's seat.

"Nothing," she said.

"I thought we'd go to Granny's. It's close and it'll be quick. That all right with you?"

"Fine," she said. She liked the down-home atmosphere of the place, and the cooking reminded her of her grandmother's. "I can taste those chicken and dumplings now."

"Me, I'm dreaming of the liver and onions."

Francine laughed. "Liver and onions? Yuck!"

"Watch it," Stuart warned. "Them's fighting words. I love liver and onions."

She tilted her head to the side and studied him. "You amaze me, Stuart."

He cast a glance at her. "I think I like that."

Not sure how to take the flirting, Francine faced forward, thankful they had already arrived in Granny's parking lot. Once they were seated in a back booth near the windows, she said, "They're busy tonight."

"It's the liver and onions."

She laughed at the twinkle in his eyes. A waiter, wearing a red-and-white-checkered apron that matched the tablecloths, brought them Granny's famous iced tea, sweetened, and offered menus which neither of them took. Francine ordered the chicken and dumplings with peach cobbler for dessert. Stuart also added the cobbler to his order of liver and onions.

"I shouldn't have ordered that cobbler," Francine said. "I'm going to be full after I eat the dumplings."

"Hey, Granny's peach cobbler has nothing to do with hunger. It's 100 percent about taste. And to show you how generous and unselfish I am, I'll share yours with you so you don't have to eat it all."

"And what will you do with yours?"

He grinned. "I'll take it home with me and eat it as a late night snack. I'm a sucker for their cobbler."

Francine shook her head. "A judge, a Corvette, liver and onions, and cobbler. Something about this picture doesn't fit."

"It fits all right. You just don't know my background."

She leaned forward and rested her forearms on the table. "I'm listening."

He told her the story of growing up a preacher's kid in a rural southern Alabama town. "I'll take Granny's over Justin's any day."

Francine chuckled. She knew Justin's was P. Diddy's upscale

restaurant in the expensive Buckhead section of Atlanta. She could definitely picture Stuart better in that atmosphere than in this one with its battered oak tables and chairs and rickety ceiling fans. "I like Justin's," she said. "Not that I don't like it here."

He smiled. "I like Justin's too. We'll have to go there sometime."

Francine didn't answer. Since he still wore his wedding ring, she didn't quite know how to take his comment. She told herself to take everything he said as from one friend to another, a brother in Christ to a sister in Christ. Any other ideas would only lead her to a broken heart. She was saved from responding when the waiter brought their food. That was another point in Granny's favor—they served solid home cooking in fast-food time. After Stuart blessed the food, Francine dug into her dumplings.

"Hmm," she said, closing her eyes to savor the taste.

"That good, huh?"

She opened her eyes and found him smiling at her. "That and I'm hungry. An unbeatable combination. Thanks for thinking of this place. It's perfect." She pointed her fork at his plate. "How's that yucky stuff?"

"Don't disparage my food. It's delicious."

"I don't believe you."

Stuart chuckled. "Eat your dumplings and leave my food alone."

Francine took his advice.

"You know, I had ulterior motives for wanting to have dinner with you."

She peered up at him. "What?"

"I wanted to ask you to come to the teen fathers' group that I lead every week." He sprinkled hot sauce on his entree. "The group started a couple of years ago. Faith Central has always had a strong youth ministry. This group grew out of that. Some of the boys from the church began to bring their friends and a great many of them were fathers. This group is a safe place for them to talk and learn what it really means to follow the Lord."

"That's a great idea for a ministry." She thought about Toni, wishing her friend had had some place like a women's group where she could have gone. "So many times when people fall into sexual sin and its results, they feel there's no place for them. I'm glad Faith Central has made a place."

"Me too," Stuart said. "It's a really effective group. The boys are learning what it means to walk with God, and I'm learning a lot from them. You'll love them and they'll love you."

"It sounds like a good group," Francine said, "but why do you want me to come?"

"Because of what you said during service yesterday. Your testimony is powerful. Kids, especially these kids, need to see people make mistakes and recover. They need that hope. You know, kids are resilient but they're also really hard on themselves. It's sometimes difficult for them to believe God forgives them, because they can't forgive themselves. They need to see what victory looks like, and that's you."

Francine sat back in her chair. "Your words sound wonderful, Stuart, but they don't sound like they should be applied to me. I don't see myself as anybody's example."

He reached across the table for her hand. "That's the beauty of your testimony. You didn't set out to be an example, but God made you one. You said so yourself. It was His choice and He chose to use you to meet the needs of other believers."

She tried to absorb his words. "Somehow the words sound different when you say them. When I think about it, I think about how good God was to take a life that I'd about ruined and use it to help somebody else the way He did yesterday. That's all my testimony is."

"That's what the boys need to know. A couple of them were in church yesterday and you can be sure we're going to talk about what you said when we meet tomorrow. I'd love for you to be there. If you can't come this Tuesday, pick any Tuesday and you're welcome to join us."

"You know," Francine said, "God never ceases to amaze me. I came back home scared to death at the reception I would get, and, for the most part, all He's given me is love. When I left here five years ago, I thought I had to leave to find purpose in my life, to do something for God. Now I know that I don't have to do things for Him. I have to let Him do things through me. Such a simple lesson but so difficult for me to learn." She met his smiling eyes. "Thanks, Stuart, for inviting me to come to your group. I'd love to come one of these Tuesdays."

CHAPTER 18

D awn went straight to the refrigerator when she entered the house. She pulled out a cold diet soda, some tuna salad, and some bread. She'd eat a quick sandwich and then seek the quiet refuge of her room. Sylvester entered the kitchen as she was putting the remaining tuna salad back in the refrigerator.

"Leave that out, please," he said. "I guess I'll make it my dinner too. You don't mind if I eat with you, do you?"

"Of course not." She placed the plastic container of tuna on the table. Then she went to the pantry and brought back a bag of potato chips. She seated herself at the table and took a bite of her sandwich. When Sylvester sat next to her, she said, "You wanted to talk to me about something?"

He put two slices of bread on his plate. "Huh?"

"At the funeral home you told Francine you wanted to talk to me about something."

He grinned. "Oh, that. It was an excuse to keep from going out with them."

"So you're matchmaking?"

He shrugged. "I like to see the people I care about happy. I think Francine and Stuart could make each other happy. No harm in that, is there?"

She popped a chip in her mouth. "I didn't say there was."

He propped his elbows on the table and brought the sandwich to his mouth. "We're not going to argue about this, are we?"

She shook her head. "I don't want to argue."

Sly wiped his mouth with a paper napkin. "Good. Neither do I." He sipped his drink. "I want to apologize for Sunday. I shouldn't have raised my fists to Walter."

"No, you shouldn't have. You were totally out of line."

Sly placed his sandwich down and met her gaze. "Not totally. I'm sorry for almost physically assaulting Walter, but I'm not sorry for what I said, because it's true."

"It's—"

"Okay, Dawn," he challenged, "look me in the eyes right now and tell me that Walter hasn't propositioned you." When she didn't speak, he said, "I know what I'm talking about and I want to save you the pain that I suffer."

"You're not the only one who suffers, Sly," she said quietly.

"I know," he said. "Francine was right on the money yesterday. Sin has far-reaching consequences."

"Too bad you didn't think of that then."

Sly nodded. "You're right. I wasn't thinking, but you won't have that excuse, Dawn." He rubbed his hand across his head. "Who am I kidding? I didn't really have it as an excuse myself."

"I'm glad you realize that."

Sensing that this line of conversation was leading them to the same familiar dead end, Sly said, "I think we made good progress this evening."

Dawn nodded. "You know, I think this could work and take Amen-Ray to a whole new level."

"Me too. I'll get started on that business plan tonight."

Dawn looked at him for a long moment, considered what she was about to say. "Since I'm here," she said, "I could help." When he looked at her, she added, "If you want a second head to work on it."

"I thought you were tired."

She shrugged. "I wasn't as tired as I thought. Besides, if we work here, I can put on something a bit more comfortable, kick off my shoes, and put my feet up while we work."

"Well, two heads are always better than one," Sly said. "I'd appreciate your help. We may be able to work through this a lot quicker than Stuart thinks. I've already been thinking about the funeral homes we'd visit on our initial road show."

"Which ones?"

"Vines in Fort Lauderdale is at the top of the list." He rattled off a few others. "Of course, Peterson here in town."

"Good choices," Dawn said.

"Well," Sly offered, "we can make the first road trip together, if you like. We can start pulling the presentation together as we work through the business plan, since that's what we'll be presenting anyway."

"That's a good idea," Dawn said, though she was unsure about the part with them traveling together. Then she asked, "Have you talked to your grandparents about these plans for the funeral home?"

Sly shook his head and sat back in his chair. "I don't want them to worry. I haven't even told them about Easy Rest. They have enough on their minds when they should just be enjoying their retirement."

Dawn smiled. "You've always been protective of them."

"I wouldn't call it protective."

"What would you call it?"

"Responsible. When I was growing up, going to college, I never had to concern myself with the business. The business became partly my job when I joined Grandpa, and all of my job after he retired. He's carried the load long enough. It's my turn now."

"It's not just you, Sly," Dawn said. "Francine and I are with you in this as well."

"I know," he said.

She shook her head. "I don't think you do. I think you hold yourself solely responsible for what happens at the funeral home. That's too much, even for you." Sly studied her for so long without speaking that Dawn felt uncomfortable. She picked up her glass of soda to have something to do with her hands. "What?" she asked.

"You. I never know what to expect from you."

"And?"

"To be honest, it makes me nervous. Yesterday, you were distant and disconnected. Today, you're concerned about my taking on too much and wanting to work with me on this project. I wonder what tomorrow will bring."

She met his gaze. "Let's not worry about tomorrow. Why not take what we have today and work with it?"

"Is that the best you can offer?"

She nodded. "Is it enough?"

He studied her long seconds before answering. "I guess it'll have to be."

"Good. Now enough analysis. Let's eat so we can get to work."

Nodding, Sly dug into his meal.

Two weeks later, Stuart sat in the Genesis House Community Center in southwest Atlanta in his meeting with his teen fathers' group. He covered his anxiety over Francine's impending arrival by preparing his boys for her visit. "Okay, guys," Stuart told the gathering of nine teenaged boys. "Ms. Amen is going to join us today. I told you about her, remember?"

"We remember, all right," Jimbo said. He was a tall, lanky boy, a basketball star at a local high school, and the father of a two-year-old girl. "Judge has a woman."

"Bet," chorused a few of the other boys. They usually followed Jimbo's lead.

"She's not my woman," Stuart tried to explain.

"Yeah, right," somebody said. "Tell us anything, Judge."

Stuart tried again. "I'm serious, you guys. Are you going to feel free talking in front of her? Is there anything you'd like to talk about before she gets here?"

"Nah, man," said Hank, the seventeen-year-old son of one of the local ministers. Hank had a seven-month-old son. "We can't wait for her to get here. We want to see what kind of woman you can get."

"Man, she's fine," another boy said, nudging his neighbor with his elbow. "We saw her at church."

The other boys howled at that comment. Stuart bit the inside of his lip to keep from smiling. Some days he forgot how young they were. They were fathers, but they were also kids. It struck his heart deeply, as it always did, to realize how irrevocably their lives had changed with the birth of their children. As he looked at them, Stuart saw where he could have been had it not been for the grace of God. His life had been lived in much the same fashion as theirs—careless and carefree. The only difference was, his actions hadn't caught up with him in the form of an unplanned and unwanted pregnancy.

Stuart glanced out the window just in time to see Francine get out of her car. He stood up and pointed a finger at his crew. "I want you to be on your best behavior. I know you know how to treat women, and I don't want you to get so comfortable with teasing me that you forget. Got that?"

"Got it, Judge," they chorused.

"I'll be right back," Stuart told them. He left the room to meet Francine. When she came around the corner and faced him, he asked, "Are you ready?"

"I guess," she said, a smile lifting the corners of her mouth. "Are they ready for me?"

"More than ready. As Hank said, they want to see what kind of woman I can get."

"Woman?"

Stuart grinned. "What can I say? They're young."

She cocked her head to the side. "What if I don't measure up?"

Stuart's gaze traveled from the top of the French braid on her head to her simple white blouse to her standard denim jeans. He had no complaints. "Not a chance," he said in all seriousness. All nine heads turned as the two of them entered the room and Stuart read the acceptance and, for a few, recognition, in the teenaged eyes now focused on Francine.

"You done good, Judge," somebody said.

"Okay, gang," Stuart said, "I'd like you to meet my friend, Miss Francine Amen. A couple of you have seen her around Faith Central. Francine, this is my crew, also known as TFMA, Teen Fathers Making Amends. Why don't you introduce yourselves to Miss Amen?"

Stuart kept Francine's hand in his during the introductions. When they had gone around the circle, Jimbo asked, "Are you the judge's girlfriend?"

Francine cast a sidelong glance at Stuart. "Well," she said, "I'm a girl and since I'm his friend, I guess that makes me his girlfriend. What do you think, Judge?"

Stuart smiled down at her. "Good answer." Then he turned to the young men gathered in the room. "Who wants to start?"

There was murmuring among the group before Timothy, the newest member, spoke. Timothy had two children by two different girls. "I'll go," he said. Twirling a pencil in his fingers, he began, "I went to see Tisha last week like I said I would. I tried to tell her how sorry I was about everything, but she didn't want to hear it. She kicked me out, said I was a no-good user."

"Did she let you see your baby?" another boy asked.

Timothy shook his head. "She said if I didn't want to see him when he was born, I couldn't see him now, said I could go see my other baby."

"That's rough, man," Jimbo said. "But you hurt her real bad when you said the baby wasn't yours."

"Jimbo's right, man," Hank chimed in. "It's like the judge said. When you hurt somebody, the hurt doesn't go away for them because you say you're sorry."

"I'm trying to do the right thing," Timothy said, now sounding much younger than his seventeen years. "But she won't let me. She's the one wrong now."

"That doesn't matter," Stuart told the boy. "It doesn't matter what she does. What matters is what you do." This was his mantra to the boys—take responsibility for your actions and accept their consequences.

"Why does she have to act so crazy?" Timothy asked.

Stuart turned to Francine. He felt her spirit reach out to the young men as they spoke, so he wasn't surprised to see the tears building in her eyes. "You're a woman," he said to her. "Can you offer Timothy any insight on why Tisha acts the way she does?"

Her widened eyes told him that he had put her on the spot. He guessed she wasn't sure if she had any words to offer Timothy. Since he was sure she did, he waited and prayed.

"Well," Francine began. Stuart squeezed her fingers. "Let's think about the situation from Tisha's perspective. Did you ever tell her you loved her?"

Timothy gave a barely perceptible nod.

"Did you mean it?"

"I thought I did at the time."

She waited.

"Well, maybe I liked her," Timothy added.

"Okay," Francine said. "Did she tell you that she loved you?" Timothy nodded.

"Do you think she meant it?"

Timothy nodded again, this time more slowly.

"How do you think she felt when she found out she was pregnant?"

Timothy lifted his slim shoulders. "I don't know. Scared, maybe?"

"Yes, she probably was scared. Now, who do you think was the first person she told?"

"Me," Timothy said, his eyes watering.

"What did she say?"

Timothy wiped at his eyes. "She said she thought she was pregnant. She asked me what we were going to do."

Francine tightened her grip on Stuart's hand as if needing his strength. "And what did you say?" she asked Timothy.

Timothy squeezed his eyes shut and tears leaked down his cheek. "I asked her why she was telling me. It wasn't mine."

Stuart knew his eyes were wet now too. As he scanned the room, he saw that the eyes of most of the boys in the room were wet. Wet because they too had similar stories to tell; wet because they'd learned that being a man meant having feelings, not hiding them.

"And then she started crying," Timothy continued. "She started crying and I left her there crying."

Francine wiped her own tears. "It hurts you now to think about what you did, doesn't it, Timothy?" she asked, her words comforting, not accusing.

Timothy nodded.

"Well, you hurt, and you said those words. Imagine how much worse it feels to be the receiver of those words. Imagine how much worse they hurt Tisha. It may be a while before she comes around, and it's possible she may never come around."

Stuart squeezed Francine's hand, proud of the way she'd handled the situation, but in no way surprised.

"That's one of the things we as men have to live with," he told the boys, "the consequence of our actions. We don't have to beat ourselves up about it every day, but we have to know that our actions have consequences and sometimes those consequences live with us forever. Our challenge is to learn from our mistakes, not repeat them, and to help someone else along the way."

As the meeting settled into what Francine imagined was its standard rhythm, she studied Stuart's interaction with the teens. It was obvious that they respected him and that his opinion carried a lot of weight with them. It was equally obvious that he cared about them and respected them as men. She felt good inside, to see him at work. She guessed it was something she needed to see: a sincere man of God doing the work of the Lord without fanfare and without thoughts of gain. It was refreshing and encouraging to observe. She appreciated as well the way he included her and allowed her to share with the boys whose hearts he prayerfully protected. He demonstrated a level of trust in her that made her ashamed at the lack of trust she'd originally held for him. How badly she'd misread him!

After about ninety minutes, the meeting ended with a prayer led by Timothy. "I like them," she said after the last young man had left.

"You're a natural with them," Stuart said, smiling at her. "Have you worked with young people before?"

She glanced away before answering. "Before I left here, and at the last church I went to."

He leaned against one of the metal folding chairs. "The memories of that place aren't all bad, are they?"

She shook her head. "Some of them are really sweet, really wonderful."

"Why not focus on those memories then? Look at the good that God did."

Francine knew Stuart had no idea how much she wanted to embrace his words. "How can I when so much ugliness was there?"

"Because it's a reminder that in the midst of whatever atrocities are at work, God will make Himself known to hearts that are open to Him. It's about God, Francine, it's not about the evil-doers. Focus on what God did, not what they did."

"It's hard," she said. "It's hard to separate them in my mind. When I first went there, I fully associated everything there with God."

"But now you know that isn't true?"

She nodded.

"Do you think everybody there was insincere?"

"Not everybody. There were people who came through who thirsted after God, but I wonder how many other people we corrupted? How many did Bishop Payne manipulate and seduce? How many hearts open to God were closed because of what they experienced there?" She squeezed her eyes shut. "There were so many souls, Stuart. I still see them in my heart. I see their need in a way that I didn't see it when I was there. They were so hungry for some direction in their lives, and that made them prime targets for manipulation. Do you know that there were some people there who sought the Bishop's advice on every—and I do mean *every*—decision they made?" Opening her eyes, she said, "I should have seen it, the evil, I should have seen it earlier."

"You had no clue?"

She looked deep inside her heart before answering him. "In hindsight, I saw some things that concerned me but I explained them all away. For example, I knew that we grossly mismanaged

the money—I have the past-due credit card bills as evidence—
but that was okay because we were supporting the ministry. Our
all-night Bible studies promoted irresponsibility at work, but
that was okay because we needed the Word more than we
needed our jobs. So what if the members seemed to rely on
Bishop Payne more than God? He was the shepherd God had
placed to guard their souls, so that was all right too. But the illicit sex, I couldn't explain away the sex. The predatory nature of
the sexual abuse could not be ignored." She cast a self-conscious
smile at Stuart. "Whew, I bet you didn't expect all of that, did
you? I'm sorry."

He shook his head. "Don't be sorry. I'm glad you felt comfortable enough with me to share what you did. You have a lot
going on inside."

"I guess I do," Francine said. "The most difficult for me is
thinking about the people, the souls, still there. That's hard."

"Have you been praying about it?"

"I'm ashamed to say that I haven't been, not really."

He took her hands in his. "Then why don't we start tonight."
He bowed his head. "Father God, I thank you for my sister
Francine. I thank you for the heart she has toward You. I thank
you for the heart she has for Your people. I pray You give her
clarity of thought and prayer about the lives she left behind in
Ohio. I pray that each soul in Temple Church that is truly seeking You will find You. I pray that the abuse and the abusers will
be exposed and demolished. Thank You for being able to make
a way out of no way, to find solutions when we can't even ver-
balize the problems very well. We thank You for being God. In
Jesus's Name. Amen."

"Amen," Francine said. "Thanks, again, Stuart. I seem to find
myself saying that a lot around you."

"That's good," he said with a smile. "I like hearing it."

She took her hand from his and wiped at her eyes.

"Have you heard of Sister Betty?" he said, leading her out of the meeting room.

"The Christian comedienne?" When he nodded, she said, "Yes, she's hilarious. I have all her books and a couple of her tapes."

"Well, she's going to be in town at the Comedy Club next week. Would you like to go? Genesis House is sponsoring the event. Sister Betty is a big supporter."

Francine hesitated, thinking about the wedding ring Stuart still wore, but she decided to go with her heart. "I'd love to."

CHAPTER 19

S tuart and Sly stayed in the meeting room after the other members of Faith Central's Leadership Team exited their regular monthly Saturday morning meeting. Rev. Thomas had asked for a few minutes with them before their prayer partners' meeting.

"I won't keep you long," Rev. Thomas said as he sat down. Instead of choosing his regular seat at the head table, he sat at the table with Stuart and Sly, facing them. "How are things going with Ted Campbell and BCN, Stuart? I deliberately didn't bring him up in the meeting this morning, but I do want an update."

"He took our comments into consideration," Stuart told the pastor. "But there's a clause in his proposal that still needs some work. I passed along to him a similar clause from the Genesis House contract as an example of something that Faith Central could support. It has provisions for profit sharing by individual contributors as well as guidelines for the selection of a Board of Directors."

"What's your read on this guy?" the pastor asked.

Stuart shrugged. "I don't want to make any hasty judgments."

"I'm not asking you to," Rev. Thomas said. "Give me your impressions."

"To be honest, he didn't seem too happy that I had changes for his revised proposal, but I get the feeling that he really wants Faith Central on board so he's willing to be accommodating."

"But you don't think he's coming from a good place in his heart?" Rev. Thomas said, getting to the core of Stuart's concerns.

"I didn't say that," Stuart said.

Rev. Thomas chuckled. "I heard what you said and I also heard what you didn't say." He glanced at Sly. "What did you hear, Sly?"

"The same as you, Pastor. Stuart has some reservations about the guy, but he's not ready to put them on the table yet."

"That right, Stuart?"

"Yes, sir. Let's wait and see what he does with the Genesis House clause. His actions there will tell where his heart is."

The pastor tipped his chin downward. "I agree with you. I think the Lord is doing something here with us and with Campbell. But it's not clear to me that He's leading us to be a part of BCN. I don't think that's the issue. We need to keep Campbell in our prayers so we don't miss what God's trying to do. Agreed?"

Both Sly and Stuart nodded.

Rev. Thomas directed his attention to Sylvester. "Sly, I'm going to do something I don't usually do. I'm going to talk to you about something that normally I would discuss in private."

Sly sat up straighter in his chair. "Sir?"

"Since you and Stuart are prayer partners, I'm going to say my piece to both of you."

"I can wait outside, Pastor," Stuart said.

Rev. Thomas waved off his offer. "No need. You two don't have many, if any, secrets from each other, do you?"

Sly and Stuart looked at each other and shook their heads.

"Okay, then," Rev. Thomas said, his gaze holding Sly's. "Sly, I much prefer it when people come to me with their problems, rather than me go to them. Even though you haven't come to me, your situation has been brought to my attention."

Sly shot a glance at Stuart.

"No, Stuart hasn't mentioned anything to me, if that's what you're thinking."

"That's not what I was thinking," Sly said.

"The run-in between you and Walter Andrews at Mother Harris's picnic a few weeks back was brought to my attention. A thing has gone too far when people outside of it start telling me about it."

Sly felt Stuart's eyes on him. He could feel his friend's surprise at the pastor's revelation. "I was going to tell you about that today, Stuart," he said.

Stuart nodded, but he was on alert.

"Why don't you tell me about it?" Rev. Thomas asked. "I know you and Dawn are having problems." At Sly's raised brow, he added, "Don't look so surprised. I'm the shepherd responsible for your soul, Sly. Not much gets by me. I've got connections in high places."

"So I see," Sly murmured.

"That doesn't mean I know all your business, but I do know something's not right with you and Dawn. The fight with Walter suggests to me that he's somehow involved in the trouble you're having. Is that right?"

Sly nodded. "But it's not what you think."

"Why don't you tell me what it is then."

"I'd rather not," Sly told the pastor. "Dawn asked that I not speak of it outside our home."

Rev. Thomas glanced at Stuart. "But you told Stuart?"

Sly nodded. "I needed some help and I knew he'd keep it quiet."

Pastor folded his arms across his chest. "So you think I'm going to blab your business all over town?"

"No, no," Sly rushed to say.

"Then what is it?"

Sly dropped his head. "I don't want to tell you because I'm ashamed. I don't want you to think less of me and I know you will when you hear the details."

Rev. Thomas sighed. "Sly, Sly, I thought you were smarter than this. What's done is done. Now, today, we're about you being able to accept and walk in the forgiveness that God gives. If you're on the verge of fighting at Sunday afternoon church functions, I don't think you're there yet."

Stuart rested a hand on Sly's shoulder. "Tell him, Sly. You've been holding this in too long."

The story tumbled out of Sly, punctuated by his tears. "Dawn's having a hard time forgiving me," he said as he finished the story. "The incident that Sunday was because I think Walter's coming on to her. They talk a lot and I'm afraid she's going to end up doing the same thing I did."

Pastor nodded. "She might if she's not careful."

"That's what I keep telling her, but she won't listen."

Pastor turned to Stuart. "What's your counsel in this situation, Stuart?"

"I think they need to talk to a third party."

Pastor glanced at Sly. "Why haven't you?"

"Dawn doesn't want to and I can't force her."

"What about you?" Reverend asked Sly.

"Me?"

"Yes, you," Pastor said. "It's better if both of you seek counseling, but you need to even if she doesn't."

"But—"

The pastor leaned forward, his arms folded on the table in front of him. "No buts, Sly. You came very close to engaging in fisticuffs at a church function. Things have gotten out of hand. Don't you see that?"

Sly wiped his hands down his face. "I guess I haven't wanted to think closely about it."

"I guess not," Rev. Thomas agreed. "Well, I'd like to counsel both you and Dawn. If she doesn't want to do this for herself or for the good of your marriage, you might suggest to her that she do it for the ministry. You both are part of the Leadership Team at Faith Central and you have to set the example. We all fall short of what God wants from us at one time or another, but that doesn't give us the freedom or the leisure to wallow in falling short. It may not be fair, but the standards are even higher for you and Dawn because you're leaders."

"I understand, Pastor," Sly said. "You're right, of course. I'll talk to Dawn."

Rev. Thomas nodded. "Good. I believe she'll do the right thing, but even if she doesn't, I want you to schedule to meet with me next week, all right?"

Sly nodded. "Yes, sir."

"Good, good," Rev. Thomas said. He glanced again at Stuart. "You have anything you want to add here?"

Stuart shook his head. "No, sir."

"Okay, then," Pastor Thomas said, "if all minds and hearts are clear, let's pray." He closed his eyes and bowed his head. "Father God, we thank You for loving us when we are most unlovable. We thank You for meeting us where we are. This morning I bring my brother Sly and my sister Dawn before You. Lord, You love them individually and You love them as the one they are in marriage. Restore their union, O Lord, to the fullness that only You can give. Use a situation—a sin— that could destroy their marriage to make their marriage stronger. Only You can do that, Father, and we humbly ask now that You do. Father, we also pray this morning for Rev. Campbell. We don't know yet why You brought him into our

THE AMEN SISTERS 239

lives, but we know You did it for a purpose. We pray so that You keep our eyes, ears, and hearts open to Your will that we may deal with him according to Your purpose. We pray all these things in Jesus's name. Amen."

After the prayer, Rev. Thomas left the two men to their prayer partner meeting.

"As usual," Sly said, "my issues have dominated our time together."

Stuart slapped him on his shoulder. "Don't think of it that way. We bear each other's burdens. You're there for me when I need you. You were there during Marie's sickness and when she died. I can never repay you for that."

"It isn't about payback," Sly said. "Now, what's up with you this week?"

"You sure you don't want to talk about what happened with Walter or what's going to happen when you talk to Dawn?"

Sly shook his head. "I'll talk to Dawn tonight. If I focus on it too much, it'll only add to my stress." He chuckled. "Believe me, after what just went on with Rev. Thomas, I welcome the opportunity to talk about you."

Stuart chuckled too. "Okay, I believe you."

"So what's up? I meant to thank you again for working with us on the proposal for the funeral home. Dawn and I started working on the business plan, and it's shaping up nicely. We should have a draft for you and Francine to review soon."

"Good," Stuart said. "Let me know if there's anything else I can help with."

Sly nodded. "So how did dinner go with you and Francine?"

Stuart twisted the wedding ring on his finger. "It went well. I enjoyed her company and I think she enjoyed mine. I invited her to come to my TFMA group and she did."

Sly leaned forward, quickly latching onto the positive topic. "I didn't know about that."

"It wasn't a big deal," Stuart said, even though he knew it was. "The boys liked her and she liked them."

"What about you?" Sly asked. "Do you like her?"

Stuart met his friend's gaze. "I asked her to go to see Sister Betty with me next weekend."

Sly slapped him on the back. "Well, that was quick work."

"Don't get too far ahead of me," Stuart warned. "We're friends and we're going out. That's all."

"As long as Francine knows that, it's okay with me. I don't want her to be hurt. She's been through so much already."

Stuart understood Sly's concern for his sister-in-law. "We've talked about Marie."

"Good," Sly said. "Francine needs friends and she couldn't do any better than you."

Stuart slapped him on the back. "Thanks for the character reference."

Sly laughed.

Seated at a back booth at Friendly's restaurant on Saturday evening, Francine rubbed her palms together when the waitress brought out a huge banana split made of five different flavors of ice cream. "I'm going to enjoy this," she said to Dolores.

"A Jim Dandy," Dolores said with a shrug. "I've never heard of it."

Dipping her spoon into the vanilla ice cream portion of the outrageous dessert, Francine said, "Are you sure you don't want one?"

Dolores scooped her spoon into Francine's dessert. "Sure, I want one," she said, "but mine would show up on my hips before I got out of the door."

Francine chuckled. "You're too funny."

"Please. I'm not even joking. I already have hips for days."

"There is nothing wrong with your hips," Francine told her big-boned and well-proportioned friend. "You don't have a weight problem."

Dolores started to dip her spoon into the ice cream again, but then placed her spoon down on the table next to her. "I would if I had Jim Dandys every day."

"So would I," Francine said, "which is why I only have them on special occasions."

"What special occasion is this?"

Francine tilted her head toward Dolores. "I feel like I've made a new friend."

Dolores smiled. "So do I. You know, I'm glad you suggested seeing a movie. I needed to get out."

"Workaholic, huh?"

Dolores's shoulders lifted slightly. "That's the way it is when you have your own business. There's always something else to do."

"Well, the invitation was the least I could do after you fitted me in for an appointment today. With the job at the bookstore, there was no way I could make that appointment with Dawn."

"No problem. As you can see, I didn't have anything else to do." Dolores sipped from her glass of diet Coke. "I have even more free time now that Monika's old enough to entertain herself."

"I can't even imagine rearing a child alone. You've done a wonderful job with Monika."

"These days I wonder about that," Dolores said.

"You're thinking about her father?"

Dolores cupped her hands around the sweating glass of soda. She hadn't thought about much else for the last few weeks. How could she? "I've been doing a lot of that lately. I used to wonder how people who once loved each other could come to hate each other. Now I know."

Francine reached a hand across the table and her friend grasped it. "You have every reason to hate him, Dolores."

Dolores lifted a brow. "That doesn't sound very Christian."

Francine removed her hand and sat back in her bench seat. "I know," she said. "But some things, some actions, are deserving of our hate. Sometimes it's hard to separate the person from the act."

"You're telling me. You know, I could slap him silly. I really could. I think if I were a violent person, I would kill him. Not for what happened between us—no, I assume responsibility for my role in that—but for what he's doing to Monika. His lack of concern for her and how it affects her, for that, I think I could kill him. I really do."

"But you won't," Francine said.

Dolores released a long, soulful sigh. "No, I won't."

"But you can make him accountable."

Dolores met Francine's gaze. "How?"

"By refusing to keep his secret." Francine leaned forward. "Don't you see, Dolores? You're letting him get away scot-free."

"But what can I do that won't hurt Monika? I have to think about her. I *am* thinking about her."

"I know you are. I know you have to. You wouldn't be the good mother you are if you didn't. But she's hurt anyway. You're hurt. And he goes on with his life. There's no way that's right."

"I know but—"

"No buts," Francine said. "He has to be stopped and you have the power to do it."

"I already talked to him. He told me what he'd do if I told Monika. I can't allow that to happen. I'm going to try talking to him again. Maybe he'll change his mind. He's not a totally bad person."

Francine let her skepticism show in her eyes.

"Well, he's not," Dolores insisted.

"That's not what you were saying a minute ago."

"Why are you pressing me about this? It's my decision."

"Because I don't want you to look back on this and wish you had done something. That's an awful feeling, Dolores. I know. I've been there. I *am* there."

"I'm sorry, Francine. I forgot about what you went through with your friend, but that was different. It really was."

Francine shook her head. "I don't think it was that different. Your story is a lot like Toni's. A pastor she loved took advantage of his relationship with her and she ended up pregnant."

"That's why she killed herself?"

Francine looked away, unable to meet Dolores's eyes. "No, she killed herself because she knew no one would believe her. She had no one to stand with her against him. He was the one with the good reputation, so who would believe her? I didn't and I'll always regret it." She met Dolores's gaze. "I don't want you to have that regret at some point down the road."

Dolores studied her glass of diet Coke. "So what happened when you exposed that pastor?"

"I didn't. He's still there, still bishop. The negative publicity surrounding Toni's death made them go underground for a while, but they'll resurface. No doubt they're saying they're suffering because of the gospel."

Dolores looked at her. "Why didn't you expose him?"

"I couldn't. Who would believe me? He'd already gotten the congregation to buy into his spin on the story before Toni's death. In some ways, I was like Toni. I stood alone against him."

"The same way I'd be alone."

Francine shook her head. "It's not the same at all. You'd have me, and Stuart, and Mother Harris with you, just to name a few. You wouldn't be alone at all."

"You make it sound so simple."

"I know it's not simple, Dolores. I know it's not easy. It's hard. Probably the hardest thing you'll ever do."

A part of Dolores wanted to expose Teddy, but she knew her motives related more to making him pay for not acknowledging his daughter than they did to doing the right thing. "I'll think about it," she said. "That's all I can promise."

Francine reached for her hand. "Why don't you pray about it too?"

"I can do that."

Francine sat back in her seat. "Good." She released Dolores's hand and dipped into her ice cream again. "Still glad you came out to the movies with me?"

Dolores smiled. "Yeah," she said. "It's been a long time since I've been out to the movies on Saturday night without a date."

Francine chuckled. "I know what you mean. I betcha some of the people in the theater thought I *was* your date."

Dolores laughed. "They probably did. There was a time when thoughts like that would have kept me home on a Saturday night rather than going out with a girlfriend. I thank God that a little bit of wisdom comes with getting older."

"Amen to that."

Dolores sipped from her drink. "So, are you seeing anybody?"

Francine thought about Stuart and shook her head. "You?"

"Nah, and it's been a while. I've almost given up on meeting Mr. Right or even Mr. Almost Right. Doesn't Sylvester know any worthwhile eligible men?"

Again, Francine thought about Stuart. "Now, you know I don't want my sister and brother-in-law playing matchmaker," she said. "I don't even want to go there."

Dolores laughed. "I know what you mean." She paused. "What about Stuart?"

"What about him?"

Dolores shrugged. "I wondered if maybe something was going on between you two. He's an available brother."

Francine smiled at her friend. "Are *you* interested in him? You've known him longer than I have."

"To be honest," Dolores said, "for a hot minute after his wife died, it crossed my mind. But Marie is still too close to my heart for me to even consider it. You never met Marie, so you don't have that hindrance."

Francine thought about the plans she and Stuart had to see Sister Betty. "Well, Stuart and I are just friends."

"That's the best place to start."

"Don't even try it," Francine said. "Stuart and I are friends. In case you haven't noticed, he's still wearing his wedding ring. He's obviously not ready for a relationship and I'm not sure I am either."

Dolores shrugged. "If you say so."

"I say so."

CHAPTER 20

Don't do this, her spirit warned, but Dawn ignored its counsel. "Nothing's going to happen," she said aloud as she drove her car into the parking lot of Friendly's, where she was to meet Walter. When she pulled into a parking space away from the door, she noticed that he pulled in next to her. He quickly got out of his car and opened her door.

"Hungry?" he asked.

She shook her head. "Not really."

"Then let's walk instead of going inside. There's a nice breeze."

She fell into step with him, again ignoring the warning bells issued by her conscience. The parking lot was over half empty, so they had plenty of room to roam.

"It's been a while," he said. "After that Sunday, I'm surprised you're still speaking to me."

She cut him a sideways glance. "Sly was wrong to raise his hand to you, but you did push him. I think you wanted him to hit you so you'd have an excuse to hit him back. You want to get physical with him again, don't you?"

Walter rolled his shoulders forward. "I wouldn't mind going a round or two with him. Do you blame me?"

"Not really," she said. "I've had thoughts of doing some serious hair-pulling myself."

Walter chuckled as they continued their walk. After a few minutes of silence, he said, "They were together that day."

"Exactly what do you mean by together?"

"No, they didn't sleep together, but they did talk after the funeral."

"How do you know?" Dawn asked. "You weren't there."

"I hear things," he said.

"Right."

"All right, Freddie told me."

Dawn stopped walking. "You've seen her?"

He turned to face her and gave a dry laugh. "All of her."

"What do you mean by that?"

"She was in my bed when I got to my buddy's crib on that Sunday night. She wants to get back together. She told me she spoke with Sylvester after the funeral. She got the impression he wants to get back with you as much as she wants to get back with me. Apparently, he didn't talk with her too long. You've got him on a short leash, don't you?"

Dawn was glad to learn that Sly had let Freddie know what his marriage meant to him. "I wouldn't say that," she said.

"Anyway, Freddie thought a roll in the sack would get us back on the right road."

"Did it?" Dawn asked, studying his face.

Walter put his hands in the pockets of his slacks and lifted his head to the slowly darkening sky, his eyes closed. "Not exactly."

"So you slept with her and then told her to get out?" Dawn thought that was cold, even if Freddie did deserve it.

"I wish." He opened his eyes. "Actually, I tried to sleep with her, but every time I touched her, I thought about Sly touching her. The images of them together are branded on my brain and I can't get rid of them. He's in my head and in our bed and I can't get him out." He looked down at her. "Have you and Sly . . ."

"That's not your business."

"I take that to mean you haven't. Why haven't you? You're still living in the house with him."

Dawn didn't answer.

"You haven't for the same reason I couldn't. You can't get the pictures of them out of your head either. There are three people in your head." He took her hand in his. "Maybe even four." He pressed her fingers to his lips. "You're there too," he said, "in my head. When I was holding Freddie, I thought about her and Sly and I also thought about you and me." He kissed her now fisted hand. "We'd be good together," he whispered. "I'd make it good for you."

Dawn knew it had been wrong to come here tonight. Why hadn't she listened to her conscience? She tried to pull her hand and her gaze away from Walter, but he held both tightly.

"Don't you miss it, Dawn? The closeness, the intimacy you and Sylvester shared. I thought Freddie and I had a pretty good sex life and I miss it. I know you have to miss it too." He pulled her fist open and kissed the palm of her hand. "I can feel the passion in you. Don't you want to be held, touched, loved?"

Dawn wanted those things. Oh, how she did! But did she want them from this man or from her husband? Would being with Walter help to erase the demon pictures of a naked Sly and a naked Freddie rolling around together in the bed of that hotel? Would it make her forget how much she hurt because of his betrayal? She raised her eyes to Walter and the darkening of his told her that he was going to kiss her. *Step away,* her spirit shouted. *Step away now.*

Ignoring the internal warnings, Dawn closed her eyes, giving silent consent for Walter's kiss. When his lips touched hers, her hands automatically went to rest on his waist. Walter was a bulkier man than Sly, and Dawn felt smaller in his arms than she did in Sly's. She was kissing a man other than Sylvester for the first time in almost five years. The kiss itself was pleasant, but any embers of passion were doused by her growing sense of guilt. Though her body would gladly follow Walter's lead to an anonymous bed somewhere, her heart wouldn't let her. When Walter lifted his head, she opened her eyes and saw in his the question of how far they would take this. She stepped away.

"You shouldn't have done that," she said.

"Me?" he challenged with a lifted brow. "I don't think I was the only one participating in that kiss."

"You weren't," she admitted. "*We* shouldn't have done that."

"I don't regret it," he said, smoothing a finger down her cheek. "You shouldn't regret it either. We're human. We have needs. I'll make it good for you, Dawn," he promised again.

Dawn stepped away from him, fighting the desire to step closer. "It's not going to happen, Walter. I'm not going to sleep with you."

"You want to. I know you want to. I can tell when a woman wants me."

"It doesn't matter what I want or what you feel. I'm not sleeping with you." Dawn's resolve strengthened with each denial. "It's not me you want anyway. It's Freddie. Why don't you go to her? It seems she still cares for you." Dawn couldn't believe she was making Freddie's case for her.

Walter shook his head. "I can't."

Dawn responded to the pain she heard in his voice. She pressed a soothing hand on his back. As she stood there, she felt a rumbling in his body and realized that he was crying.

"Why did she go to him, Dawn? I loved her so much and I thought she loved me. Why did she do it?"

Tears stung Dawn's eyes. "I don't know, Walter. Only Freddie can answer that. Why don't you ask her?"

Walter shook his head as the rumblings in his body subsided. "I can't."

"Why not?"

"I think you know the answer to that," he said. "Have you asked Sylvester?"

Dawn dropped her hand from him, breaking the contact.

"No, you haven't," he said when she didn't answer. "You haven't asked him because you don't want to know the answer." He gave another dry laugh. "I've never admitted it before, but I wonder if Sylvester is a better lover than I am. Is that why Freddie went to him?"

God help her, but Dawn had wondered the same thing. What if Sly enjoyed being with Freddie more than he enjoyed being with her? What if they couldn't recapture what they had, what she thought they had? She couldn't bear the rejection, not again. A new thought occurred to her. "Is that why you want to sleep with me, Walter? So you can find out how you compare to Sylvester?"

She felt him stiffen next to her but he didn't look down at her. He didn't answer.

"That's it," she said. "I know that's it."

He looked down at her then, the pain in his eyes making it almost unbearable for her to maintain eye contact. "I wouldn't use you that way, Dawn, not after the way we've both been hurt. I'd soothe you, the way you'd soothe me. We'd be good together."

"It wouldn't be any good, Walter. There'd definitely be four people in any bed you and I shared. You need to go home to your wife and figure out how to make your marriage work, and I need to do the same with Sly. Either that or we need to walk away. I don't know about you, but I can't go on living this way much longer."

Francine paced in front of the fireplace in the Amen-Ray living room, praying her eyes had deceived her but knowing all the while they hadn't. That had been Dawn she'd seen kissing some man in the Friendly's parking lot. Now Francine understood the source of the problems between Dawn and Sylvester—Dawn was having an affair! How could her sister be so reckless? And so careless? She was right out in public in the Friendly's parking lot where anybody could see her. Didn't she have any sense of shame?

Francine shook her head. Dawn was still the reckless sister she'd always been. Francine should have known she hadn't changed. When she saw the headlights of a car, she pulled back the curtains of the front window in the living room and peeked out, praying Dawn was arriving home before Sylvester. She needed to have a talk with Dawn without Sly present. Yes, she had a few words to say to her baby sister.

A few moments later, after parking her car in the garage, Dawn entered the house through the kitchen. "Francie," she called out in a bright voice.

"I'm in the living room," Francine said, preparing herself for the confrontation.

Dawn strolled into the room as if she hadn't a care in the world, as if she hadn't recently had her lips plastered across another man's face. "I saw your car outside. How was the movie?" Dawn slipped off her shoes, sat on the couch, and folded her legs under herself. She appeared to be settling in for an evening of chitchat.

"It was good. You and Sly should go see it," Francine said.

"Maybe we will," she said. "So, what else did you and Dolores do?"

Francine sat down next to her sister on the couch. "We went for a Jim Dandy at Friendly's."

Dawn's smile faded a bit. "You did?"

Francine nodded. "I only got back a short while ago."

"Oh."

Francine decided to give her sister a chance to come clean. "I thought I saw your car there."

Dawn lowered her feet to the floor. "I met a friend for a cup of coffee."

Francine captured her sister's gaze. "Did you drink it from his mouth?"

Dawn lowered her eyes, then snapped them back up. "What are you talking about?"

"You know what I'm talking about, Dawn. I saw you."

Dawn stood up. "I don't know what you're talking about. I'm going to bed."

Francine stood and took her sister's arm to stop her departure. "Oh, no, you're not going to run away from this. I saw you, Dawn. I saw you kissing that guy. Who was he? What are you doing cheating on Sylvester? How can you do something so cruel, so self-destructive?"

Dawn shook Francine's hand off her arm. "Don't butt into something that's not your business, Francie. Things are not always what they seem."

"What I know is what I saw. Are you saying you weren't kissing that man?"

Dawn sighed, folded her arms across her chest. "I'm saying it's not your business. I'm saying what's between me and Sly is between me and Sly. Now I'm going to bed." She turned her back to Francine and marched toward the stairs.

Dawn's callous attitude about something that Francine considered deadly serious caused her temper to snap. "How can you do this to Sly, Dawn? You're as selfish as you've always been. I don't know why I'm surprised. You've never been satisfied with what you had. You always wanted what somebody else had."

Dawn turned on her. "What does that mean?"

"It means you wanted Sly when I had him, and now that you have him, you want somebody else. Same old Dawn."

Dawn staggered under Francine's condemnation and sat back down on the couch. "You knew about my feelings for Sly?"

Francine rolled her eyes. "Please, Dawn. I've known you all your life. You only wanted Sylvester because I had him, the same way you only wanted whatever toy I had because I had it. If nothing else, you're consistent." She stared down at her sister, condemning her with her eyes. "I thought things were different with Sly. I thought you two had found something special. I thought you loved him. I know he loves you. How can you hurt him this way, Dawn?"

Dawn didn't answer. She just stared at Francine as if she could sear a hole through her with her stare. Francine felt uneasy under Dawn's hot perusal. "What?" she asked, when she couldn't take any more. "Don't you have anything to say?"

Dawn shook her head. "What can I say? You've got it all figured out. You've judged me and convicted me. I'm not the only one who hasn't changed, Francie. You're as judgmental now as you were before you left town. Was all that stuff you said in church that Sunday just words?"

"Oh no you don't," Francine said. "I'm not going to let you turn this on me. You're the one committing adultery."

Dawn threw her head back and laughed. When she stopped laughing, she said, "No, Francine, I'm not. Sly had the affair."

"I don't believe you."

"I can see that," Dawn said, her watchful eyes holding Francine in place. "But I wonder why you don't believe me. Is this the way you were with Toni? Were you so sure she was lying that you didn't even bother to listen to her?"

Dawn's words made Francine's knees grow weak and she had to hold on to the back of a nearby chair to keep from falling.

"The truth hurts, doesn't it?" Dawn taunted.

When Francine said nothing but continued to stare at Dawn with dead eyes, Dawn rushed to her side. "I'm sorry, Francie," she said, pulling her sister's tense body into her arms. "I shouldn't have said that. I was trying to hurt you."

When Dawn ended the embrace, Francine walked around and sat in the chair. "If you were trying to hurt me, you found the most effective way to do it."

"I'm sorry," Dawn said again. "But you really don't know how things are between me and Sylvester. I've asked you before to leave it alone and now I'm asking you again."

Dawn's harsh words still echoed in Francine's head. Why had she been so quick to believe the worst of Dawn? Was she being judgmental or was she merely reacting rationally to what she'd seen? "I love you, Dawn," she said. "I only want to help."

Dawn gave a wry smile. "I know you do, but you can't fix this for us. We have to fix it ourselves."

"Sly was wrong to sleep with another woman, very wrong, and I want to wring his neck for doing it, but I don't see how your kissing another man is going to fix the problem in your marriage."

"Neither do I," Dawn admitted. "I know what I did wasn't right, and it won't happen again. You have to believe that I haven't cheated on Sly."

"But he cheated on you?"

Dawn sighed. "You're not going to give up on this, are you?"

"I don't see how I can. You do love Sly, don't you?"

Dawn nodded.

"Then who is this other guy and why were you kissing him?"

Dawn expelled a long breath. "Since you're so determined to know the details, I'll tell you. The man you saw me kissing was Walter Andrews, Mother Harris's nephew, the husband of the woman Sly had the affair with. Walter and I are not having an affair."

"Then what are you doing?"

"Trying to make it through the pain together. He's the only one who understands how I feel, and I understand him."

"So you kissed each other so you'd feel better?"

Dawn cut a wary glance at her sister. "I can do without the sarcasm, Francine. I knew you wouldn't understand."

The accusation in Dawn's voice cut Francine deeply, but she refused to allow it to make her lose focus. "I bet Sly won't understand either."

"You're not going to tell him." It was a command, not a question.

Francine shook her head. "No, I'm not going to tell him, but someone else might. You were out in the open, Dawn. Anybody could have seen you. What will this do to Sly if he finds out? What will it do to your marriage?"

"Sly's not going to find out," Dawn insisted. "I know it was wrong and it won't happen again. Walter knows it too. Trust me. It won't happen again."

CHAPTER 21

S ly rubbed his hand down the back of his neck as he made his way down the upstairs hallway to the bedroom that was his alone. He glanced across the hallway at the closed door of Dawn's bedroom and felt a sense of relief that he wouldn't have to talk to her tonight. He suspected she would not be enthusiastic about a command counseling session with Rev. Thomas.

He stopped suddenly when he entered his bedroom, then blinked twice. No, he wasn't seeing things. Dawn lay asleep in the middle of his bed, her gown twisted about her thighs. He looked at her and wanted her, but he was afraid to hope that her presence in his bed meant she wanted him as well. He thought about leaving her there and sleeping across the hall, but before he could decide, her lashes fluttered open and she saw him.

"Sly. It's you." She quickly sat up, pulling her gown down in the process. No, she hadn't come because she wanted him.

"Who else would it be?" he asked, disappointment making his voice gruff. "It *is* my room."

"I know," she said. "I'm here because I wanted to talk to you."

He turned to the dresser and pulled off his watch and ring. "It couldn't wait until morning?"

"No," she said. "I don't think it could. I saw Walter tonight."

He turned to face her, trying to read in her expression whether he still had a marriage. Seeing nothing there, he offered, "You're seeing an awful lot of him, but I've told you that already."

"Yeah," she said, "you have."

"Yet you continue to see him. Why, Dawn? Are you trying to push me away?"

She shook her head. "No, I'm not." When he smirked, she said, "I'm really not. I won't be seeing him again."

He eyed her suspiciously. "What brought this on?"

"Does it matter? Isn't it enough to know that I won't be seeing him again?"

"No, it's not enough. Why aren't you going to see him again?"

She met his gaze, her eyes clear. "Because I want our marriage to work. Because I love you."

Sylvester wanted to believe her. "Did you sleep with him, Dawn?" he asked, voicing the question he wasn't sure he wanted answered.

"No, I didn't."

He studied her, needing to believe her but needing more to know that she was telling him the truth.

"I didn't sleep with him, Sly. Do you believe me?"

He nodded because he did. He hoped he wasn't being a fool to trust her.

"Well, that's something," she said. "How do we do it, Sly? How do we put it back together?"

He sat down on the bed next to her. Though he wanted to pull her into his arms, he held himself back. "I don't know," he said, "but I think both of us wanting to put it back together is a good start."

"Maybe we should do that counseling you mentioned," she

said. "It's still hard for me to deal with the feelings I have about what happened, and I seem to get angry every time we talk about it. That can't help."

Sly took a risk and covered her hand with his. "I spoke to Pastor today. He wants us to come for counseling with him."

Her eyes widened. "You told him about us?" There was no accusation in her voice, only surprise, and Sly took that as a good sign.

He shook his head. "Somebody told him what almost happened between me and Walter at Mother Harris's picnic, and he put two and two together. So, what do you say?"

Dawn bit down on her lower lip. "I hate that people will know. It makes me feel so humiliated."

Sylvester's heart wrenched in his chest, knowing he was the cause of her pain. "It's my humiliation, Dawn. I'm the one who sinned."

"But it's still humiliating for me." She lowered her eyes. "Why did you go to her, Sly? Was something missing in our relationship? I thought you were satisfied with all parts of our life together. What did you have with her that you didn't have with me?"

Sly felt as though sharp knives pierced his chest. "It wasn't about you, Dawn. I know that's hard for you to believe, but it really wasn't about you. It was all about me. I saw something that was available for the taking and I took it, disregarding the cost. It wasn't worth it. You have to believe that. Not one minute of it was worth it. If I could undo it, I would."

"Is that because you got caught? Would it still be going on if Walter and I hadn't found out?"

Sly squeezed her fingers. "I don't know, Dawn," he answered honestly. "I'd like to think I would have come to my senses, but I don't know. I really don't know."

She lifted her tear-filled eyes to his. "That hurts, you know. It hurts a lot."

He wiped her tears with his fingertips. "I know it does and I'm sorry, but I'm trying to be honest."

"If given the opportunity, would you do it again?"

Sly shook his head. "Never. I don't ever want to see these tears in your eyes again and know that I caused them."

"I want to believe you," she said. "I need to believe you."

"It's going to take some time and I'm willing to give you all the time you need. I just need to know that you're willing to work at forgiving me. Do you think you'll ever be able to forgive me?"

"I think so," she said, "but I don't know if I'll ever forget."

He accepted the truth of her words. "That's all right. Maybe neither one of us needs to forget."

"But it hurts so much to remember. I can't live with this kind of pain forever."

"Let's pray that what we remember will be how we made it through, how we had a chance to see how valuable, how precious, what we have together is."

"That God will work this awful situation for our good?" When he nodded, she said, "I'll try, Sly, and I'll meet with Rev. Thomas for counseling."

"Thank you," he said, "for giving me another chance. You won't regret it."

"I hope not. I can't go through this again."

"You won't have to," he promised. Holding her hand again, he said, "It's been a while since we've prayed together. How about we seal our new beginning with a prayer?" When she bowed her head, he did the same. "Father God," he said. "Thank You for giving me this wonderful woman to wife. Thank You for the light she's been in my life and in my heart. I thank You, Father, that You've opened her heart to me again after I hurt her so badly. I know the damage I've done to our relationship with each other and our relationship with You. I ask Your forgiveness and Your mercy. I pray especially for my dear sweet Dawn, that

You would heal the hurt I've caused in her heart, that You might allow love to grow afresh out of the deep wells of pain, that You might fill her heart and mind with hope for the future You have in place for us as a couple. Thank You for bringing us together and for keeping us together. In Jesus's name."

"Father," Dawn said softly, tears in her voice. "I know the right thing to do, but I don't know how to do it. Please show me and help me. Give me confidence in Sly again. Let me see him as the man of God You've called him to be, a man I can trust with my life and my future. Forgive me for my unwillingness to forgive before. Show me what true forgiveness is. Be true to Your word and work all this for our good. In Jesus's name."

Sly squeezed her fingers again as they said together, "Amen."

Still holding her hand, Sly said, "I want to hug you, but I don't want to make you uncomfortable. Is it okay?"

Dawn nodded and he pulled her into his arms and held her. Her hot tears burned his shoulder as he held her tightly against his chest. In his heart, he promised to never hurt her this way again. When she pulled away a few minutes later, he said, "I've been thinking." She looked up at him. "Why don't we take a trip, a short vacation, just the two of us?"

"I don't know, Sly. I'm not ready—"

He pressed a finger against her lips. "I'm not asking for more than you're ready to give. I just want some time alone with you. We're about finished with the proposal for the collective. A couple of weeks tops and we'll have a decent draft. Why don't we take a short trip to Florida? We can try out the proposal on Mr. E-Z at Vines Funeral Home, stop in to see my grandparents, and spend a day or two at the beach."

"No pressure?"

"None at all," Sly said. "I won't deny that I want to be with you again, but I can wait until you're ready to be with me."

She studied his face as if assuring herself that she could trust him. "Okay," she said. "I'll go."

❧

Sister Betty brought the house down with her Friday night performance at the Comedy Club. As she left the stage with her trademark Sister Betty Bounce done to "Reach Up," her theme song, the crowed roared with laughter. Clapping enthusiastically at Sister Betty's outlandish antics, Francine cast a happy smile at Stuart. "She's wonderful," she told him. "I'm so glad you invited me to come with you."

"I'm glad you came," he said as the applause died down. "It's a good thing we did the early show. I have a feeling the late show is going to be even more packed."

George Roberts got Francine's attention when he took to the stage after Sister Betty. Dressed in a black tuxedo that seemed to be especially made to fit his muscular body but that made him distinctly out of place in the middle of the more casually dressed audience, George removed the microphone from its stand. Just as he was about to speak, a male voice in the crowd yelled out, "What's up with the tux, man? You and LaDonna get married tonight?"

George gave a broad smile as the crowd broke up with laughter. "I wish," he said good-naturedly, with a wave of his hand to the heckler. "But since you brought it up, I am feeling a bit lonely up here." He extended his left hand to LaDonna, who was seated at a table to his far left. "Come on up here, baby."

As LaDonna made her way through the crowd to join him, George thanked everyone for attending the event and for supporting the ministry at Genesis House. When LaDonna reached his side, dressed in a floor-length, strapless black gown with a white pearl necklace and matching earrings, George pulled her close and said in a teasing voice, "Look, but don't touch."

The crowd, including Francine and Stuart, broke up with laughter. When the laughter died down, George said, "We're overdressed because we had a reception at the Governor's Mansion tonight. But governor or not, we couldn't miss this event, because we love and support the ministry of Sister Betty and because we love and support the ministry of Genesis House. It's a real blessing for the two ministries to come together tonight for one purpose: to lift the name of Jesus, not just in word, but in deed. Both Genesis House and Sister Betty have touched hearts and changed lives. It is our prayer that your hearts have been touched tonight. Because we know Sister Betty, we know they have been." With one arm still around LaDonna, he waved his other arm toward Sister Betty. "Come on up here, Sister Betty. You've ministered to us. Now it's our time to minister to you."

As Sister Betty came up from the right side of the room, a young man came up from the left and handed what looked to be a large gold key to LaDonna. When Sister Betty reached his side, George dropped his arm from LaDonna and pulled Sister Betty into an embrace. "We love you, Sister Betty, and we thank God for your ministry." He turned to LaDonna and she handed him the key. "On behalf of Genesis House and the city of Atlanta, I present you this key to the city. Since you already have the key to our hearts, this was the best we could do."

Francine watched with tears in her eyes. This warm, funny, loving man was the George Roberts she knew, the George Roberts she hadn't seen since Toni's death. It did her heart good to see him here tonight. She prayed she'd see him again.

"You all right?" Stuart whispered as George, LaDonna, and Sister Betty made their way back to their tables.

"I'm fine," Francine said. She looked around the already crowded dining room while giving her emotions some time to settle. "Sister Betty really brings a crowd, doesn't she? Though I like the dinner-theater atmosphere here, I have a feeling that her next visit is going to be someplace like the Fox Theatre."

"You're probably right, but I like this venue better too," he said. "Hungry?" At her nod, he said, "Good, our meal should be here pretty soon. They're really good here about timing meals to coincide with the end of the show. That's another thing I like about this place. A brother gets to laugh and then he gets to eat."

She chuckled. "So does a sister."

As if he'd heard their conversation, the waiter brought their dinner salads and a basket of rolls to the table. He was soon followed by another who topped off their drinks. Francine tasted her Caesar salad and was about to tell Stuart how good it was when a voice interrupted their meal. "I didn't know you were friends with Francine, Stuart," George Roberts said, staring down at her. Not the cheerful and loving George Roberts of a few minutes ago, but the hateful George Roberts who'd surfaced after Toni's death.

Stuart removed his napkin from his lap and placed it on the table next to his plate. "Good to see you, George." He glanced up at the man and then flashed Francine a broad smile. "Yes, Francine is a very good friend."

George huffed. "Then you might consider being more selective in your choice of friends."

"That's enough, George," Stuart said, standing. "Either you apologize right now or you leave. Better yet, why don't you apologize first and then leave."

George sneered at Francine. "I apologize for interrupting your meal, Stuart, but let me give you a word of advice. Once a murderer, always a murderer. I'd think somebody being considered for the Georgia Supreme Court would have better judgment."

"George—" Stuart warned.

"I'm leaving," he said. "Enjoy your meal. If you can."

Stuart watched him stalk off and then took his seat. "I'm sorry about that," he said. "George was way out of line. Does he get in your face this way often?"

"Don't apologize for him." Francine was more concerned

about George's unspoken threat. Something told her that he'd been intentional and purposeful in bringing up the Georgia Supreme Court. "I'm sorry he caused a scene," she said. "What was he talking about with the Georgia Supreme Court?"

Stuart placed his napkin back on his lap and picked up a roll. Breaking it in half, he said, "I've been approached about a possible seat on the court. Nothing's been announced yet, but presumably it will be soon."

"Congratulations, Stuart!" she said. "What an honor! I can't think of a more deserving person. I know you'll do well on the bench. We need people like you making those kinds of decisions and judgments."

"Thanks," Stuart said. "But it's not official yet. I'm not even supposed to be talking about it until it's announced. George was way out of line to bring it up the way he did."

"How did he know? Is he involved in the selection and nomination process?"

Stuart shook his head. "Not that I know of. But he's served in the Georgia legislature for a long while now, so he has quite a few connections. I'm not surprised he knows."

The waiter came, removed their salad plates, and replaced them with the main course. After he was gone, Francine asked, "Can George cause trouble for you?"

"Why would he?" Stuart asked. "But to answer your question, no. The Lord opened the door and only the Lord can close it."

Francine heard his words and knew he was right, but she still worried about George. Was she making too much out of what he'd said? Stuart turned her attention back to the present when he asked about her week at work, and they spent the rest of dinner swapping amusing stories about happenings on their respective jobs.

Later, as Stuart escorted her to her front door, he said, "You've been quiet. Is something wrong?"

She shook her head. She didn't want to tell him she couldn't get George's interruption out of her head. He'd only tell her not to worry about it. "Nothing's wrong," she said. "I had a good time tonight. Thanks again."

He grinned down at her. "Stop thanking me," he said. "It wasn't actually a hardship for me to take an attractive and intelligent woman to dinner. I should be thanking you. I had a very good time too."

"You sound surprised."

"Maybe I am," he said.

She chuckled. "Don't go overboard on the flattery, Stuart, I don't think my ego can take it."

He laughed with her. "That's not what I meant. I haven't done this since Marie died. I haven't wanted to do it."

"I understand," she said.

He shook his head. "I don't think you do, because I don't think I did until this moment."

He leaned toward her and Francine knew he meant to kiss her. She turned her head to the side so that his lips missed hers and pressed against her cheek.

He stepped back from her. "I'm sorry," he said. "I thought—"

"Don't apologize, Stuart," she said. "You didn't do anything wrong. It's just that I can't let myself get involved with you when you're not over your wife. I've had too many disappointments lately. I can't deliberately set myself up for another one."

"I wouldn't hurt you, Francine."

"I know you wouldn't intend to, but my heart could be broken all the same." She inclined her head down to his wedding ring. "Your heart's not free, Stuart. It still belongs to Marie. Let's work on friendship for now."

"For now," he repeated.

CHAPTER 22

On Sunday morning, Francine exited the ladies' room at Faith Central and was about to make her way back to the sanctuary when she bumped into George. "We've got to stop meeting like this," she said, without thinking. "Or you've got to stop hanging around outside bathroom doors. You're going to get a bad reputation if you don't watch it."

She moved to step around him, but he grabbed her arm. "You think you're so funny," he said. "You always did have a smart mouth. Always knew better than everybody else."

She tried to ease her arm away, but George held on. She was about to snatch her arm out of his grip when another woman headed for the bathroom. Not wanting to cause a scene, she smiled at the woman. "Let me go," she bit out after the woman entered the bathroom.

He leaned his mouth so close to her ear that she could feel his hot breath on her skin. "My sister is dead and you're living life like you'll live forever. You've gotten in good with Mother Harris, everybody here at the church, and now you've set your sights on Stuart Rogers. I bet you're thinking marriage and children, aren't you? Stuart's a good catch, I have to admit."

She struggled against him. "I don't want to hear this, George. Let me go."

"Don't get too pleased with yourself." He tightened his hold on her arm. "I can guarantee you this thing with Stuart isn't going to last."

"That's none of your business."

He gave a harsh laugh. "Oh, but it is. I think the selection committee for the next Georgia Supreme Court justice would be pretty interested to know that their top candidate is dating a cultist murderer. It should make for good headlines. For the opposition."

"You're not serious, are you? What's Stuart done to you?" she asked.

"This isn't about Stuart. It's about you trying to have the life my sister will never have. If you care about Stuart, and I'm not sure you do, you'll walk away from him so he can have his future. If you don't, I guarantee you his candidacy for the court will be quashed amid a flurry of rumor and conjecture."

"Do you hate me that much?"

George looked at her for a long minute. "I hate you more." He let go of her arm and strode back toward the sanctuary. Francine turned, almost bumping into the woman leaving the bathroom, and went inside. She stood by the sink and covered her face with her hands. Why, Lord? she asked. Why was the past reaching out to destroy her future? Why was it reaching out to destroy Stuart's future? What was she supposed to do?

"Francine," a soft voice called.

She looked up and saw LaDonna. "Hey, girl," she said, forcing a smile on her lips.

"Did George say something to you?" LaDonna asked.

Francine considered lying because it was easier, but she nodded her head in assent.

"What did he say? I knew something was up when he left the sanctuary right after you did."

"He really hates me, LaDonna," Francine said. "I knew it, but I think I never understood the depth of it until today. He hates me so much that he says he'll hurt other people to get back at me. Do you think he'd really do it—hurt somebody else to get revenge on me?"

LaDonna looked away. "At one time, I would have said no, but he's changed, Francine. I can't say what he would and wouldn't do."

"What do your instincts tell you?"

LaDonna sighed deeply. "I wouldn't put anything past him if it meant a way for him to hurt you. He wants you to pay for Toni's death. It's an obsession with him." She lifted her shoulders in a slight shrug. "He couldn't get that Bishop Payne or that church, so he's set his sights on you. He needs to make somebody pay and you're the closest target."

"You were right, LaDonna," Francine said. "I shouldn't have come back here. I've only caused trouble."

"I'm still willing to give you some money to help you get settled someplace else," LaDonna said. "I know it's not fair, not right, but I love George and I'm going to stand by him."

"Even if he ruins Stuart in the process of trying to get back at me?"

LaDonna nodded. "But I don't want that to happen. Do us all a favor and leave town. It'd be best for Sly and Dawn, too. We all know they're having problems, and your staying there can't be helping them. If you won't leave for George's sake, then do it for your sister." As strands of music from the choir filtered into the bathroom, LaDonna looked at her watch. "Think about what I've said," she said. "It's best for everybody concerned." She leaned over and gave Francine a quick hug. "I'm sorry it has to be this way." Then she turned and left the bathroom.

Francine stood there quietly for a few minutes and then decided she needed to get some fresh air. She took a slow turn around the church parking lot, her mind filled with questions: What was she going to do? Where was she going to go? How would she support herself? By the time she returned to the front of the sanctuary, people were coming out the doors. Stuart stopped her just as she was about to go inside and get her purse.

"Hi," she said.

"Hi yourself. It's good to see you."

She gave him the smile she thought he wanted. "You too."

"Hey, a couple of friends of mine, Nate and CeCe Richardson—I told you about them. They run Genesis House."

"I remember."

"They're throwing a big party for the teen fathers' and teen mothers' groups on Saturday. Since you got along so well with the boys, I thought you might like to attend. You'd also get to meet Nate and CeCe."

It sounded like a wonderful idea. Francine would love to meet the couple who ran such a unique ministry, but she wasn't sure she should go. Stuart's wedding ring was an obstacle to a romance between them, and now it seemed George's threat was an obstacle to their friendship. Who was she kidding? Any sort of relationship with Stuart was impossible, since she was leaving town. "I don't think so, Stuart."

"We'd go as friends, Francine," he said, correctly reading a portion of the cause for her reluctance. "I'm not asking for more."

"I know," she said, "but I still don't think it's a good idea for us to start going places together. People will get the wrong idea."

"Maybe you're right," he said. "But I still want you to come. If I give you directions, will you come on your own?"

She nodded because it was easier. "I'll think about it."

"If that's the best I can do, I'll take it. Wait here while I get some paper. I want to make sure you have all the information before you leave."

Sitting in his courthouse chambers on Friday morning, Stuart twisted the wedding ring on his left hand, his thoughts on Francine. He'd been thinking a lot about her and the wedding ring since their date—yes, he now knew it was a date—to see Sister Betty a week ago. What did he want from her—friendship or something more?

His office door opened. "The judge is here," his clerk said.

"Thanks, Matt." Stuart stood to meet Judge Mac. He greeted him at the door and led him to the corner chairs where they'd sat the first time the older man had come to visit. "Judge," Stuart said, extending a hand to the older man. "I was surprised to get your call this morning."

After shaking Stuart's hand, Judge Mac sat down. "I'm not going to mince words with you, Stuart," he said. "I assume you know George Roberts."

Stuart nodded. "Very well."

"Is there anything you need to tell me about that relationship?"

Stuart frowned. "What do you mean?"

"George has been making calls this week and one of them weaved its way back to me, which was probably his goal."

"I'm not following you, Judge."

Judge Mac met his gaze. "George Roberts is trying to derail your nomination."

Stuart sat back in his chair. "You must be mistaken. Why would George do something like that?"

"That's what I wanted to ask you."

Stuart shook his head. "I can't believe it. Is there any possibility you're mistaken?"

It was Judge Mac's turn to shake his head. "None." He paused. "Stuart, when you enter politics at the level you're entering it, the stakes are high and nothing's off limits. Your personal life is not something you can keep personal. Your entire life is an open book. If our opponents can find anything in your past, your present, or your future that can embarrass you or the governor, they'll use it."

"And you think they've found something? George has given them something?"

"It hasn't gone that far yet. On the surface, George's statements could be viewed as a warning from a political ally of possible trouble ahead, but my gut tells me it's more than that." He eyed Stuart. "Have you recently gotten involved with a woman?"

Stuart was about to say no and then he thought of Francine. How would he describe their relationship? "What have you heard?" he asked, instead of answering the question.

"That you're involved with some woman who was involved in a Jim Jones–type cult that led to a young woman's death."

"Francine," Stuart murmured, more to himself than to Judge Mac.

Judge Mac sighed. "So you do know this woman?"

He nodded. "We're friends. We go to the same church."

"Is what George said about her true?"

"It's probably a good spin on the truth. The perfect sound bite. Unfortunately, the truth requires an explanation that can't be boiled down to a single sound bite."

"Why don't you try explaining it to me? I've been at this a lot longer than you have. There could be a sound bite in it after all."

Stuart gave Judge Mac a truncated version of Francine's decision to leave town five years ago and the events that led to her return home. When he was finished, Judge Mac sighed. "Poor girl."

Stuart was heartened by his reaction.

"But you're right," Judge Mac continued, "the explanation is too complex. Takes too many words. People don't want to hear it." He met Stuart's gaze. "How serious is this relationship?"

"We're friends."

The corner of the older man's mouth turned up in a smile. "Are you sure it isn't more than that? I can tell you care about the woman from the way you talked about her."

Stuart remembered the aborted kiss. "It could grow into something more," he admitted, "but right now, we're friends."

Judge Mac sat back in his chair. "Then we have a problem, Stuart." Stuart opened his mouth to respond, but Judge Mac held up a hand to stop him. "Hear me out," he said. "I didn't say it was a problem we couldn't handle."

The notion of his friendship with Francine being a problem didn't sit well on Stuart's shoulders, but he kept his thoughts to himself.

"There are a couple of ways we could handle this," Judge Mac explained. "The best would be for you to put this relationship on hold until after the election." He peered over his glasses at Stuart. "The worst would be for us to tough it out, since that would mean your friend's life would become fodder for our opponents and ultimately the press."

Stuart pressed his fingers against his nose. "So my options are to give up my friendship with Francine or have her name scandalously dragged through the papers? I have to tell you, Judge, neither option appeals to me."

"I didn't think they would," Judge Mac admitted, "but you needed to know. We have our people looking into the situation and what happened. Maybe there's another spin we can put on it."

"I hear a *but* in there somewhere."

Judge Mac sighed. "Unfortunately, there is. You were so attractive to us, Stuart, because we didn't think we'd have to worry about these kinds of issues with you. Your record speaks for itself, but today people not only care about what goes on in the office, they also want to know what goes on at home. That makes your friend an issue."

"Are you telling me that I could lose the appointment because of this?" Stuart asked. In asking, he realized how much the judgeship had come to mean to him.

"I know it doesn't sound fair, but it's a possibility. This is a religiously conservative state. Unfortunately, our opponents could spin your friend's background in worse ways than George did. Right now, you're still our man, but I'd be lying if I said we didn't have some concerns."

"I see."

"I hope so." Judge Mac studied Stuart for a long moment. "Is this relationship that important to you? If you had to choose between your friend and a seat on the bench—"

"Don't even ask, Judge," Stuart said. "I couldn't do that to a friend, not after what she's been through. When you first came to me with the possibility of a seat on the bench, you said you wanted me for the man I was. Well, I wouldn't be that man if I walked away from a friendship. I don't think I'd like myself very much if I did that."

Judge Mac was unfazed. "How much will you like yourself if you lose a seat on the highest court in the state of Georgia because of a friendship? Is one person really more important than the thousands of people, millions of people, that you could impact on the bench? Why don't you think about that? Talk it over with your friend. Maybe she'll decide you two can put your relationship on hold until you get the seat."

Stuart had no doubt that Francine's solution would be to end the relationship. "I won't tell her because it's not her decision to make, and anyway, if she knew, she'd be hurt."

"You're not listening to me, Stuart. With politics at this level, all decisions are interrelated. If this young lady is going to be in your life and you maintain an interest in the seat, then she has to know what she's letting herself in for. You don't have a choice in letting her know what to expect." On those words, Judge Mac stood. "Thanks for meeting with me on such short notice." He extended his hand. "I'm sorry the news wasn't more positive.

Why don't you try talking to George? This thing might die down if he doesn't fan the flames."

Stuart shook the older man's hand. "I'd already planned to talk to George," he said. He opened the office door for Judge Mac.

"Good," the older man said. "You let me know what happens with him." He eyed Stuart. "And with your lady friend."

Stuart nodded. When he closed the door, he knew he had some praying to do. Then he'd call George.

CHAPTER 23

W e did it," Dawn said, lifting her naked arms in the cool Fort Lauderdale night air. She was glad she and Sylvester had decided to spend the night at a hotel on the beach after their Friday afternoon meeting with Mr. Ezekiel "E-Z" Vines at Vines Funeral Home. Tomorrow or the day after, they'd drive to Tampa to visit his grandparents. Being out here tonight, with the ocean and the sky spread before her and colliding with each other, she felt free, powerful. This was the best high she'd had in a long, long time. "We really did it. We sold Mr. E-Z on the collective."

Responding to his wife's playful mood, Sylvester snaked his arm around her waist and pulled her to him. "We make a good team, Mrs. Amen-Ray."

Dawn looked at him, their closeness, the brightness of his eyes. She knew he wanted to kiss her and she wanted his kiss. "I have to agree with you, Mr. Ray." Because she wanted to, she leaned up on her toes and pressed a soft kiss against his lips, the first such kiss she'd initiated since she found out about his affair.

His arms tightened around her. "Dawn, my sweet, sweet

Dawn," he murmured against her lips, before deepening the kiss.

She gave herself over to her husband and his kiss, and in so doing she felt hope, real hope, for their future together. When he lifted his head, she remained in his arms. "I love you," he said.

She ran her fingers across his lips. "I know."

He lowered his head again and kissed her deeply. She read the question in his touch and she saw it in his eyes when he lifted his head. She cupped his jaw in her palm. "I love you too, Sly," she said, "but I'm not ready to make love with you. Not yet."

His arms tightened around her again. "Why not?" he asked. "You can't deny that you want to be with me. I can feel it in your kiss." He brushed her hair back from her forehead. "I know your body as well as I know my own, and I know you want me. Don't hold back, sweetheart. Take a leap of faith."

Lowering her eyes, she stepped out of his embrace and turned to face the ocean. "No pressure, you said," she reminded him.

He rested his hands on her shoulders. "I meant it."

"I'm not playing games with you, Sly."

"I know you aren't."

Dawn thought about Pastor Thomas's advice that she share her feelings with Sly so he'd not have to guess. Though she had dreaded counseling, she had to admit that their first session had been helpful. If nothing else, it helped her to get rid of some of the shame she felt at what had happened between Sly and Freddie. "I'm afraid to make love with you again," she whispered.

He turned her to face him. "Why are you afraid? I'm not going to hurt you."

"Not physically." She didn't doubt physical pain would be easier to endure.

"Not in any way." When she didn't respond, he said, "You're thinking about Freddie."

Her last conversation with Walter filled her mind. Four in a bed. Knowing that she had to be honest with Sly if their mar-

riage were to ever be restored, Dawn pushed past her need to
protect herself and let him see her vulnerability. "How can I not?
She was the last woman you were with. I can't help but wonder
if you're going to compare us and where I'll come out in the
comparison. What if you find that you enjoy being with her
more than you enjoy being with me?"

He sighed deeply. "That won't happen."

"How can you be so sure?"

"Because what I want from you is more than a sharing of bodies." He pressed his palm against her cheek. "I want a mingling
of spirits, a sharing of hope, love, and respect. I can only get that
from you. You're my wife, the good thing in my life that's talked
about in Proverbs."

Dawn knew the next logical comment was that he had gotten
something out of his relationship with Freddie or he wouldn't
have kept it going, but what good would it do? What could he
say that could make her understand and believe him? Nothing.
Sly was right. Her decision to make love with him again would
have to be an act of pure faith. Was she ready to make it? "I want
those things too, Sly, but not tonight."

He pressed a kiss against her forehead. "I can wait." He took
her hand and led her to a log near the edge of the water. "There's
something I wanted to talk to you about."

"This sounds serious," she said, a bit anxiously.

He squeezed her hand. "It is. I've decided to step down from
my position as church trustee."

"Why?"

He lifted a brow. "Because of the affair. It's the right thing to
do. I realize that what I did wasn't just a slipup or a mistake. It
was a sin against you, the church, God, even against Freddie and
Walter. I need to do something to show that I understand the
gravity of what I did."

"Did Pastor tell you he wanted you to resign?"

He shook his head. "I haven't discussed this with him. This is about me and you."

"Me?"

He smiled. "If there's one thing I've learned, it's that every decision I make is about you and me. That's what marriage is about."

She liked hearing him speak of their marriage in such terms. "So what will you tell people?" She had visions of him making a statement in church the way Francine had. She wasn't sure she was ready for that.

"I won't tell them anything," he assured her. "I'm not doing this to embarrass you, Dawn. You're the innocent in all of this."

"Not so innocent," she murmured.

"What did you say?"

She debated telling him about kissing Walter. "I've taunted you a lot with other men, Sly," she said. "But I never really wanted anyone else. I only wanted to hurt you the way you'd hurt me."

"I understand," he said. "And it worked. You did hurt me."

"I'm sorry."

He pressed another kiss against her forehead. "I forgive you. That's the past. Let's look to the future."

"Walter kissed me," she said after a few moments of silence. "And I kissed him back."

He pulled away to look down at her. She saw the hurt on his face, saw him wipe it away quickly. "It doesn't matter."

"It does," she said. "It matters because that kiss made me realize what I was doing, what Walter and I were doing. Walter never wanted me, Sly, and I never wanted him. We both wanted to hurt you and Freddie. Everything between us was about you and Freddie. We were two hurt people trying unsuccessfully to ease our pain."

He pulled her to him. "I'm so glad I didn't lose you. I don't know what I'd do without you. I was so scared."

"I was scared too."

He tightened his hold on her. "I know you probably don't want to hear this, but I feel badly for Freddie and Walter. I know I betrayed Walter, but I feel I betrayed Freddie too."

Freddie's name on Sly's lips combined with the concern for her in his voice grated on Dawn. "I'm not ready to hear you talk about Freddie, Sly. Maybe one day, but not now."

"All right," he said, easily dropping the subject. "I've been thinking that since I'm not going to be on the trustee board, we could start participating in the couples' ministry again. We used to do that when we first got married, and then we stopped. I'd like for us to start doing more church things like that together. What do you think?"

"I think it's a good idea," she said. "We had some good times there." She smiled up at him. "You could always join the gospel choir."

Sly nipped her bare shoulder with his teeth. "You know I can't see a tune, much less hold one."

She grinned and snuggled deeper in his embrace.

"Cold?" he asked. "You want to go inside?"

"No," she said. "Let's just sit here and be thankful for the second chance we've been given."

He pressed a soft kiss against her lips. "Sounds like a plan to me."

Having decided against Stuart's suggestion that she attend Nate and CeCe's party alone, Francine spent a quiet Saturday night at home. Dawn and Sly were still away on their working vacation in Florida, which she hoped boded good things for their marriage. She surfed the Internet for a couple of hours, looking for jobs in Alabama, Florida, and North and South Carolina—she didn't want to stray too far from home. Weary

with that task, she went in search of Aisha Ford's book, *Flippin'
the Script*. A good story would take her away from her own
problems, if only for a short while. The phone rang as she
headed out of the family room to get the book from her bedroom. "Hello," she said.

"Francine, it's me, Stuart."

She leaned against the wall, her mind scrambling for a reason
he would accept for her not attending the party. "Hi, Stuart."

"Look," he said. "I'm on my way out the door. Dolores just
called. Monika has sneaked off to Savannah with some older
guy that Dolores doesn't know."

Francine slid down into the chair next to the phone table.
"What?"

"I know how you're feeling. It surprised me too. The good
news is that I was able to make a few phone calls and the state
patrol spotted the guy's car. They're bringing her back home
now. She should be here in about three hours."

"Thank God for that."

"I have," he said. "Anyway, I'm calling because I think Dolores
could use a friend right now. I'm on my way over there, but I
know she'd appreciate your presence as well. I called Mother
Harris but she's not home."

"I'm on my way over now, Stuart," she said. "Thanks for calling me."

"No problem. Dolores needs her friends around her. She's
pretty broken up over this, blaming herself."

"I can imagine," Francine said. "Let me hang up so I can get
over there."

"Right," he said. "I'll see you there."

Twenty minutes later Francine was knocking on Dolores's
door. "Stuart called me," she said when Dolores opened the
door.

Dolores pulled her through the marble foyer. "I'm glad he
did," she said. "I can't believe Monika did this. It's not like her."

"What exactly happened?"

Dolores dropped down onto the sofa in the living room. "She told me she was spending the weekend with a girlfriend. Of course, I talked to the girl's mother to confirm everything was okay. But then, apparently, Monika called the mother at the last minute and said she couldn't come after all. I ran into the mother at the market after work and found out about the last-minute cancellation. She talked to her daughter and we finally got the truth out of the girl. Monika planned to spend the weekend in Savannah with some boy. Apparently, they were going to some weekend music festival. She's never lied to me before, Francine. Not like this."

Francine rubbed her friend's shoulders. "Stuart told me the authorities tracked her down."

"Thank God for Stuart," Dolores said. "He called one of his police friends and they set everything in motion. They found them in about thirty minutes. I'm going to kill that girl when she gets home."

The doorbell rang. "I'll get that," Francine said. "It's probably Stuart." She opened the door to him.

"How is she?" he asked.

"She's holding up pretty well." Noticing the tiredness in his eyes, she asked, "How are you?"

"Shaky, but good. When I think about the danger Monika put herself in, it scares me. I could kill her."

Francine chuckled. "Dolores just said the same thing. Come on in. She'll be glad to see you."

Stuart followed her into the living room. "Who's going to kill her first, Dolores, you or me?"

Dolores smiled. "Kids," she said with a shake of her head. "I think I get first turn at her, since I gave birth to her."

"Just be sure to leave some for me."

"I will," Dolores said. Then she dropped her head and began to cry. Francine glanced at Stuart. "This is all my fault," Dolores said. "She's been defiant over this thing about her father. I know she's acting out because of it."

Francine rubbed the distraught woman's shoulders.

"You can't beat yourself up about this, Dolores," Stuart told her. "Monika's safe and she'll be home in a few hours."

"That's not going to solve the problem. I've got to talk to her father again, make him see how much she needs to know about him."

Francine glanced again at Stuart.

"You don't have to do this alone, Dolores," he told her. "We can go with you the next time you talk to him."

Dolores looked between the two of them. "I don't know—"

"That's the biblical way to do it," he explained. "You've already tried to get him to do the right thing. Now it's time to bring in witnesses."

"He won't like it."

"That's the whole idea," he explained. "Maybe we can make him see the error of his ways. This is about him as much as it's about Monika. You told us he was a pastor. Well, he needs to come clean before you and Monika, but most importantly, before God. Maybe we can get him to see that."

Francine saw the skepticism on Dolores's face and feared the woman wouldn't have the courage to do what she knew was right. "Stuart's right, Dolores. You're not in this by yourself. You have all the support and love you need."

Dolores pulled a Kleenex from the box on the end table next to the sofa and blotted at her tears. "His name is Teddy Campbell. He's the pastor of Pilgrim Community."

"Theodore Campbell?" Stuart asked.

"That's him," Dolores said. "Do you know him?"

Stuart nodded. "Though not that well."

"You believe me that he's Monika's father, don't you, Stuart? You don't think I'm lying, do you?"

Stuart pressed his hand against Dolores's shoulder. "Of course

I believe you. I haven't changed my position. We need to talk to him. I'll talk to Pastor and he and I will go with you to talk to him."

"You will?" Dolores asked.

"Of course we will." He looked at Francine. "I'm going to give Pastor a call right now and let him know about this." He looked back at Dolores before Francine could tell him that she wanted to be in on the confrontation with the so-called pastor too. "Is it okay if I use your phone?" he asked Dolores.

"Of course," she said, a bit dazed. Francine knew she had to be thinking about how fast things were moving.

"It's going to be all right, Dolores," Francine said.

"I certainly hope so," she said. "I can't help but wonder what good it does Monika if he only wants to meet her because we force him into it."

Dolores had a point but there were other perspectives to consider. "Just think about the number of times you've had to be forced to do the right thing. It's still the right thing regardless of why you do it."

"I hope you're right, Francine," Dolores said. "My daughter's life depends on it."

Stuart came back into the room. "I spoke to Pastor. He suggested that the three of us try to talk to Rev. Campbell tonight. If he doesn't come around, then Pastor will take it to the next level."

"Tonight?" Dolores said in a high voice. Francine knew things were moving much too fast for the woman.

"Do you think you can get him to come over here?" Stuart asked.

Dolores twisted the Kleenex between her fingers. "I don't know."

"Can you give him a call and see?" Stuart asked again. "I'd suggest another place but we need to be here when Monika gets home."

"He's not going to come," Dolores said.

"Try calling him," Stuart urged.

"What should I say?" Dolores asked.

"Tell him you need to talk to him about Monika and it can't wait."

Dolores eased up from the sofa. "I'll try, but I don't think he's going to come."

After Dolores left he room, Francine asked Stuart, "Do you think he'll come?"

"He'll come."

Wondering at his confidence, Francine asked, "How can you be so sure?"

"This is a God thing now. He has no choice."

Dolores returned to the room. "He'll be here in twenty minutes."

Stuart looked at the two women. "Let's pray."

CHAPTER 24

This is difficult for her," Francine said to Stuart. They stood in Dolores's kitchen, with its pristine white cabinets, black countertops, and black-and-white-checkered ceramic tile flooring, both holding cups of recently brewed coffee. Dolores had asked for a few minutes to herself while they waited for Rev. Campbell.

"She's strong," he said. "She's going to have to be."

Francine nodded. "What do you think is going to happen?"

Stuart rolled his shoulders in a tense shrug. "He's either going to admit he's Monika's father or he's going to deny it."

"He'll deny it," Francine said, Toni's tale of Bishop Payne's denial ringing in her ears. "I know he will."

"You can't be sure."

She thought about her last visit to Temple Church, when she'd spoken with Cassandra. The woman had been too bold in her attitude and lies. "You forget, I've been through this before. He's going to deny it until it's impossible to do so, and then he'll put his own spin on it and beg his congregation for forgiveness. His life will go on without a hitch."

"This is not the same situation. These are not the same people."

Francine wasn't so sure. "If it looks like a dog—"

The doorbell rang before Stuart could respond. He and Francine joined Dolores in the living room, and Stuart encouraged Dolores to go to the foyer and answer the door. He and Francine remained in the living room.

"You know better than to call me at home," they heard a masculine voice say after Dolores opened the door. "You'd better get that daughter of yours in check. Between the two of you, you're going to ruin everything."

The voice grew louder as Rev. Campbell and Dolores came closer to the living room. Rev. Campbell stopped on the threshold of the room, his eyes taking in Stuart and Francine. "Judge Rogers," he said, trying unsuccessfully to hide his annoyance.

Stuart stood and extended a hand to him. "Rev. Campbell." He glanced at Dolores. "Why don't we all have a seat?"

Dolores sat on the couch next to Francine. Stuart sat next to her, leaving Rev. Campbell to take the high-backed chair.

"What's this all about?" Rev. Campbell asked Stuart. "I can't believe you want to talk to me about BCN."

"BCN?" Dolores asked.

Stuart turned to the women. "Rev. Campbell approached Faith Central a while ago about participating in a project he's started to develop, a black Christian television network, BCN." Looking at Rev. Campbell, he said, "May I introduce Francine Amen of Amen-Ray Funeral Home. She's also a member of Faith Central."

"Nice to meet you," Rev. Campbell said automatically and with no emotion.

"I didn't know you were interested in television," Dolores said, turning everyone's focus back to her.

"Well," Rev. Campbell said, "there's probably a lot about me you don't know. We don't know each other that well."

Francine shot Stuart an "I told you so" glance while Dolores sucked in a surprised gasp.

"Let's get to the point, Rev. Campbell," Stuart said. "We asked you here tonight because Dolores's daughter, your daughter, Monika, has run off to Savannah with some guy. We believe she's acting out because Dolores won't tell her who her father is. Dolores isn't telling her because she has some crazy idea you'd deny parentage."

Rev. Campbell sat straighter in his chair. "She's right. I'm not the child's father, that's the truth. I don't know why Ms. King persists in making that claim."

Stuart eyed the man, daring him to repeat the lie. "Are you saying there's no way you could be Monika's father?"

Rev. Campbell was good. He didn't even blink. "That's exactly what I'm saying. I did know Ms. King some years back, but we never had a physical relationship."

"Oh, Teddy," Dolores cried, "how can you lie like this?"

Rev. Campbell ignored her. "This type of thing happens a lot, I'm sad to say." He directed his comments to Stuart. "Women get a fixation on a pastor. I try to counsel them, which is why I came over here tonight, but as you can see, some cases are too far gone."

Stuart fisted his hands at his sides, determined not to let Campbell see his rage. "We could easily resolve this matter if you would take a paternity test."

"No," Rev. Campbell said. He straightened the crease in the leg of his dark brown slacks. "That's a road I refuse to travel. Once it starts, I'll be doing it every time some sick woman makes an accusation."

"Wouldn't a paternity test be the easiest way to stop the accusations?" Stuart reasoned. "Why would women continue to make false charges against a man with a record for successfully proving them to be liars?"

Rev. Campbell pursed his lips in annoyance. "It's obvious

you're not married, Judge Rogers. Regardless of what the tests show, the allegations would reach my wife and they would hurt her. I can't allow that to happen. We have to stop this lie right here, right now. I'm glad you're both here. Now I have witnesses."

"He's lying," Dolores appealed to Stuart and Francine. "You have to believe me."

Francine patted her hand. "We believe you." She shot an accusing glare at Rev. Campbell. "He's the liar."

Stuart ignored the women, keeping his focus on Rev. Campbell. "The paternity test doesn't have to get back to your wife, and neither does the allegation—if the test proves false. We can keep this between us. You have my word as a judge and a brother on that. If the tests show Dolores is lying, we can get her the help she needs. If they show you're lying, you can repent."

"I take exception to your tone, Judge Rogers," Rev. Campbell said in indignation. "You sound as though I'm already guilty."

"Forgive me," Stuart said quickly. "That's not the impression I want to give at all. Now, what do you say about the paternity test?"

Rev. Campbell looked between the three people. "I'll think about it," he said.

Stuart stood. "You do that. Rev. Thomas will be following up on your answer in the next few days."

"Rev. Thomas?" Rev. Campbell stood, uneasy now. "Why do we have to bring him into this?"

"He's already in it," Stuart explained. "As soon as this matter involved a member of Faith Central, he became involved."

"Dolores—uh, Ms. King—is a member of Faith Central?"

Stuart shook his head. "Monika is."

Having no response to that, Rev. Campbell took his leave.

After he left, Dolores said, "He lied like a dog. He sat there and lied like a dog."

"I know he was lying," Stuart said, "and he knows he was

lying. Now he's trying to figure out how he can get out of this with the least negative impact to him and BCN. He's going to do something. I'm just not sure what it'll be."

"What options does he have?" Francine asked. "He has to admit it. He can't bluff a paternity test, can he?"

Stuart shook his head. "Not hardly. If he's smart, he'll come clean with his wife before Rev. Thomas gets to him."

"Is that why you didn't press him tonight?" Francine asked. "You wanted to give him a chance to make it right with his wife?"

He dipped his chin. "She deserves that much."

"She does." Dolores sat back down. "I've only thought about how this is going to affect Monika. I haven't really thought about his wife. I guess I never thought about her, especially not when I was having a relationship with Teddy." She looked down at her hands. "How in the world do I explain all this to Monika?"

"Prayerfully and honestly," Stuart suggested. He sat next to her on the sofa. "The half-truths aren't working, Dolores. You need to tell Monika the truth and trust God to protect her heart when you do. You need to trust God in this. You can't fix it yourself."

Francine noticed the set of headlights in the driveway at the same time that Stuart and Dolores did, but Dolores beat the two of them to the door. She pulled it open and ran out to meet her daughter. Francine and Stuart followed behind her, with Francine smiling as Dolores pulled Monika into her arms. She stood back while mother and daughter reunited and Stuart thanked the officer.

Dolores pulled Monika to her in a tight hug. "Don't you ever scare me like that again, young lady." She pulled back and studied her daughter's face. "You took a good ten years off my life."

"I'm sorry, Momma," Monika said when Dolores enfolded her in another embrace. "I didn't want you to worry."

Dolores pulled back from her daughter again. "You lie to me, you go traipsing off to south Georgia, and you don't want me to worry? Well, you have a funny way of showing it."

Monika lowered her head. "I only wanted to go to the music festival."

"That's no excuse. You should have asked. Why did you have to lie and sneak away?"

Monika didn't answer immediately.

Stuart asked the officer, "What about the boy?"

"Man," the officer corrected. "We couldn't hold him on anything, so we let him go. We have all of his information in case we need to get in touch with him. We also gave him a long talk about underage girls." The officer tipped his hat to Francine and Dolores. "Y'all have a good night." To Monika, he said, "Listen to your mother, young lady. She's been where you're trying so hard to get."

"Yes, sir," Monika said.

The officer pulled off, leaving Monika and the three adults standing in the driveway. "I'm going to kill you *tomorrow*," Stuart said to Monika, "but tonight I need a hug."

Monika walked into his arms. "I didn't mean to worry everybody."

Stuart pulled away from her. "You should have thought about that before you lied to your mother. There's never a reason to do that, Monika."

Monika cut a glance at her mother. "She lies to me."

Dolores walked over to her daughter. "I guess I deserved that," she said. "Well, my lies end tonight and so do yours."

"Listen to your mother, Monika," Francine said. "She loves you and only wants what's best for you. So do we." She pulled the girl into her arms for a quick hug. "I'll talk to you tomorrow."

The teen rolled her eyes. "You're not going to kill me too, are you?"

Francine shook her head, a smile on her face. "By the time you get to me, I have the distinct feeling you'll already have been killed a couple of times."

When Dolores led Monika to the front door, Stuart and Francine stayed in the driveway. "Aren't you coming back in?" Dolores asked.

Stuart shook his head. "We'll talk to Monika tomorrow," he said. "Give me a call if either of you want to talk later tonight."

"The same goes for me," Francine said.

Dolores left her daughter at the door and went back to hug her two friends. "Thank you both for being here tonight. I'm not sure what I would have done without you."

When Dolores and Monika were safely in the house, Stuart turned to Francine. "Going home?" She nodded. "I'll follow you."

"You don't have to do that."

"I know," he said, "but I will."

After escorting her to her car, he walked to his. He pulled out first, waited in the street until she pulled out, and then followed her the short distance to her home. He got out when she did.

"Thanks," she said.

Shoving his hands into the pockets of his slacks, he asked, "Aren't you going to invite me in for coffee?"

"We've both had too much coffee. How about a soft drink?"

Returning her smile, he said, "Sounds good to me."

He took her key, opened the front door, and then followed in after her. "Make yourself at home," she said, leaving him in the family room. "I'll get the drinks."

Familiar with the home, Stuart plopped down in the armchair and placed his feet on the matching ottoman.

"Here you go." She handed him a tall glass of diet Coke. "It's caffeine free."

He took a long swallow. "Just what I needed."

She sat down in the chair facing his. "You were good with

Rev. Campbell tonight, much better than I would have been. I would have pressed him too hard to confess. I was so angry with him for lying that I could have hit him."

"Let's pray he does the right thing."

"I don't hold much hope for the guy myself. He's rather smarmy."

Stuart chuckled. "Don't hold back. Tell me what you really think."

"You think I'm being too hard on him?"

He sipped from his soda. "Sometimes it's hard to see what the Lord is doing."

"You think he's doing something with Campbell?"

Stuart leaned forward and rested his arms on his knees. "We've been working with him on the planning for BCN. It's never been clear that we—Faith Central, I mean—would get on board with it, but the Lord had us keep the lines of communication open with Rev. Campbell. I'm beginning to think this situation is the reason why. It's all a part of the Lord's plan to give him another chance to mend his ways."

"So you don't think it's about Monika and Dolores at all?"

"Of course it's about them too. The Lord's going to teach them something, the same as He's going to teach the two of us something. That's the way He works."

She arched a brow at him. "So what's the lesson for us?"

"What do you think it is?"

"I haven't really thought about it in that way, but I have wondered if the Lord was giving me a chance to help make a wrong situation right," she said. Maybe that was why she had come back home, and when that job was completed, it would be time for her to leave.

"Because you couldn't with Toni?" When she nodded, Stuart raised a brow. "Are you sure that's not vengeance talking? Your desire to avenge Toni's death, which you think was caused by another cheating minister?"

"Does it matter? If it is, it's a righteous vengeance."

Stuart didn't speak for a long while, and when he did, he surprised Francine by changing the topic. "Why didn't you come to the teen fathers' and mothers' get-together tonight at Nate and CeCe's house? I thought you were coming."

She put her glass to her mouth and didn't answer him immediately.

"You were home when I called about Monika," he persisted, "so I assume you didn't have other plans for the evening. Am I wrong?"

"No," she admitted. "You aren't wrong."

"Then why didn't you come? I know you liked being with the boys, and you would have enjoyed meeting Nate and CeCe and the girls."

How could she explain it to him in a way that he would accept, without going into all the details? "I didn't think it was a good idea."

"Because I invited you?"

She glanced away from him. "That was a part of it." She turned back to him. "I thought it would be easier."

"Easier for whom?"

"For both of us. I think you're attracted to me and I admit that I could be attracted to you. It's safer all the way around for us not to get too attached."

He held her gaze with his own. "I took off my wedding ring," he said with meaning.

Her eyes widened and then lowered to his left hand. She met his eyes again. "When did you do that?"

"Yesterday."

"Why did you do it?"

"Because I'm ready to put the past in the past. I loved my wife, but I'm ready to look to a future without her. For the first time, I can actually see a future without her."

She looked back at his bare finger. "I'm happy for you."

"So, would you have come to CeCe and Nate's if you'd known I'd taken off the ring?"

She thought about George's threat and LaDonna's advice. "Probably not." She stood and turned to face the window. "I have a past that some people would call sordid. You don't need that, especially not with your plans for the Georgia Supreme Court. The Lord has great things in store for you."

Stuart put his Coke down and came to stand behind her. He turned her to face him. "Have you ever thought that maybe you're one of those great things?"

She shook her head. "I come with too much baggage, Stuart. You're ready to soar. I'd only hold you back."

He placed his hands on her shoulders. "Your past is a part of who you are. You don't have to run from it or be ashamed of it. I thought you knew that."

"I do," she said, "but I don't want it to hurt you or anybody else."

"So your avoiding me is your way of protecting me?"

She looked down at her hands. "Something like that."

He tilted her chin up and grinned at her. "It's sweet but unnecessary."

Taking comfort in the warmth his eyes offered, she asked, "So you'll risk your chances for the bench for a relationship that hasn't even started yet?"

He pushed her hair back off her forehead with his hand. "I'd risk it for a friendship, any friendship. If I have to deny my friends to get the position, what's the point in having it? God opens a door, God closes it. If the position's for me, it's for me. I won't have to compromise my principles or my friends to get it. How much would you risk for a friendship?"

She moved away from him and sat back down. "What do you mean?"

"Suppose somebody does try to make your past an issue. Are you willing to endure that kind of scrutiny because of your friendship with me? To have all of it, including Toni's death, become a topic of discussion, not just among people who know you, but the general public?" Francine lifted her empty glass to her mouth. Stuart took it from her and placed it on the cocktail table. "Would you endure that scrutiny?" Stuart asked again.

"I don't know," Francine said. "If it was just me, I would, but what about the others involved? What about George and his family?"

"What if George is the one starting the talk?" Stuart asked. "He's already started making waves."

"Oh, no." Francine pressed her fist against her lips. "What's he done?"

"He made a few phone calls to a few influential people. I got a visit from the judge who originally approached me about the seat on the court."

"What did he say?"

Stuart sighed. "He said a lot but the gist of it was that if George continues with the talk, your past could become an issue in the judicial selection and election processes."

Francine sank back in her chair as if seeking refuge in its deep cushions. "That's what I'm trying to tell you. George isn't joking around. He hates me so much that I believe he'd actually torpedo your chances for the bench to get back at me."

"So your answer is to get out of his way?"

"What else can I do?" she asked, thinking about the list of jobs she'd scanned on the Internet. Surely, she could get one of them.

"You tell Dolores and Monika they should fight. Why aren't you fighting?"

"Fight George? What do you mean?"

"He's verbally assaulted you more than once. Do you think that's right?"

"It's not right, but I understand he wants somebody to pay for what happened to Toni. So do I."

"Ah, vengeance again," he murmured. "But you're not the person at fault, so why are you taking George's trash?"

"Because I *am* at fault."

Stuart shook his head. "You can't have it both ways, Francine. Either you believe God forgives you and you move forward, or you don't and you wallow in the past. Your letting George abuse you the way he does, letting him dictate your life, is a way of wallowing in the past. Can't you see that?"

"It's not the same," she said. "It's not the same at all."

"Tell me how it's different."

"I wasn't there for Toni when I should have been."

"And letting George abuse you somehow makes up for that? Is that your tribute to Toni? Does it in any way help you to make sense of her death?"

"You don't understand," Francine said.

Stuart placed his glass on the counter. "I think I do understand," he said. "You're more interested in vengeance, making people pay, than you are in listening to God's voice and being obedient to Him." He shook his head sadly. "Maybe I don't know you as well as I thought I did."

Francine felt his disappointment in her but she had no defense. She watched in silence as he opened the door and left.

CHAPTER 25

With closed eyes, Dawn listened to the back-and-forth conversation between Sly and his grandfather as she rocked in the wicker swing on the deck of Grandpa and Grandma Ray's patio. The cool breeze from the ocean near the senior condo complex, the sound of the male voices, and the sway of the swing combined to give her a feeling of total relaxation.

"I like this collective idea a lot, Vester," Grandpa Ray said. "I'm so proud of what you're doing with the business. You're going to make it so much more than what we gave you. I know Willie and Grady are looking down on you with big smiles."

Dawn smiled at that notion. She liked to think her grandparents were happy with the way she and Sly and Francine were taking care of the business that had been left to them.

"I hope so, Grandpa," Sly said. "Your approval means a lot to us. We want you to be proud of us."

Dawn opened her eyes as Grandpa reached out and placed a strong, callused hand on Sly's knee. "There's never been a time we haven't been proud of you, Vester. You're a son and grandson any man would be proud to have."

"I had a good teacher," Sly said. "You're the best, Grandpa."

"The best at what?" Grandma Ray called from the door. "Somebody had better be the best at opening doors. If I have to open it, I may drop somebody's cobbler on the floor."

Grinning, Dawn got up and slid open the screen door for Grandma Ray. "Let me help you with that," she said, reaching to take the tray from the older woman.

"I can do it," Grandma Ray insisted. "When I get too old to carry a tray of dessert, I'll be the first to tell you about it. Now you sit back down."

Sharing a quick smile with Grandpa Ray and Sylvester, Dawn sat back down in the swing while Grandma Ray placed the tray on the wicker table. She handed bowls of apple cobbler with rich French vanilla ice cream to Sly, Grandpa Ray, Dawn, and finally herself. "I hope you like it." She took a seat on the glider next to Grandpa Ray.

Grandpa Ray took a big scoop and put it in his mouth. "Ooh," he said. "Doris, this dessert is about as sweet as you are."

Sly chuckled. "Stop flirting with my grandma. She's a married woman."

"I know," Grandpa said. "I like 'em married."

"Stop acting silly, Lee," Grandma said. "Dawn is going to think you're getting senile in your old age."

Grandpa wriggled his brows. "I'm not getting older," he said. "I'm getting better." He leaned over and kissed his wife's cheek. "You tell 'em, honey."

Grandma Ray pursed her lips together, but Dawn caught the twinkle in her eye. "Pay him no mind, Dawn," she said. "Sly, I hope you have better manners with your wife than your grandpa has with me."

"I think Grandpa has it right, Grandma. I think I ought to follow his example." Sly leaned down and pressed a soft kiss on Dawn's lips, giving her a taste of his dessert in the process.

Grandpa Ray chuckled. "I always knew the boy was smart."

Grandma just shook her head. "What are we going to do with them?" she asked Dawn.

Grandpa Ray gave Dawn a big wink. "I can think of a few things," he said to his wife.

Sly laughed outright. "You two haven't changed a bit," he said.

Grandpa Ray huffed. "Why mess with perfection?"

Grandma Ray took a big spoon of ice cream from her bowl and shoved it into Grandpa's mouth. "That ought to keep him quiet for a minute or two."

Dawn loved seeing the playfulness of this couple. They'd been married for more than fifty years and they still enjoyed each other. Her grandparents had been the same way. She so wanted that for herself and Sly. She wanted to grow old with him. She wanted to sit out on the porch with him and toss teasing words back and forth with their grandchildren. She wanted a family. She cast a glance at Sly. She wanted her husband.

Grandma Ray asked a question that brought Dawn back into the conversation. They chatted about one thing and then another for over an hour, until Grandpa stretched his arms above his head. "I don't know about y'all, but after all that good dessert, I know I'm going to sleep well tonight. You ready, Doris?"

"I guess so," Grandma said. "It's getting to be our bedtime. You go on, Lee. I'll be along as soon as I put these dishes in the dishwasher."

"Go on to bed, Grandma Ray," Dawn said. "Sylvester and I'll clean up."

Grandma looked from her grandson to his wife. "Are you sure? You two must be tired from that drive from Fort Lauderdale this morning."

"We're not that tired, Grandma," Sly added. "You go on to bed with Grandpa. We'll take care of everything."

"But—"

Grandpa stood and took his wife's arm in his. "Let the young folks take care of it, Doris. They don't need half as much sleep as we do."

"Okay, then," the older lady said. She leaned down and placed a kiss on Sly's jaw and then Dawn's. "Sleep well, you two. We'll see you in the morning."

"Bright and early for you, Sly," Grandpa said. "You promised to hit a few golf balls with me."

"I'll be up, Grandpa," Sly said. "See you in the morning."

Grandpa clapped Sly on the back and kissed Dawn on her cheek. "It sure is good to see the two of you. You have to visit us more often. Your happy faces make me feel young again."

"You are young, Grandpa," Dawn said.

"Come on, Lee," Grandma said, "and stop fishing for compliments."

Grandpa smiled at his wife. "She's a bossy bit," he said to Dawn with another big wink. "But I guess I'll keep her."

Grandma murmured a retort that Dawn missed because of the noise of the screen door opening and closing. "They're wonderful," she said to Sly when the older couple was out of earshot. "I'm so glad we came down. Grandma's right. We should visit more often."

Sly draped an arm around her shoulders and pulled her close to his side. "So you're enjoying yourself?"

"A lot. We needed to get away."

He pressed a kiss against her hair. "It's been special for me too."

She turned her head and kissed him full on the lips. He returned the kiss, showing her how much he loved her. When she would have deepened it, he pulled away. "While I enjoy kissing you more than you can know, I can't take too much of it."

Dawn knew he referred to their physical abstinence. With an inner sense of well-being, she decided to end the drought. "Let's clear the dishes so we can go to bed," she said.

"You go ahead," Sly said. "I'm going to stay up a while longer. I'll put the dishes in the dishwasher before I turn in."

Dawn knew he was continuing the pattern he'd taken on for their trip. He'd let her go to bed and to sleep before he'd join her. She didn't want him to follow his routine tonight. "Let's do it together, Sly."

He looked up at her with a question in his eyes.

"I want us together," she repeated. "In all ways."

When he continued to stare at her without speaking, she grew self-conscious. To hide her nervousness, she stood and reached for the tray of dirty dishes. He covered her hand with his to stop her. "What are you saying, Dawn?"

She lifted her eyes to his. "I'm saying I want a full marriage, Sly. I want to make love with you again. Tonight." When he still didn't say anything, she added, "If you want to, that is."

A wide grin broke out over his face. "I want to," he said. "I'm just trying to figure out if Grandma and Grandpa will be upset if we don't take the time to put the dishes in the dishwasher."

Dawn smiled at his quip and rewarded him with a kiss that he returned in full measure.

On Sunday morning, Francine dressed for church after a sleepless night. She'd tossed and turned all night, her thoughts going around and around, from Rev. Campbell's lies about his relationship with Dolores, to Stuart's challenge to her about George, to her job search and relocation plans. She needed some peace about all three and hoped that today's service would provide some answers.

With Dawn and Sly still out of town, it seemed pointless to brew coffee or make breakfast, so she decided to grab a breakfast bar and bottle of water to consume during her drive to church. The phone rang as she passed it en route to the refrigerator. "Amen-Ray residence, good morning," she said, remembering her manners. She took the handset with her and opened the refrigerator door.

"Miss Francine?"

Monika's frantic voice stopped Francine's perusal of the refrigerator contents. "It's me," she said. "What's wrong, Monika?"

"I want to see my father," she said.

Francine closed the refrigerator door. "Where's your mother? Did you and she talk last night?"

"Momma's gone to church."

Francine waited for Monika to address her second question, and when she didn't, she prodded, "And?"

"We talked. She told me who he was." The girl gave a sigh so full of anguish that it should have come from a much older and life-worn woman. "I looked up his church in the phone book. I want to go there this morning."

Francine braced herself for the direction she feared this conversation was heading. "What did your mother say?"

Silence. Then, "I didn't ask her."

"Monika—" Francine chided.

"Miss Francine, I have to see him, and Momma won't go with me, I know she won't. Since he doesn't want to meet me, she thinks we should leave him alone, but I want to see him. I've never seen my father and I want to see him. Please go with me. I just want to see him."

Francine's heart ached for the teenager. She wished she could contact Dolores and get her permission, but there was no way of doing that now. She didn't doubt that Monika was well aware of this. The teen might be hurting but that hadn't interfered with her plotting skills.

"If you don't go with me," Monika threatened, "I'll take a cab and go by myself. I have money."

"You will do no such thing, Monika. Wait and talk with your mother."

"I'm not waiting, Miss Francine. I'm going this morning—either with you or without you. Please go with me. I'm scared."

Francine copied Monika's earlier sigh. "You stay put," she told the teenager, "until you talk to your mother."

"She's not going to let me go. I just know it. I'm calling a cab."

"No, Monika—"

Instead of getting a response, Francine got a click followed by a dial tone. She took the phone from her ear and stared at it. Monika had actually hung up on her. Having no idea how to contact Dolores, Francine dialed Stuart's cell. She wasn't surprised when he didn't answer. He'd probably turned it off for church. She left a message on his voice mail that she was going to try to intercept Monika at Rev. Campbell's church.

Francine hung up the phone and rushed out of the house, praying that she'd get to Monika before the girl got inside the church. Her prayer was answered and she caught up with the teenager just as she was walking up the concrete steps leading to the doors of Pilgrim Church. When Francine called to her, she turned and gave a smile that didn't quite reach her lips. "I love you, Miss Francine," she said. "Thank you so much for coming. I knew you'd help me."

As Francine fell into step with the girl, she had the feeling she'd been conned by the teenager. "I love you too, Monika," she said, "but you should have talked to your mother before coming here."

Monika kept walking as if she hadn't heard Francine speak. When the two of them reached the top step, Monika took Francine's arm and stopped her. "I'm scared," she said. "What if he recognizes me?"

Francine thought it was a bit late to consider that possibility. Besides, even if Rev. Campbell didn't recognize Monika, Francine knew he would remember *her* from the disastrous meeting she, Dolores, and Stuart had with him last night. A part of her was glad of that. The more she thought about it, the more she was convinced that Rev. Campbell would weasel his way out of the situation with Dolores and Monika. She could feel it in her bones. Well, he might try to weasel his way out of it, but with their presence this morning, she was going to make sure he squirmed. "We can turn around and go on to Faith Central," Francine offered, though now she was psyched at the idea of shaking up Rev. Campbell's world a bit.

Monika shook her head and took the last step to the landing of the church. "I want to see him," she said aloud, though Francine felt she was talking to herself. "I just want to see him."

The church secretary was reading the week's announcements when Francine and Monika slid into a pew about midway down the center aisle of the sparsely populated sanctuary. The low turnout surprised Francine. She estimated two or three hundred people in a sanctuary that could easily hold twice that many.

The announcements finished, the secretary read the names of the visitors who had submitted visitors' cards, asked them to stand, welcomed each one individually to service, and invited them to stay for the visitors' reception in the pastor's lounge immediately following the service. When she asked if there were other visitors who had not completed a card, Francine was unsure if they should stand. How much did she want to throw their presence in Rev. Campbell's face? From her seat, she could glimpse him in the pulpit when he leaned over to whisper to the man sitting next to him. Otherwise, he was pretty well hidden by the podium. Monika ended Francine's internal debate when the young girl stood up. Francine felt compelled to stand with her. She took great pleasure in seeing Rev. Campbell lean to the side when he heard their names. She met his eyes and issued a taunting smile. Yes, he remembered her, and she bet he knew who Monika was too. If he didn't, she bet he wondered.

After they sat down, Rev. Campbell stood at the podium.

Francine glanced to her side to see how Monika was doing. "Are you okay?" she whispered.

The girl nodded, but otherwise her eyes remained fixed on her father. He had all of the teen's attention.

Francine turned her head back toward the pulpit. She watched Rev. Campbell but she couldn't focus on his words. She wondered how he could stand before these people and preach when last night he'd lied about being Monika's father. She allowed her gaze to roam the congregation. Did any of them know the kind of man he was? Would they do the right thing if they knew, or would they go along with the status quo? She wasn't sure, but her instincts and past experience gave better odds to maintaining the status quo. Then she wondered if they were already keeping secrets for him. Were there other Doloreses seated in the sanctuary today?

When the service was over, Monika spoke for the first time since they'd entered the church. "I want to go to the visitors' reception," she said. "I want to see him up close."

Francine studied the girl. "Are you sure you want to do this, Monika?"

"I'm sure."

Francine wasn't so sure though. Monika was a mature fifteen, but she was still a child. How would meeting her father affect her?

"I'm not going to throw a tantrum or anything," Monika said. "I just want to see him up close. I think I have his nose and eyes. I just want to see him."

Francine couldn't fight the sentiment in those words. She followed Monika to the back of the church where the ushers were directing visitors to the lounge. An usher dressed in all white greeted them at the entrance, asked them to complete the visitors' cards, and gave them visitors' badges to wear. They took the offered cards and badges and then sat at one of the six-foot-long metal folding tables to complete them.

"He'll come, won't he?" Monika asked anxiously.

"I don't know," Francine said. Rev. Campbell might be such a coward he'd come up with some fake excuse so he wouldn't have to face them. She glanced around at the other visitors mingling with church members. The visitors, with the exception of her and Monika, were easily identified by their blue-and-white name badges.

When they had completed the visitors' cards, Francine and Monika returned them to the usher and went to join the others congregated around the refreshment table. A petite woman with honey brown skin turned and greeted them with an open and loving smile. Francine couldn't help but smile back.

"Welcome to Pilgrim," she said, giving first Francine and then Monika a warm hug. "I'm Sister Campbell."

His wife. Did she know she was married to a monster? Francine wondered.

"We enjoyed the service, Sister Campbell," Monika said to the older woman.

"I'm glad you did, and I'm sure the reverend is too. He should be in here in a few minutes to greet you. Do you have a church home in the area?" she asked.

Francine nodded. "Faith Central," she said. "Rev. Thomas is our pastor."

"That's right. I remember now." The woman smiled broadly. "I know Faith Central and Rev. Thomas. Both have excellent ministry reputations. I believe my husband is doing some business with Rev. Thomas. We'll have to ask him when he shows up." The woman glanced up, and Francine watched as her smile softened with love. "There he is now."

When Sister Campbell waved her husband over, Francine felt Monika stiffen beside her. She hugged the girl to her side briefly in a show of support and love, and felt some of her tension ease.

"Reverend," Sister Campbell said, reaching out her hand to

pull him into their circle. "You have to meet these two visitors. Francine Amen and Monika King. They're from Faith Central."

"Oh, yes," he said, "Rev. Thomas's church. You have a good ministry there." He shook both their hands. "We're glad to have you here, but I can't imagine you're looking for another church home."

That comment was directed to Francine. She knew it was, because he had yet to meet Monika's eyes. Francine had no sympathy for him. Her esteem for him went even lower because he refused to look at his daughter. "We decided to go visiting today."

"Are you by any chance related to the Amens of Amen-Ray Funeral Home?" Sister Campbell asked.

"My grandfather was one of the founders."

"How wonderful," Sister Campbell said. "Amen-Ray has done a funeral or two here. Always a very professional job. It's a wonder we haven't met before."

Francine saw no need to go into her history, so she didn't. "You're probably familiar with Monika's family too. Her mother owns Kings and Queens Day Spa."

Sister Campbell smiled at Monika, but for some reason the smile didn't seem to reach her eyes. "Why, this is wonderful. I've heard so many good things about that establishment. I've been meaning to go in for a treatment myself. You must be really proud of your mother."

When Monika answered, she let her gaze slide from Sister Campbell to the father she was meeting for the first time. "I'm very proud of her," she said. "She's worked really hard to build a good life for us. She's the best mother in the world."

Sister Campbell tilted her head toward her husband. "Now, this young lady appreciates her mother. I hope the boys say such glowing things about me." She turned back to Francine and Monika. "We have three sons. Two are grown and married, and one thinks he's grown. Our baby is in college. In fact, he's in summer school now."

"No daughters?" Monika asked, her glance sliding back to her father.

"We weren't so blessed," Sister Campbell said, "but we always wanted a girl." She glanced up at her husband. "Didn't we, Reverend?"

"All children are a blessing," he said, not answering the question. "Well, it's been a pleasure talking to you, Ms. Amen, Ms. King. If you're out visiting again, we hope you'll stop in here at Pilgrim. Our door is always open."

Sister Campbell took one of their hands in each of hers. "You'll have to come again, I've enjoyed talking with you so much I almost hate to stop, but we do have to greet the other visitors. Enjoy your day."

Francine and Monika murmured good-byes. When the couple were out of earshot, Monika said, "I wonder what my brothers look like."

Francine smiled down at the girl, proud of the way she'd handled herself. She'd been more of an adult than Rev. Campbell had. "I'd bet they're handsome."

She nodded. "I look a little like him, don't I?"

Francine considered the man in question. Monika did have his wide brown eyes, slight nose, and full mouth. "There's a resemblance."

"He had to notice it, didn't he?"

He'd noticed all right, though Francine was sure he hadn't wanted to. "I'm sure he did."

Monika nodded. "Me too." She released a sigh, this time a lighter one, as though she was getting rid of a long-held burden. She looked up at Francine. "I'm ready to go home now."

Francine took one final glance at Rev. and Sister Campbell mingling with the visitors. Then, shaking her head, she turned to follow Monika out of the lounge and to their car. She pulled up short when she made eye contact with Toni's mother, Mary Roberts. Acting on impulse, she raced toward the older woman, stopping within arm's reach. "I'm so sorry," she began, tears on her cheeks. Mrs. Roberts placed an index finger on Francine's lips and, without saying a word, pulled her into a warm embrace. There in the arms of the mother of her dead best friend, Francine released the full grief she felt over her friend's death.

When the women pulled apart, their cheeks were damp and their eyes red. "I want—" Francine began.

Mrs. Roberts shook her head. "I can't talk about it, Francie," she said. "It's still too raw."

Saddened, Francine sucked in her grief and nodded. She watched Mrs. Roberts turn away from her and head down the hallway, away from the pastor's lounge.

"Francine?" Monika called. "Are you all right?"

Though Francine wasn't sure she'd ever be all right again, she gave Monika an affirmative nod. "We can leave now," she said. And they did.

CHAPTER 26

For Francine, the drive from Pilgrim to Monika's house seemed much longer than the initial drive to the church. She couldn't shake the pain she'd seen in Mrs. Roberts's eyes. As evidence of the stress she was under, she was relieved to see Stuart's car in the driveway when they arrived, despite the awkward ending of their last conversation.

Monika turned to her. "You called him, didn't you?"

"I thought he could help."

The teen folded her arms across her chest. "Help what? Can he make my father want to know me? I don't think so."

"Monika—"

"Don't," Monika said, getting out of the car and slamming the door behind her.

With a sigh, Francine opened her door and followed the teenager, whose mood had grown progressively worse during the drive home. Dolores pulled the front door open before they reached it. "You have some explaining to do, young lady," she said to Monika.

"Not now, Momma," the girl said, walking into her mother's open arms. "I just wanted to see him."

Love softened the concern in Dolores's eyes. "What did you think of him?" she asked, after they all were seated in the living room. Monika sat on the couch between Dolores and Stuart, while Francine sat in the chair facing them.

"I look like him," Monika said.

Dolores pushed her daughter's locks back off her forehead. "A little."

She met her mother's gaze. "More than a little. Enough that he knew who I was."

Dolores turned to Francine. "He said he knew who she was?"

"Not exactly."

"There's no 'not exactly.' He hardly even looked at me," Monika explained, her calm maturity surprising the adults. "But he knew who I was." She dropped her eyes from her mother's. "His wife was nice."

Dolores lifted her daughter's chin with her palm. "It's all right, Monika. She's not at fault in this."

Francine wasn't so sure about that, but she kept her thoughts to herself.

"You've met him, Monika," Stuart said, "so now what?"

The girl met his gaze directly. "I want to meet my half-brothers and my grandparents, if I have any."

"Oh, Monika," Dolores said. "I knew this was going to happen. I knew you weren't going to be satisfied with meeting him." She pressed her forehead to her daughter's. "We can't make him want to know you, sweetheart."

"I know that, Momma," Monika pleaded, "but his family may be different. Maybe they'd want to know about me."

Dolores brushed her hand across Monika's head. "Sweetheart, I can't help but think you're setting yourself up for a big heartbreak."

Monika took her mother's hand. "My heart's already broken, Momma. I'm trying to fix it."

Dolores couldn't fight those words. Instead, she had to fight tears. "What can we do?" she asked Stuart. "I've talked to him, you've talked to him. Nothing works."

Stuart shook his head in disagreement. "We started the process, but we haven't given it time to work." He inclined his head toward Monika. "Our young lady here got a bit ahead of us."

"What do you mean?" Francine asked.

"I mean we didn't allow Jesus's three-step process to work through. Rev. Thomas still has to talk to Rev. Campbell. If that doesn't work, we'll go to his wife and the Board of Trustees at the church. And if all those fail, there's still the civil court system. We can't make him *want* to do the right thing, but we can make him do it. Don't ever doubt that."

"What's the point if he's not interested?" Dolores wanted to know.

Though Dolores had addressed the question to Stuart, Monika answered, "Because they're my family and I want to get to know them. If they don't want to get to know me, at least I'll know I've tried. Otherwise, I'll always wonder."

Dolores pressed her daughter's head against her shoulder. "I don't want you disappointed, sweetheart."

Monika wrapped her arms around her waist. "I'm already disappointed, Momma," she said. "Let's finish this now."

"For what it's worth," Francine said, "I think Monika's right and I think both of you are very brave for going ahead with this."

Dolores hugged her daughter to her side. "We couldn't have done it without your support, you and Stuart both. You've been there for us."

"And we'll continue to be there," Stuart added. "We'll see this through to the end."

"Whatever that may be?" Dolores said.

Both Stuart and Francine nodded. "Why don't we pray?" Stuart offered. The four people clasped hands and prayed. When the last "Amen" was uttered, Francine stood and said, "I'm going to head on home."

"I'll walk with you," Stuart said, standing as well.

When they were alone outside, Stuart asked Francine, "Are you all right?"

"I'm fine."

He tilted her chin up. "You don't look fine. What happened? Did seeing Rev. Campbell again upset you?"

She shook her head. "Not that. I saw Toni's mother."

"Ah . . ."

"She's hurting so much, Stuart."

Stuart pulled Francine into his arms. "She's not the only one, is she?" he murmured.

Francine let herself accept the comfort Stuart offered until the bulk of her sadness passed. She pulled back and looked up at him. "I'm sorry, Stuart."

"Don't be," he said. "Crying can be good for you."

"But it doesn't solve anything," she said. "Actions speak louder than words or tears." She looked away from him to the immaculate lawns of the homes across the street, debating whether to tell him her plans. Seeing Mrs. Roberts this morning had settled it for her. She was definitely leaving town as soon as this matter with Monika was settled. She knew it would be best for everybody, just as she knew Stuart wouldn't agree. "I've started looking for another job."

"You're leaving the bookstore? Why?"

She exhaled a deep breath and turned to him. "I'm leaving Atlanta, Stuart."

"So you've decided to run away?"

She shook her head. "I've decided to do what's best for the

people around me. You didn't see the look in Mrs. Roberts's eyes. She couldn't even talk to me."

"In time, she'll get past it, Francine. She needs time to grieve."

"How can she if the wound's reopened every time she sees me?"

Stuart stared down at her and she knew he wanted to shake some sense into her. "You've made up your mind, haven't you?"

She nodded.

"You're going to do what you're going to do, but I have to tell you I think you're wrong. Running away is not going to help you or George or Mrs. Roberts or anybody else. In the end, your martyrdom will only make you bitter because you'll realize all you had to give up." He eyed her suspiciously. "Maybe that's what you want? Maybe this is the ultimate penance for the wrong you felt you did to Toni? That's it, isn't it?"

Francine didn't answer. He'd come too close to the truth.

"It's not going to work, Francine, because God doesn't work that way. The only answer to sin is obedience; the only answer to wrong past behavior is obedient present and future behavior. You can't live your life making up for the past; you have to live it being obedient to what God has for you *now*. That's the only way to make up for the past."

Francine grew weary at Stuart's words. "I know you don't agree, Stuart, but it's my life and I have to do what I think is best."

Stuart shook his head. "You're wrong. What you have to do is what the Lord tells you. You'll never know what that is if you spend your life running from the mistakes of the past."

Francine frowned as she hit the Return key on her sister's computer to submit her resume to the four most promising listings on monster.com later Sunday evening. She hoped the Internet would land her a position, but if it didn't she had a backup plan in the stack of newspapers from Charleston, Raleigh, Charlotte, Birmingham, Montgomery, and Jacksonville. Though she was applying for jobs, her heart wasn't in it. She was glad to be back home surrounded by people who loved her. She didn't know how she'd make it without that support system, but she owed it to the people she loved and cared about to give it a shot.

The doorbell gave her the excuse she needed to get up from her job searching, though she did wonder who'd be visiting at this hour. It was a little after eight. She pulled up short when she saw through the sidelights that her visitor was Sister Campbell. Taking a deep breath, she pulled open the front door.

"Sister Campbell," she said. "This is a surprise."

The older woman's gaze didn't waver. "I know it's late," she said, "but I'd like to talk to you about something. Is it all right if I come in?"

Francine stepped back so the woman could enter. "Forgive my manners. You caught me off guard. As I said, seeing you at the door was a big surprise." Francine led the woman to a seat on the living room sofa. "Can I get you something to drink?" she offered.

Sister Campbell shook her head. "I won't be here that long."

"Oh," Francine said, sitting on the couch next to her. "Well, what brings you by tonight?"

Sister Campbell met her eyes. "I want to know the real reason you and that young girl came to Pilgrim this morning."

"What?"

"You heard me. I want to know the real reason you were at Pilgrim this morning. I'm not stupid enough to think you were just out visiting churches. You see, I know who owns Kings and Queens Day Spa."

Francine slumped back on the sofa. "You know?"

"I know that woman was after my husband fifteen years ago and I guess she wants to start her games again. Were you her emissary? Are you trying to ruin my marriage?"

"You've got this all wrong, Sister Campbell. No one is after your husband."

"You're a liar," Sister Campbell spat. "I know all about you. You had another little girlfriend who messed with a minister, and now you come here and take over where you left off. Well, you and Dolores King are not getting my husband."

The woman's anger unsettled Francine. She stood. "Look, Sister Campbell, I don't know what you're talking about. Nobody is trying to get your husband. You need to talk to him about his relationship with Dolores and Monika."

"There is no relationship!" the woman screamed. "I told you, Dolores King has been after my husband for years. I don't know what her game is this time, but she won't get him. And you can tell her for me that sending that girl around is not going to help her cause."

Francine's eyes widened. "You know, don't you? You know about Monika."

Sister Campbell stood and took a step toward Francine with a menacing glare. "I know my husband, and I stand behind my husband. You and your friend need to understand that. A number of women like you and Dolores King have come against our marriage, looking at my minister husband like he was a chocolate bar with your name on it. Well, he was mine then and he's mine now. There's no way some little skeezer like you or your friend is gonna come between us." She poked Francine's chest with her finger. "You'd best understand that."

Francine stood speechless as Sister Campbell strode out of the room, and the house, slamming the door behind her. When she heard the car start, she collapsed onto the couch and covered her face with her hands. When she had calmed down sufficiently, she picked up the phone and called Stuart.

When she finished telling him the story, he said, "Are you okay? Do you need me to come over? Sly and Dawn aren't back yet, are they?"

"I'm fine," she told him. "And even though Sly and Dawn aren't back yet, I don't need you to come over and sit with me. I'm a big girl."

"And you can take care of yourself? Okay, I hear you."

"I'm more concerned about Dolores and Monika. Do you think we need to tell them about Sister Campbell's visit, the things she said?"

"I don't think so," Stuart said. "It would only upset them. Let's wait until we hear back from Rev. Thomas's efforts. I have a feeling that all this is going to wrap up rather quickly. Besides, I don't think Sister Campbell wants a face-to-face with Dolores. She gave *you* the message, hoping you'd pass it along, when she could have gone straight to Dolores if she'd wanted."

"That's what I figured," Francine said. "She knows about Dolores and Monika, doesn't she?"

"Either that or she suspects. It sounds like she and Rev. Campbell have been through the other-woman thing before, more than once."

It did, but Francine could feel no sorrow for the woman. Instead of defending her husband, she should have been thinking about the lives that lay in ruins because of him. "How can she support him, Stuart? She's the one who could stop him for good, at least get him out of a position where he continues to harm people."

"He's her husband, Francine, whatever else he is, he's her husband and the father of her children. She's probably protecting her children as much as she's protecting him."

Francine didn't believe that. "Her children are grown with their own families. They can handle the truth. A better guess is that she's doing it for herself. Maybe it's important for her to be First Lady, more important than anything."

"Maybe," he said. "I really don't know."

Francine sighed. "Look, I've kept you on the phone long enough."

"No problem," he said. "I'm glad you called. What were you doing anyway?"

Francine paused, not wanting to tell him. "I was updating my resumé and sending it out online."

"Oh," he said.

"I know how you feel, Stuart, so before we argue about it again, let's just say good night. Okay?"

"Okay," he said. "Good night."

"Good night." She held the phone until he hung up. Then she went back to look at the want ads in the newspapers she'd bought.

At work on Monday morning Francine found herself smiling as she thought about the giggles she'd heard coming from the master bedroom of the Amen-Ray home when she'd gotten up. Evidently, Sly and Dawn's working trip had led to a reconciliation.

"What's on your mind?" Mother Harris asked. "You've been going from broad smiles to flat frowns all morning."

Francine looked up from her task of counting the money in the cash register. Mother Harris was right. She had a lot on her mind today. She was grateful for the happy thoughts about Dawn and Sly. They were a welcome relief. "Well," Francine said, grinning, "I'm hearing things and they're sounding like Sly and Dawn have worked out their problems."

"Praise the Lord," Mother Harris said. "I'm happy for them. They've always been a special couple, one of my favorites."

"They are special people," Francine agreed absently, her thoughts now turning to Monika's situation. That girl was spe-

cial and she didn't deserve the treatment Rev. and Sister Campbell were giving her. Thank God, the teen was also strong, willing to fight for a chance to know the family she'd never met.
Thank God, too, she didn't have to fight alone.

Mother Harris nudged her arm. "Now tell me what's making
you frown."

Francine glanced at the clock. Since they had about fifteen
minutes before the store opened, she sat down on the stool next
to Mother Harris. "It's Monika. Well, not exactly Monika, it's
her father."

"Stuart's been keeping me updated on that."

"So you know Monika and I went to his church yesterday?"

"What?"

Apparently, Stuart hadn't gotten around to calling Mother
Harris with the latest news. "Yes, ma'am, Monika tricked me
into following her to her father's church yesterday." Francine
gave Mother Harris the details of the call Monika had made to
her on Sunday morning. "The sorry excuse for a minister basically pretended he didn't know who we were. I could have
slapped him, but Monika seemed fine with it. She handled the
situation very well. Almost too well. You know what I mean?"

"You expected her to get upset?"

Francine knew she would have been more upset than Monika
had been. She had even been upset on Monika's behalf.
"Wouldn't you expect that?"

"I'm not sure," Mother Harris said. "We've all been praying
for Monika. Maybe the Lord's protecting her heart the way we
asked Him to."

"I hadn't thought about it that way," Francine said, liking the
idea of the Lord keeping Monika safe. Either you believed in
the power of prayer or you didn't. "I hope you're right. Monika
is a great girl and Rev. Campbell should be happy to have her as
a daughter. His wife—now, she was a trip—was all nice at

church. She told us they had three boys and always wanted a girl, and he stood there like a jerk. Can you believe it?"

"Unfortunately, I can. I'm sure you didn't expect him to acknowledge Monika right then and there, did you?"

"I'm not sure what I expected, but it certainly wasn't all the pleasantness. His wife seemed to be a nice woman, a godly woman, but she showed her true colors when she showed up at my house last night."

"What?"

Francine told Mother Harris the details of Sister Campbell's visit. "The woman knows the kind of man she married and she's covering for him."

Mother Harris got up and wiped down the counter that Francine had already cleaned. "Don't be so hard on her. She's his wife. What did you expect her to do?"

Francine waited for Mother Harris to turn to her. "Well, if she knows the kind of man he is, she needs to stand up for what's right. That's the Christian thing to do. If she doesn't, she's letting him do the things he does, which makes her as much to blame as he is. The only reason he can get away with anything is because people keep quiet, or worse yet, cover for him." Francine knew that to be the case with Temple and Bishop Payne, and she could see little difference between him and Rev. Campbell. They were cut from the same cloth.

"You're being awfully harsh, Francine."

"I'm not being harsh," Francine said. "I'm telling the truth. If Sister Campbell sits there next to Rev. Campbell and pretends he's all that when she knows he's not, she's perpetrating a fraud, as the brothers would say, and she ought to be held accountable."

Mother Harris put the cleaning cloth down and went to flip over the Closed sign and unlock the door. "You've got pretty strong opinions on this subject," she said when she came back to the counter.

"Of course I do," Francine said. "After what I've been through, I should." She studied Mother Harris. "I'm surprised you don't hold stronger opinions."

Mother Harris's lips curved downward in a slight frown. "Oh, I do hold opinions," she said.

"Well, tell me. If you think I'm wrong, I want to know."

Mother Harris sat down and folded her hands primly on her lap. Then she raised sad eyes to Francine. "You're so harsh. Don't you have any compassion for Sister Campbell? You didn't know what was going on at Temple. Why is it so hard to believe she doesn't know what's going on with her husband?"

"Whew!" Francine reeled from the blow of that comparison. "Maybe I deserved that, but I wasn't married to Bishop Payne. I wasn't sleeping with him. A wife has to know, doesn't she? How could she not know, especially after all those years?"

"What if she did know, and didn't do anything? What penalty would you assign to her?"

Francine shrugged. "I know I'm not the one who hands out penalties, Mother Harris, and I'm not saying I should. It's just that he wouldn't get away with it unless she allowed it. There are probably a lot of preachers' wives out there right now covering up for their husbands, and the way I see it, they're as guilty as their husbands. Besides, Sister Campbell does know. I know she does. She's just blaming the women like her man is some kind of catch."

"She does have a point, Francie," Mother Harris said. "Some women do go after pastors. You know that."

"I know, but that's not the case here." *And it wasn't the case with Bishop Payne.*

"I hear you," Mother Harris said.

"But you don't agree?" Mother Harris looked away, causing Francine to wonder at her anxiousness. "Is something wrong, Mother Harris?"

Mother Harris met Francine's gaze and took her hand. "I'm

going to tell you something, Francine, that I've never told anybody. Not anybody."

Francine felt a shiver of fear trickle down her spine. "What is it?"

"I was one of those wives."

"What are you talking about?"

Mother Harris took a deep breath. "I was a wife who turned a blind eye to her minister husband's philandering."

Francine couldn't have been more surprised if Mother Harris had said she'd gotten drunk and done lap dances at a local bar last night. "What?"

"You heard me. In the early days of our marriage, Rev. Harris wasn't as faithful as I expected a husband to be."

"And you did nothing?" Francine accused, unable to fathom the strong, godly woman she knew Mother Harris to be doing nothing.

"What was I supposed to do? Tell me, what was the right thing to do?"

Because Mother Harris had asked it, Francine fully considered the question before answering. A compassion she hadn't felt for Sister Campbell flowed through her being. "What did you do?" she asked. "I know you did something."

Mother Harris glanced at the door, making Francine wonder if she was praying for a customer so they would be forced to end the conversation. "I did what any good wife would do. At first, I pretended I didn't know, and when that became impossible, I told my mother I was leaving him." She gave a wry smile. "Do you know what she said to me?"

Francine had no idea, and the ghosts reflected in Mother Harris's eyes made her wonder if she wanted to know.

"She told me that preachers were different men. She said some things had to be overlooked if I wanted to have a happy home." Mother Harris laughed, a hollow sound. "I remember how crushed I was. Betrayed first by my husband, the man I loved, and then by my mother, the woman I thought would always have my best interests at heart."

Francine draped an arm around the older woman's shoulders. "So you kept quiet?"

"For a while. It was a few years before I took a stand. And the stand I took was much worse than keeping quiet."

Not imagining Mother Harris doing anything really awful, Francine waited for more information.

"One of them got pregnant. Rather, he impregnated one of them, a woman in our first congregation. She told him. He told me. I think that was the eye-opener for him. He wanted to confess all, take responsibility for the child."

"That was a good thing. Your husband sounds like he learned his lesson."

"He did, but I didn't." She lowered her head. "He asked me to stand with him, to forgive him. He said we could weather it together. I told him that if he acknowledged that child, I'd leave him and let everybody know this woman wasn't the first."

Francine's arms dropped from the other woman's shoulders. She couldn't believe what she was hearing. "Mother Harris?"

Mother Harris glanced over at her. "Yes, Mother Harris did that. Of course, I wasn't Mother Harris then. I was Sister Harris, Pastor's wife."

"What happened?"

"We didn't publicly acknowledge the child, but we did provide financial support, generous financial support. Reverend looked for and got an appointment in another town—that's when we came to Faith Central—and we continued to live our lives, build a ministry." She looked at Francine, her lips curving in a smile at some secret memory. "He was a changed man afterwards. I'm sure he never thought about cheating again and I'm also sure his heart was broken that he could never acknowledge his child. We never discussed it again, not even when we wrote the checks each month."

Francine pulled Mother Harris into her arms. "I'm so sorry," she said, wishing she could absorb the woman's pain. After all these years, her pain remained alive.

When Francine pulled away, Mother Harris said, "It's fitting, don't you think, that we never had children of our own? Do you think that's enough penalty for the pastor's wife who didn't want to face her husband's sin, and who, as a result, committed an even worse sin?"

Francine didn't know what to say. She wanted to comfort Mother Harris but she didn't have the words. "What happened to the child?"

Mother Harris smiled, a real smile this time. "She grew into a lovely young woman and she came looking for her father."

Francine couldn't help but notice the similarities with Monika. "What happened?"

"Nothing. She was a married woman with children of her own. She didn't want to be acknowledged. She only wanted to meet him."

Francine thought that maybe the woman had wanted Rev. Harris to *want* to acknowledge her, wanted him to publicly claim her as his daughter despite her words to the contrary. "Neither of you tried to change her mind?"

"We tried, but she didn't want it for her children, her family. They were happy," Mother Harris said. "She just wanted to meet him, thank him for the money over the years, and let him know things had worked out well for her. By then, Reverend was well known and a child of his past would have become a major scandal, much more so than it would have been at the time the child was born."

Francine thought the entire situation was sad. Reverend and Mother Harris had missed out on children and grandchildren for no reason at all. "Do you still keep in touch with her and her family?"

"It would be hard not to. She lives here in Atlanta and she and her son go to Faith Central."

Francine's mouth dropped open. "What?"

"It's a real mess, isn't it?"

Francine thought it was, but she didn't say so. She wondered who the son was but she didn't ask.

"It's George Roberts," Mother Harris said. "George is my husband's grandson."

Francine slumped back on her stool. "George?"

Mother Harris nodded. "Now you understand his hostility. It's not all about you."

Francine's heart ached anew for George. She'd known about the pain he felt because of the closeness he'd shared with his sister, but to have that burden added to the burden of the circumstances of his mother's birth must be nearly unbearable for him. "Does he know?"

Mother Harris rubbed her hands together and pressed them to her mouth. When she lowered them, she said, "I'm sure his mother told him, though we've never spoken of it."

Francine could hardly believe what she was hearing. "But you see him every Sunday."

Mother Harris released a heavy sigh. "I know. There have been times when I've wanted to say something, times when I'm sure Rev. Harris wanted to say something, but too much time had passed and it was easier to leave things unsaid."

Francine felt an overwhelming sadness for Mother Harris and for George and his mother. How could they live with the lie all these years? "Oh no," Francine said, a new thought occurring to her. "Did Toni know?"

Mother Harris squeezed her eyes shut. "I'm sure she did."

"But she never said anything, not even to me, and I was her best friend."

Mother Harris reached for Francine's hand. "That's the way

things were," the older woman explained. "Nobody talked about it. It was an awful secret that was forced on them all."

"How did they live with it?" Francine wondered aloud.

Mother Harris lifted her slight shoulders in a shrug. "Rev. Harris was dead by the time George and Toni were old enough to understand, so it wasn't as if they had to see him every Sunday. Their mother had made peace with it, the secret, a long time ago."

Francine didn't bother to wipe at the tears that rolled down her cheeks afresh as she thought about the torture Toni must have gone through knowing that she was repeating her grandmother's pattern. *Why didn't I listen to her? Why didn't I try to understand?* "Toni must have felt so alone," she told Mother Harris. "I can see how she would have been reluctant to bring her problem to her mother and George. I was truly the only person she had and I turned my back on her. How could I have done that, Mother Harris?"

Mother Harris squeezed Francine's hands. "You thought it was the right thing to do at the time, Francie. You can take comfort in the knowledge that your intentions were good. I don't have that excuse. I wanted to punish my husband and save face because of my pride, no other reason."

"Good intentions won't bring Toni back or lessen George's pain. What are we going to do, Mother Harris? How are we going to make it right?"

Mother Harris gave a light laugh. "That's my Francie," she said, "always wanting things to line up in a way that makes sense. Some things just don't make sense. Some things can't be made right because they can't be undone."

Francine shook her head. "I can't accept that," she said. "There has to be something." Those words ended their conversation as the door chimes signaled the arrival of the day's first customer.

CHAPTER 27

Francine was still reeling from her morning conversation with Mother Harris when she got home Monday night. You never really knew what other people were going through, she thought to herself. She never would have guessed any of the things Mother Harris had told her this morning, and if anyone but Mother Harris had told them to her, she wouldn't have believed them. At least now she understood where George's hatred of her was based and she better understood the depth of Mrs. Roberts's pain. Much of it had nothing to do with her, Francine now knew, and accepting this made her realize how much she'd taken on herself unnecessarily.

Francine wished there were something she could do for them. She now agreed with Stuart that allowing George to berate and blame her was not helping him, and that her leaving town would not help George or his mother. But there had to be something she could do, she thought as she climbed the stairs, heading for bed. When she reached the landing of the second floor, she stopped in surprise at the sight of Dawn trooping from the guest room to the master bedroom, her arms loaded down with clothes. "Somebody moving?" she asked with a knowing smile.

Dawn returned the smile. "My husband is moving back to our bedroom."

"You go, girl!" Francine said. "I thought the giggling I heard this morning was a good sign." Francine laughed at the blush that graced her sister's cheeks and widened her eyes. "All I heard was giggling."

Dawn chuckled, then beckoned her sister to join her in the master bedroom. "I'll have to tell Sly about the giggling. He may never be able to face you again."

"Don't you dare," Francine said.

Dawn dumped the clothes on the bed, then began picking them up a few at a time and returning them to their rightful closet. "You'd better be nice to me then."

"I'll think about it," Francine said, sitting down on the side of the bed. "So all is well with you and Sly?"

Dawn glanced down at her sister. "It's much, much better. We're working through our problems together."

"All I have to say is, y'all do some loud work."

Smiling, Dawn tossed one of Sly's shirts at Francine's head. "You're bad."

Francine pulled the shirt off her face. "I'm not the one throwing stuff at people, you are." Tossing the shirt back to Dawn, she asked, "I know y'all got busy in Florida, but did you do any funeral home business?"

Dawn lifted her chin in mock consternation. "Of course we did." The corners of her mouth turned up in a smile. "Mr. E-Z loved the idea. His funeral home is on board."

"That's great, Dawn. Ezekiel Vines is no pushover. I know Sly was happy."

Dawn smiled a secret smile. "He was. About a lot of things. It was a good trip all around. Sly plans to call a meeting later this week to update you and Stuart and to make plans for our next steps."

"Sounds good to me," Francine said.

Dawn sat down next to her sister. "We want you to think about heading up the collective, Francie." When Francine would have interrupted, Dawn said, "I've always thought your job at the bookstore was temporary. I know you've needed the time to get adjusted to being back home, but you belong at Amen-Ray. It's your heritage. It needs you and you need it."

Francine knew her sister was right. Amen-Ray was her heritage, a part of her, but was she ready to reclaim it? "I don't know, Dawn," she said. "I'll think about it."

Dawn placed a reassuring hand on her sister's shoulder as she stood. "That's all we ask." She went across the hall for another load of clothes. When she dumped her second load on the bed in the master bedroom, she asked, "How was your weekend?"

Francine sobered as she thought about her conversation with Mother Harris. "Eye-opening."

Dawn arranged the shoulders of one of Sly's shirts on a wooden hanger. "What in the world does that mean?"

Francine gave her a brief update on her conversation with Mother Harris and the Monika saga. "You know, when I was going through the fallout at Temple," she said to Dawn, "it never occurred to me that other people were going through, or had gone through, what I was experiencing. Now it seems everybody has a story, a secret story."

"Well, I know about secrets," Dawn said. "I had my own. I didn't want anyone to know about my problems with Sly. It was too embarrassing. Maybe that's a part of it too, for the people with stories about illicit sexual encounters with members of the clergy, including the wives. I can only imagine the embarrassment and humiliation a minister's wife, this woman whose marriage is supposed to be an example to the entire congregation, would feel if she had to go through what I went through with

Sly." She lifted her shoulders in a shrug. "You know, you said all this when you made your confession at church. It's odd how I didn't hear it then, or at least I didn't see it as applying to me. I guess you really don't hear things until your heart is ready to hear them."

"You must be right." Francine remembered the words she'd shared about sin and shame. At the time, she'd been thinking of herself and not anyone else. Even when Pastor Thomas had opened up the prayer time for the church, she'd still focused on herself. She realized now that even back on that day, Mother Harris and Dolores had struggled with their own sin and shame. Even the innocents, like George and Monika, suffered as a result of the sin. She guessed even Sister Campbell suffered.

"You know," Dawn said, "since we're being honest with each other, I have to tell you I've been a little jealous of your past relationship with Sly."

"There was no need for you to be."

Dawn chuckled. "Jealousy isn't a rational emotion. I was insecure about my relationship with Sly, so it didn't take much to make me jealous. Thank God, that's over."

"So you're okay with me and Sly, our friendship?" Francine was ready to give the relationship up if she thought it would cause continued problems in her sister's marriage. In fact, she'd been ready to leave town.

"More than okay," Dawn said. "You know, the Lord used your coming back home to bring things to a head between Sly and me. If the anger and hurt between us had been allowed to simmer over a long time, the way it was doing, I'm sure our marriage would have died a courteous but slow and agonizing death. So I guess I owe you one."

"No, you don't," Francine said. "If anyone does any owing, it's me."

Dawn looked down at her sister. "Okay, let's not get into an argument over who's the better sister. Let's just agree you're my best sister and I'm yours."

"I like the sound of that," Francine agreed. "Anyway, it's good to know my coming back was good for one person."

"It's been good for more than just one person, Francine," Dawn said. "Just look at how your testimony at church affected people. Then the way you've been there for Monika and Mother Harris. I don't think either of them would agree with you."

"All I did was listen," Francine said.

"Maybe that's all they needed, somebody to listen. But you know what? People have to feel that they can *trust* that somebody. Apparently, you made them feel free to talk. You gave them a safe place to share their feelings. Don't discount how important that is."

Francine stared down at the floral comforter that covered the king-sized bed. Her sister's words were confirming a lot of things in her heart. "What about what you said to me a few nights ago when I confronted you about what I saw at Friendly's?"

"What'd I say?"

She looked up at her sister. "You said I was being judgmental toward you, believing the worst before I had all the facts, just as I had done with Toni. Mother Harris said basically the same thing about my attitude toward Sister Campbell. She said I was harsh, but I think she meant judgmental."

"Don't be so hard on yourself. I was pretty angry that day when I said that to you. And if Mother Harris really thought you were judgmental, she wouldn't have shared her secrets with you. Face it, Francie," Dawn said, "you have a gift. Don't run from it, embrace it."

"The gift of listening?" Francine scoffed. "I don't think I've read about that one."

"No, but you have read about hospitality, mercy, and encouraging. If you haven't, check out First Peter 4 and Romans 12."

Francine considered her sister's words. They did describe the person she'd been before she left town with Bishop Payne and Company, and they even described the person she'd been in Temple Church. Until Toni. "So what do you think happened with Toni?"

"I don't know, Francie, and I'm not sure it matters." Dawn put down the shirt she was holding and sat next to her sister. "I went through this with Sly. I kept asking myself and him why he slept with somebody else. Then I wanted some tangible proof that he wouldn't do it again, but I finally realized that Sly could never explain what had happened to my satisfaction and that there was no way for him to prove to me that he wouldn't cheat again. I had to decide if I wanted to trust him and God and try to move forward with the marriage I wanted. I decided I did."

"You make it sound easy."

"Oh, but it wasn't. I wanted to love Sly again and live a full marriage, but I wanted to feel safe before doing it. I found out that the feeling of safety came *after* I allowed myself to love him." She cast a glance at her sister. "I think you're going to have to do the same."

"Do what? How?" Francine asked.

Dawn rested her forefinger against her chin. "Well, maybe instead of focusing on what happened with Toni, you can focus on what the Lord would have you do now. It's all right to figure out why we made mistakes, but it's no good to study the past so much that you end up wallowing in it at the expense of moving forward."

Dawn's words, an echo of those Stuart had spoken, made a lot of sense. Francine smiled at her sister and took her hand. "I'm glad you're my sister, Dawn. I love you very much."

Dawn smiled back at her. "I love you too. Now, would you like to pray together?"

Francine nodded and they did.

The next day Dawn made a step of faith like the one she had discussed with Francine. She wanted the future that lay before her, and to have it, she knew she had to close the door on the past for good. Instead of taking a booth in the back of Friendly's the way she normally did when she met with Walter, Dawn took a seat near the front that gave her a good view of the entrance. She glanced at the clock above the door. Her three guests, scheduled to arrive in fifteen-minute intervals, should start arriving any minute now. To ease her anxiety about the upcoming talks, she scanned the menu even though she knew she'd only order coffee.

"I didn't expect you to call so soon," Walter said, sliding in across from her in the booth. He leaned toward her, flashing what some women would regard as a sexy smile. "I'm glad you did though."

Dawn knew Walter thought she had called him here to take him up on his offer of sleeping with him. "Sly and I are back together," she said without preamble. She needed to get that truth on the table quickly.

He sat back against the wall of the booth. "So Sly talked his way back into your bed, huh? What exactly is it that this guy has?"

Dawn's heart went out to the man seated across from her. "I love him, Walter. I never stopped."

"Despite what he did?"

Even though those words made her sound weak, Dawn knew she wasn't weak. She'd had to be strong to try again. She took comfort in her strength. "Yes. Despite what he did."

"How do you know he won't cheat on you again?" he challenged. "You know what they say about leopards and spots."

Dawn shook her head sadly. "I know what God says about

forgiveness and I know He can change a person. You should know it too, Walter."

Walter gave an empty laugh. "So Sly pulled the God card on you, huh? Gave you some sob story about sin and repentance and you fell for it." He moved his head from side to side. "Sly's proof that a man can get a woman to believe about anything he wants her to believe."

Though Walter's words hurt, Dawn refused to allow them to settle in her spirit. "I wanted you to hear it from me," she said, choosing not to respond to his taunts. "If Sly and I can work things out, maybe you can work things out with Freddie. You still love her, Walter."

"Sometimes love isn't enough," he murmured.

"What else is there, beyond love and forgiveness? What do you want from Freddie? She's asked you to forgive her. She's told you she wants to come back home. What more do you want from her?"

He glanced away from her. "I want her to make me believe she won't do it again."

Dawn reached out for his hand. "Oh, Walter. You ask the impossible. She can't do that, only you can."

Walter turned her hand over in his. "Sly's a lucky man," he said. "I hope he knows that."

A voice beyond their table said, "He does."

Walter and Dawn looked up at Sly. He frowned down at them. Dawn saw his internal struggle with jealousy and accusation. Saw it cross his face and pass. He chose to trust her. She saw the decision reflected in his face when he made it. "Join us, Sly," she said, sliding over to make room for him to sit next to her. She pulled her hand out of Walter's and slid it into her husband's. Pressing a kiss against his cheek, she said, "Thanks for coming."

"No problem," he said, but he was staring at Walter.

"What's going on, Dawn?" Walter challenged. "Did you bring

me here to throw your reconciliation with your husband in my face?" He turned hard eyes to Sly. "You know I only came because I thought she was ready to sleep with me, don't you? I knew I was wearing her down."

Dawn squeezed Sly's hand and was proud of him when he didn't react to Walter's charge. "My wife is only sleeping with me," Sly said. "And I'm only sleeping with her."

"Today, you mean," Walter said. "What about tomorrow?"

"Today, tomorrow, all the tomorrows," Sly said.

Walter sat back and folded his hands over his stomach. "I have to give it to you, man," he said. "You got her to believe that trash."

Dawn looked from one man to the other. "This is getting us nowhere," she said.

"Depends on where we're trying to go," Walter said. "Why don't you tell us, since you arranged this little party."

Dawn looked up at her husband. She hadn't prepared him for this meeting any more than she had prepared Walter, but she trusted his heart and she knew he'd do the right thing. "Don't you have something you want to say to Walter?"

Sly's eyes widened in question before they smiled in understanding. He squeezed her fingers and turned to face Walter. "I was wrong, Walter," he said. "I was wrong to betray our friendship. I was wrong to sleep with your wife."

"You've got that right," Walter said. "And for the record, we were never friends."

"All right," Sly said, accepting the denial. "If I could go back in time, I wouldn't make the same mistakes, but I can't and unfortunately all of us have to live with it. I ask for your forgiveness, but I understand I may never get it. If there was any way I could restore to you what I've taken, I would."

Dawn's heart grew proud at her husband's words. She wasn't sure how Walter was receiving them, but she hoped he heard the sincere regret in Sly's voice.

Walter studied him. "There is a way that you can make it up to me," he said. "Let me sleep with your wife."

"Not happening," Sly said, his eyes hard. "No way, nohow."

"I guess your little apology wasn't so serious after all," Walter challenged. "You sleep with my wife and all I get is a kiss from yours."

Dawn felt Sly flinch at the mention of the kiss, and she was glad she'd already told him about it. He didn't say anything. Both men stared at each other. Dawn looked toward the door, thinking this would be the perfect time for her next guest to arrive. A few seconds later, the door opened and Freddie entered. Dawn lifted her hand and waved her over.

"What's she doing here?" Walter demanded of Dawn.

"You told me once that there were four of us in your bed, Walter. Well, I figure two of us need to get out."

Walter grudgingly slid over when Freddie arrived at the table, and she sat down next to him. She glanced at the three faces present. "Well, this looks like fun."

Walter cut her a scathing glare. "You're in no position to make jokes."

She met his stare. "What do I have to lose, Walter? I've lost everything that matters to me."

"Whose fault was that?" he shot back.

"Mine," she murmured. "Not yours. Mine."

"At least we agree on that."

Dawn was struck that the circuitous conversation of Walter and Freddie sounded very much like the ones she and Sly had engaged in. She knew it would lead nowhere productive. "I asked you to come here," she told Freddie. "And it was one of the hardest things I've ever done. I think I could live my whole life without ever seeing you again." Sly's hold on her hand tightened. "But that's not possible or right." She inhaled a deep breath and let it out. "When I saw you at Kings and Queens a while back, I got the impression that you were trying to apologize to me. Were you?"

Freddie lifted damp green eyes to Dawn. "I'm so sorry, Dawn," she said. She glanced at Sly. "Sly was a good friend to me and I took advantage. I guess I was jealous of the two of you. Sly seemed content with all the time he spent alone while you and Walter worked with your choirs, but I was so lonely I thought I would die. I wondered how Sly could not be lonely, so I played on that." She looked away. "I did it, and I did it on purpose."

"Why, Freddie?" Walter asked, pain filling his voice.

Freddie looked at her husband. "Because I was lonely, Walter, so lonely."

"But I was there. I loved you. I never thought about cheating on you. I was happy and I thought you were too."

Freddie shook her head. "You weren't there for me, Walter. I love you, but sometimes I wasn't sure if you loved me."

"What are you talking about, Freddie?" Walter accused. "Don't try to turn this on me. I didn't cheat. You did."

"I know that, Walter. Believe me, I know it."

"Then what are you saying?"

"I'm saying you spend more time at church than you spend at home. I'm saying you say you want children but I'm afraid I'll have to raise them alone because you'll always be off doing something for the church."

Walter looked away. "If things are so bad, then why do you want me back?"

"Because it's worse being without you."

Walter didn't say anything. He juggled a pink packet of sugar substitute from one hand to the other.

"I'm sorry too, Freddie," Sly said. "It wasn't all your fault."

She accepted his words with a slight inclination of her head.

"Isn't this nice," Walter smirked. "We're all sorry. What is this? Good Christian Week or something?"

Dawn chuckled, a sound that reflected the lightness she felt in her heart. Though it would take time, she felt Walter and Freddie had a fairly even chance of making it back to each other. "This does sound like a *make nice* party, doesn't it?" she agreed. "The truth is, the four of us will never be friends. I think that's a bit much to ask of any of us. But we can go forward from here having learned something that will make us work harder at keeping what we have." She looked at her husband and her lips curved in a smile. "I wish none of this had ever happened, but I'm happy to be back on the road with my life partner." She turned to Walter. "Today is about the rest of your life, Walter. Sly and I are walking out of here as a unit. We're no longer a part of your marriage. What you and Freddie do or don't do can no longer be laid at our feet."

Sly slid from the booth and took Dawn's hand. "I pray the best for both of you," she said to the couple they were leaving behind. Then she walked out of the restaurant, her hand folded in the hand of the man she loved. After they exited the restaurant, Sly pulled her into his arms and shared with her a kiss full of love and hope. Then they walked to their cars as one.

CHAPTER 28

Francine hadn't been able to stop thinking about Mother Harris all day on Tuesday. Though the older woman wasn't scheduled to be in the bookstore, Francine needed to see her to assure herself her friend was well. Their Monday conversation played over and over in her mind. George was Rev. Harris's grandson and Mother Harris had lived with the shame of it for more years than Francine wanted to think about. After closing the store, she called Mother Harris with the intent of going over to her house. When no one answered, she decided to swing by the Genesis House Community Center on the off chance of catching Stuart after his TFMA group meeting. She wanted to tell him that he was right and she wasn't leaving town after all.

She breathed a sigh of relief when she pulled into the Community Center parking lot and saw Stuart's Corvette parked there. Scanning the group of young men playing basketball on the nearby court, she grabbed her purse and slid out of her car. Stuart wasn't among their number, so she assumed he was still meeting with his group. Not wanting to interrupt them, she headed in the direction of the basketball players and took a seat on one of the benches a good ways away from the play. The seat gave her a good view of the game, the Community Center entrance, and Stuart's car. Confident there was no way she could miss him, she settled back to enjoy the game.

"You're like a bad penny. You turn up everywhere."

Francine tilted her head back so she could look at George, praying for wisdom as she did so. "Your material's getting old," she said to him. "Can't you come up with something more original?"

"Why waste my time trying to do that? You're not worth it."

Francine sighed. "Why don't we have this out like two adults, George, and quit all the sniping?"

He stared her down. "What you really mean is, you want a chance to make more excuses for what you did to my sister."

Tired of holding her head back, Francine stood and faced George. "That's not what I mean at all."

He folded his arms across his chest. "You've got three minutes," he said.

Francine wasn't sure how to begin.

"Two minutes and fifty seconds," he said.

"Honestly, George, I don't know where to start. You've known me all my life. You know I wouldn't do anything to hurt Toni. I loved her. You have to know that."

George dropped his arms and leaned his face close to hers. "What I know is that my sister is dead because of you."

She shook her head. "Not because of me, because of them, because of what they did to her." When he would have turned away, she grabbed his arm. "We're on the same side, George. LaDonna told me that you tried to get charges filed against them. Well, I think you were right to try. They should pay."

"So should you."

"Don't you think I've paid?" she asked. "You say I'm responsible for Toni's death, and I feel responsible. I brought her there, but I was as innocent as she was. I didn't know what was going on. I was deceived too."

George looked away from her but not before she could see the dampness in his eyes. "I can forgive you for taking her there, but I can't forgive you for turning your back on her when she needed help." He turned his eyes back to her. "Can you imagine how alone she felt? I can't forgive you for leaving her alone like that."

"I'm sorry I didn't stand with her, George. I'll always regret that. But the reality is that I couldn't imagine a pastor doing what Bishop Payne did to Toni and the other women in the congregation. There was nothing in my experience to prepare me for that. I couldn't believe her because what she said seemed impossible to me. I now know that, unfortunately, it's very common. That things like that kind of misconduct go on is one of the best-kept secrets in the church."

"You've got that right," George said.

Francine placed her hand on his arm, and he surprised her by not shaking it off. "I'm sorry about your grandmother, George. It shouldn't have happened to her either."

His eyes turned cold and he shook off her hand. "Stay away from me," he said. "You know nothing about me or my family."

Francine's hand tightened on his arm to keep him in place, though she knew he could have pulled away from her if he really wanted to. "Your mother deserved to know her father and you deserved to know your grandfather."

He shook her hand off again. "Too bad people don't always get what they deserve. Especially people like you. What you deserve is to pay for my sister's death, but you're coming out of this whole thing smelling like a rose. When Rev. Thomas held you up in church that Sunday as an example of what it meant to be a Christian, I wanted to throw up. You've even got Pastor and Stuart talking to me about *my* attitude." He shook his head. "You've really got them fooled. You don't know how many times I've thought about changing my membership since you've been back. I still don't know if Faith Central is big enough for both of us."

"George—" she began.

He waved her off. "Forget it. I don't want to hear it. Your three minutes were up a long time ago."

Francine watched him stalk toward the Community Center entrance. Though the conversation hadn't gone the way she wanted, she was glad she'd had a chance to say the things she did. She prayed the Lord would use her words to soften George's heart.

When George opened the Community Center door, Stuart was coming out. They shared a few words and then Stuart glanced over at Francine. George said something else and Stuart shook his head. Then he clapped George on the back and headed in her direction.

"What brings you by?" he asked Francine when he reached her side. "You should have come in and said hello to the guys."

Still thinking about George, she said, "I didn't want to interrupt."

"Did you and George have words again?"

She looked at him. "What did you and Pastor say to him?"

Stuart grinned. "He told you about that, huh?" When she nodded, he said, "We just talked about what it meant to be a Christian. We didn't think blackmailing sisters or sabotaging brothers was part of the description. George agreed." Stuart studied Francine closely. "Rather, he said he did. What did he say to you?"

"It doesn't matter," she said. "What matters is that he's no longer after you."

He tapped her nose with his finger. "What matters is that he works this out with God. This is not just about me and George, or you and George. It's about George and God. That relationship can't be doing too well if he's treating his brothers and sisters the way he was treating us."

"You're right," Francine said. "You're so right. That's why I wanted to talk to you."

He pointed to the bench she had recently vacated, and they sat down. "What did you want to talk about?"

"A few things. First, I wanted to tell you I've called off my job search and I won't be leaving town."

He grinned at her. "Now, that's good news."

"Aren't you going to ask why?"

He smiled. "I think I have a pretty good idea. Mother Harris called me over last night, told me about your conversation with her, and told me her plan for trying to make up for the injustice she and her husband did to George's family."

"Plan?"

He nodded. "She's some lady."

"What's she going to do?" Francine asked.

Stuart shook his head. "That's for her to tell you and I'm sure she will. She thinks you walk on water."

"What?"

He chuckled at her wide-eyed expression. "She appreciates your being there and letting her work through what was bothering her. She said that even though it was tough to do, she felt a burden had been lifted."

Francine bowed her head to hide her tears. "I didn't know," she said. "I was a bit worried I'd done more harm than good."

He tilted her chin up. "When you said you weren't leaving town, I thought you'd finally gotten it. When are you going to see what a blessing you are to people around you? You sell yourself and God short when you don't."

Francine knew he was right, and she wanted to live the rest of her life like she believed it. No more recriminations for the past. No more feeling unworthy. If she'd realized anything in the past few days, she realized what she'd experienced at Temple needed to be public knowledge. She didn't want people to be as naive as she was. She wanted people to know what was possible so that people who needed help—people like Toni, Mother Harris, George and his mother and grandmother, Monika and Dolores, even Sister Campbell—could find that help. She was about to tell Stuart this when his cell phone rang.

"Rogers," he said. He stood up. "I'm on my way." He reached for her hand as he flipped his phone over and tucked it back in his pocket. "We have to get to the hospital. It's Mother Harris."

"What happened?" Francine asked as he pulled her to his car. She got in, not bothering to point out that she had her own car.

"I don't know the details," he said. "Rev. Thomas just said we needed to hurry."

"George," Francine said as Stuart put the car in gear. "We need to get George. He needs to be there."

Stuart looked over at her, as if debating her request. "Stay put," he said. "I'll get him." She watched as he sprinted into the Community Center. No sooner had he entered the door than he and George rushed out. Stuart ran back to his car and George hustled to his own. The two-car convoy made it to the hospital in record time. Rev. Thomas met them at the entrance to the emergency room.

"How is she?" Stuart asked, his hand holding tight to Francine's. George stood next to him, his heavy breathing indicative of his concern.

Rev. Thomas shook his head. "I'm sorry," he said. "She's gone."

"Nooo," Francine cried, turning into Stuart's arms.

Three days later Francine sat in Rev. Thomas's office with Stuart, Sly and Dawn, Monika and Dolores, George and his mother, and Freddie and Walter, waiting for Mother Harris's will to be read. She still couldn't believe that her good friend and supporter was gone. A massive heart attack, the doctors had told them. Mother Harris had known about the condition of her heart and so had her doctor, but she hadn't chosen to share that knowledge with anybody else. As the doctor explained, when he'd warned her about her condition, she'd blithely told him, "I'm old, parts are gonna wear out, but I'm not going anywhere until the Lord calls me." And that, he'd said, was that.

Francine glanced around Rev. Thomas's office at the lives Mother Harris had touched. The older woman had said she had no children, but as Francine looked around, she realized that wasn't true. Mother Harris did have children—children of the faith, brothers and sisters in Christ she'd nurtured and supported as much as any parent could have. Francine blinked back tears as she looked into the faces that represented Mother Harris's legacy. What would her own legacy be? she wondered.

The door opened and Rev. Thomas joined them. "I'm sorry I'm late," he said, "but another appointment ran long." He glanced over at Stuart, who sat in a chair close to Rev. Thomas's desk. "Did you bring the documents?"

Stuart handed Rev. Thomas a manila folder. "Stuart could have done this without me," Rev. Thomas told the assembled group from his perch on the front edge of his desk, "but Mother Harris wanted it done this way. Since we've always followed what she wanted us to do, I didn't see any reason to stop now." The comment brought a soft chuckle from the group that Francine knew was coupled with individual and specific memories of a Mother Harris moment. "I have Mother Harris's will in front of me and you're all here because you're all named in it." He glanced down at the papers. Then he looked over at George, who was seated next to his mother. "The bulk of Mother Harris's estate, including her home, the bookstore, and the proceeds from Rev. Harris's life insurance, which Mother Harris never touched, go to his only child, Mary Roberts, and his only living grandchild, George Roberts. If Mother Harris had any regret in her life," Rev. Thomas told them, "it was that she and Rev. Har-

ris never publicly acknowledged his child. She had plans to correct that error but the Lord saw fit to take her home before she
could do it." He handed George and Mrs. Roberts envelopes
with their names on them. Mrs. Roberts squeezed hers tightly
in her fist and turned her face into her son's shoulder and
weeped. "She informed me that she wrote these letters," Rev.
Thomas told them, "to say what she should have said years ago."

He turned to Monika and Dolores. "Mother Harris knew
how much you wanted a family, Monika, and more than anything, she wanted you to know she considered you and your
mother her family." He handed envelopes to both Monika and
Dolores. "Like any grandparent would like to be able to do for
a grandchild, Mother Harris left money to cover your college
education and the down payment on your first house." He
smiled at the teenager. "She said she'd leave the car up to your
mother. She didn't think her heart could take you behind the
wheel of an automobile." Monika squeezed her eyes shut but
tears still leaked from her closed lids.

Rev. Thomas now turned to Walter and Freddie. "What
Mother Harris wanted most for the two of you was reconciliation and restoration." He handed each of them an envelope.
"She knew how hard it was to forgive an unfaithful spouse," he
told Walter, "and she wanted you to do a better job of it than she
did. In addition to a substantial sum of money from her personal
life insurance policy, she signed you both up for marriage counseling."

Next Rev. Thomas turned to Francine, Dawn, and Sly.
"Mother Harris kept a warm spot in her heart for you, the much
loved grandchildren of her dearest friends. Because she knows
how much the legacy of your grandparents means to you, she
wanted to support that legacy by investing in the funeral home.
Francine told her about the venture you were planning, and she
left a substantial investment in the collective. She asks that the
proceeds from her investment be donated to Genesis House."

He handed an envelope to Francine and one to Sly that was for him and Dawn. "Dawn and Sly, Francine told Mother Harris about your reconciliation and that made her happy. Francine, she loved you dearly. She wanted you to know, really know, that your coming back here changed a lot of lives, no one's more than hers." Francine's heart contracted with love and loss for the dear woman who had herself changed so many lives.

Finally, he turned to Stuart. "I know this surprises you, Stuart, but she had something for you too. She wanted you to know that she and Marie have your back. She didn't see a need for a letter to help explain that." Stuart lowered his head.

Rev. Thomas looked across the room at the group. "That's it, except for a rather large donation that she left to the church." George and his mother were the first to stand. "Thank you for everything, Rev. Thomas," Mrs. Roberts said, her voice still clogged with tears. Francine stood and hugged the older woman, hating the stiffness in Mrs. Roberts's body as she embraced her. Francine didn't say anything, because there was nothing left to say. George leaned toward her and whispered, "You're fired. Don't even think about coming back to the bookstore." Then he turned and led his mother out of Rev. Thomas's office.

When Francine turned back to Rev. Thomas, he said, "Mother Harris expected that response and you should have too. Read her letter and you'll understand better." Rev. Harris turned to Dawn and Sly. "Would you two give us a few minutes? I need to discuss something with the others that has nothing to do with the will."

Dawn hugged her sister and then she and Sly left the room.

"This is not the best time for this news," Rev. Thomas said to the assembled group, "but I thought you'd appreciate it." He looked at Monika. "Your grandmother and your three brothers want to meet you," he told her.

Monika's mouth dropped open.

"What?" Dolores asked.

"Rev. Campbell's three sons and his mother want to meet their newest relative."

"When?" Monika asked.

"Whenever you're ready to meet them."

"What about my father?"

Rev. Thomas's lips curved downward in a frown. "He's not there yet, Monika." At the dismay on her face, he added, "Don't take it personally, sweetheart. It's no fault of yours. It's his problem and he has to work through it on his own. If it helps you any, he's not close to your brothers either."

Monika nodded as she turned into her mother's embrace, and Dolores led her out of the room. Stuart and Francine stayed behind.

"What happened when you talked to Rev. Campbell?" Francine asked.

"I didn't talk to him," Rev. Thomas explained. "I made a few investigative phone calls, found out a few things, and then I called his oldest son. He's pastor of a small church in southern Alabama. Excellent reputation and a strong ministry of reconciliation. Anyway, I told the son the story and he took it from there."

"What about BCN?" Stuart asked.

"It's not clear yet. It's my prayer it's something the son will want to take over. The only thing that's clear is that Rev. Campbell won't be a part of it. I told Rev. Jr. that you'd be in touch with him, Stuart."

"Will do," Stuart said.

"What about Sister Campbell?" Francine asked with a new compassion for the woman.

"She's standing by her husband's side. They resigned their pastorate but I'm not sure what they'll be doing next." Rev. Thomas glanced at Francine. "Stuart and I are going to keep Dawn and Sly company for a few minutes." He inclined his head toward the envelope she still held in her hands. "You should take a few minutes and read that."

When she was alone, Francine took her seat and opened the envelope with her name printed in Mother Harris's bold script.

My dear Francie,

I remember clearly the day you walked into the bookstore after you returned home. Your eyes were clouded with uncertainty, as if you thought I'd turn you away. I knew then you'd be a blessing to us all. Little did I know how much of a blessing you'd be! Even as I write these words, I know they'll be hard for you to hear, but you need to hear them and you need to believe them.

One of your most endearing qualities is that you're always ready and willing to put yourself under the Lord's microscope so He can point out and fix your imperfections. To balance that, you have to remember He'll be fixing those imperfections until you join Him, and me, in glory.

Dearest, you have to let Toni go. There is no other way to say it. She had her own relationship with the Lord. You couldn't live that relationship for her. If she'd turned to Him, He would have been there for her. He was waiting for her to do it, wanting her to do it. It was her moment, not yours. I know these words are hard for you to hear, but you need to hear them and believe them. They are life to you.

The Lord has much in store for you because of what you've suffered. Your experiences will only make you better able to minister to others who have suffered similarly, and I hope you know by now that there are many. I was one. So are Monika and Dolores. So are George and his family. So are Sister Campbell and her children. These are lives that the Lord has allowed you to touch in the short time you've been back, but it's just the beginning. Open your eyes and your heart so He can show you what He's doing with you already and what He wants to do with you in the future. Stop looking back. Focus on what the Lord is doing now. It's enough to keep you occupied.

I feel pretty certain that with George in charge, your days at the bookstore are numbered, but don't fret about that. I always knew it was a temporary place for you. The Lord opens doors and He closes them. It's no more complicated than that. Just keep your eyes and heart open for the next door He opens for you. He has great plans for you, dearest!

I love you, Francie, with the love of the Lord. Thank you for being a sister to me, for giving me a place to voice and face a shameful part of my history. You'll never know the burden that was lifted just from sharing with you. I had a chance to make it right before the Lord, so I'm ready to leave here. I think now I was waiting all this time for you to come home so I would be ready to go home. Know that I'm happy, I'm free, and I'm ready to meet the Lord.

Your sister in Christ,
Mother Harris

Francine waited for tears to come, but they didn't. Instead her heart filled with an incredible joy. After a while, she heard Dawn call her name and the door open. "Are you all right, Francie?" Dawn asked.

Francine stood up and smiled at her sister. "Better than I've been in a long time," she said. "Let's go home."

EPILOGUE

Francine sat on a bench in Dayton's McArthur Park on an early Sunday morning before the crowds arrived, and waited for Cassandra. The Ohio park held bittersweet memories for her. Temple had held many church services here on cool spring and fall Sunday mornings as well as on hot summer ones. She had especially enjoyed the outdoor sessions. There was something freeing about praising God in the wide open spaces.

A smile on her face, Francine glanced across the children's play area to the surprise couple of the year, Stuart and Dolores. The recently engaged couple sat hand in hand at a redwood picnic table. When the two of them had found out that Dawn and Sly wouldn't be coming with Francine because of Dawn's pregnancy—or rather, Sly's overprotectiveness of his pregnant wife—they'd decided to come along. When she'd tried to explain that she didn't need chaperones, they'd ignored her, unwilling to hear of her meeting Cassandra or anybody from Temple all alone. They still didn't trust the woman, or anybody at Temple, and frankly neither did Francine. She didn't trust them, but she now had more compassion for them. When she'd come to see Cassandra after leaving the hospital almost two years ago, she'd seen her ex-friend as an enemy, an abuser, a co-conspirator with Bishop Payne. Time and experience had shown her she'd been wrong. Cassandra had been a victim as much as she and Toni had been, as much as many others at Temple still were. It was her acceptance of Cassandra as a victim that had encouraged her to give the woman a call.

Of course, she'd had a team of people praying for her. In the past year, she'd founded a new ministry, called "A Safe Place," for women involved in, recovering from, or impacted in some way by illicit relationships with members of the clergy. She hadn't set out to found a ministry; rather, it had seemed to spring up around her. And it had all stemmed from Stuart's nomination to the Georgia Supreme Court. As he'd warned her, and despite George's efforts to stop the mudslinging he'd deliberately started—efforts George had undertaken for Stuart's sake, not hers—she'd had a few moments in the spotlight. But the publicity had had a different impact than she'd expected. Calls and letters had poured into the funeral home, where she now served as Coordinator of Cooperative Services. There had been an outpouring of support from women who'd suffered through similar situations as well as women who were still suffering. It had been Stuart's friend CeCe, who was also now her friend, who had suggested starting a support group at Genesis House. The turnout had been overwhelming. That first group at Genesis House had grown to a national network of more than one hundred groups.

Between A Safe Place and the cooperative, which now boasted 150 family-owned funeral homes, she had a full life, but more importantly, a purposeful life. She attributed it all to the growing relationship she had with the Lord. Over the last year, she'd finally learned what Dawn, Mother Harris, and Stuart had tried to tell her: The Lord had a wonderful plan for her life. She still had questions about that plan, but she'd learned to live with them. For a while there, it had looked as though she and Stuart might become something more than friends, but the Lord had had other plans and now Stuart and Dolores were planning their wedding. She celebrated their relationship because she loved them, individually and as a couple, but it did leave her with a big question mark for her own life.

Francine glanced at her watch. Though Cassandra was already fifteen minutes late, Francine didn't want to give up on her. She could afford to wait another fifteen minutes, but not much longer, because she, Dolores, and Stuart had an invitation to a very special surprise birthday party that Monika's brothers had planned for her. The boys doted on their little sister, and Francine loved them for filling the gap left by the inattention of her father.

Francine glanced over at Stuart and Dolores again, thankful for their support, and caught sight of Cassandra in her peripheral vision. She stood and watched as her ex-friend strode toward her with that long-legged gait of hers. "Hi, Cassandra," she said when the woman reached her. She gave her a brief hug, and stepped back to read the surprise in Cassandra's eyes. "Thanks for coming," Francine said.

Cassandra pushed her sunglasses up on her forehead. "I don't know why I did. We don't have anything to say to each other. I think we said it all two years ago."

Francine shook her head. "I wanted to thank you again for calling Dawn when I was hospitalized."

"You've already done that," Cassandra said. "What do you really want, Francine? I have things to do."

Francine pulled a brochure describing A Safe Place from the side pouch on her black leather handbag. "I wanted to apologize for accusing you of enabling Bishop Payne. You're a victim as much as I am, as much as Toni was."

"I'm nobody's victim," Cassandra declared. "I don't know where you get that from."

Francine wasn't fooled by the false bravado. "I got it from you, Cassandra. You told me when I was here the last time that your life with Bishop Payne was better than your life on the street. I just wanted to tell you that if you wanted a *real* life, the life you talk about in Bible Study, that you can have it."

Cassandra said, "I don't know what you're talking about."

"I know you don't, but you can," Francine said, and handed the brochure to Cassandra. "When you get tired of the life you have with Bishop Payne and you decide you want a real life, you can call me at the number on this brochure. What you have with Bishop Payne is a poor imitation of what life in Christ is about, Cassandra. I think deep down inside you know that. There's a place inside you that yearns for more than you have, a place that hurts because you want more, need more."

"You don't know what you're talking about."

Francine just smiled. "But I do," she said. "I know and I also know that even though life with Bishop Payne is not what you want it to be, it's comfortable for you. I just want you to know that when you're ready to trust God, there's a safe place for you to go."

Cassandra looked annoyed, but Francine noticed that she tucked the brochure in her purse. *Thank you, Lord.*

"I met with you like you asked, but now I have to go," Cassandra said.

Francine hugged her again. "Take care of yourself, Cassandra, and remember that Jesus loves you more than anybody does."

With a frown on her face, Cassandra turned and strode from the park. Dolores and Stuart made their way to Francine. "How'd it go?" Stuart asked.

"Perfect."

"You ready to go home?" Dolores asked.

She nodded. She was ready to go home.

READING GROUP GUIDE

Discussion Questions

1 Guilt. Forgiveness. Responsibility. Consequences. Francine and Sylvester are wrestling with many of the same issues—albeit in very different situations. When have you had to wrestle with the fallout of sin? How did you handle these issues? What Scriptures convicted and encouraged you?

2. In chapter 1, Francine's therapist told her, "You always have options," and now in chapter 2. Rev. Thomas offers to hear whatever options the BCN group comes up with. Options, choices, decisions . . . we are faced with them every day. How do you weigh your options? What influences your everyday decisions? What role (if any) do prayer, faith, Scripture, and the counsel of others play in your choices?

3. What experience have you had with groups such as the proposed BCN (in chapter 2) or with individuals like Bishop Payne? Are you quick to support such ventures or follow such people? Why or why not? How have "scam artists" exploited Christians—especially new believers, seniors, or folks with few resources of their own? What might make people of faith vulnerable to being exploited?

4. Mother Harris says, "I hope you've learned that some things don't make sense, no matter how hard you try to make sense of them." Do you agree or accept that? Why or why not? When have you confronted uncertainty, confusion, and apparent chaos in your life—and how did you handle it? What, if anything, allows you to accept when life just refuses to make sense?

5. Both the single women and the married ones in the spa agree that loneliness is a struggle. How might a single person handle loneliness differently from a married person? When "lonely meets *you* at the door," how do you greet it? What are the pitfalls in the struggle? What strategies do you have for dealing with loneliness—and what benefits might there be to accepting it?

6. Already we have seen many different faces of grief in this story—Stuart's for his beloved Marie; Sly and Dawn's for their marriage, their trust, and their dreams; Glenda's for her spouse; Francine's for Toni and for past mistakes. How have you experienced grief in your life (whether you named it as such or not!)? How do you respond to its different emotions and stages—anger, guilt, denial, acceptance?

7. A theme in this chapter seems to be communication, especially in decision-making—between husbands and wives (Sly and Dawn) and between parents and children (Dolores and Monika). Is it okay for Sly not to involve Dawn in discussions about the collective? If you were Dawn, would you want to participate? Why or why not? Think about your relationship with your parent—or child—and how you communicated about important issues or decisions. Do you think the communication was appropriate or sufficient? Why or why not? How do you choose whom to consult or in whom to confide?

8. In this chapter, a recurring issue is truth and lies—between spouses, between parents and kids, even between "me, myself, and I." The Bible says "the truth will set you free"—and yet none of us ever tells the whole truth all the time. Diplomacy and wisdom often seem to counsel discretion and even caution in speaking truth. When, if ever, is partial truth acceptable or appropriate? How do you choose what to say and what to hold back? How does the age of the listener, for example, affect that decision? Do you think Dolores's decisions to withhold some things from Monika were appropriate? When, why, or why not?

9. As adults, we say things like "honesty is the best policy" and "the truth will set you free," but the fact is, sometimes we don't really want to know the truth. In chapter 8, Dolores told Monika, "A lie is easier," and she meant, easier for the teller. In other circumstances, however, it may be that the person lied *to* prefers the lie to the truth. When have you, like Walter and Dawn and Francine, found the truth so painful that you almost wished you could turn back time and return to the days of believing the lie? How willing are you to accept the truth—about yourself and about your situation—and let God work out the pain into something liberating, healing, and redemptive? Why?

10. To what extent, if any, do you feel sympathy for Sly? Why? How *should* a cheating spouse, who is now intent on repentance and reconciliation, expect to be treated? With anger, hurt, coldness, violence, hostility, vengefulness, ambivalence—all of the above and more? It is natural (if not right) for the wronged spouse to strike out in a variety of ways—or to become caught in an emotional limbo or in pendulum mood swings. What should a man like Sly be willing to accept from his wife? Where, if at all, should he draw the line and refuse to subject himself to "ill treatment"? Can you think of any Scriptures that might offer counsel to Sly or someone like him?

11. Mother Harris speaks to Francine with almost brutal honesty. How does her truth contrast with some of the other truths and lies of this story? What do you think makes the difference? (See Psalm 15:2; Zechariah 8:16; and Ephesians 4:15, 25.)

12. What lesson do *you* take from Scripture's frequent "case studies" about men "led astray" by beautiful women (e.g., Samson, David, even Hosea)? Is Rev. Ted's interpretation legitimate? Why or why not—or to what degree?

13. Sly despairs that he has a wife who doesn't want to sleep with him—but Stuart points out that she *does* want to work with him. How might working together be a foundation for rebuilding their marriage? What different forms of intimacy and expressions of trust have you experienced in a relationship? What other options might you explore in rebuilding your own foundations of trust and intimacy? Be creative!

14. If you had been at Faith Central that day to hear Francine's testimony and Rev. Thomas's altar call, would you have stood and gone forward? Why or why not? How has shame acted to reinforce sin's hold on your life? How might the courage to confess free you?

15. Francine is awed to realize that God took her sin and shame and miraculously transformed it into a testimony that convicted, encouraged, and healed. When have you seen God do the same in your life? How might God do it again one day very soon? How can you cultivate a spirit of openness and humility that might allow God to do such transformations more often?

16. Stuart says, "I think a lot of churches look for good leaders rather than good shepherds." What is the difference between a leader and a shepherd? What do they share in common, if any-

thing? What place is there for both in the church? What are the right reasons for entering ministry—or any position of leadership, for that matter?

17. The beauty of Francine's testimony, according to Stuart, is that she didn't set out to be an example; God made her one. What is the beauty of *your* testimony? If you don't know its beauty, ask someone else! If you don't know what your testimony is, ask God to show it to you.

18. How did you feel about Timothy's experience and relationship with Tish? How does it compare or contrast with Sly and Dawn's situation? For whom do you feel more sympathy—and why? How does hearing the stories of others who have come through similar circumstances influence and nuance your understanding of the issues and your ability to feel for individuals on both sides of those issues?

19. You've heard the expression "hate the sin; love the sinner." Yet Francine admits, "Sometimes it's hard to separate the person from the act." Be honest with yourself (and with one another, if you're in a group). Can you do it? Why or why not? If you believe you can, what does that paradoxical position look like? Does Christ's life offer any examples?

20. Do you think Dawn was right to tell Francine to "butt out"? Why or why not? What are the pros and cons of involving a close family member or friend in such a difficult relational challenge? What are the pros and cons of involving a third party of another kind—such as a support group, pastor, or other counselor?

21. Dawn tells Sly that she wants to forgive him, but isn't sure she can ever forget. He responds by reflecting that perhaps

neither one of them *should* forget. Francine wrestles with a similar issue in trying to forgive herself for her past mistakes. What is the benefit of "forgive and forget"? What benefit might there be to forgiving but *never* forgetting? What kind of remembrance of such a past is healthy in a relationship? What remembrance is destructive and self-defeating? How do you embrace one without the other?

22. When have you had to choose between a professional opportunity and a personal one? How did you weigh your options? Whom did you involve in the decision? What finally decided the matter for you—and why?

23. Dolores worries that Teddy will only agree to acknowledge Monika if forced to do so. "It's still the right thing, no matter why you do it," her friends point out. Is there value in being compelled to do the right thing? Why or why not? How does that principle relate to sentencing a criminal to community service or to a person who seeks to make amends only out of a sense of guilt or shame? In what way does such "compulsory righteousness" bear out the promise in Romans 8:28?

24. Stuart asks Francine, "How much would you risk for a friendship?" How would you answer that question? How have you done so in the past? What was Jesus willing to risk? (See John 15:13.) What kind of life have you been willing to lay down for your friends?

25. The visit to Sly's grandparents seemed to be a source of inspiration and encouragement to Dawn. Why? What is it about being with other people who have "been through" and survived to tell the tale with humor, dignity, and faith that encourages and inspires you? Seek out such mentors—in marriage, in busi-

ness, in ministry, in *life*. Listen to their wisdom, emulate their example, and be encouraged to press on.

26. Again, Mother Harris challenges Francine about her need for things to "line up in a way that makes sense." What examples of that are evidenced in this story? "Some things can't be made right because they can't be undone," Mother Harris says. Francine can't accept that. Can you? Why or why not? When faced with such a situation, what is our responsibility? How do you think God expects us to respond?

27. What do you think about Dawn's "make nice" party? Was it foolish and futile? Was it appropriate and effective? Was it cruel and manipulative? Was it gracious and healing? Why? What scriptural principles might undergird such a meeting between transgressors and victims? (See, for example, Matthew 5:21-26.)

28. How comfortable are you with the idea of being under God's microscope? Are you encouraged or discouraged by the idea that such scrutiny—and the discipline and correction it involves—is a lifelong process? Why?

29. How difficult is it for you to see women involved in illicit relationships (especially with clergy or a married man) as victims? Why? What impact have such relationships had on you? How have you seen the church handling such relationships? How could the Body of Christ respond differently—for the redemption of all people involved?